The Fire Reapers

PATRICIA ROBERTSON

Lp

LINNAEA PRESS

The Fire Reapers
© 2013 by Patricia Robertson
All rights reserved.

First Linnaea Press Edition, November 2013

Linnaea Press
Box 31811, Main Street PO
Whitehorse, Yukon
Canada
Y1A 6L3
www.patriciarobertson.net

Typeset at SpicaBookDesign in Book Antiqua
Cover illustration by Chris Tougas

Library and Archives Canada Cataloguing in Publication

Robertson, Patricia, 1948-, author
    The Fire Reapers / Patricia Robertson.

ISBN 978-0-9689354-3-9 (pbk.)

        I. Title.

PS8585.O3218F57 2013   jC813'.54   C2013-906606-3

Printed and bound in Canada.

The Fire Reapers is printed on FSC-certified 100% recycled paper.

For Ceilidh and Mhairi

❦

for Owen and Quinn

❦

and for Luke:

❦

the next generations

And the leaves of the trees were for the healing of the nations.

– based on Revelation, 22:2

The only hope, or so it seems to me, lies in a re-enchantment of the world.

– Morris Berman

If we surrendered to earth's intelligence we could rise up rooted, like trees.

– Rainer Maria Rilke

Table of Contents

The House in the North

eil stood in the front yard of 207 Golddust Avenue, staring. Was this really going to be their new home—this wonky old cabin? Holy crap. It had logs for walls and a leaning tin chimney and antlers that might be caribou nailed above the front porch. Huge iron tubs filled with weeds guarded the front gate. Why did they have *teeth* along one edge?

"What do you think, sweetie?" His mother put her arm round his shoulders and squeezed, hard. "You're awfully quiet."

"It's sure different from our old place," Neil said. "It's just— weird." But then everything in the Yukon was weird. Here it was, ten o'clock at night in early July and still light as day. His mother had told him and Katie that in the summer you could read a book outside at midnight, but he hadn't believed her. And now his uncle had gone and picked something for them that wasn't even a real house.

"It looks like someone just dragged it out of the bush," he said.

"Oh Neil!" His mother shook him gently, smiling. She hadn't smiled very much in the last year, and he liked seeing her happy again. "You know what it reminds me of? Where we spent summers when I was little, out at Fox Lake."

"But why can't we find a house like the one we had? With a garage and a basketball hoop and—"

"What are these tubs, Mom?" His sister was leaning over the gate and running her fingers along the metal teeth.

"Dredge buckets, sweetie. From the big gold dredges they used to use in Dawson City."

"They look scary. Like dragon mouths!" Katie made her

1

hands into claws, opened her mouth in a snarl, and charged toward him. Neil dodged away. He wasn't in the mood for silly games, especially after spending four days driving up the Alaska Highway to somewhere he hadn't wanted to go in the first place.

He raced for the tangle of bushes at the back of the house and crawled into them just as Katie rounded the corner. "Neil! Hey Neil!" she called, pulling aside branches. Now his mother was calling too. Well, let them. If it had been up to him he'd have stayed behind in Vancouver and started Grade 7 with Jasper and Eli at his old school. He could live with Jasper's family—they had a spare bedroom now that Jasper's older brother had gone off to university. He'd even thought about running away, about living on that small patch of beach near the marina and sleeping under the logs at night. His friends would bring him food. And by September, when school started, even his mother would have to accept that he wasn't ever ever *ever* going to the Yukon.

Their voices faded, then disappeared completely. He stuck his head out warily. They must have gone back to Uncle Dan's—they were all staying there till their furniture arrived. As he crawled out, his T-shirt caught on a nail poking from a loose plank. He yanked it free, tearing it—crap—and stood up.

The plank, it turned out, was part of the wall of an old shed, hidden in the overgrowth. There was a padlock, but it was broken. Neil pushed open the warped door. In the dim light he could make out bits of machinery and rusty tools—the kinds of things the old miner who'd lived here might be expected to have. He'd been a prospector near Dawson City before retiring and building this place, Uncle Dan had said.

There was something weird in the shed, too—a tall round clay cylinder, almost as tall as he was, covered with painted spirals and circles. Neil lifted the lid off, releasing a choking cloud of dust and a couple of frantic beetles. Whatever it was, it hadn't been used in years. Coughing, he dropped the lid back in place, stepped out into the light, and pushed the door shut behind him. The whole place gave him an odd shivery not-quite-right feeling.

The hinges of the front gate squeaked and he glanced up. Katie was running toward him, carrying an armload of vivid blue flowers. "Look what we found! Delphi—delphin—"

"Delphiniums," his mother said, coming up behind her. "I'd forgotten they grow wild here." She reached Neil and patted his arm. "We figured we'd let you stay and fight the dragons while we went for a walk."

Neil wrenched himself awake and sat up in bed, breathing hard. That nightmare again. It was always the same. First the smoke— thick, choking smoke, filling his lungs, making it impossible to breathe. He was in a forest of pine and spruce and birch some- where and the whole thing was ablaze. Above him the flames leapt from treetop to treetop, racing ahead so fast he knew he'd never outrun them. A wolf came dashing out of the trees, stared at him in panic, then plunged back into the smoke and disap- peared. He yanked his jacket over his head and curled up into a ball, but the flames were all around him now, towering above him, coming closer, closer ...

He threw back the sheet, feeling shaky, and went to open the window. Twilight still leaked round the edges of the pinned-up blanket in his cousin Matt's old room, though the clock said two a.m. He'd had the nightmare almost every night since his mother told him they were moving. Once they got to the Yukon, he'd thought, it would stop. But it hadn't. Did it have something to do with his dad? If it did, for the life of him he couldn't figure out what.

He reached for his father's walking stick, the one his dad had whittled from a piece of oak. He liked holding its smooth nubbly length against his body, especially when he couldn't sleep. Sometimes he even talked to his dad, though he'd have died before telling anyone. "Guess what, Dad? We're here in the Yukon, and I'm still getting those nightmares. Crazy, huh?"

His father, he knew, would have had an answer. His father had had an answer for everything—well, nearly everything. It was impossible to believe he was gone, that he'd never see him again. Could it really have been only ten months? Ten months, two weeks, three days ...

He brushed away the wetness on his lashes angrily. He'd be twelve in November. Too old for tears. He climbed back into bed and made himself think of something else. Like the photos of the trip he'd sent Jasper and Eli: the moose and her calf in that swampy meadow near Fort Nelson, the flock of curly-horned wild sheep crossing the highway at Muncho Lake. And then there'd been the lake itself—the owner of the lodge there said no one knew how deep it was—and those grizzly-claw marks on the front door of their cabin in the morning. At least that's what the owner said they were, though Neil was pretty certain he'd been kidding.

He clutched the walking stick under his pillow, cool and smooth and comforting in his hand, and fell asleep.

But it's all right now, in fact it's a gas, But it's all right, I'm Jumping Jack Flash ...

Where was he? He sat up, startled. Oh yeah—the Yukon. Some early-morning car was going past, its radio blaring. Good. He'd wanted to wake up early. He wanted to explore those high sandy cliffs at the top of the street. "They go back to the last Ice Age," Uncle Dan had told him the night before, "and they're flat like that because they used to be the floor of a glacial lake." Maybe there were fossils up there, like the ancient snails his father had studied.

Uncle Dan had already left for work, but everyone else was still asleep. He wouldn't have to explain to anyone where he was going. He let himself quietly out the front door and walked past the silent yards, past a woman pushing a stroller. The air smelled dry and piney, not like the rainy ocean smell back home, and the biggest, blackest birds he'd ever seen—ravens, his mother said—floated above the cliffs.

To get up there, though, he'd have to climb a trail that snaked skyward through dense bush. He stopped at the edge, hesitating. What about wolves, or grizzlies? There couldn't be any this close to town, could there? *Don't be a wimp. You live here now, remember? I bet Yukon kids go up there all the time.*

A hundred metres in, the trail became much steeper. He struggled onward, grabbing at branches as he climbed. The ravens skrawked above him, and once or twice he heard the high, alarmed squeak of a gopher. At last the trees opened out and he scrambled the final few metres through sand and gravel to the top.

Far below him was the wide greeny-gray Yukon River, with the little town spread out along its banks like so much Lego. He walked along the cliff edge, checking each rocky outcrop for signs of ancient life. All he found were some interestingly shaped stones and a branch that looked like a snake with its mouth open. Already he was sweating in his T-shirt—he hadn't thought a northern summer would be so hot. Just before he headed back down, his hiking boot struck a chunk of rock flecked with fool's gold. Iron pyrites, so his dad had taught him, not gold at all, but pretty and shiny. Katie would like it.

He shoved the rock in his shorts pocket and slid the first few sandy metres downhill. He was thinking about Jasper and Eli and the upcoming bike race round the Vancouver seawall—the three of them had signed up in the Junior Division weeks ago—when he saw a man sitting under a tree in a patch of sunlight. He was wearing a ratty-looking jacket and holding a bottle of something.

5

"Feel like joinin' me?" The man's low guttural voice made him sound older than he looked. He lifted up his bottle and saluted. "Could tell you a few things, you know. Seein' as how you're new here."

How does he know that? Probably just a guess. Probably he's lonely and wants to talk. "Like what?" Neil said, stopping warily a few feet away.

"Oh, all kinds of stories. Like about old Tombstone Charlie, eh? He was a friend of mine."

Neil stared. What kind of name was Tombstone Charlie?

"Pretty strange, eh, what happened to old Charlie. One day he's there and the next—boom!—he disappeared, just like that. Folks figured he went off on a trip and got lost in the bush."

Neil nodded politely and began slowly backing away. Why was the man telling him all this stuff?

"Just wanted to let you know, seein' as how you're livin' in his house." The man grinned, revealing gold upper teeth. "Too damn bush-smart to get lost, that Charlie. He was lookin' for the door to the future. And he found it."

The door to the *what?* Holy crap. He'd been right to be wary. The guy was crazy after all. Or drunk. But he merely waved the bottle at Neil and grinned again, as though doors to the future opened every day.

"Sure," Neil muttered. "Thanks." And then he took off as fast as he could down the trail, slipping on the pine needles. When he reached the street he stopped to look back, but the trail was empty.

"Come *on*, Neil! Hurry *up*!" Katie was jumping up and down in the driveway of his uncle's house. He wiped his sweaty forehead with his arm, suddenly thirsty. "Where were you? We've been waiting *hours*!"

"*There* you are!" His mother was coming out of the house

with Auntie Trish, frowning at him. "Where on earth have you been?"

"Oh, around," he said lamely, and waved the snakelike branch at Katie to forestall any more questions. "Look what I found!"

But she didn't take the bait. "Race you over there!" she shouted, and took off before he could say anything. It was way too hot to run. He trailed along through the streets behind his mother and aunt.

In the bright morning sunshine the new house looked ordinary—not strange at all. There was a big wood stove in the living room—"just like the old days," his mother said happily—and a battered gold pan propped on a shelf. Up the uneven stairs, with their driftwood railing, was what would be his bedroom—a small loft with a sloped ceiling and a wide seat under the window. He stared out at the houses opposite and the hills in the distance. His old bedroom had looked out on the North Shore mountains, and on a morning like this Jasper would be coming over so they could bike down to Stanley Park together. Neil hoped his new bike would arrive on the moving truck in one piece.

"Come look, Neil!" Katie cried from downstairs. His mother had opened the door of the wood stove to show how the damper operated to control the air flow. How could they even *think* about the stove on a day like this?

"See these tin sheets?" Auntie Trish was pointing at the wall behind the stove. Neil looked more closely. *Very* weird. Empty tins of motor oil, old brands he didn't recognize, had been hammered flat and nailed in place. "They protect the walls and reflect the heat back out into the room," his aunt said. "An old prospector's trick."

That reminded him. "Auntie Trish, what happened to the guy who built this place?"

"No one really knows." His aunt looked sad. "It's too bad, because he was always so friendly. People thought maybe he fell in the river. He was getting—well, a little senile, people said."

7

"What's 'senile'?" Katie wanted to know.

"When your mind doesn't work as well as it used to," his mother said. "It happens to some old people."

"What was his name?" Neil hoped he sounded casual. He didn't want his mother to know he'd run into some drunken stranger.

"Hebbs," his aunt said. "Charles Hebbs. His mining claim was near Tombstone Mountain, so people called him Tombstone Charlie."

Holy moly. There really *was* a Tombstone Charlie. He thought he saw his aunt and his mother exchanging glances. Standing here in broad daylight, he felt suddenly shivery again. The whole place seemed crazier than ever.

A Talking Dog

eady, kid? Got your fishing rod? Then let's hit the road."

It was another hot morning and the air inside the truck was already suffocating. Uncle Dan swung himself up into the cab and slammed the door. Ever since Neil had arrived, his uncle had been promising to take him to Dawson City sometime when his job as a wildland fire officer took him there. That way Neil could actually see the place where the big gold rush began.

They climbed the long hill out of town and turned onto the Alaska Highway, heading north. "I remember back when this road was still gravel," his uncle said, easing the truck into the passing lane. "Jarred the teeth right out of your head, let me tell you."

"Did you and Mom go to Dawson often?"

"Every summer. Your grandpa had a gold claim up there, on Hunker Creek."

A gold claim! His mother had never told him that. "Wow! Did he make a lot of money?"

"Nope. Just like most other prospectors." Uncle Dan laughed.

"But the guy who built our place did, didn't he? Before he— disappeared?" A cold breeze brushed the back of his neck.

"He was lucky. And persistent. Look." Uncle Dan pointed to a distant smudge of smoke on the horizon. "We got word of that one this morning. Lightning strike. Small fire, fortunately." Even as they watched, a helicopter clattered overhead, large metal bucket dangling. "We got a crew in there right now dealing with it," Uncle Dan said. "Good thing it's small. We don't have any more men to spare."

They were passing Braeburn—just a gas station and café—and the helicopter was dwindling to a small speck in the distance. "Have *you* ever been in a forest fire, Uncle Dan?" Neil said, remembering the nightmare.

"I used to be a smoke jumper. The guys who jump out of planes to get to the fire. That's how I put myself through university."

"Was it dangerous?"

Uncle Dan frowned. "One time, in Alberta, we were trying to contain a fire and the wind changed on us. Very nearly caught me and several other guys in a downdraft. We had to make a run for it through the flames." He pointed to some whitish patches on his arm. "That's where I had to have skin grafts to cover the burns."

Neil looked at his uncle with new respect. He'd actually out-run a fire! He remembered the flames in his nightmare and shuddered.

"It's almost like a fire has a mind of its own," his uncle said. "I wanted to learn how to outsmart them."

Neil had a lot more questions, but a call came through on his uncle's radio phone—something about "number fifteen" and "jumped the line" and "emergency call-out." His uncle frowned again and shook his head, and there was a flurry of calls to and from various places. Neil decided it was best to keep quiet and watch a movie on his cell phone, and the next thing he knew they were pulling into Dawson. What a cool place! It looked like a Western movie set. All the buildings had false fronts, and the gravel streets had wooden boardwalks, and the swinging front doors of the hotel made it look like a saloon.

It was dinner time, and a good thing, too, because he was starving. Two other fire officers and a conservation officer joined them in the restaurant. "Got a bad one just over the border in Alaska," one of the fire officers said, slicing his steak. "I hear they're bringing crews from as far away as Florida."

The conservation officer gave a low whistle. "And a new outbreak today right close to town."

"I've never seen anything like it." The other fire officer, an older man with weathered skin, shook his head. "Worst summer I can remember. Isn't that right, Dan?"

Uncle Dan nodded, and for the first time Neil noticed the lines in his face. "The weather's changed a lot since I was a pup. And if the spruce beetle starts moving west from Watson Lake ..."

The men around the table looked grim. "What happens then?" Neil wanted to know.

"The spruce beetle kills spruce trees, and that makes them dry and brittle," the conservation officer explained. "Perfect tinder for fires."

"The winters aren't cold enough anymore to kill the beetles off," Uncle Dan added.

It was hard to believe, Neil thought, that the north was actually getting warmer. His mother had often talked about going snowshoeing and cross-country skiing when she was younger, sometimes right outside her front door.

"Does that mean we won't have any snow this winter?" he asked a little anxiously. He might not have wanted to come to the Yukon, but his mother *had* promised him a snowboard.

The men laughed. "No such luck!" the conservation officer said. "Maybe one day, but it won't happen any time soon."

"Besides," Uncle Dan said, rumpling Neil's hair, "you have to make it through a *real* winter if you want to be a sourdough—a true Yukoner. Now, your mother would say I was keeping you up far too late, wouldn't she?"

Two years ago life had been perfect. Two years ago he'd lived in a big yellow house near Kitsilano Beach with his father and mother and Katie. He was in Grade 5 at Gordon Elementary, he loved soccer and skateboarding. Most of all he loved biking with Jasper and Eli all the way along the beaches as far as the university where his father taught. His biggest hero was Ryder

Hesjedal, the first Canadian to win the toughest bike race in the world, the Giro d'Italia. One day he was going to own a Cervelo bike just like Ryder's and win the pink jersey for Canada. Meanwhile he and Jasper and Eli entered every race they could.

But the fall he turned ten, his father got sick. He was tired all the time and his voice became hoarse. There were tests, and visits to specialists, and more tests. A tumour in his dad's lung, they said, but the treatments only seemed to make him worse. He lost weight, and his hair fell out, and he slept all the time instead of going to his teaching job at the university. Neil couldn't believe it. His tall, healthy dad, who biked to work and took him fishing and camping every summer!

And then he got better. "Remission," the doctors called it. The tumour had stopped growing because of the drugs. Little by little his dad got stronger, and his face wasn't so pale anymore, and he even went back to teaching part-time.

It lasted three months. Then the illness started all over again. And nine months later, on a clear and cloudless September day, the perfect world came crashing down.

Neil dawdled along the riverfront, kicking stones in the strange half-light. The sun was a glowing orange through the smoke and Dawson City seemed shrouded in fog. Uncle Dan had said he'd be tied up in meetings for most of the day, so Neil would be on his own. Maybe he'd take his fishing rod and head upriver. The conservation officer had talked about a spot just outside town where grayling were supposed to lurk in the deeper pools.

He found the spot, or thought he did, and spent an hour or two casting, without success. The smoke was making his eyes smart, and besides he was feeling lonely. He was just about to give up when he heard movement in the bushes behind him. He whirled round but saw nothing. Maybe he'd imagined it.

No, there it was, half-hidden in the willows—a pair of

glinting eyes, a brown wolvish snout. He grabbed his tackle box with some vague idea of defending himself, but the wolf, if that was what it was, had vanished again. He shouldered his rod and started back toward town, glancing behind him uneasily from time to time.

He was almost at the first houses when he heard whimpering and turned. There, between the bush and the road, stood a dirty brown dog, thin and bedraggled-looking—not a wolf at all. Relief flooded him, then sheepishness. "Hey, buddy," he called, and got down on one knee.

But the dog only stood there shivering, its tail between its legs, a piece of rope dangling from its neck. Its fur was singed in patches and the left leg was matted with blood. He tried walking toward it but it backed away, the whites of its eyes showing. A water bomber roared overhead, spooking it so that it turned and ran, stopping some distance from him. "Come on," he urged, trying to make his voice reassuring. "It's okay, you know. I won't hurt you."

Suddenly he remembered the granola bar in his pocket. He tore the wrapper off and held it out. The dog sniffed at it suspiciously, then lunged for the food. Neil managed to grab the rope as the dog struggled, leaping and twisting. "We're going to get help," he told it in his firmest voice. "You'll just have to trust me."

With the dog still struggling, though less frantically, they made their way into town. At the hotel he sneaked it up to the room and filled the ice bucket with water, which the dog wouldn't touch. Instead it paced between the door and the wall, howling. When he tried to hold it, the dog shot under the bed and lay there panting. It was a long afternoon.

"It's terrified, poor thing," Uncle Dan said when he finally turned up and Neil told him what had happened. They knelt down, lifted the comforter, and stared at the two golden-brown eyes staring back at them. "We'll have to pull it out of there so we can take it to the vet."

It took the three of them to hold the dog down in the vet's

tiny office. "Pretty thin, but she'll look a lot better when she fattens up," the vet said, gently palpating her stomach as she yelped and squirmed. "She got that leg caught on barbed wire, is my guess. Must have been in a forest fire, too."

"What kind of dog is she?" Neil asked, staring at her foxlike face.

"Husky and yellow Lab, I'd say." The vet was bandaging the dog's wound, over her objections. "And who knows what else? Yukon trail mix, like most of the sled dogs."

Back at the hotel they found a cardboard box and an old towel and made a bed for her. She inhaled the canned dog food they'd bought, but she jumped back, growling, when Neil tried to stroke her. "She'll come round," Uncle Dan said. "Just give her time. You want to keep her, don't you?"

It was a question that didn't need an answer. He'd wanted a dog forever, but his mother had always said no. Why would she say yes to this scrawny animal?

"You leave your mother to me," Uncle Dan said firmly. "This one could use a good home. She's a toughie—she deserves one. Besides, she chose you."

When Neil woke in the night she was curled nose to tail beside the cardboard box, as though disdaining the comfort of a bed. Yes, she was a toughie, all right. And she had chosen him. She'd followed him because she needed help.

For the first time in a long time, the nightmare didn't come.

"This one walked right out of a forest fire and talked to Neil," his uncle told his mother the next day when they got home. She was standing by the truck, staring in alarm at the new arrival. "Guess you're just going to have to keep her, Lesley."

It was true, about the talking. That morning the dog had sat down, lifted her head, and produced a loud roo-roo-roo to let them know she wanted more breakfast. Uncle Dan said she must have malamute in her—malamutes were pretty vocal. Out in the street she'd told several passing strangers all about her adventures. People stopped and smiled. "Quite a dog you got yourself there," one man said. Neil couldn't believe his luck. Who knew a dog could talk?

"I might have known you'd find him a stray, Dan," his mother said, looking rueful. "You always were attracting them."

"But not *talking* ones." His uncle grinned. "This one's special. Besides, she picked Neil out herself."

His mother shook her head, but the dog stayed. "We can't call her Doggie forever," she said at the end of the week, after Neil had tried out and rejected a dozen names. "What about Freya?"

The name stirred a dim memory in him. "Don't you remember the stories about the northern lights?" his mother asked. "About where they come from?" She'd often told him and Katie about seeing them as a little girl from her bedroom window—"like white and green and pink ribbons that ripple up and down very fast, as if someone was shaking them," she'd said.

"*I* remember." Katie leaned forward eagerly. "Something about wolves and Val—Valky—"

"That's right. The Valkyries were the warrior maidens of the ancient Norse people. They rode through the sky on their wolves at night. And the northern lights are really their sparkling breastplates and helmets."

It was a nice story, even if it was make-believe. "And Freya?" Neil asked. "What did she do?"

"Freya was the Valkyries' leader. *She* rode on a golden boar. And it was her job to collect the souls of dead warriors from the battlefield. She wasn't only beautiful, she was smart and brave."

Smart and brave and beautiful. A northern name for a northern dog. It was perfect.

Freya filled out nicely, just as the vet had said she would. Slowly the gash on her leg healed and the singed patches grew back in. As for the dull brown coat, it turned a deep red-tinged gold, shading to cream on her belly and paws. She was quick to learn—even his mother admitted that—and her cringing fear soon vanished. Neil took her with him everywhere till summer ended. He taught her to come and sit and stay, though she offered a grave paw to visitors without any prompting. At night she slept curled up on his bed, ignoring the one they'd made for her under the stairs.

Neil had worried all summer about his new school, a big grey junior secondary surrounded by bush. On his first day he walked there by himself, determined to be brave. In his home room, when the other kids talked about summer trips Outside— meaning down south—or about getting their moose later that fall, he felt lost and strange. But the boy who sat across from him had a dog, too, a German shepherd mix named Taku. All that fall, as the aspen leaves turned gold and then brown and then blew off the trees altogether, Neil and Luka took the dogs for daily walks along the river. Freya and Taku raced each other along the trails or chased squirrels or argued over sticks. Freya also hunted and caught voles, much to Neil's admiration and disgust, crunching them noisily in her mouth.

Taku was a great dog, but Freya was in a class of her own. She figured things out so quickly it was scary. And she stood growling, hackles raised, between Neil and anyone she considered a threat—because he'd rescued her and she was returning the favour, so Uncle Dan said.

There was only one thing she was afraid of: the sight of fire. When they used the wood stove for the first time in October, she wouldn't go near it.

The Tunnel of Smoke

eil was raking leaves in the backyard one bright fall Saturday, feeling sorry for himself. He'd promised his mother he'd finish the job before the snow came, which meant he was missing out on watching a seniors' league soccer game with Luka. Considering how warm October was—the weather report said the Yukon was the hottest place in the country right now—snow didn't seem likely anytime soon. Why had he gone and promised? And why did trees have to have so many leaves anyway? He'd just tossed another load in the wheelbarrow when a burst of rooing came from the other side of the tangle of bushes behind him.

Holy crap. Freya must be in Grumpus's yard!

He hadn't met Grumpus—she went away in the summers—but he'd heard her moving around her yard just that morning. Some crazy oldtimer, according to the other kids. She'd once chased Jimmy Nesbitt down the street with a bowie knife because he'd tried to steal her snow shovel, or so she claimed. She drove around town in an old truck with a bumper sticker that said *Save the wolves, shoot a human.* "And she wears this old leather hat all the time," Luka's friend Jackson told Neil, "with this big brown feather in it. She *says* it's a pterodactyl feather. As if!"

What if she hurt Freya?

He raced to the bushes and scrabbled through, thorns scratching his arms. At last, panting, he reached the sagging remains of a fence and peered over. There was Freya, trotting across the yard, rooing her head off. And there was Grumpus herself, complete with leather hat, advancing toward her. Neil's heart hammered in his ears. She was carrying an axe!

17

He took a deep breath. "Sorry about my dog," he shouted as loud as he could above the rooing. Should he go get her? Stay where he was?

"Who are you?" Grumpus stopped and stared at him, her voice gruff and unfriendly. He could have sworn she gripped the axe more tightly.

"I'm Neil. Neil Grescoe." His mouth was dry. He waved a hand at the house behind him. "We moved in back in July."

"Huh. That so." She still sounded unfriendly, but the hand on the axe slackened. "You must be Dan Tremblay's nephew then." It was a statement, not a question. She grinned wolfishly at him. "Been choppin' my wood for the winter—if it ever gets here. Now don't just stand there, come on over."

Grumpus's yard was much neater than Charlie's, with a greenhouse and a plot for vegetables and a toolshed. A big black soup pot hung on a hook outside the kitchen door—"for boiling small children," she told a startled Neil when she caught him staring at it, "and pesky animals."

"I'll make sure Freya doesn't—" he said quickly.

She grinned her wolfish grin again. "Just kiddin'. I'm Dee." She stuck out a grubby hand. "Deanna's the real name, but way too fancy-dancy. You partial to peanut butter cookies?" And with that she wheeled off into the house and came back with two glasses of root beer—"homemade, of course," she said—along with the cookies. There was even a bone for Freya.

They sat on a couple of battered lawn chairs while Freya gnawed on the bone. Dee took out a pouch of tobacco and papers and began rolling a cigarette. "So. You all settled in Charlie's place?"

"Ye—es." He hesitated. "But ..."

"But what?"

"It's weird. Different."

Dee gave a humph, whether of agreement or annoyance Neil couldn't tell. "Charlie was different all right. Too bad more folks ain't like him. Near broke my heart when he disappeared. I felt better with him keeping my back, so to speak. Safer."

Maybe *she* knew the real story. "My aunt said he—"

"Fell in the river. I know what folks said." Dee lit her cigarette and blew out a stream of smoke. "Charlie would've been *mortified* if he knew."

"Then what happened to him?" What the man in the bush had said was coming back, making his heart beat faster.

"Ah, now *that* I can't tell you. Well, I can't tell you for certain. But I have my suspicions." Dee took a swig of her drink and stared into the distance as if she was deciding how much to tell. "All I know is, he ain't dead. You been in the shed?"

Startled, he went blank, then nodded.

"You seen that furnace? That big clay pot? You know what it's for?"

He shook his head dumbly.

"It's for cookin' different kinds of potions, I guess you'd call 'em. Charlie studied alchemy for years. Said it was a kind of early chemistry. Everyone thinks it's about turnin' lead into gold, but Charlie said more gold was the last thing he needed, and besides—" She shook her head. "I'm rattlin' on here, ain't I? Point is, Charlie was studyin' all kinds of things. Time travel, quantum physics, you name it. Smarter'n a dozen university professors rolled together, Charlie was." She blew out another stream of smoke and narrowed her eyes at him. "Can you keep a secret?"

"Uh, yeah, of course I can," Neil stammered.

"Because most folks—well, they'd laugh outright." She leaned forward, watching him with a fierce disconcerting gaze. "It sounds loony, I admit. But Charlie told me he was lookin' for a way into the future. Said he'd got it almost figured out."

Neil's heart was thumping so hard he was sure Dee could hear it.

It wasn't possible.

It *couldn't* be possible.

"I met this guy ..." He swallowed and started again. "He said—said Charlie had found ..."

"The door to the future?" Dee nodded. "Musta been Sammy Jim. He and Charlie were good friends."

"But how did he—I mean, how do you know he—?"

"I don't know *anythin'* for certain. But if anyone could do it, Charlie could. He said anythin' was possible if we kept our minds open. Said he was working on a new science. He called it 'quantchemy'."

Neil stared at her. It was beyond loony. It was about as crazy an idea as he'd ever heard. Dee and Sammy and Charlie must *all* be crazy. He could just imagine what his father would have said. *I need proof. I'm a scientist. Show me the proof.*

But aloud he said, "That's—uh—really interesting."

"Interestin'?" Dee snorted. "It's downright *amazin'*. Charlie said past, present, and future were—what did he call it?—simultaneous. All going on at the same time. He said time machines were old-hat, we didn't need all that flim-flam." She stared out across the yard. "And he said if he ever disappeared, I'd know he'd made the leap."

Neil cleared his throat. "When did he—uh—leave?"

"Three years ago. November 17th, to be exact. I remember the day because I slipped on the back stairs and broke my damn ankle."

November 17th—Neil's birthday! Another weird coincidence. It was all too much. "I better get going," he told Dee. "My mother'll be getting home soon."

"Sure thing. Now come back anytime, okay? And bring your girl there with you." She nodded at Freya. "You got yourself a nice little Yukon husky. You should try hookin' her up to a sled this winter."

One day it was mild and sunny, and then the temperature plunged overnight. On Thursday it began snowing heavily, and by three-thirty, when Neil walked home, drifts were piling up and the snowplows were out. Maybe school would be closed the next day. But Luka just laughed when Neil asked him. "No way! They don't close till it drops below forty."

"Cold!" Dee said when he saw her out shovelling the sidewalk. "This ain't cold. Cold is sixty below for three weeks straight. I remember when I was cook at the Newgold mine camp, back in the seventies. It was so cold my tush got frostbit!" She pointed to the spot on her behind. "And I still feel it every winter, dammit."

It still seemed pretty cold to Neil, even if it was only minus twenty-two. He walked to school in his new parka and felt-pack boots, feeling like a polar explorer. "Maybe it isn't getting warmer after all," he said to Dee, but she just shook her head.

"We got cougars here now, and deer, and robins—never used to have 'em before. The squirrels are breedin' earlier, too. Everything's changin'."

It was a bad time to be having problems with the wood stove. It smoked all the time, even after the repairman came. Neil's mother kept adjusting the damper, but it didn't seem to help. "Maybe the wood's green," she said, frowning. "Though Dan said the guy who sold it was reliable." For the umpteenth time she scraped the embers into a shovel and threw them out the back door into the snow, then turned on the furnace they'd had installed as backup.

He texted Eli and Jasper to tell them how the hairs in his nose froze when he went outside, and how he'd gone snowboarding on his new board with Luka. But Eli texted back to say the Vancouver seawall race was that weekend and he and Jasper had been practising every day with Eli's dad, who'd been a racer.

Neil's own bike—it had arrived safely after all—was tucked away in a corner of the mud room. He wouldn't be able to ride it till April at least. He sat staring miserably at his cell phone. He'd never win that pink jersey for Canada now—not if he could only practise in the summers. Stupid snowboard anyway.

Stupid snow, stupid winter, stupid *everything*. How had he ever thought it would be fun? Fun was a zillion kilometres away, in his *real* life, with his *real* friends. He snuffled back tears.

If only it were true, about Charlie and time travel! If he had the chance, he'd go back to the past instead of the future, to when his dad was alive and everything was okay. "And I'd *stay* there," he whispered vehemently, clutching the phone. "I'd stay there forever. I'd never come back."

In November he got to go on a winter camping trip with his class, and learned all about building snow houses and how to find dry wood to start a fire. Then November 17th arrived—his twelfth birthday. He got a titanium watch with Ryder Hesjedal's signature on the back from his mother, and a knife from Uncle Dan with a handle he'd carved from sheep horn. Katie gave him a book about prehistoric animals, Luka a headlamp he could wear for snowboarding in the dark. Even Dee gave him a present—one of Charlie's old alchemy books. He looked at the strange illustrations with their green lions and two-headed people, but he couldn't make head or tail of the writing.

After pizza and ice cream and red velvet cake—his favourite—he and Luka took Freya and Taku for a long walk. Freya loved the snow. She leapt gleefully into the deepest drifts she could find, sometimes disappearing altogether. She even hunted for voles in the drifts, pushing her nose ahead like a shovel. Dee said she could smell them.

"We're going skiing up at Mount Sima on Saturday," Luka said, "me and my dad. Want to come?"

Neil did, very much. He'd sometimes gone skiing with his parents and Katie at Cypress Bowl back home. But for a moment—a brief, horrible moment—he couldn't say anything because he suddenly hated Luka. How come Luka still had a dad? Luka's dad had been sick, too—he'd had a heart attack two years ago—but now he was on a diet and everything was fine. Some people, it seemed, got a second chance.

Why couldn't *Luka's* father have died instead?

And then he felt awful. He *liked* Luka's dad. He was always joking and teasing, and he told fascinating stories about being a policeman in Croatia before they'd moved to Canada.

"Sure," he forced himself to say. He hoped he sounded more enthusiastic than he felt. "That'd be great."

It was strangely hot upstairs when he went to bed that evening—the thermostat must have been turned too high. He forced open the frozen-shut window and let cold fresh air rush in. Narrow bands of cloud were swirling overhead, making strange vibrating patterns.

Wait a minute. Not clouds. Those must be the northern lights!

They widened into shimmering white and green bands, then narrowed again, then leapt across the sky. Neil stood watching, open-mouthed. They made him feel—he didn't know exactly, but sort of funny and tingly and excited. He tried taking a photo, but all he got was a blur. Standing there in his pyjamas he was soon freezing, so he shut the window reluctantly. He'd text Jasper and Eli first thing in the morning and tell them about it.

The helmets and breastplates of the Valkyries—he'd seen them at last ...

In the middle of the night a cold wet nose nudged him awake. He rolled over groggily. The clock on his night table said 3:17. Freya was sitting upright, staring at him.

"No, Freya," he said firmly. It wasn't like her to do this. "Lie down." He lay back down himself but she bumped him again with her nose, twice, three times.

He sat up and switched on his bedside lamp, annoyed. "What's the problem, huh?" She looked at him steadily with those big brown eyes of hers, then ran to the door, whining.

There was no help for it. He climbed out of bed, shivering. The room, so hot earlier, was freezing. He flung on his bathrobe and, at the last minute, grabbed his cell phone, just in case. As he opened the door, Freya shot downstairs ahead of him, making her warning sound in her throat—*ouf, ouf.* He tiptoed after her, the hairs on the back of his neck prickling. Was someone in the house?

Shakily, he switched on a light. And then he laughed out loud. Freya, still *oufing*, was creeping toward the wood stove, body held low in hunting position. So that was it—the dreaded stove monster! She must have heard something and decided the stove had come to life.

"Silly girl," he said affectionately, running his hand over the worry wrinkles on her forehead. "It's okay, you know. Nothing to get bent out of shape about." She turned and looked up at him with hurt dignity, so he bent forward to open the broken stove, determined to show her it was harmless. "See?"

But the handle was *warm*. Then he noticed the smoke. Thick white curls of it, billowing out round his legs and across the floor. *What the—?* He tried to slam the stove door shut but it wouldn't close. He flapped his arms frantically, but it was useless. Already he could barely breathe, and the room was getting warmer. A *lot* warmer. Holy crap. He had to wake his mother and sister up, get them outside before—

He stumbled blindly in what he hoped was the direction of the hall. Freya was right behind him, growling low in her throat. Ahead of him a sort of ragged opening was appearing, as if someone was tearing a hole in the smoke. And licking round the opening—*ohmygod*. Flames! Leaping red and orange flames, hissing and crackling.

He stopped, paralyzed. Behind him, still growling, Freya nudged him forward, hard. "Cut it out!" he yelled, and pushed her away. He must be having his nightmare again. That was it. *Okay, this is when I wake up. Any time now ...* The opening was growing wider, and through it he could see what looked like daylight. The flames leapt higher, hissing and flickering. The air was thick as cotton wool, sweat trickled down his face.

Please, whatever's happening, get me out of this, now!

Behind him Freya gave a ferocious growl and lunged past him. Was she nuts? He tried to grab her but missed. She gathered herself, paused, then leapt through the flaming opening and vanished.

"Freya!" he screamed. "Freya!"

Nothing. Only the crackle and roar of the flames.

He felt as if he was going to throw up. The room, the whole house, seemed to be spinning round him. He staggered and fell. The floor tilted beneath him and he slid toward the opening. He opened his mouth to scream but nothing came out.

Instinctively he yanked his robe over his head and curled into a ball. The flames singed his back as he passed through, and then he was falling, falling, though how could he be falling when no wind moved through his hair? Terrified, he braced himself for a landing, but it never came. Instead he shot out as if from the end of a tube into blinding sunlight. He lay there for a moment, the wind knocked out of him. He could feel ground beneath his fingers, but it wasn't earth or snow. It was sand.

The Prisoner in the Desert

Neil sat up and stared round, blinking. He seemed to be in the middle of a vast desert that stretched away on all sides. There were no signs of life anywhere—no birds, no animals, certainly no people, just the odd withered-looking bush. Above him the sun was a blinding copper penny in a cloudless sky.

He stood up, feeling wobbly and nauseous. Apart from having no idea where he was, he seemed to be fine. No bruises or broken bones, anyway. But where was Freya? He couldn't have been more than a minute behind her. He looked round and whistled and called, but there was no response. He couldn't even see any paw prints.

It was scorching hot and the sand was burning his feet, so he took off his bathrobe and sat down on it. It hadn't been burned at all. Strange. And how had he ended up here, of all places? He'd only ever seen deserts like this in pictures—the Sahara, for example. But that was impossible.

Unless it had something to do with—but no, that was *way* too crazy.

Only he couldn't think of any other explanation.

"Way to go, Charlie," he said out loud, angrily. Exactly how he didn't know, but he was pretty sure Charlie and his weird experiments were responsible. How else would he have got here—wherever *here* was? Still, getting angry at Charlie wasn't helping. Somewhere in this vast place was Freya, and he had to find her.

He took out his cell phone. No signal, just as he'd expected. He stared as hard as he could in every direction. The sweat trickling down his face made it hard to think. What would his father have done? *First things first*, his father would have said. Water and shelter. And on a hot day, in the desert, Neil was pretty sure water came first.

Far in the distance, almost invisible in the heat shimmer, he could see a faint line of reddish cliffs on the horizon. Maybe they were sandstone. You could find water in sandstone rock formations. He'd learned that the summer they'd hiked through the strange-shaped hoodoos along the Milk River in southern Alberta, him and his dad and Jasper and his dad. Neil's dad had shown him a spring that bubbled up from an underground aquifer. That had been the summer before his dad got sick—the last trip they took together.

He stood up resolutely. This was no time to start feeling bad again. He'd head toward those hills and look for Freya at the same time. Maybe he'd stumble across her tracks. But he was horribly unprepared. Here he was, no water bottle, no shoes, and wearing (of all things) his babyish PJs, the ones with the penguin design his great-aunt Irene had sent last Christmas. They didn't even fit him anymore. His father would have been distinctly unimpressed.

He tied the sleeves of his bathrobe round his waist and set off. The sand made for difficult walking, and sharp black pebbles and thorns stung his feet. Now and then he stopped to catch his breath, panting. What he would have given for something to drink! For the first time he understood what *dry as a bone* meant.

He walked for what seemed like hours. The copper penny grew low in the sky, but the red hills didn't seem to be getting any closer. A wind sprang up, kicking great swirls of dust in his face. He took off his pyjama top, tied it round his mouth and nose, and pressed on. Still no sign of anything, just the withered bushes and the endless sand, rising here and there into low dunes. His feet hurt. When he stopped to look at them, they were cracked and blistering.

In the fading light something pricked him, hard. He felt a

trickle of blood down his left arm. A bush, that was all it was—a bush with large spikes. He licked off the blood, grainy with sand.

He was beyond thirsty, but he'd never make those hills now. Besides, he was so tired he could have fallen asleep standing up. It was getting too dark to see anything anyway. He collapsed on the sand and slept. Or must have, because a few moments later a distant sound jerked him awake. He lay there listening, but it didn't come again. It couldn't be Freya, could it? Suppose it was a wild animal? Did they come out at night to hunt? He shivered a little. What he needed was a fire.

That winter camping trip with his class the week before! Hadn't he shoved matches in his PJs pocket? Yes, to his immense relief. The thorny bush was dry and brittle and its branches snapped off easily. He dug a hollow, filled it with twigs, then piled the larger branches on top. It took three matches before the twigs caught. He sank back on his heels, exhausted, as the flames flared up. They seemed alive and reassuring, and he watched them, worrying about Freya, until he couldn't keep his eyes open any longer.

He was wakened by voices. He sat up, immediately alert, and looked round. At first he could see nothing. The fire had died down, though a flame or two still flickered. Then he heard the snap of a twig. There, a few hundred metres away—shadows crouched against the night blackness. Human shadows.

The fire had been a mistake. It was too late to hide now. As the shadows began to move, he flattened himself against the ground, his stomach tightening. Running bootsteps thudded into the ground toward him. He tried to wriggle deeper into the sand but it was useless. The next thing he knew the shadows had leapt on top of him, shouting and yelling in words he couldn't understand. They pinned his arms behind him and dragged him to his feet. Someone shone a light, a tiny glowing stone bright as sunlight, in his face. Blinded, he staggered and almost fell. One of them kept repeating something loudly over and over. They searched his pockets and seized the cell phone and the matches. They even forced his mouth open and thrust their fingers inside. Then they bound his wrists together behind his back and flung him to the ground.

He struggled into a sitting position, heart thudding, and spat sand from his mouth. His captors—there might have been twelve or so—had formed a circle round the dying fire. They wore uniforms and strange triangular caps, and glowing translucent tubes were slung from their shoulders. They paid no attention to Neil. They were watching a man, their leader perhaps, who stood apart, closer to the fire. He interlocked his hands and raised them above his head, index fingers pointing upward like a steeple, and as he did so the others bowed their heads. Then he began chanting loudly, his voice rising and falling, the others chanting in response. This went on for a long, wearying time.

At last they stopped, and their leader motioned to the two soldiers nearest him. They produced a small shining box, knelt at the edge of the fire, and carefully scooped some of the dead embers into it. Then they handed the box to their leader, who raised it above his head and chanted some more words. Finally he brought the box to his lips and—Neil couldn't believe it—*kissed* it.

What was so special about embers? The whole thing was crazy.

But more important, what were they going to do with *him*?

He didn't have long to wonder. Two of the soldiers grabbed him by the arms and yanked him to his feet as their leader shouted an order. Then, in pairs, they set off at a brisk pace, Neil and his guards bringing up the rear.

It was hard to walk with his hands tied behind him, and besides he was exhausted. He stumbled along, half-walking, half-dragged by the soldiers. His bare feet burned with every step, and his tongue felt swollen to twice its normal size. Every time he fell they yanked him up again, yelling at him. *The next time I fall I just won't get up. They'll have to carry me.* But suppose they hit him instead? Or, worse, just left him there?

He was about to collapse when he saw, in the distance, the flicker of flames. Another fire, he thought groggily. Then the black outlines of tents loomed out of the darkness, with human shapes moving among them. The leader shouted another order and the soldiers came to a halt. Neil, sagging between his guards, was hauled upright. Some of the human shapes were coming to meet them.

There were five or six of them, long cloaks swirling from their shoulders. They came to a stop right in front of him. One of them, the tallest, wore an elaborately decorated cap, and he was flanked by two others carrying glowing stones. He had a narrow, clean-shaven face, and the light carved deep shadows in it. He waved aside the leader's explanations and stared straight at Neil. "Your name, prisoner," he said, in an accented English Neil couldn't place.

"Neil." His lips were parched and only a croak came out. He tried to stand up straighter. "Neil Grescoe. And I don't know why you're—"

"Silence!" The tall officer lifted his arm imperiously. "Where are you from? And what are you doing in the Drear Lands?"

"I don't know." Neil shrugged helplessly. "What I mean is, I *do* know, sort of, but—"

"If you'll permit me, Flame-Protector Arngrim." A younger officer stepped from the group. She spoke with an even more marked accent, and she glanced at Neil with contempt. "Judging by his clothes, the *fangi* comes from the Hot Regions. Perhaps he's the son of an Aqua Libere." Hisses and sounds of disgust from all round. "Perhaps he's a spy."

"Of course I'm not," Neil said indignantly. "And I don't know anything about any Hot Regions." A wave of nausea and dizziness washed over him. "I'm from the Yukon. And before that Vancouver."

The tall officer stared grimly at Neil. "Yukon? We've never heard of it." He folded his arms, his nostrils flaring. "And as for Vancouver—it disappeared many years ago, in the Great Drowning."

Many years ago? And Vancouver *drowned*? Neil's head whirled.

"Suppose," said the younger officer, her voice soft and menacing, "you tell us the truth instead. We have ways of finding out if you don't."

"But I *am* telling the truth," Neil said desperately.

"Then prove it." The tall officer folded his arms and smiled contemptuously as the others grinned and nodded.

His phone. They'd have newer ones now. He jerked his head at the guards. "They took my cell phone."

At an order from the tall officer, the leader produced it. The officer took it and studied it, frowning, turning it over and poking at the screen.

"Just as Flame-Defender Gunnlaug said." His voice dripped scorn. "It's precisely the kind of primitive techno used in the Hot Regions." He handed the phone to his aides and flicked a hand at the guards. "We're wasting our time with him. Take him away."

They threw him down on a patch of stones at the edge of the camp. As their bootsteps crunched away, Neil lay on his side, barely moving. His whole body ached. If only he was where he ought to be, in his own bed! He drifted in and out of vague half-dreams—he was lying in soft sheets, Freya was licking his face—when suddenly a rough hand jerked him upright. "Here," a voice said in disgust—a man's voice speaking English with a Russian accent. "Drink. Me, I think better to let you rot."

31

A container was tilted to his lips. It wasn't water, but it was cool and minty and marvellously thirst-quenching. Neil drank, gasping, until the container was pulled away. Then the man took something from his belt, yanked Neil's left pyjama leg up, and pressed the thing against his ankle. An electric shock sizzled through Neil's skin, shooting such intense pain up his leg that he saw stars. He collapsed on the ground, writhing and moaning. "What did you do to me?" he screamed.

But there was no answer. The man bent over him, sliced through the cords at his wrists, and disappeared into the darkness. Neil pushed himself up, shakily. The pain seemed to be subsiding. He touched the spot on his ankle tentatively. There was no welt or puncture, though it still throbbed. He eased his shoulders—they felt as if they'd been pulled from their sockets—and rubbed his chafed wrists. How had he got himself into this nightmare? If only he hadn't let Freya out of the bedroom ...

He'd never been so exhausted in his life, but he forced himself to stay awake. He couldn't fall asleep just yet—he needed to figure things out. Like where he was, and who these people were, and why they'd captured him. They must have mistaken him for someone else. Saying he was the son of an Aqua-something, or a spy. As for being from the Hot Regions, wherever they were, it seemed hot enough right here.

He couldn't make sense of any of it. Another bolt of weariness shot through him, and though he fought to keep his eyes open, he fell almost instantly into deep, still sleep.

When he woke, the sky was lightening and he couldn't remember where he was. He sat up, rubbing his eyes, and stared about him. Of course! How could he have forgotten? He was a prisoner, trapped in a vast sandy desert by a bunch of crazed soldiers at some unknown time in the future. And he hadn't a clue what to do about it.

His ankle was throbbing again and he bent over it. Even in the dawn light there was nothing to see, not even a mark or bruise. He rubbed it slowly, feeling small and alone and frightened. Back in the Yukon his mother must be worried sick about him. She must have gone upstairs hours ago and found his bedroom empty. Crap. *Double* crap. And where was Freya? Was she lost somewhere in the desert, too? Or was she in some different time period altogether?

Two soldiers were approaching. One was middle-aged and burly; the other was taller and younger, thumb hooked nonchalantly under the strap of his translucent tube. In the daylight, Neil could see the pattern on their uniforms, flame-like swirls in desert browns and ochres. Flames decorated their shoulder badges, too—two red flames for the older man, one for the younger. Something to do with their rank, Neil guessed.

The older one, his expression sour, flung a tiny metal container at Neil's feet. He stared at it warily. "Open," the man commanded, and Neil realized it was the soldier from the night before. "Eat."

Cautiously he picked it up. It was almost weightless. He barely had time to wonder how to open it when the lid dissolved in his hand, revealing a tiny plastic leaf. He sniffed it, experimentally.

"Is not poison," the man said, almost jovially. "Go on, eat!"

Was it really food? He picked the leaf up and nibbled an edge. Amazingly, it tasted of cheeseburger—spanking hot cheeseburger, with mustard and relish and warm toasted bun. He stared at it, then crammed the rest in his mouth. It was all too weird, but he was far too ravenous to worry about it. When he'd finished, surprisingly, he felt quite full, and his aching body didn't hurt quite so much.

"... usually five days' march to the Fortress," the younger soldier was saying in English. He wasn't much more than a teenager, with thick sandy hair and freckled arms. He pulled out a tiny vial, tapped a pinch of some red powder onto the back of

33

his hand, and inhaled it. "Now it'll be seven at least, thanks to that piece of dirt we captured. Of all the lousy luck." He threw a disgusted look at Neil, who pretended to be still absorbed in eating. "Though he doesn't look like Aqua Libere to me. More like a Bestia. Or even an Arbolé."

The older man grimaced. "Better you watch your mouth. Also taking *threk* on duty." He looked disapprovingly at his colleague, then glanced round nervously and dropped his voice. "Besides, there is bounty for prisoners, for *fangi*. Five hundred *Flammunir*. And if he is spy ..."

"He's just a kid," the other said scornfully. "He can't know much."

"That is reason they use him," the burly one said darkly. "So young, we don't suspect. Or maybe he is decoy. Something important happening other place."

The younger soldier kicked a stone, hard. "Whoever he is, we're stuck with him. And in this Flame-forsaken place!"

"You have been to Fortress before?" the older one asked. Neil wondered why he was changing the subject.

"Yeah. Once."

"You have seen Interrogation Centre?" The man's voice thickened with excitement, and he licked his lips.

"You mean the Truth Chamber?" The younger soldier gave the older man an amused, superior glance. "I've heard stories. Like what they did with the Arbolé leader. Ever heard of *Bréinnthir*?"

The older man, face sullen, shook his head. "You know I speak only little bit Nordlandish. I transfer from United Chinese Empire last year."

The younger one grinned. "It's an interrogation method. Guaranteed to produce results. In UL it's called the Plane of Oblivion." He glanced in Neil's direction and dropped his voice to a whisper. After a minute or two he said, louder, "They say the Arbolé scum lasted only three days. Best way we've found for eliminating terrorists. And spies."

Neil, the little metal container trembling in his hand, pretended he'd heard nothing.

"What are we doing here anyway?" The younger soldier jerked his head at Neil. "He can't escape."

"Okay for you." The older one gave him a resentful glance. "You are native Nordlander, they trust you. Me, I must prove myself. The little one is my special prize. Go. I keep watch."

After the younger soldier marched off, Neil sat stunned, trying to make sense of what he'd heard. *What are we doing here anyway? He can't escape.* Why not? Because he could be seen for miles in this open landscape? Because there was nowhere to go? And who were the Arbolé and the Bestia and the Aqua Libere? Why did these soldiers hate them? It was all baffling.

The day wore on, getting steadily hotter, while the burly soldier paced nearby. Neil watched him, half-seeing, his thoughts in turmoil. The Fortress, the Truth Chamber, the Plane of Oblivion—it all sounded terrifying. If he couldn't convince them he wasn't a spy, his fate seemed sealed.

He was nodding off, half-drugged by the remorseless sun, when he noticed the soldiers were breaking camp. The tents in the distance were being taken down, the bedding and other equipment packed away. Everything seemed to collapse into tiny packages that fitted into various pockets in their uniforms. As evening came on, some of the soldiers sat and cleaned their weapons, while others built up the fire in the central fire pit. The burly soldier went off to join them, leaving Neil alone.

He puzzled over this for a while before it hit him. His ankle! The man must have embedded something in his ankle—a microchip or something they could use to track him down if he tried to run. Any thought of escape was obviously useless.

A sudden burst of music from somewhere almost deafened him. The soldiers were forming a circle round the fire, just like

35

the night before. As the music faded, an officer stepped forward and began that weird chanting, the soldiers taking up the chant whenever he stopped. It went on forever. Neil dozed, woke, dozed again. And then the burly soldier, still looking sour, was shaking him awake. Two other soldiers were with him: a short, round-faced woman and a younger man with a scar along his jaw. The woman produced a pair of lightweight boots that sealed shut after she'd jammed them on Neil's feet.

He was yanked upright, still half-asleep, and they set off briskly. The moon had risen, bright and full, illuminating the way ahead of them. The boots must have belonged to a much bigger soldier—Neil felt as if he was wading in them— and in spite of them his feet still hurt. After a couple of kilo- metres or so, to his relief, they slowed down a little. There was no sign of the rest of the troops—they must be far ahead. His guards seemed to huddle closer, and the woman and the younger man muttered between them in what he supposed was Nordlandish.

They travelled all night across an endless sweep of sand, broken here and there by a dry streambed. Still Neil saw no other living thing of any kind—no trees, no birds, no noc- turnal animals. Here and there they passed what must have been buildings once, or highways—slabs of crumbling asphalt, shattered plastic and concrete. Before dawn they stopped for a brief rest. Neil, drooping with fatigue, collapsed to the ground. Several containers of the leaf-shaped food were handed round, and the burly guard and the young round-faced soldier got into an argument about giving Neil any. Neil was too exhausted and dispirited to be hungry, anyway.

The sky was pinkening in the east when their little group caught up to the other troops. They were sprawled in the shadow of a dune, asleep except for a guard detail. Neil, half- dead with thirst and exhaustion, was shoved to the edge of the sprawled bodies. He fell asleep almost instantly and dreamed about a strange wolf-like creature, half-human, who came over the horizon and stood watching him with its fierce golden eyes before loping away.

They slept all that day. In the evening, after a quick meal, they set off again—roughly, Neil thought, to the east. Why did they always travel at night? Because of enemies? The daytime heat? The land was changing into a kind of sparse prairie, with rolling hills and scrubby low bushes and sharp coarse grass that cut his ankles. Several times, in the distance, he saw what looked like burnt and twisted trees, their limbs frozen at grotesque angles in the moonlight.

Apart from the burly guard, the troops no longer paid any attention to him, and Neil was left to stumble along at the end of the file. Sometimes he slept standing up. Once he thought he saw the strange wolf creature in the distance, and once, his heart quickening, he was sure Freya stood outlined on the horizon, waiting for him. He burst into tears when Freya turned out to be a large reddish stone.

"Fresh meat and Flamme ale!" the burly guard said when they stopped to rest. "I can almost taste!" And he threw away half of his leaf-shaped meal. "There is no farm somewhere? No village?"

"If you count the Ash-Gatherers," the scar-faced soldier said. "Pagans, the lot of them." He quickly laced his fingers together and raised them above his head in the way Neil had seen the night he was captured. "The First Flame himself knows how they survive."

Neil pricked up his ears. So there were people living nearby. People the soldier didn't like. Perhaps the Ash-Gatherers, whoever they were, didn't like the soldiers, either.

Just before sun-up they made camp in a sort of dry ravine. Neil stumbled down its sides, slipped, and lay there as if dead. Every cell in his body ached. Even his molecules ached. How would he ever make it through another night of this forced march?

He woke in the deep heat of noon to the sound of murmuring somewhere near him. The scar-faced young soldier sat a few metres away, holding a book of some sort and mouthing

37

the words softly. Now and again he glanced round nervously, as if afraid of being caught.

> *I heard the spring light whisper*
> *Above the dancing stream,*
> *"The world is made forever*
> *In likeness of a dream."*

Neil sat bolt upright in astonishment. The guard wasn't only speaking English, he was speaking words Neil recognized! "We read that in school!" he blurted out. "It's a poem. It's—"

Startled, the guard stared at Neil, then hastily glanced round. "You didn't see anything, okay? Understand?" He shoved the book under his jacket and leaned menacingly toward Neil. "Otherwise it'll be game over." And he sliced his finger across his throat.

Neil stared back at him, too baffled to be frightened. "I don't get it. It's just a poem."

"It's a book, okay?" The guard glanced about warily again, keeping his voice low. "We're not supposed to have books. And especially not books in UL."

"Why not? And what's UL?"

"Don't they teach you anything these days?" The guard shot him a contemptuous look. "Or" —his face darkened—"were you kept at home so they could turn you against us?"

"I'm not a spy," Neil said wearily. "I'm not anything. I'm just a kid."

"And that accent." The guard eyed him suspiciously. "I've never heard it before. Where did *you* learn Universal Language?"

Neil digested this in silence. UL must be what they called English here. "In—er—the United Chinese Empire," he said, adding, "in a very small village. Very isolated."

The guard looked puzzled. "I thought only Mandarin and Russian were permitted." He gave a sudden snort. "That's the official line, but who knows? We're not supposed to speak UL, anyway."

"Why not?"

"Because everyone's supposed to speak Nordlandish. We're in the Arctic Wealth Alliance! Nordlandish is the AWA's official language."

"We're in the *Arctic*? With all this heat and sand?"

The guard stared at him as if he were mad.

"What did you expect? It's always been like this." His eyes narrowed. "You're a weird one. You speak UL fluently, but you don't know anything."

"Why do you have a UL book if you're not supposed to?" Neil said before the guard could ask another awkward question.

The soldier hesitated and glanced round again. "It belonged to my mother," he said finally. He pressed his hand against the hidden book, his face softening. "It's the only thing I have of hers. She died when I was ten."

So this man had kept his mother's book, just as Neil had kept his father's walking stick. "Can I see?" he asked.

After another hesitation the guard slowly withdrew it from his jacket. "Be very careful with it," he said, holding it out reluctantly. "It's from BGD. Before the Great Drowning," he added at Neil's puzzled look.

It was a textbook, of all things. An English textbook called *Words to Live By*. The cloth cover was rubbed almost to nothing and many of the pages were missing or discoloured. A name, almost completely faded, had been written on the flyleaf— *Candace Burns? Brown?* he wasn't sure—and *Middlebury Junior High, School District No. 27* was stamped on the title page.

Neil stared at the book and then at the guard. "I don't get it. This Candace—she can't be your mother."

The guard grinned for the first time. "She was my great-great-great—I forget how many greats—grandmother. Her family emigrated to the AWA from someplace called ..." He frowned, trying to remember. "New Mexico, I think it was. After the first Great Burning."

Neil was afraid to ask what the first Great Burning was, or

what had happened to New Mexico. Instead, as he handed back the book, he said, "What part of the AWA are we in?"

"Nordlandia, of course." The guard stared at Neil with wide eyes. "We led the mineral discoveries in the Nordish DeadSea," he added proudly. "We produce more gigillium from our sea-bed mines than any other region in the AWA. And we were the first to prospect in the asteroid belt with the Federation of GalactiCorps."

So the whole world had completely, terrifyingly altered—the climate, the countries, everything. "What year is this?" Neil asked weakly.

"Ár-Flamme 39," the guard said promptly. "Flame-Year 39 to you. Five more months and it'll be Ár-Flamme 40. There'll be big celebrations in the City." Without waiting for a response he thrust the book at Neil again. "Maybe you can help me with the words in here. Half of them don't exist anymore. I've never had much practice reading UL anyway."

A glimmer of an idea began forming in Neil's head. "All right. It's a deal." He'd have to be careful, though. He didn't want it to lead to any more questions about where he'd come from.

"Read the one on page 149," the guard said eagerly. "It was my mother's favourite."

Neil turned to the page and read the poem aloud softly.

Loveliest of trees, the cherry now
Is hung with bloom along the bough,
And stands about the woodland ride
Wearing white for Eastertide.

Now, of my threescore years and ten,
Twenty will not come again,
And take from seventy springs a score,
It only leaves me fifty more.

And since to look at things in bloom

Fifty springs are little room,
About the woodlands I will go
To see the cherry hung with snow.

"What does 'threescore' mean?" the guard asked. "I don't remember."

"Three times twenty, I think," Neil said a little uncertainly. "He's talking about how many years he has left to see cherry trees in bloom."

"Read it again," the guard said. And after Neil did so: "That's beautiful," the guard said dreamily. "It sounds like music. I didn't know you could use words like that."

"But don't you have poetry?"

The man looked shocked. "It's not allowed. It's forbidden by the Archons." He seized the book from Neil's hands and shoved it under his jacket again. "I shouldn't be doing this. I really shouldn't. And all that stuff about cherries and snow—it's nonsense, it's a lie." He glared at Neil as if it were all his fault. "Just remember. You didn't see anything, okay?" And he sliced his finger across his throat once more.

On the march that night, Neil was even more tired than usual. He kept stumbling and falling. "We should just leave him here!" the scar-faced guard exclaimed.

Scar-Face must be mad because Neil knew his secret, he decided. So much for his dumb idea that he could persuade the guard to help him escape in return for more help with the poems.

"Yeah, let the Ash-Gatherers find him," the round-faced woman said sulkily. "See what *they* do to him."

It can't be any worse than ending up at the Fortress after this horrible march. Aloud he said, "Are there any of them around here?" He tried to keep his voice casual, but Scar-Face looked at him sharply.

41

"Why?"

"Oh, I just—you know. I wanted to learn more about the AWA," Neil said lamely.

"Must be primitive, no, these Ash-Gatherers?" the burly guard said.

"They collect ash from the Burnings and make *bricks* with it," Scar-Face said in disgust. "Can you imagine? Bricks. It's desecration, that's what it is." And he raised his laced fingers again.

Neil desperately wanted to ask more questions, but he didn't dare. One thing was clear—he had to escape. As soon as possible. Apart from the dangers of the Fortress, Scar-Face had a reason to get rid of him now, too. Who knew what he might do?

But what about that microchip or whatever it was in his ankle? He didn't know how it would react, but he'd just have to take his chances. He forced himself not to think about what might happen if he was recaptured.

Several tedious hours later, the burly guard went off to pee. As soon as his back was turned, the two younger guards pulled out their vials of threk and took a furtive sniff or two each. Within a minute or so they were giddy and light-headed, especially Scar-Face. He staggered and fell, giggling. The woman, unsteadily, tried to help him up. Then they were both on the ground, helpless with laughter.

He would never have a better chance. He edged toward the nearest clump of bushes, never taking his eyes off the guards. As soon as he was out of sight he started to run. In the dark he stumbled through tussocky grass, splashed through a marsh. Behind him, in the distance, he thought he heard shouting. He was forcing a path through tall, sharp-edged grass when that searing electric pain stabbed through his ankle.

He managed to haul himself upright and stagger onward. The shouts were getting nearer now, and he could feel the thud of running feet. Another stabbing burst exploded, this time in his groin. He fell and got up, fell and got up again, sweat pouring down his face.

Just ahead of him was one of those blackened trees. He reached out for it and half-fell, half-rolled into a hole beneath the roots. Earth and twigs showered over him, filling his mouth and nose. He bit down hard on a root fibre to stop himself crying out and lay as still as he could.

Moments later dozens of bootsteps thundered past. Men shouted to each other, their voices panicked. An officer screamed out orders. Gradually the sounds faded away, then, shortly afterward, returned. They were circling like dogs tracking his scent. The ground shook. He lay still, heart in his mouth, whimpering a little, almost passing out with the pain. At long last the voices faded again and didn't come back.

He waited, shaking and nauseous, before crawling out of the hole. When he stood up his legs wobbled beneath him. What was it his father had always said on their long hikes? *One step at a time, that's all. You just have to take one step at a time.*

The pain had faded but his left leg seemed numbed, weakened. He dragged himself forward, muttering under his breath. *One step. Just one. One more. And another.* He lost track of how many times he stumbled and fell. He had no idea where he was. He just hoped he wasn't going in circles.

Morning dawned, grey and muggy. His mouth seemed stuffed with cotton wool. Then he heard his father calling to him. *This way, son! This way. Atta boy.*

I'm coming, Dad. I'm coming.

The bushes and grass and sky around him were fading weirdly in and out. Maybe he'd just lie down for a bit. Just till he got his breath back. His father would understand. He'd lie down for a few minutes and then he'd get up again.

Just a short rest, Dad. Won't be long.

A huge wave of blackness moved toward him. He stood there swaying, and then the blackness rolled over and engulfed him.

The Ash-Gatherers' Village

Astra pushed back the scarf that had slid down over her eyes and stood up. She'd been working in the village vegetable garden all morning and she was tired and hungry. It was a lot of work, growing your own food—digging up the soil, adding goat manure, planting seeds—not to mention having to cook it, too. In the City it was so much easier. You just went to a nutristation and ordered whatever moodfood you wanted. When she'd first arrived in Ashgård, the idea of eating food grown in dirty soil had been so horrible she'd barely been able to choke down what was on her plate.

Several children were heading home past the garden for lunch. Astra waved her trowel at them. What she missed most of all were Stroorberrie Joywafers—flat bright-red wafers, the size of her palm, that came in packages of six. Fru Berta claimed there were real stroorberries that grew out of the earth, with delicious heart-shaped fruit—but that was probably just another of those fairy tales from the Better Times.

One more row of weeding, then she'd head home for lunch, too. As she knelt down, a shrill buzzing split the air. The alarm! She leapt to her feet. Omi Rajavi and his little sister rushed past, their eyes wide with fear, then a surge of adults from the brick kiln. "Strangers! Take cover!" Froken Bensimbra gasped as she ran by. Astra flung her trowel down and ran, racing out of the garden and up the dirt road to the house.

Fru Berta was waiting tensely for her at the front door. "Get along with you!" she hissed, flapping her apron in the direction of the cellar as if Astra were a stray chicken. Astra scrambled down the stairs and into the arms of her father. They lowered

44

themselves through the trap door into the root cellar, her father being careful with his bad knee as always, and squeezed between the sacks of yams and turnips. From upstairs came the sound of Fru Berta's footsteps as she crossed the kitchen and stationed herself by the window—armed with her late husband's rusty Kalashnikov, no doubt. Despite her fear Astra couldn't suppress a giggle. "Imagine Fru Berta with that old weapon!" she whispered.

"Even without the Kalashnikov she's pretty formidable!" Her father put his arm round her and drew her closer. She loved it when he held her, but now she felt the tension in his muscles and her throat tightened. How long were they going to have to live like this? "I don't know, *elskede*," her father always said, sighing, "but nothing lasts forever." Which was a totally unsatisfactory non-answer.

She nibbled her fingernails while they sat in the dark, holding their breath. There hadn't been an Útlagi attack on Ashgård for a long time now—there was so little left to take as booty. As for the FUAZ, the climate illegals—she could never remember what the initials stood for—there were fewer of them these days, too, though the reason wasn't clear. Rumours of a sonar stun fence round the coasts of the Arctic Wealth Alliance—spearheaded, so her father said, by the Nordlandish government—had reached the village. The fence instantly killed those who tried to cross it.

Which left *Them*—those terrifying soldiers whose uniforms flickered like fire and whose real name was never mentioned in any of the villages. Were *they* the reason for the alarm? But they certainly couldn't be mistaken for strangers. So who had arrived at the main gate, and why?

The front door suddenly opened and Fru Berta's footsteps tapped away down the path and along the road. What was she doing? The all-clear hadn't sounded! Astra reached out for her father's hand and held on tight. After what seemed like hours the front door opened again. Fru Berta's heavy tread sounded above their heads, followed by their pre-arranged signal on the cellar door: triple knock, pause, triple knock. Astra fairly leapt to her feet, almost banging her head on the trap door, and rushed up the stairs.

"What happened, Fru Berta? Who are they? Are we safe?"

"Good heavens, child! I can't answer three questions at once!" But Fru Berta was smiling. "Yes, we're safe. Everyone got so excited they forgot to ring the all-clear. It turns out there's *one* stranger. A boy about your age. He collapsed near the gate and some of the men carried him in."

A strange boy wandering out of the Drear Lands? *"Heilagr aska!"* she said, but under her breath, because it was one of *their* swear words and her father didn't like her using it. Who'd ever heard of such a thing?

"Who is he? What does he look like? Is he a villager? Or is he—" Astra was breathless with excitement "—is he one of the Others?" She'd heard only the dimmest stories about the Others—the strange hybrid beings who, the villagers whispered, lived in hidden places on the outskirts of society. She wasn't even sure they were real.

"More to the point, is he all right?" her father said, limping into the kitchen with a look of concern.

"He's sunstruck and very dehydrated." Fru Berta was distractedly putting jars and bottles in a basket and taking them out again. "Dr. Forberg's looking after him. I'm taking along my sun-heal balm and a few other things."

"Oh, Pappa, let's go! Right now!" Astra tugged at her father's sleeve. What a weird week! First there'd been the dog that had followed old Herr Branhammer home from his daily walk outside the gate. At least, everyone said the golden-furred creature was a dog; Astra had never seen one. Where it came from, and how it had survived, was a mystery. And now this boy. And once again, everyone in Ashgård knew about it before she did. It was so unfair!

"Dr. Forberg doesn't need everyone crowding round him, elskede—"

46

"They already are," Fru Berta said with exasperation, snapping the basket lid shut. "Whether they're useful or not." And with that she strode off out the door. Astra, after a moment's hesitation, raced after her. She couldn't wait while her father, always slow and deliberate, got his hat and walking stick. Not when something *this* exciting was happening!

Dozens of other villagers were coming out of their houses and joining the crowd flowing up the hill. Of course—the men of the village reserve would have taken the boy to the Mayor's. Astra caught up with Fru Berta and ran past, dodging in and out of the crowd. Mayor Landholm's house was right at the top, its ash-brick walls and straw-bale roof distinguished from the others only by the village crest—a hand holding a sheaf of millet—on the wall.

A throng of people stood in the open doorway. Astra pushed her way through. The strange boy was lying on a sofa, eyes closed. His face and neck were deeply sunburnt, his feet filthy and badly blistered. His dark-brown hair was cut girlishly short round the ears and he wore the strangest clothes—loose pants and a jacket, badly torn and patterned with fantastic birds. He must have been out in the Drear Lands for some time.

Dr. Forberg was bending over him, holding a small medicine bottle and a dropper. He straightened and looked round at the crowd. "I've given him something to make him sleep. He was delirious and hallucinating. Now off, scoot!"—this was addressed to the horde of small children at the front. "Let the boy sleep. There'll be plenty of time to find out more when he wakes."

"Can't be up to any good, wandering around in the Drear Lands like that," Herr Bradley's wife muttered, as others turned away grumbling.

Astra stepped forward boldly, eager to get a closer look. "Where do *you* think he's from, Dr. Forberg?"

"I really don't know, Astra." Dr. Forberg stood there frowning. "It's quite baffling."

Astra stared at the sleeping boy. Whatever happened in the world, her father said, happened for a reason—because human beings had lessons to learn, for example. The Great Pervader, the force that flowed through everyone and everything, brought such opportunities to all. Her father sometimes quoted a poet who'd lived long ago on the Scattered Isles in the North Atlantic DeadSea, back when they'd been a single island called Britain. "He called it 'the force that through the green fuse drives the flower,' " her father said.

Astra felt sure that this boy, too, had arrived for a reason. What it was she didn't know, but she shivered a little, out of both fear and excitement.

The boy slept for twenty-four hours. So said Fru Berta, returning from a second visit the next afternoon. Dr. Forberg had been back to check on him, too. The boy had drunk several cups of water and a bit of broth, though he hadn't yet been able to answer any of their questions. The Mayor was busy trying to find clothes for him. There was also the matter of a place for him to stay—the Mayor's house, which doubled as her office, was too small.

Astra, in the middle of a mathematics lesson, wanted to dash over there at once, but her father laid his hand on her arm. "Let the boy have some peace and quiet. Besides, you have to finish your lesson."

"But I *am* finished, Pappa. Look." Astra scribbled something in her notebook and held it up. "There. There's the answer. Can I go now?"

"So like my Toivo at that age!" Fru Berta said indulgently, taking a bowl of bread dough from the top of the oven where it had been rising. "Let the child run along, Professor."

Dear Fru Berta! But her father shook his head. "She needs to learn a little self-discipline. Her mother was the same: full of passion and energy, but impulsive."

Astra hated it when her father talked about her mother like that. She *liked* being like her mother—the same red hair that turned gold in the sunlight, her father said, the same way of smiling—though she'd died when Astra was just four. She let out a gigantic sigh and glared at her notebook. It wouldn't do any good—once her father had made his mind up there was no changing it.

She'd just picked up her pencil again, sulkily, when there was a knock at the door. One of the children with a note from Mayor Landholm, requesting the attendance of Astra's father at a special village council meeting that evening. The strange boy was awake and alert and doing better. Now what were they going to do with him?

Soon after supper Astra and her father stood on Mayor Landholm's doorstep, Astra holding a plate of Fru Berta's buttery *serinakaker* and quivering with excitement. "I thought it might be less intimidating for the boy if another child was present," her father explained when the Mayor opened the door. "Astra understands that this is a formal meeting and that she must keep silent."

The Mayor squeezed Astra's shoulder and ushered them into the small central room. The other members of the Council were already seated. To Astra's disappointment there was no sign of the boy. She and her father squeezed themselves onto the one remaining chair, between Herr Grünewald and Fru Vleinigen.

"I thought it might be best to have a discussion among ourselves first," Mayor Landholm said, sitting down heavily. "Before we bring the boy in."

"I disagree." This was Herr Bradley, the manager of the brick kiln, in his funny nasal UL. "I think we need to question the boy first. How do we know what to do with him if we don't know who he is?"

"Two things we know for certain," said Herr Grünewald

bluntly, pushing his wire glasses up his thin nose. He was the village optometrist—a rare skill these days—and had been expelled from the City after retinal implants made glasses obsolete. "We know he was wandering in the Drear Lands. And we know he can't have been there by accident."

"How do we know that?" Froken Bensimbra asked.

"My dear Raquel." Herr Grünewald looked down at her condescendingly. "Think about it. Would anyone wander into the Drear Lands by mistake?"

Poor Froken Bensimbra sank back, blushing, but Fru Vleinigen, who baked bread for the village, leaned forward, frowning. "Could he be a spy for—for *them*? An infiltrator?"

"He's rather an unlikely candidate, isn't he?" said Mayor Landholm. "A mere boy? And anyway, he'd hardly have been left to wander—"

"Sigrid's right," said Herr Grünewald. "It's a ruse, to catch us off guard. Perhaps he's the son of a senior officer."

"They start them young these days," added Herr Bradley. "I saw it all back home. Boys of eight and nine wearing those shoulder patches, being drilled in formation." Herr Bradley was from the Nation of Arkansas, Fru Berta had told Astra. It was one of the tiny statelets that were forever at war in the vast VilderRegion between the Pacific and Atlantic DeadSeas.

Several people shifted in their chairs uncomfortably. "I spoke to him myself at some length when he woke up," Mayor Landholm said sharply. "In UL—he doesn't speak either Old or New Nordlandish. *I'd* say he's simple-minded. He doesn't seem to know where he is or where he came from."

"Then how did he get here?" demanded Herr Bradley.

"Didn't it occur to you he might be a very good actor?" Herr Grünewald said. "That's one of the skills—"

"May I speak?" Astra's father leaned forward in his calm, focused way. "Why don't we ask the boy to come in? Then we can all judge for ourselves. He may be a little frightened, but we'll do our best to reassure him."

50

Most of the council members nodded, though Herr Grünewald gave Astra's father a dark look and Fru Vleinigen squeezed her hands together nervously. Mayor Landholm left the room and returned with the boy. He'd had a bath and his hair was combed, though the work tunic and shabby trousers he wore were at least two sizes too big for him. His eyes flicked warily round the room.

"This is our village council," Mayor Landholm said, laying her hand gently on his shoulder. "They have some questions they'd like to ask you." And she motioned him to her own chair.

"What's your name?" Fru Vleinigen said—rather rudely, Astra thought.

"Neil," the boy said, after a moment's hesitation. "Neil Grescoe." A strange name, perhaps from somewhere else in the AWA, or even the VilderRegion. And the accent! Astra had never heard anything so weird.

"Please, explain yourself," Herr Grünewald said. "Where are you from? And what were you doing in the Drear Lands?"

This is awful, Astra thought. This isn't helping at all. And before anyone else could say anything or her father could stop her, she said, "I'm Astra," looking straight at the boy.

Uh oh. How often had Fru Berta said "You watch that impulsive tongue of yours"? Mayor Landholm frowned and Herr Grünewald looked scandalized, but she rushed on. "I know just how you feel, because I was scared, too, when we—when me and my father left the City and came to live here. But we just want to help you. We all wanted to meet you and—and help you."

It hadn't come out in exactly the way she'd intended, but the boy looked relieved. "Really, Astra, I do think—" Fru Vleinigen began, but Herr Bradley broke in.

"Obviously your daughter doesn't understand the danger, Hallvard," he said, glaring at Astra's father. "Perhaps you ought to explain a few things to her."

Astra, clenching her fists, looked at her father, who had gone quite pale. "On the contrary," he said. "I think Astra and I may claim to have experienced the danger first-hand before we ever came here." He took a deep breath and went on. "We are pre-judging the situation before we have the facts. Let the boy speak openly."

Mayor Landholm cleared her throat. "I'm going to let him explain in his own words how he got here," she said firmly, and sat down on the floor.

In the sudden silence the boy hesitated, clearing his throat. "I know this'll sound strange," he said slowly, "but I don't know how I got here. Not exactly. I know where I started out, though. In a place called the Yukon."

There were murmurs of surprise. Mayor Landholm raised her eyebrows as if to say I told you he was simple.

"Yukon," Astra's father said, frowning thoughtfully. "That was the old name for one of the provinces of Beaufortia, if I remember correctly. It was renamed about two hundred years ago when the new regional boundaries were established."

Everyone stared at the boy again. "It's illegal to use the old names," Mayor Landholm said. "Weren't you taught that?"

"But I'm not—I'm not from your time." The boy lifted his chin and spoke in a rush. "I come from the past. And I somehow ended up in the future."

"Heilagr aska!" Herr Grünewald exploded.

"I'm sure you'll understand if we say that—well, that's very difficult for us to believe," Froken Bensimbra said gently.

The boy nodded vigorously. "Oh, I know. It's difficult for *me* to believe. But it's true."

"If I might be so bold," Astra's father said, his face intent. "I can't speak more openly, but there may be something to what the boy says."

Astra's heart leapt into her mouth. Her father must believe there was a chance, however tiny, that the boy's story was true. Could he *really* have manifested out of the past?

"The wood stove in my house—" The boy broke off uncertainly and rubbed his forehead. "It wasn't lit that night. It didn't work. But somehow the house filled up with smoke anyway, and then my dog disappeared—" He choked up and shook his head. "I landed in a desert. In your time. I don't know where it was. I walked a long way. I was heading toward some red cliffs. And then that night I made a fire, and the next thing I knew these men in uniforms grabbed me."

Here there were sharp intakes of breath all round the room. Herr Grünewald said *"Tythinggeir!"* under his breath, which Astra knew was a very bad swear word.

"We marched for several days, I think. They said they were taking me to the Fortress." The boy paused and licked his lips. "But I managed to get away. I think maybe I wandered in circles for a while. They thought I was a spy," he said, near tears, "but I'm not."

"That's the most amazing story I've ever heard," Froken Bensimbra said, staring at him in admiration.

"An amazing imagination, certainly," Herr Bradley said dryly. "But if he is an escaped prisoner, we're in danger as long as he stays here."

"We're not in the business of putting terrified children out in the street," Mayor Landholm said firmly. "Or the Drear Lands, in this case. Dr. Forberg says he's disoriented, perhaps in shock. He needs time to recover."

"I would have thought," Herr Grünewald said with disdain, "that the decision was obvious. We can't risk sheltering another refugee." And he looked meaningfully at Hallvard and Astra.

"But he's had a terrible ordeal," Fru Vleinigen ventured. "And he does look very tired." In fact, thought Astra, he looked exhausted.

"Perhaps Fru Berta would not be averse to having the boy stay with us," Astra's father said quickly, "since she's already sheltering fugitives." Astra could have sworn there was a hint of sarcasm in his voice.

"An excellent suggestion," declared Herr Bradley. "No need to endanger anyone else."

"Then I take it I'm outvoted," Herr Grünewald said sullenly. "I hope, for all our sakes, that my fears prove groundless."

As the meeting broke up, Astra's father lingered, talking in a low voice with Mayor Landholm. The boy stood by himself, looking lonely, and Astra went up to him. "Fru Berta's very kind," she said, "and Pappa's very persuasive. I'm sure she'll take you in."

"All I really want," the boy said, "is to go home. If anyone knows how to get me there. Just as soon as I find my dog."

"You're very quiet, elskede," Astra's father said as they walked home together. "Is something troubling you? Are you worried about the boy living with us?"

Astra shook her head. Should she tell her father what she was thinking? She was quite sure, but would anyone else believe her?

"I think I know where the dog came from, Pappa."

"The dog?" She could hear the smile in her father's voice.

"I think it belongs to the boy. I'm sure of it. Only Linn'll be so upset if she has to give it up." Linn was Dr. Forberg's daughter, a thin little girl of eight who was often ill.

Her father was silent for a minute or two. "The dog will decide," he said at last.

Neil Learns a Thing or Two

eil woke with a start, his pillow drenched with sweat. Around him was only darkness, and for a few terrifying moments—but no, here he was, lying on a cot in the Mayor's office in an Ash-Gatherer village, no longer a prisoner. He felt weak with relief. In his dream he'd been back in the clutches of those soldiers, the ones the villagers referred to as *they*. Only now *they* had Freya, too, and they were threatening to take her away forever if Neil didn't tell them who he was spying for.

He stared up at the ceiling, feeling sick. Where *was* Freya? How was he ever going to find her? His ankle was throbbing again and he sat up, rubbing it anxiously. Suppose they could track him down here?

He pushed the thought away quickly, slipped out of bed, and groped for the too-big trousers and tunic. He still felt battered and wobbly, but he certainly wasn't going to get back to sleep now. Besides, he didn't want to return to that bad dream.

He crept as softly as he could to the door. If he woke Mayor Landholm up, she might tell him to go back to bed. Quietly he let himself out and stood on the porch, staring about him. The little village, spread out below him in the moonlight, was tiny—not more than a couple of dozen houses, with a grassy area in the middle. A single unpaved road ran round it. There were no streetlights, or even any light in the windows.

He set off down the hill. The houses were all made out of the same ugly ash-coloured brick—Scar-Face had talked about them, he remembered—with roofs of straw. He passed a shed with goats inside—he heard faint bleats—and a beehive-shaped building with a chimney sticking out of its roof. Where they made the bricks, maybe. Piles of them were stacked outside.

He continued on round the village, feeling strangely disoriented. The soldiers had those glowing weapons, those tiny lighted stones, but these people—it was as if they were living in the past, not the future. He passed a vegetable garden, and a field with trees, and came to a fence that separated the village from the Drear Lands. Not much of one. It was patched together from old iron rods and bits of wire and rusted machine parts. He could make out a section of hood from a Ford truck, a rusted Caterpillar tread.

He was about to head back to Mayor Landholm's when howling broke out nearby. The goats across the way began bleating and shrieking, and from somewhere came the bray of what must be a mule. They'd scented a wolf, maybe, or a coyote, with the pack right behind it. He stared round wildly but saw nothing. The doors of the nearest houses were flung open and people rushed outside, shouting to each other, brandishing weapons.

"What do you think you're doing out here, young man?" It was Dr. Forberg, who grabbed him by the shoulder.

"I was just—I couldn't sleep—I wanted to—"

And then, over Dr. Forberg's shoulder, he saw the wolf. It was tied to a stake in someone's yard and it was leaping and yipping and howling. It suddenly stood on its hind legs and let out the most heartrending roo-roo-roo he'd ever heard.

Ohmygod. Not a wolf at all. It was Freya!

The next moment she was in his arms, sobbing and howling, and tears were streaming down Neil's face. Freya! His very own Freya! "Never again," he whispered through his tears, "we're never going to be separated again," to which Freya sobbed roo-roo-roo in reply.

Mutters of confusion and amazement went round the crowd. "That's a wild animal," someone said in alarm.

"It's Freya—my dog—she was missing, I—" Neil stammered, between his tears and Freya licking his face.

"I suppose *she* came from the past, too?" a man said, pointing an old hunting rifle at Neil.

"Now, Henk." A tiny woman gently pushed the rifle aside. "I'm sure the boy can explain."

"There's no need," Mayor Landholm remarked wryly. "Seems to me the dog's made it very plain."

"But Smilti's *my* dog," a little girl said. She was standing beside the doctor in her nightgown, gulping back tears.

"She had a gash in her paw," Dr. Forberg explained to Neil, "and a torn right ear, which I treated. And after that—well, my daughter Linn fell in love with her. Pets are forbidden, but I couldn't very well turn the dog out."

Neil looked up at Linn earnestly. "You gave Freya a home until we found each other again," he said. "As long as I'm here, you can take her out for a walk anytime you want."

Linn, her lower lip trembling, managed a quavering smile. Everyone else began drifting away, muttering about interrupted sleep, or about how the dog and the boy had thrown the whole of Ashgård into uproar. Some, more darkly, said none of it boded well.

Neil and Freya, pressed so close to each other they might have been welded together, walked back up the hill with Mayor Landholm. What had happened to Freya since she'd jumped through the smoke tunnel? He'd probably never know. But that was okay. Amazingly, they'd found each other again, and that was the only thing that mattered.

He examined her carefully when they got back to the house. She looked a little thinner, but otherwise she seemed okay, and her paw and the torn right ear were both healing. "We're going to be together for always," he muttered sleepily into her fur when they were curled up together on his cot. "Always. I promise." And Freya licked his nose by way of reply.

It was bright daylight when he woke. Freya was still pressed against him, tail draped over her muzzle. In Mayor Landholm's tiny kitchen he found a note. *Dear Neil, There is cereal and fruit for you in a bowl on the table. Also scraps for Freya. Please walk down to Fru Berta's house—the one with the sunflowers.*

It was late morning, judging by where the sun was overhead, and stiflingly hot. For the first time since his ordeal he was starving. He ate the nutty-tasting cereal hungrily and fed Freya the scraps. Then he opened the door and stepped outside. Freya shot off after something—a rabbit, maybe?—and he headed down the hill.

By daylight the village seemed even smaller and shabbier. He was passing one of the houses when the door opened and Astra's father came out. He turned to shake hands with another man—one of the council members, Neil thought—and after a few moments the other man went back inside the house as Astra's father waved a greeting. Neil waited for him to come down the path.

"Hello, Mr. —" he began, and realized he didn't know his name.

"You must call me Hallvard," the man said. He was very tall, with a small neat beard and kind, sad eyes. "I just had a long chat with Herr Grünewald about you."

"About me?"

"There's been—well, some concern in the village about your being here. As you know."

"They think I'm a spy," Neil said, crestfallen.

"They're afraid." Hallvard laid a hand on Neil's shoulder. "They're worried about what might happen because you're here." Freya, having given up her hunting, rushed past them to the Forbergs' to see if Linn was there. "*They* are bound to be looking for you," Hallvard went on, "and if they find you in our village ..." He paused, and Neil felt as though a dark cloud had just passed over the sun. "They'd take you away, of course. But they'd also take revenge. Destroy our homes, perhaps. It's happened before, though not here. Not yet."

Neil shivered and looked about him, as though black shadows lurked round every corner. "Does that mean I can't stay here?" He felt his eyes watering.

"No, no, no." Hallvard was emphatic. "Fru Berta is more than willing to have you stay with us. But it might be best for you—well, to keep out of sight for a while. Not draw attention to yourself. They *do* have spies—real ones. Not to mention airborne spying devices."

Neil stood stock still for a moment. "But who *are* they?" he burst out. "And why do they want me? I don't know anything. I'm no use to them."

"You and I know that, but *they* don't. You escaped before they had a chance to question you, and they'll want you back." Hallvard sighed. "It's a long story. A very long story. It's the reason my daughter and I are here in Ashgård, too."

"Did you escape from them as well?" Neil wanted to know.

"No, not exactly. But we *are* in danger from them." They'd reached Fru Berta's house, where chickens pecked in the dirt and sunflowers brightened the dull walls. "Come on in. I'll tell you the whole story at dinner this evening."

When Fru Berta saw Neil, her mouth fell open and her blue eyes widened. "By Thor and Odin!" she said. "I hadn't seen before how much you look like Toivo!" She wiped her ash-covered hands on her work clothes—"my turn in the brick factory," she explained—and tilted up his chin. "It's uncanny, that's what it is. Same mouth, same nose. Though Toivo had a mole, right here—" and she pointed to a spot just below Neil's left ear. "It meant good luck, so we always said."

Her face crumpled, and she looked so close to tears that Neil didn't dare ask about Toivo. Instead he asked the question that had been worrying him since Dr. Forberg had said pets were forbidden. "Can Freya stay with me? She won't be any trouble."

Fru Berta smiled and bent to scratch Freya's ears. "It's been a long time since there was a dog in Ashgård. And with an Old Nordlandish name yet!" Freya rooed happily and wagged her tail, and Neil felt a rush of relief. "As long as she hates them as much as I do," Fru Berta said fiercely, "she's welcome. Forbidding pets indeed!"

Astra joined them, and over dandelion-and-peavine salad and rabbit stew, Neil told them about Charlie, and the mysterious smoke tunnel, and how Freya had disappeared through it, which was why he'd ended up here in the first place. And how he'd landed in that vast sandy desert—"Lake Mjøsa, it used to be, once," Fru Berta muttered—and how he'd walked all day looking for water. But he skipped over the part about being captured by the soldiers and how he'd escaped. He'd told some of that story already, and Fru Berta looked so angry when he even mentioned it, and Astra so frightened, that he decided it was best to leave it out.

"So you have no idea how it happened," Hallvard said, leaning forward intently. "The business about the smoke in the stove, I mean. And the tunnel or whatever it was you fell through."

Neil shook his head. "Though it must have had *something* to do with Charlie. With his experiments, I mean. Maybe—I don't know—maybe *he* made that tunnel through the smoke." It sounded ridiculous, stated like that, and he stroked Freya's ears to hide his embarrassment.

"My own investigations—" Hallvard began, and broke off as if he'd changed his mind. "This Charlie ... You don't know anything more about him?"

Fru Berta set down her cup of chicory coffee with a snort. "It all sounds like a load of codswallop to me. All this business about mysterious smoke and travelling into the future." She shook her head. "You don't have to be afraid of us, you know, lad. You can tell us the truth."

"But it is the truth," Neil said, his heart sinking. So Fru Berta didn't believe him either. Only Hallvard had been willing to listen. *There may be something to what the boy says,* he'd said.

"*I* believe the boy," Hallvard said, and Neil looked at him gratefully. "For one thing, extraordinary as the possibility is, it's too fantastical a story to make up. And for another ..." He paused, and a long glance passed between him and Astra, who so far had been quite silent. "I might as well admit, Berta, that I had my own reasons for asking the boy to stay here. But I must ask you to keep your counsel. What I'm about to tell you is known only to Astra and myself."

Neil shivered, and Fru Berta's eyes grew round. "I know you're doing some sort of secret research," she said, "but by Thor and Odin, I've never pried. Never," she added stoutly.

"And I've been very grateful for your discretion. Now, it seems, I must take you into my confidence—you and the boy, too." He paused, looking round at them gravely. "I worked at a research institute in the City—the Research Institute for Temporal Investigations, it was called. Many scientists worked there. We were investigating the nature of time. Several of us were working on projects about time travel." He paused again, as if choosing his words carefully. "We believed that, if it was possible to gain access to the wisdom of the past, this might help us with the great dangers of our own time."

Neil's heart leapt into his mouth. So *that* was why Hallvard believed him! A million questions crowded his brain, but he forced himself to listen.

"They were also interested in our work, of course," Hallvard was saying. "Very interested. As they gained more power, they began trying to control what we did. Just before they seized the Institute, a number of us fled." Hallvard reached out and took Astra's hand. "Astra and I were fortunate. We managed make our way here. Others were—not so lucky." A kind of shiver went round the room. Freya gave a short, sharp bark, as if she sensed danger.

"I was fortunate in finding Fru Berta," Hallvard went on.

"She allowed me to convert a room in her cellar into a laboratory so I could continue my work, in secret. Both for my own sake and that of the village, I wanted to avoid discovery. And as you've found out, Neil"—he smiled slightly—"people tend to be skeptical about such research anyway."

Fru Berta's eyes had grown even rounder, if possible. She opened her mouth as if to say something and then shut it again. Neil said eagerly, "So did you find a way? Can you travel back to the past?" Maybe Hallvard could help him and Freya get home!

Hallvard glanced at his daughter again before answering. "With Astra's help I'm carrying out certain ... experiments. I won't go into more detail; that would only endanger you and Fru Berta. But we've made a great deal of progress. I'm certain that one day people will be able to physically enter the dimension of time as easily as they now move in the dimension of space. It seems, in fact, that you may have succeeded."

So the answer was no. Neil slumped back, dejected. Hallvard reached forward and ruffled his hair gently. "I'm sorry I can't give you the answer you wanted, lad. Perhaps—who knows?—there'll be an unexpected breakthrough. Your miner friend Charlie found a way."

He isn't my friend, Neil thought sulkily. In fact I hate him. It's all his fault I'm here. But Fru Berta shook her head and got up from her chair. "It's all getting a bit much for my old brain," she said, clearing away dishes with an energetic clatter. "Time travel into the future, indeed! The lad looks pretty solid to me!"

Even Neil had to smile at this, but Astra frowned. "You were so brave, escaping from those soldiers," she said. "I don't know how you did it. I couldn't have done that."

This wasn't, of course, the full truth, and Neil looked down guiltily. Should he tell them about the thing in his ankle?

"You know, Pappa, I've been thinking," Astra went on. "Neil's actually time-travelled. Maybe he ought to see what we're doing."

Hallvard glanced at his daughter, his eyes narrowing. "It's

a dangerous proposition, Astra. We mustn't take unnecessary risks."

"But things can't be more dangerous than they already are. Besides, who knows?" Astra's eyes lit up. "Maybe he can help us."

Neil found himself sitting on the edge of his chair. But Hallvard shook his head firmly. "The risks are too high. I can't take responsibility for what might happen—if only at the physical level."

"I don't see how there's a risk." It was obvious Astra didn't give up easily. "Not if he's only watching." She paused and laid a hand on her father's arm. "Please, Pappa."

Hallvard's face softened, but all he said was, "Let me think about it. I need to sleep on things, elskede, you know that."

Astra thrust her lower lip out and frowned. She must be used to getting her own way, Neil thought. When Hallvard wasn't looking, she slid her eyes sideways at Neil and winked.

The Memory Stone

Neil slept late on the makeshift bed in the cool cellar, with Freya tucked beside him. When he came into the kitchen the next morning, Astra was sitting at the table drumming a pencil on a pad of paper. "I have to write an essay for Pappa," she said, and made a face. "It's about a famous Old Nordlandish novel, *Kristin Lavransdatter*. Have you heard of it?"

Neil helped himself to a cool glass of goat's milk—he was sweating even indoors—and shook his head. "Can't say I have."

"It's set such a long time ago," Astra said, sighing. "And I don't understand half the words." That reminded Neil of Scar-Face and his poetry book, a memory he pushed quickly away.

"Why do you have to write an essay for your dad?" he asked. Freya was letting him know she wanted a walk by pushing her nose into the back of his knee over and over.

"Because if I go to school I have to be registered, and it's best if there's no record of me being here," Astra explained. Which didn't really help, but Astra was rushing on. "The book says they had something called ice. Pappa says it's solid water, can you imagine? It's ridiculous."

Neil stared at her. "We had it in my time, too."

"You did?" Astra looked at him in amazement. "Most people here don't believe it ever existed. What's it like?"

"Well, it's cold," said Neil uncertainly. "And smooth, like glass. And you can skate—" he stopped, because of course she wouldn't know what that was. "You can wear these boots with blades so you can move on the ice."

"You're kidding, right?" Astra shook her head and laughed. "How can you walk on water? You'd fall down." She looked

64

skeptically at Neil. "My grandmother said there actually used to be snow, too, but I don't believe her. I think she got it from this book. I think the author made it all up."

"Of course she didn't—" Neil said, annoyed, but Astra bent her head over her work again. Freya, meanwhile, was trotting to the door and back with more and more urgency. "Fine. Believe what you want. I'm taking Freya for a walk."

"Pappa says it's best if Linn takes her out," Astra said, glancing up. "She'll be over any minute."

Neil stared at her again. Surely Hallvard didn't expect him to stay inside all the time? He'd only just been reunited with Freya—more than anything he wanted a long romp with her. "Can I use your phone? I'll tell Linn she doesn't need to—"

"A phone? Oh, you must mean a devcom," Astra said. And when Neil looked blank—"Short for 'communication device.' We don't have them here," she added. "They only work in the City."

Neil looked aghast. "Then how do you—?"

"We send notes." Astra held up her pencil, grinning. "I know, I couldn't believe it either. No devcoms, no imagescreens, no moodfood. It was horrible." She laughed. "Coming to live in Ashgård was the best thing that ever happened to me, Pappa says. He says I had to learn to use my imagination."

No texting, no computer games, no iPods—he stared at her, appalled. What was he going to do all day? How did Astra stand it? He wandered listlessly into the main room and flung himself on a chair, or a sort-of chair—it was made of old iron rods and rough woven cloth. What would have happened if he *hadn't* found Ashgård? Freya would have forgotten all about him. Maybe she'd have been perfectly content. He stared out the window, itching to be out in the fresh air and sunshine. Double triple *quadruple* crap. What did it matter if he went outside? Everyone in the village knew he was here anyway.

A sudden knock on the door interrupted his dismay. Linn stood there, flushed and smiling, while Freya rooed and wriggled excitedly. She snapped on the leash she'd brought and the two of them went off happily together. Restless, Neil jumped up and wandered round the room, noticing for the first time the old-fashioned lamps—what did they use instead of electricity?—and the other handmade furniture.

On a shelf made out of an old car bumper, hammered flat, was a small framed picture of a boy. A portrait, not a photo, drawn in pencil. The boy looked a little older than Neil, with thick curls and a confident smile that contained a glimmer of Fru Berta. This must be Toivo, then, though he didn't see much of a resemblance to himself. What had happened to him?

He was turning away disconsolately when the door to the cellar opened and Hallvard stepped into the room. "You know," he said, "I've been giving a lot of thought to Astra's suggestion."

Neil's stomach flipped over. "For real?"

"She's right about your experience. Much more prescient than I am, as usual."

Astra was standing in the doorway, her eyes shining. "So what does that mean, Pappa? Does it mean ...?"

"It means I'm inviting Neil to a demonstration. If you're both willing."

"Right now?" Neil and Astra said simultaneously, and Astra added cautiously, "I haven't finished my essay."

"Essays be damned!" Hallvard said with surprising impatience. "This is much more important. Or"—he glanced mischievously at his daughter—"would you rather stay behind and keep working on it instead?"

Nervous quivers went through Neil's stomach as they went down the stairs and across the cellar. Hallvard was placing a lot of faith in him. He didn't want to disappoint him and Astra by showing how little he really knew about time travel.

At the back wall Hallvard turned and looked hard at Neil. "You must promise me," he said, "to say nothing of what you witness. Nothing to anyone—even Fru Berta. Is that understood?"

Neil swallowed hard. "I promise," he said.

Hallvard nodded gravely, turned to the wall, and felt with his fingers between two of the upper bricks. He must have found what he was looking for, because the next moment, with a faint groaning sound, a whole section of the wall began sliding smoothly back. Neil's jaw dropped. A false wall!

A set of steps appeared, cut into the earth and vanishing into darkness. Hallvard picked up a nearby lantern, lit it, and stepped through the opening, followed by Astra, then Neil. Immediately the wall slid back and shut with a dull thunk. Except for the flickering lantern, they were in complete darkness.

Nervously Neil followed them down the stairs. At the bottom a long, narrow room opened out, stretching away into dimness. Along one wall was a workbench covered with beakers and test tubes and centrifuges. Above it, shelves contained bottles and jars filled with liquids and other substances. Neil had often visited his father's lab at the university, with its petrographic microscopes and its X-ray diffractometer, but he'd never seen one like this.

"Rather old-fashioned compared to my lab at the Institute," Hallvard was explaining apologetically, "but it's the best I could do here."

He placed his fingers under the bench and pressed something. A sliver of a drawer opened, so tiny you'd never have known it was there. Very gently he drew out a small cloth pouch that glowed faintly in his hand. He opened the pouch, reverently removed whatever was inside, and held it out to Neil.

It was a chunk of pale pink quartz, about the size of Neil's fist. Neil, who'd seen dozens of quartz samples in his father's lab, stared at it in disappointment. What was so special about a chunk of quartz? And what did it have to do with time travel?

But Astra was gazing at it fixedly, her eyes shining. "Look more closely," Hallvard urged.

Neil bent over it. Inside it was a dazzling multi-coloured wheel with shimmering spokes, or else a sun radiating light. It spun on its axis at the same time, creating wave forms that travelled outward and in turn became wheels or suns. It was mesmerizing. He stared, unable to look away. When he moved his head the image moved, too.

"It's—it's a hologram!" he blurted out.

Hallvard nodded with satisfaction. "I didn't know holograms had been discovered in your time," he said. "But yes, indeed, it is. And the wheel is an ancient symbol for the circularity of time."

"I've seen holograms on credit cards and—oh, all kinds of things," Neil said eagerly. "What does this one do?"

Hallvard laughed. "Then your era hasn't discovered their magnificent potential. We can enhance crystals with certain asteroidal minerals so that they generate these complex images. And by using the laws of quantum physics, we can actually merge with the crystals and manipulate the images." He indicated the quartz with pride. "This is a Memory Stone. It's something I've worked on for many years. But it's still an early prototype—an early version. It's all I managed to take with me from the lab."

Quantum physics—just what Charlie had been studying. Neil knew a little about it from his father—how an electron spinning at one end of the universe had a "sibling" electron at the other, and whatever you did to one electron happened at exactly the same moment to the other. Though no one really knew why—only that it meant that somehow everything in the universe was connected.

"... best results using rose quartz as a transmitting medium," Hallvard was saying. Neil realized guiltily that he hadn't been paying attention. "It helps to transform our consciousness from the physical to the psychic level. And when it's treated with pixillite, we can tap into the past. Into memory."

Neil wasn't really following Hallvard's explanation about transforming consciousness, so he stared at the crystal again.

Up close it glittered with an iridescence that was almost painful to look at. "What makes it sparkle like that?" Neil asked.

"The pixillite. It used to be mined with robotic devices on the asteroid Antikleia, until extraplanetary mining became too expensive."

"So it's like—stardust?" Neil stared in amazement at the crystal.

"Yes, I suppose you could call it that." Hallvard nodded. "Unfortunately, it's extremely rare, even on Antikleia. The tiniest amount here on Terrania costs a lot. But it's an essential component for time travel."

"But what does it do? How does it work? Can I touch it?"

After a moment's hesitation Hallvard placed the crystal on Neil's palm. It was surprisingly warm. "It feels like it's pulsing," he said after a few moments.

Hallvard looked startled. "Yes, you're right, it does pulse. But normally it takes several sessions before—"

"How do you operate it?" Neil said.

"You have to learn to listen for its sound. That sound is made by billions of phonons, which vibrate at a particular frequency, depending on the crystal. Then you have to attune yourself to the sound vibrations. It takes a lot of practice. Astra's much better at it than I am." Hallvard smiled at his daughter, who was still gazing at the crystal. "When you're vibrating at the same frequency, you can merge with the crystal—physically enter it."

Neil's face must have betrayed his skepticism, because Hallvard went on patiently, "We think rock is completely solid, but that's an illusion. Everything in our world is moving, even at the subatomic level—vibrating at incredible speeds. We've done a great deal of work on energy signatures in the last fifty years. So now we know how to move between energy levels."

What was it Dee had said about Charlie? Something about time machines being old-hat and how you didn't need mechanical flim-flam. Had Charlie known about these crystals?

"But I still don't get—I mean, once you're inside the crystal—"

"Then you can mentally manipulate the hologram—the Wheel, in this case—to go where you want to go."

"Then"—Neil's heart was beating faster—"I *can* go back home."

But Hallvard shook his head. "At the moment, no. You can return to the past, but you cannot materialize there. You can see an entire past moment, but you cannot participate."

"The people are so real it's scary," said Astra. "You can see and hear everything, just as it happened. But they can't see or hear you."

"But—why not?" Neil asked.

Hallvard shrugged. "If we knew the answer, we could solve the problem. Something to do with the correct vibrational level, I suspect. Our ability to adjust vibrational levels is still very crude. I think, however, we are close to a solution. And your own materialization here convinces me of the possibility." His eyes gleamed in the half-dark. "That's what so exciting about your arrival. People really *can* materialize out of the past—and dogs," he added, smiling. "And if we can do that, we ought to be able to do the reverse—send people from today's world back to the past."

But that might take years to figure out, Neil thought, and by then he'd be grown up. He'd have to find some other way of getting home. He looked so unhappy that Hallvard said quickly, "I promised you a demonstration, and here we are talking. Astra, why don't you begin? I'm sure it'll clear up a lot of Neil's questions."

Astra stepped forward, her hands cupped together. Her father placed the Memory Stone gently in the bowl her hands made. She closed her eyes, her expression intent. Hallvard stepped away from her and motioned Neil to do the same. "She's listening for the vibration I told you about earlier," he whispered. "She's using thought to align her own energy signature with the crystal's."

This made no sense at all, at least from the science Neil knew. Still, he watched alertly, wondering what would happen. At first, nothing. Maybe it was just an illusion. A kind of conjuring trick. And then Astra's hands and forearms began turning pink, as if absorbing the glow from the quartz. The glow infused her torso, her head, her whole body. The next moment it was as though Astra herself was shimmering, vibrating so fast it made Neil blink. Suddenly, though Neil couldn't have described how it happened—perhaps he'd blinked at the wrong moment—she was inside the crystal. Though "inside" wasn't quite the right way to describe it. She seemed to be outside it, too, as though she and the crystal had merged into one being. Unbelievable—he couldn't believe it even as he watched—but true.

"Now what?" Neil whispered, awestruck.

"She'll use the Wheel to choose the time she wants to visit," Hallvard said softly. "Though she always chooses the same year." He shook his head. "The last one her mother was alive."

What had happened to her mother? wondered Neil. But all Hallvard's attention was on his daughter. Eyes still closed, she stood within the Wheel, which began tilting, infinitesimally, toward her.

"Away from you is the future, toward you is the past," Hallvard explained softly, "though for some reason we are unable to go into the future yet. Astra is going back only eight years—not much time at all."

Astra opened her eyes. She seemed to be watching something in front of her. Then her face shone and her lips parted.

"There she is." The words were said so softly that Neil nearly missed them. Astra had leaned forward, biting her lip. Different expressions—a laugh, a sigh, a frown—passed across her face. Then the light went out of it and she stood there slumped and dejected. The Wheel moved back to its upright position, the vibrating shimmer returned, and the next moment Astra had somehow dissolved out of the crystal and stood in the room with them. Her face was tear-streaked and she pressed her fingers to her temples as if in pain.

Hallvard put an arm round his daughter and dropped a kiss on her hair. "Sometimes I think this is too much for you."

"No—oh no. I love seeing her. But afterwards it always hurts."

Neil could hardly contain himself. "What did you see? How do you get in and out like that? And why does it hurt?"

"We don't know the answer to the last question," Hallvard said. "I've tried the Stone myself without any ill effects. Perhaps it's only Astra who's affected like that, or only certain people. As for what she saw—" He stopped and looked at his daughter.

"She was wearing a lightdress," Astra said softly, "and she had her hair all done up"—she held her fingers above her head—"and she came into my sleeproom and began to tell me a story ..." Her voice wavered and broke off; she looked away and blinked back tears. "You know, Pappa, her voice is just the way I remember. Sort of low and soft. It always makes me think of Stroorberrie Joywafers."

Neil's heart was beating so fast he was sure the others could hear it. He knew exactly what memories *he'd* want to see if he could use the Stone. Except he'd want to watch for much longer than Astra had.

"It requires a lot of practice to reach the vibrational level of the crystal," Hallvard said gently, "and still more to adjust the Wheel. Astra here has had much more practice than I have, and yet she can hold the memory for just a few minutes."

If only he could try it! He looked longingly at the Stone as Astra handed it to her father, who gently tucked it into its pouch and placed it in the hidden drawer. What a lot of power was locked in that tiny piece of pink rock! And once you could make the past come back ... no wonder *they* wanted it.

Neil couldn't explain why he felt so wobbly and exhausted after watching the demonstration, though Hallvard thought it was because he was still recovering from his ordeal. He slept for the rest of the afternoon, with Freya curled up on the mattress beside him. By the time he wandered upstairs, rubbing his eyes, the house was filled with the deep gold of a late-summer northern evening.

Fru Berta had prepared *pølse med lompe*—or potato flatbread with sausages, in what he was learning to call UL—and what with the delicious food and a glass of apple cider, he began to feel almost normal again. Freya lay under his chair, where he fed her bits of the flatbread and sausage when no one was looking. When everyone had finished, Hallvard pushed his own chair back, turning the stem of his glass in his fingers.

"Yesterday, Neil, I promised you a full accounting of events—of how we arrived at the grave situation we find ourselves in."

"In that case," Fru Berta said, rolling her eyes, "we'll need a little more fortification." She cut pieces from a fruit cake and set the plate on the table. She closed the curtains, too, and lit a fat candle that threw shadows on their faces.

"It all begins—well, I suppose it all begins back in your century," Hallvard said, looking tired and drained—even old, Neil thought with a pang. "With the Oil Wars. I've read about them, but I don't remember all the details. And it's impossible, now, to obtain books about it. Only books issued by the Department of National Recollection are permitted."

Neil stared. "But—what about libraries? Or the Internet?"

"Information is highly controlled, and in the City only certain people are permitted—"

"What's a library?" Astra wanted to know.

"There, I think, is your answer." Hallvard sighed deeply. "It's a criminal offence to keep records or mementoes of any kind other than the approved ones."

So *that* was why the soldier who'd kept his mother's book had been so afraid. Neil couldn't believe it.

"The Oil Wars overlapped with the Water Wars and the Land Wars," Hallvard went on. "Meanwhile, the icecaps began melting—"

"But that's already happening." Neil leaned forward, his face sombre. "My uncle says that soon there won't be any ice in the

Northwest Passage in summer. And the permafrost is thawing, too. He says the climate everywhere is really changing."

"Yes. That was the beginning." Hallvard nodded gravely. "The melting icecaps meant that sea levels rose all over the world. Many coastal towns and cities were flooded."

So that was what had happened to Vancouver. The Great Drowning, the military leader had called it.

"The changes brought drought and new diseases and crop failures, too. A wide belt around the equator—the Hot Regions—had to be abandoned because of the heat. That meant we had climate refugees: millions of people flocking north to escape from places where no one could live anymore. Officially they're called FUAZ—Fugitives from Uneconomic Administrative Zones."

Fru Berta, who had picked up some sewing, set it down again. Even Freya was still.

"You can imagine what happened. The northern countries couldn't cope. For one thing there were no fish anymore, because the Arctic Ocean had turned completely acid." Hallvard leaned forward and refilled his glass. "Eventually the governments built huge gated cities with climate-controlled domes and left everyone else to fend for themselves."

It all sounded terrible. More than ever, Neil wanted to go home. But it still didn't explain about the soldiers and why they wanted him back.

"Some people and governments tried to take action, though in many places it was too late," Hallvard went on. "For example, all over the world, trees became protected species. There were major planting campaigns. People finally understood that without more trees to soak up carbon dioxide, the planet literally couldn't breathe."

"*Most* people," Fru Berta corrected.

Hallvard nodded. "But already, in your time, there were those who had other ideas. It started in ... California, I believe. Am I saying the name right?"

Neil nodded, wide-eyed. "It's in the United States. Or it was."

"Certain people there decided they had to help God destroy the world as quickly as possible, so a new and better world would rise from the ashes. They carried signs saying, 'Wake up, America, the enemy is here.' By that they meant the people trying to save the trees."

"But that's crazy!" Neil stared at Hallvard in disbelief.

"Indeed." Hallvard nodded. "I'm merely telling you what happened. They opposed the planting campaigns. They began deliberately setting fire to the forests."

Astra slumped in her chair. Fru Berta muttered something under her breath.

"Their ideas spread to other countries—what you once knew as Australia and Brazil, among others." Hallvard stared into his glass as if it was all taking place before him. "It became a religion, with rituals in which they worshipped fire. They also venerate ash, because it's the evidence of fire's power to destroy. They have a Book of Prophecies that predicts how the world will end."

Neil sat riveted, shaken to the core. That strange ceremony he'd witnessed the night of his capture—the soldiers gathering ash, their leader kissing the box! "Yes, I saw that!" he burst out. "The soldiers did that after they put my campfire out."

"But the worst was yet to come." Hallvard sat silent for some moments. "About five years before Astra was born, they were elected to the Council of Twelve—the council that rules Nordlandia—for the first time. They began taking over in other regions, too. Often by force. They imposed a different form of Nordlandish—we call it New Nordlandish—on everyone."

Fru Berta, who had picked up her sewing again, stabbed her needle into the tunic she was making. "It's all the fault of that old Leader of the Council—what was his name ...?"

"Galderup," said Hallvard quietly, "and his GlobenSalven party. Yes, they tried to work with the new members of the Council, and failed. But we're all at fault, really. We didn't resist them enough."

"What's their real name?" Neil asked.

Hallvard's expression was one of revulsion. "They call themselves the Fire Reapers. The Fire Reapers of Planetary Redemption."

Fru Berta startled everyone with a sudden exclamation—she'd pricked a finger with her needle. "Believe me, I'll do anything I can do to get rid of those *beisten*," she said grimly. "They took away the most precious thing in my life. I want them destroyed."

No one stirred. In the silence no one even seemed to breathe. The fat candle sitting on the table flickered and went out. It was as though the Fire Reapers had spoken.

The Shadows Fall

Neil slept fitfully that night, troubled by dreams of soldiers in desert uniforms brandishing torches of fire. He fell into a deeper sleep just before dawn and woke late. In the kitchen he helped himself to a handful of millet crackers while Freya, just back from her morning walk, pawed at him and rooed loudly.

"A rabbit? *Two* rabbits?" Munching, he squatted down to listen to her. "And you caught both of them? Good for you, Freya!"

"D'you *really* understand her?" Astra asked from her place at the kitchen table among her books and papers.

"Of course!" Neil tried to keep a straight face, though a smile flickered at the corners of his mouth. "Don't people understand Doggish nowadays?"

"Pappa says people could, in the old stories," Astra said wistfully. "But that was long ago, before the Great Catastrophes."

"Maybe they will again," Neil said lightly. "Who knows? Anyway," he added, a little sheepish about teasing Astra, "I don't understand *everything*. I mean, it takes a long time to learn, and—"

The door opened on Fru Berta, back from her morning shift in the vegetable garden. "The blacksmith is coming tomorrow," she said briskly. "We need to get those hoes repaired, Astra. And Fru Bensimbra says there's a crack in the door of the brick kiln."

A blacksmith? Repairing hoes? Neil's eyes widened. It was like living in that agricultural museum he'd seen on a school visit once. They'd had a blacksmith there, too, who showed them how to make horseshoes.

"I'm going for a nap," Fru Berta announced, and went off to her room. Astra, sighing, picked up her pencil. Maybe this is my chance, Neil thought. He waited until he heard snores coming from Fru Berta's room, until Astra, deep in thought, was writing steadily. Then he crept to the back door and opened it as quietly as he could. A moment later he was outside in the sunshine, leaping and punching the air as Freya raced ahead, ears back, golden muscles rippling.

Everyone seemed to be indoors—the children at school, the adults at work—except old Herr Branhammer, who was heading toward the gate. "Just off on my daily constitutional," he announced cheerfully as Neil caught up to him. "No naps for me, even if I am eighty-five!" He swung his cane up in the air to show how strong he still was. The teenage boy guarding the gate swung it open with a bored expression.

Neil waved goodbye to Herr Branhammer and hurried after Freya. She'd found an old rag and was shaking it back and forth as if it were prey. All of a sudden she dropped it and froze, the ridge of hair on her back standing straight up. A low, warning *ouf ouf* came from her throat. Neil looked about him but could see nothing.

Out of the corner of his eye, he caught a flash of movement beyond the fence. That searing pain suddenly burst in his ankle, surging through his whole body. He cried out and fell backward, writhing on the ground.

The Fire Reapers! They were coming to Ashgård!

Whatever happens I mustn't give myself away. Mustn't... but holy crap, it hurts ... He bit down hard on a knuckle to keep himself from crying out again. Freya flung herself beside him, whimpering softly and licking his face. "Quiet!" he hissed at her. There, a few metres away—a clump of scrubby bushes. Not much of a hiding place, but better than nothing. He crawled toward it.

There was a sudden commotion at the gate. Why hadn't the boy there sounded the alarm? Twenty or more soldiers, dressed in black emblazoned with flames, appeared in the gateway.

They had Herr Branhammer! His arms were bound behind him and he was struggling and calling out, though Neil couldn't make out what he said.

And then he forgot all about Herr Branhammer as a tall figure strode through, his flame-embroidered cape swirling about him. It was the officer who'd questioned Neil the night he was captured—Flame-Protector Arngrim! He gazed round the village as if trying to pierce the walls with his eyes. Neil crouched down behind the bushes, holding tight to Freya.

A group of villagers were hurrying toward the gate. Some of them carried old hunting rifles. They'd be totally useless against the Fire Reapers' weapons, Neil thought. Didn't they know that? Dr. Forberg, who was unarmed, reached the gate first. He said something to the Flame-Protector, who folded his arms and looked at him coldly. The officer said something in return, and gestured at Herr Branhammer. Dr. Forberg shook his head firmly. Flame-Protector Arngrim looked furious, and shouted an order. At once the soldiers set off at a jog toward the nearest houses, weapons at the ready.

Please God please. Please let Astra and Hallvard be safe in the cellar ...

When he dared to look again, Flame-Protector Arngrim was pacing back and forth, flexing his black-gloved fingers. Dr. Forberg and the others still stood there, whispering helplessly to one another. Ten minutes passed, fifteen. Neil, his body still throbbing with pain, changed position gingerly, terrified some movement of the bushes would give him away. Freya sat pressed against him, staring fiercely at the gate.

At last the soldiers came jogging back. Their leader stepped forward and saluted Flame-Protector Arngrim. Whatever he said next infuriated the officer, who glared at the villagers, shouted something, and stared round the village again, very slowly. Neil could have sworn he looked directly at his hiding place. The next moment, at a sign from the Flame-Protector, Herr Branhammer was released so roughly he staggered. Then the Flame-Protector turned on his heel and strode out through the gate, his cape swirling around him. His officers and troops swung in behind him.

Neil crawled as quickly as he could to the fence. Already the soldiers were diminishing black figures in the surrounding scrub, heading east. They passed the ruins of what might once have been a parkade, their shadows flickering in and out of its shattered concrete, and disappeared. The burning in his ankle was ebbing at last.

At the gate Dr. Forberg and Mayor Landholm were arguing with several others as more people arrived. "We *voted*," Mayor Landholm yelled. "We decided as a community. We all agreed—"

"Well, *I* didn't!" someone shouted from the back of the crowd. "And look what's happened!"

Neil hesitated. If he could just get back to Fru Berta's without being seen ... He tried to slip past, but the heavyset man who'd been at the council meeting caught sight of him. *"You!"* he exclaimed in a nasal American accent. "You're the reason they came! What are you doing out here?"

There were a few scattered catcalls, but Dr. Forberg stepped forward. "No need to terrify the boy further, Jim," he said firmly. "Herr Bradley's right, Neil. What are you doing here?"

"Umm—well—I—" Neil stammered, reddening to the roots of his hair as all eyes turned to him. "I had to find Freya. She ran off, then the soldiers came. So I hid behind those bushes over there." He pointed, his finger trembling. It was *mostly* true.

"*Tívar reiði!*" someone muttered.

"You see? What did I tell you?" Herr Bradley bellowed. He glared at Dr. Forberg and then back at Neil, who wished the ground would just open and swallow him up.

"They can't have really believed the boy was here—" Dr. Forberg said.

"Or that we'd be stupid enough to shelter him," someone else called out.

"—otherwise they'd have been much more thorough," Dr. Forberg went on. "But they may well be back. And we know their spies are everywhere. From now on, Neil, you must stay hidden, as you were told. Do you understand?"

Neil nodded, not trusting himself to speak.

"And what happens when they don't find him in the next village?" exclaimed a red-faced woman with bad teeth. "Or the next?"

At that a babble of voices broke out in English and Old Nordlandish. One group began berating Mayor Landholm; others muttered among themselves and glanced uneasily toward the gate.

"It's true, we've no time to lose," Dr. Forberg said loudly, trying to be heard over the hubbub. "We'd better get word to Ashbergen at once. Eino"—addressing a man with white-blond hair and sandy eyelashes—"you're the strongest runner. Takat"—he called to the teenage boy still quivering at the gate—"run and ask your mother to make up a food parcel."

Neil slipped away, feeling small and useless and frightened. It was all his fault, the whole terrible mess. He should have told them the truth about the thing in his ankle at the beginning. That was how they'd known where he was. He'd put Ashgård in terrible danger. And now other villages were in danger, too.

Double holy crap. Was he going to let that Charlie have it, if he ever found him.

"I knew it would be difficult, being cooped up," Hallvard said gravely when Neil and Freya slunk in with their tails between their legs. "You're a lively young boy. But this visit doesn't surprise me. Sooner or later they were bound to come."

"I'm sorry," Neil said, in a small, trembling voice. "I really am. I feel awful. I didn't think ..."

"The danger of our situation, I'm afraid, isn't something you're used to." Hallvard shook his head wearily. "You live in a more fortunate time."

"But what do we do now?" asked Astra, and glared at Neil.

"We'll do what we've been doing all along," Hallvard said firmly. "We'll continue our work on the Stone."

"You mean you don't want me to leave?" Neil gripped Freya's fur for reassurance. "Herr

Bradley—"

"I know what Herr Bradley thinks," said Hallvard evenly. "You'll continue to stay here with us. Besides"—he put his arm round his daughter—"I'm not convinced they were looking only for you."

Neil went silent. Hallvard hadn't reproached him; he was even suggesting that Neil wasn't the only cause of the soldiers' visit. He felt a rush of gratitude, though he was sure Hallvard was only trying to make him feel better. All of a sudden his left leg crumpled under him. Hallvard caught him just before he hit the floor.

"Are you all right?" Hallvard said.

"I'm just—I guess I'm still shaken up." Neil's heart was hammering.

But Hallvard was staring at his leg. "We should have Dr. Forberg take a look at that ankle. Did you injure it?"

"N-not exactly." Neil swallowed, hesitated, hurried on. "The soldiers put something in it when they caught me. A microchip or something. And it zapped me when the soldiers went past. It makes my leg weak and achy afterward."

Astra gasped, but Hallvard knelt down and ran his fingers round Neil's ankle. "So they've refined their methods," he said softly, as if to himself. "Whatever's in here, it's not a chip. Microchips are old techno."

"They must have used it to track me," Neil said, whitefaced.

"If that were true, they'd have found your hiding place." Hallvard stood up, his eyes narrowing. "But it does seem the device is activated in their presence. I wonder—" He shook his head. "They must have been here on a fishing expedition. Just to see what they could find." His face was grim. "Which means they'll be back."

Neil Tries His Hand

That evening, still shaken, Neil sat in the kitchen while Fru Berta kneaded dough for bread. She'd slept through the whole thing after taking a larger than usual dose of her naptime sleeping potion. "You mean I missed my chance to go after those beisten?" Her face was rigid with anger. "You should have woken me up! I'd have chased them all the way to the Hot Regions!"

"You said they took something from you," Neil said, remembering the conversation from the previous evening. "Something really valuable."

"They took my lad," she said, and gave the dough a savage punch. "Just nineteen, he was."

"What happened?" Neil asked, though he half-dreaded the answer.

"He'd gone and joined the Arbolé, though I begged him not to." Fru Berta sighed heavily. "They were fighting to save the last stand of *furu* on Gimsøy Island. Pine trees, I think you say in UL." She gave the dough another punch. "I've never seen him since. The worst part is not knowing. Whether he's still alive or not."

A silence, in which Neil thought of the portrait of the boy with the curly hair. Had he been killed, or was he a prisoner? "Who are the Arbolé?" Neil asked. His guards had talked about them.

"Some call them the Half-Trees." Fru Berta slid the fat sausage of dough into a loaf pan and set it on the stove to rise. "They're trying to save the last trees on the planet—here in Nordlandia especially. But the government calls them terrorists."

83

"But isn't that a good thing? Helping the forests, I mean? Why does the government hate them?"

"I'm not clever like Hallvard, I don't understand it all. All I know is my Toivo joined them when he was only seventeen." She shook her head, sadness creeping into her voice. "I hardly saw him after that. Only when he could manage to risk a visit home, because of course they were always hunting for him." She dropped her voice to a whisper. "Toivo told me the Arbolé could actually *talk* to trees. They were teaching him. He even showed me, late one night, when no one else was around."

This sounded fascinating. "Could *I* see?" Neil asked eagerly. "Could you show me?"

"Oh, I wouldn't dare." Fru Berta looked shocked. "There's folks in this village would call me a witch. You never know what people are up to," she added cryptically.

"But how did he do it?" Sometimes adults were so frustrating, especially about the really interesting things. Fru Berta shook her head firmly.

"It's too dangerous. If they ever got hold of you again, there's no telling what they'd do to you."

"Can't you give me a hint? Just a little one?" he said, in the wheedling tone that sometimes worked with his mother. The cellar door opened and Astra stood there, looking like a thundercloud.

"Pappa wants to speak to you," she said.

Uh oh. Now what?

"What about?"

"I'll let Pappa tell you," she replied brusquely, and turned on her heel. With a thumping heart Neil followed her downstairs in silence and across the cellar to the false wall. Just as before, as soon as they stepped onto the stairs the wall slid shut behind them. They were in darkness, except for the dim glow from the methane lamps below.

"Ah, there you are," Hallvard said briskly as Neil appeared at the bottom of the stairs. "Did Astra tell you?"

"Tell me *what*?" Neil said. What was going on? Hallvard crossed his arms, his expression grave, and a chunk of something like red-hot potato surfaced in Neil's throat. So this was it. He was going to be asked to leave after all. He gulped, shut his eyes, and waited.

"I'm going to teach you about the Stone," Hallvard said.

Neil opened his eyes wide. "You mean ..."

"I've been giving it a lot of thought, ever since our little visit this afternoon." Hallvard's eyes were fierce. "It's quite possible that they've found out we're living in Ashgård, Astra and I. It brought home to me the danger we're in. My life's work could be destroyed in an instant."

And it's all my fault! Neil thought again, wildly, as Astra gulped back a sob. "Up till now I thought we were safe," Hallvard went on, "or as safe as possible. Ashgård's at the edge of the Drear Lands, after all ..." He added in a low voice, as if to himself, "I allowed myself to be lulled into complacency. I should have known better."

Astra gave Neil a quick, scornful glance. "Maybe he isn't ready, Pappa."

"Of course I'm ready," Neil said quickly. In fact he was more than ready—he was trembling with excitement. He was going to learn about the Stone!

"You're quite sure?" Hallvard looked at him levelly, his expression stern. "It's a tremendous responsibility I'm asking you to take on—not something I would normally do to a child. But these are strange times. Besides," he added with a grim smile, "they won't expect that I've entrusted my knowledge to children."

"I'm sure," Neil said, as firmly as he could, and stood up straight. He thought he heard a tcch from Astra. Maybe she was jealous. She'd been Hallvard's sole apprentice up to now, after all. He felt a sudden spasm of fear. Suppose he couldn't make the Stone work?

"Very well," Hallvard said, his ice-blue eyes severe. "But I must caution you that your first results may be disappointing. Using the Stone takes practice. And there may be ... unforeseen consequences. Unpleasant after-effects, for example."

So his head might hurt like Astra's—so what? It seemed like a small price to pay if he was going to learn how to see his father!

"I'm ready," he said again, trying to control his trembling.

Hallvard was already opening the hidden drawer and removing the Stone. He lifted it from its cloth pouch and motioned to Neil to hold out his hands.

"You'll notice it gives off a slight heat. That's the pixillite." He laid the stone gently in Neil's cupped palms. "Now, since it's your first time, we need to make an energy circuit." At Neil's puzzled look, he added, "It's a method of raising the vibrational level—at least until you're accustomed to doing it on your own."

He held one hand out to his daughter, who took it and placed her other hand reluctantly on Neil's left arm. If Hallvard noticed her reluctance, he gave no sign. He placed his other hand on Neil's right arm and said, "Now, close your eyes and listen as hard as you can."

It seemed idiotic to try and listen to a piece of quartz. He felt stupid standing there holding it. Still, he wanted to be able to do what Astra did, so he stood as quietly as he could, straining to hear something. All he could hear was the sound of his own breathing. After what seemed like long minutes, he became aware of a slight tingling in his palms, a tingling that radiated slowly up his arms. Were they turning pink, the way Astra's had? He wanted to open his eyes and look but didn't dare.

"Patience," he heard Hallvard murmur. And it was at that moment that he thought he heard something after all—a faint murmuring, so low as to be almost inaudible. It vanished almost immediately. "Crap!" he said out loud.

"You're not taking this seriously!" Astra exclaimed. The next moment she'd grabbed the Stone from him as his eyes blinked open in surprise. "You see, Pappa?" She turned to her father, face flushed. "Didn't I say it wouldn't work? Didn't I?"

"He doesn't understand it the way you do, elskede," Hallvard said gently. Astra glared at Neil and clutched the Stone harder.

Crapzillion. "It just came out," Neil muttered. "I didn't mean—I mean, I thought I heard something, but then it went."

"A good sign." Hallvard nodded approvingly and motioned to Astra to return the Stone. She thrust it at him gracelessly, and once again they stood in the formation of the energy circuit. This time Neil had to struggle to pay attention. His mind kept dancing away—to his mother and how worried she must be, to Luka and snowboarding, to what they must be saying at school. When it happened he almost missed it. It was still almost outside his range of hearing, but definitely there—a low murmuring singsong, strange and wild and distant. Not what he'd expected at all. It filled him with a desperate yearning, though for what he didn't know.

The next moment his whole body began to vibrate with teeth-jarring speed. He felt as if he were being shaken loose, as if he were weirdly slipping down into his own body—into his veins, his bloodstream, into his cells and the molecules that made up the cells. And now, alongside his own, he could feel the Stone's molecules, too. For a few bizarre moments it was as if he *was* the Stone, as if his bones had turned to quartz and he knew exactly what it was like to be mineral.

He opened his eyes. He was inside the Stone! Or it was inside him, he couldn't tell. Astra and her father were faint, gauze-thin shapes floating in some other dimension. And there, right in front of him, was the Wheel, spinning and shimmering.

He tried to collect his thoughts. What time did he want to visit? That was easy. The summer he was ten—the last summer before his father got sick. It had been such a wonderful summer. He'd got a new fishing rod, and there'd been trips with his dad almost every weekend, and—

Almost at once the Wheel began to spin dizzyingly. Images flashed past like a pack of cards shuffled at lightning speed, blurry and out of focus. And then suddenly he was standing in the sunshine in front of his old house, with its yellow paint and white trim. Sounds drifted toward him—a nearby lawnmower, children's laughter, a car humming past. There was his mother, a hand shading her eyes against the sun, standing in the doorway. She was motioning at someone he couldn't see—his sister, perhaps. But where was his father?

Almost at once he came round the corner, tall, lean, a little stooped. Neil's heart leapt into his throat. He'd forgotten the way his father swung his left arm as he walked, his lopsided grin. How, he thought with a pang, could he have forgotten already? His father was wearing his favourite floppy hat and hippie sandals, an outfit Neil had always found horribly embarrassing. Now he would have given anything to have him back, sandals and all.

" ... if we want ... have lunch in ...," his father was saying to someone—to Neil himself, perhaps. His voice was broken up, as if by static. And Neil heard the fragments of his own reply: "... still looking for ... have to check with Mom ...."

It must be the weekend they went fishing up on the Similkameen River. He'd caught two fat trout and they'd grilled them over an open fire. His father was opening the door of the minivan, whistling that lame campfire song about worms and everybody hating you. Neil had detested that, too, except now all he wanted was to hear his father whistling it over and over.

He tried to open his mouth but the words wouldn't come. His father was climbing into the van and snapping on his seatbelt, oblivious. Didn't he *know*? Didn't he know this was the last real summer ever? That he was going to get sick, and he'd never get well again?

"Dad," he said, wrenching the words out with an effort. "Dad, there's something I have to tell you. You're going to get sick—very sick. You're going to—"

But almost at once the scene began breaking up, as if the reception was fading. He concentrated as hard as he could, and for a moment the scene steadied, and his father said something about did he have his anorak and began backing the van out of the driveway. And then the scene was gone. The house, his father, everything. Neil stared in disbelief. His father had been so ... so *there*. How could he just disappear like that?

He reached out with his hands, groping in the air in front of him. Almost at once the vibrating returned and he felt himself slipping again, sliding down into his cells, his molecules, faster, faster, faster ... His head and body were coming apart, he was going to throw up. And still the world whirled round him, a blur of light ...

When he came to, he was sitting on a chair in the lab and someone was bending over him, telling him to breathe, to breathe deeply. His head still spun and he felt sick to his stomach, and his whole being ached with sadness. It had been so real. Just like Astra had told him.

"Can you tell us what happened, lad?" Hallvard's face, white, alarmed, slowly came into focus. "Are you in pain?"

Neil shook his head, but that made him feel dizzy again so he stopped. He suddenly threw up over the edge of the chair. "Here. Sip this slowly," Hallvard said, holding out a glass of pale amber-coloured liquid. It tasted bitter but refreshing, and gradually his stomach stopped heaving like a ship on rough seas.

"What is that stuff?" he said.

"Cloudberry elixir," Astra said. "It helped me the first time, too," she added.

"Fru Berta's secret recipe," Hallvard explained, "using the last patches of cloudberries in the Lyngen Alps, just north of here. It helps to assuage grief, among other things."

The blurred edges of the world were sharpening, though the horrible sadness hadn't gone away. "It was amazing," Neil said. "I wanted it to last forever."

Hallvard looked troubled. "That's one of the dangers with the Stone. It creates cravings for more. Not to mention the physical reactions."

"It's okay," Neil said. "I got to see my dad. It was like he was alive again. It was wonderful."

And then he threw up again.

He heard Astra's exclamation and felt Hallvard bending over him. He lifted Neil's arm over his shoulder and hefted him up. "I think," he said firmly, "we've done quite enough for one day. Let's get you into bed."

The Blacksmith's Revelation

was foolish to allow you to use the Stone so soon,"
Hallvard said the next morning. Neil was sitting
up in bed, Freya beside him, sipping a cup of tea that Fru Berta
thought might settle his stomach. He still felt strange, though
he couldn't quite put his finger on it. It was as if a few stray cells
hadn't been fitted back together properly and were still floating
around his body.

"Your reaction was much more severe than I expected."
Hallvard shook his head, looking perturbed.

"It's okay," Neil said, putting his arm round Freya. In spite of
the weird feeling in his body, he was quite happy. The tea was
soothing, he and Freya were safe, and best of all he'd seen his
father, just as real and vivid as if he were alive again. What an
amazing invention that Stone was! If only he'd been able to stay
there with his father forever!

"Your ordeal in the Drear Lands must have weakened you.
And perhaps that device they inserted—" Hallvard broke off,
sighing. "I allowed my fear to get the better of me in suggesting that you try to use the Stone. Not to mention my scientific
curiosity."

"Honest. I'm okay. And I'm really glad I—"

From outside came the rattle of cart wheels, the surprising
sound of a mule's whinny. "There's the blacksmith," Hallvard
said. "The very man we need."

"Why?"

"Because he may know something about that device in your
ankle. He used to work in the City. He may even know how to
disable it."

It seemed preposterous that a blacksmith might know something about new Fire Reaper technology, but Neil didn't argue. All kinds of things in this future world were bizarre.

"In fact we can pay him a visit right now," Hallvard said. "If you're up to it, that is. Only we need some sort of disguise for you."

"A disguise?" Neil stared at him.

"A strange boy who escaped from them ... that kind of information's worth a lot. And the blacksmith may be willing to sell to the highest bidder."

"Maybe I should just stay here, then," Neil said, alarmed.

"I'd rather the device be removed, if possible. We don't know just what powers it has. Those beisten, as Fru Berta calls them, are capable of anything."

Half an hour later, Neil found himself hurrying awkwardly down the road after Hallvard, dressed in one of Astra's hemp tunics and her favourite bracelet, made of coloured tin. The tunic was dyed a dull orange with carrot juice, instead of the black-walnut-brown and chicory-green colours the men wore. With his short hair he could just pass for a girl, Fru Berta told him, trying to hide a smile. Astra, fortunately, was out of sight, working in the vegetable garden.

The smith was in his leather apron, hammering a red-hot piece of metal on an anvil outside an old shed on the far side of the village. He straightened and stared at them as they approached.

"Who's this?" he said, jerking his head at Neil, who fiddled with the tunic's embroidered belt, feeling ridiculous. But he kept quiet, as Hallvard had told him to.

"A visiting girl," Hallvard said.

"*A girl?*" The blacksmith raised his eyebrows. "Don't look like a girl to me."

"I'm sure," Hallvard said quietly, "you'll be able to convince yourself you saw a girl, if asked." The smith lowered his hammer, his face sullen. "And what if I do?"

Hallvard took out a change purse and extracted several coins. "Our visitor," he said in a low voice, "needs a device disabled. One designed and inserted by them." And he motioned to Neil to lift his pants leg above his left ankle.

The smith raised his eyebrows again and wiped the sweat from his forehead with a burly arm. "I can't help you. No one can. And besides, it's against the law."

Neil's heart sank. Was he stuck with the device forever?

"Then perhaps I can persuade you to help a fellow human being," Hallvard said. "Or are you on *their* side?"

The smith shifted uncomfortably. "It was easier when they used nano-chips," he said. "But nowadays ..." He glanced round furtively, then held out his hand for the coins. "They're using some sort of encrypted code imprinted on the cell membranes," he whispered. "Or so I hear."

"But *someone* must know." Hallvard's voice was low and urgent. "If you're asking a higher price—"

"It's too new. No one's found out how they're doing it. Last time I tried—" He broke off and coughed, as if he'd said too much.

"You've tried to disable one before?" Hallvard said quickly.

The man glanced round, then motioned them inside the shed and closed the door, leaving only a crack of light. "Long time ago now, it was. Must be nigh-on three years."

"It wasn't a scientist, was it?" Hallvard's voice was low but eager. "A woman about my age, tall, with a strong jaw—"

"It was an older fellow, in his sixties maybe," the smith said. "Told me he came from Beaufortia, though I didn't recognize the accent."

Beaufortia. Neil snapped to attention. Wasn't that what they called the Yukon now? "What was his name?" he blurted, forgetting he wasn't supposed to talk.

The smith stared at him. "Damned if I remember. Besides, memory just gets you in trouble these days."

"We'd appreciate it if you'd try," Hallvard said, glancing at Neil's beseeching face. He extracted another coin and held it out.

"A funny name, it was. Back-to-front, if I remember rightly." The smith paused. "It made me think of graves."

"Tombstone?" Neil said faintly, almost afraid to say it out loud.

The smith stared at him. "Yes, that was it. Tombstone. Tombstone Charlie."

Neil grabbed the blacksmith's muscled arm. "Where did you see him? What was he doing? What happened to him?"

"Whoa. Easy does it." The smith narrowed his eyes. "Why do you want to know anyways?"

"He's an old friend of our visitor here," Hallvard said quickly.

"He was in the City," the smith said, after a pause, "and he was on the run. He didn't have a permit, see? And he'd been in their clutches—" He stopped and his face went dark. "It was back when I was smithing slave-chains for them. Back before they went completely techno and expelled me, the bastards. Anyway, this particular day I'd finished my work and I was taking a shortcut home when old Disa here went lame all of a sudden. I'd got down to check her hooves when this fellow comes out of a back alley. Scared me half to death, I can tell you. I tell him I don't want no trouble and he says, 'All's I want is for you to get this thing out of my leg.' Said he'd pay me well if I kept my mouth shut." The smith licked his lips nervously. "But the nano-chip disabler I had didn't work. That's when I knew they'd changed things. He gave me some money anyway, though. Said I could use it to buy a new bridle for Disa—"

"But what HAPPENED to him?" Neil nearly shouted. "Where did he go?"

"Back into the alley, far as I saw. He'd have had a hard time of it with that code in his ankle. Me, I got out of there fast as I could, after I'd picked the stone out of Disa's shoe."

Neil's brain was dizzy with questions. Where was Charlie now? How had he ended up in the City? Had they taken him there after capturing him? But the smith was still talking. "... guess is they're using some new mineral compound for the imprinting. Something developed by one of the Mining GalactiCorps, maybe. Or in one of their own labs. Which means it'll take their know-how to remove it."

Hallvard nodded curtly. "Thank you anyway," he said. "We'll have to try something else."

"Like what?" the smith said. "Black magic?"

Hallvard did not reply. He took Neil by the shoulder and turned toward the door. The smith shouted after them, an edge of gloomy triumph in his voice. "You'll need the luck of the gods with you!"

Neil's thoughts were still in turmoil on their way back up the road. Charlie—Charlie was here, in Nordlandia, in the same time as Neil! And in deep trouble, apparently. But where was he now? Somehow Neil had to find him, though he hadn't a clue how. Charlie had brought him here; Charlie was the only person who knew how to get him back.

He was still deep in thought as they passed Fru Grünewald and Fru Bradley, standing at the side of the road with their hoes over their shoulders.

"*God dag,*" Hallvard said in a pleasant tone, but neither woman so much as looked at him. Instead they stared long and hard at Neil, then turned away in silence, resuming their conversation in whispers. Neil glanced back at them in astonishment.

"What's wrong, Hallvard?" he whispered.

"It's their fear," Hallvard said reassuringly, though Neil could see the worry in his face. "It'll all blow over eventually— you'll see."

But the stone growing in the pit of Neil's stomach told him

otherwise. A group of children were playing a short distance away. Some of them, pointing, giggled and smirked at Neil's outfit. The tallest boy yelled, "We don't like you! Go away!"

"What would your father say if he heard you?" Hallvard said quietly as Neil felt his face grow hot.

"He's dangerous. Least that's what my dad says." The boy stood his ground, chin tilted. "He made the soldiers come. And my dad says it's your fault."

Hallvard shook his head, his lips tight, and walked on. Neil hurried after him, the stone in his stomach growing heavier by the minute. A few houses from their own, Linn Forberg was standing in her yard, watching. "You haven't been over to walk Freya," Neil called out to her, but she pretended not to hear him and turned away.

If even Linn would have nothing to do with him, things were worse than he'd suspected.

"They're just as afraid as their parents," Hallvard said quietly. "Maybe more. Come, let's go in."

Dinner was quiet. Fru Berta picked at her food, and Astra claimed she wasn't hungry. Had someone said something to them? Hallvard tried to keep up a cheerful conversation, but he finally gave up. He said he had work to do and went downstairs.

Neil took Freya outside and sat on the back steps, staring into the growing dusk. Freya squatted to pee, then came back up the steps and sat very close to him, that worried triangle creasing her forehead. He put his arm round her and pressed his cheek against the top of her head. It was true, what the boy had said—he *had* made the soldiers come. Not only that, but chances were they'd be coming back. Even Hallvard admitted as much.

By the time he crawled under the covers that night, he felt as lonely and afraid as when he'd first arrived. How long would Hallvard and Fru Berta let him stay when he was putting them all in danger? It was obvious the whole village was turning against him. He couldn't believe Dr. Forberg had said anything unkind, but fear was catching. Hallvard had said so at dinner, but no one answered him.

The only good thing about the day was the news about Charlie. He'd made it to the future after all, just as he'd told Dee he would. But where was he now? Three years was a long time. How was Neil ever going to find him?

For at least the zillionth time he wished he could talk to his father. His father, he was sure, would have known just what to do.

Neil Betrays a Trust

After breakfast the next day, Neil asked Hallvard if he could help Fru Berta in the vegetable garden. He was getting bored—even weeding vegetables would give him something to do. Besides, it would show the villagers that he wasn't someone to be afraid of. He was just an ordinary kid, willing to pitch in and do his share of the chores. Plus he was feeling like his old self again, mostly. Even the blisters on his feet had healed.

Hallvard, reluctantly, agreed. "Wear a hat against the hot sun," he told Neil, "and don't look at the sky. We don't often see their spies out here, but still ... If you don't look up, they can't see your face."

"You mean like drones?" Neil asked, and when Hallvard looked puzzled, he added, "Unmanned planes."

Hallvard shook his head, tight-lipped. "Their techno has moved far beyond that. Their spies are ... alive." But he wouldn't explain further.

Neil and Fru Berta walked to the vegetable garden together. "A nine days' wonder, that's what it is, this business of the raid," Fru Berta said crossly. "They just can't stop talking about it. If anyone says anything, you just ignore them."

Neil nodded uneasily. Everyone, according to Fru Berta, had a different opinion about why the soldiers had come. Maybe it wasn't because of Neil. Maybe they'd been looking for FUAZ, or forbidden black-market goods like threk. They'd been known to raid villages for food, too—real food, not that moodfood stuff they all ate. But they'd taken nothing, not even the ancient weapons.

Other people, Fru Berta said, thought the soldiers had found out about Hallvard and his secret research project. He'd been an important scientist back in the City, after all. Wouldn't they want to find out where he was and what he was up to? There were even two or three older folk who said it had all begun with the dog. Dr. Forberg should never have taken her in. It had been a bad omen.

It felt good to be outside, even in this intense heat. Neil moved along the rows of eggplant, pulling one weed after the next, proud of himself for not complaining. All the same, he was relieved when lunchtime arrived. He was horribly thirsty and sweaty, with the taste of earth in his mouth. Fru Berta finished her row and peeled off her gardening gloves.

"There. That's the last of the eggplant. You've done very well, lad. Now, what do you say to a fresh mango from the orchard? And a tall glass of goat's milk to go with it?"

What he *really* wanted was a double ice cream cone—one scoop pistachio, one scoop chocolate—but that was impossible. He pushed the image away and followed Fru Berta along the rows to the road, then down to the orchard. Gnarled-looking trees—olive and orange and fig, Fru Berta said, pointing them out—grew haphazardly among the rough grass. Fru Berta made her way to the far side. Here, to Neil's surprise, she placed her hands on one of the tree trunks, closed her eyes, and began muttering something.

"There," she said when she'd finished. She broke off a particularly fat mango and handed it to him. "A nice ripe one."

"What were you doing?" Neil asked, puzzled, as he bit into the fruit.

Fru Berta looked uncomfortable. "I was saying thank you."

"To the tree?"

"I know it sounds ridiculous. Or it does in our time anyway. It's considered—well, pagan superstition." She glanced round. "You mustn't tell anyone, all right?"

It seemed harmless enough to Neil, if a little silly. "Is that what Toivo meant by talking to trees?" he asked.

99

Fru Berta shook her head. "Not exactly. That is, he taught me they're alive, and that it was important to respect them. But it goes much deeper than that." She looked at Neil thoughtfully. "If I show you—well, you have to promise to tell no one. Not even Hallvard. He'd think—well, he'd think I'd gone a bit daft in the head."

It struck Neil as funny that both Hallvard and Fru Berta had told him a secret that he wasn't to tell the other. But he nodded solemnly. "I promise," he said.

"Well, then." She cleared her throat. "Follow me." And she set off briskly in another direction, Neil scrambling to keep up. In a far corner were several bent apple trees, heavy with ripening fruit.

"These Pippin producers are very old," Fru Berta said in a low voice. "No one knows how old, but we've been told they're the last of their kind." She paused, approached the nearest one, put her hands together for a moment, as if in prayer, and then placed them on the trunk, just as she'd done with the mango tree. She closed her eyes and, after a moment, began what sounded like a low chanting. The murmurous singsong reminded Neil of nothing so much as the murmuring voice of the Memory Stone. His hair rose on the nape of his neck and he felt a chill down his spine.

After a minute or so, Fru Berta lapsed into silence, though she still stood with her eyes closed and her hands on the trunk. At last she opened her eyes and looked round, as if she wasn't quite sure where she was.

"What did you say?" Neil asked eagerly.

"I told them about you."

"*Me?*" Neil almost dropped the mango.

"You and Freya, yes. I'm certain there's a reason you've come. I thought the trees might know."

Neil stared at her. Trees were alive, of course—his dad had told him that trees could even communicate with each other through their pheromones, chemicals that they released into

100

the air. But getting messages meant for humans from them—that was something else.

"They don't answer in words," she went on. "But we understand each other. Though I'm afraid my Applish is very limited."

"What did they tell you about me?"

Fru Berta hesitated and looked round again. "They gave me to understand that your arrival is very important," she said softly. "It was foretold by their Elders—trees that perished long ago. You have a vital task to accomplish while you're here."

"A task?" Neil's heart was beating uncomfortably fast. "What kind of task?"

But Fru Berta shook her head. "That's all I understood. Or all they wanted to tell me, perhaps."

Neil stood holding the half-eaten mango, feeling apprehensive and uncomfortable. He didn't *want* a task. He just wanted to go home. Maybe it was all crazy. Maybe Fru Berta was just making it all up.

He wanted to ask more questions, but on the way home Fru Berta clammed up, and after that there was no chance to talk to her by herself. By the time Neil went to bed he was beside himself with frustration. He was supposed to carry out some kind of task, according to Fru Berta, only she didn't know what it was. Meanwhile, no one in Ashgård, except maybe Fru Berta and Hallvard, wanted him there. Where was he supposed to go? Especially with this skin code or whatever it was in his ankle.

Fine, I'll go, he thought angrily. I want to go, believe me. Just tell me how to get back home. But of course no one had any idea how he was supposed to do that.

He tried forcing himself to sleep—he envied Freya, twitching in her dreams—but it was hopeless. He lay staring into the darkness, clenching and unclenching his fists. Suddenly he sat bolt upright. There was a way to talk to his father—or a way worth trying, at least.

He shivered with the daring of it. Then he slid out of bed, holding his breath. Freya jumped down and he whispered to her to be quiet. Moments later he was creeping across the floor, Freya glued to his leg.

Would he be able to open the wall? *Just focus,* he told himself. That was what Ryder Hesjedal always said—focus on your goal 100 per cent. When he reached the wall he stood on tiptoe, about where he thought Hallvard had stood, and ran his fingers along the crevices between the bricks. Nothing. He tried again farther along. Still nothing. He bit his lip and tried to visualize more clearly just where Hallvard had been standing. About here, maybe? Still noth—*aha!* His fingers touched cold metal—a lever of some kind. He worked them round the lever, gripped tightly, and pulled.

A faint shuddering, as if the wall was gathering strength, and then it began sliding slowly and noiselessly back. Neil watched, half-thrilled, half-terrified. Could Hallvard or Astra have heard something? He glanced round, but all was silence. Quickly he stepped onto the first stair, Freya beside him, panicking for a moment as the wall slid shut behind him. Would he be able to find his way in the darkness?

He felt his way down stair by stair until he stood breathless at the bottom. Freya, still pressed against him, was whining softly. "It's okay, girl," he whispered, bending down to reassure her. Trembling, he groped his way across the room, hands outstretched. He hit the workbench with a bump, setting the test tubes rattling, then felt around under it. There must be a switch or lever or something that operated the hidden drawer.

But there was nothing, nothing at all. He'd almost given up when, by accident, his fingers grazed a knothole in the wood. The tiny drawer suddenly shot open. There, hidden in its pouch, glowing faintly, was the Memory Stone!

He lifted it carefully from its hiding place, scarcely daring to breathe. The Stone was so dazzling he could hardly look at it. He shivered. Did he *really* want to do this? Suppose something went wrong? Come on, he told himself sternly. Ryder Hesjedal doesn't worry about what might go wrong. He thinks about what'll go right.

Besides, he'd got this far. He couldn't stop now.

Freya was pawing his arm and whining harder. Spooking in the dark, probably. What a pest she was—just when he needed to concentrate! "No!" he told her firmly, and pushed her away. Then he held the Stone in his cupped hands, closed his eyes, and listened for all he was worth.

Somehow he missed the faint singsong altogether and hurtled straight into the teeth-jarring vibration. It was worse this time, like a violent roller-coaster ride. His stomach tumbled and roiled, his eyeballs felt shaken out of their sockets. Then abruptly the vibrating stopped and that weird uncomfortable feeling of merging with the Stone returned, as if his molecules and the Stone's were being jostled together. Only this time he felt as if he'd been split in half, with the other half of him left behind somehow in the world of the lab.

He forced himself to focus. There was the Wheel in the centre of the Stone, spinning and shimmering like before. There was the flurry of images, faint at first, then more and more vivid. After a while they slowed and he began to make out scenes. There was his old house again, but this time it was late fall, the trees bare, the sky grey. His mother was taking a bag of groceries from the car and walking up the driveway. And there, in the backyard, was his father! He was raking leaves, wearing that scarf he'd bought at some garage sale, his old work gloves.

A deep, tender longing poured through Neil. He could hear every sound—the rustle of the leaves, the slight rattle of the rake, even his father's breathing. He wanted to cry out, to rush up to his father and throw his arms round him. But when he'd tried speaking before, the scene had vanished. He'd have to be careful.

"Dad!" he said softly, cautiously. No response. His father continued his raking, oblivious. "Dad!" he said more loudly. "Dad, I need your help. I'm in trouble."

This time his father stopped and looked up, staring in Neil's direction. Was it a coincidence, or could he really hear him?

Neil rushed on, choking back a sob. "I'm stuck, Dad. I'm stuck in the future. I know it sounds crazy, but I am. And I don't know what to do."

Astra sat up suddenly in bed. She wasn't usually a light sleeper, but something had woken her. She held her breath, listening. Nothing. No, wait—there it was again. A sound—and it was coming from the *lab*. Her throat went dry. Someone, or something, was in there.

Her father was fast asleep in the bed beside hers. Better to let him sleep—he always seemed so weary these days. She climbed out of bed and began tiptoeing across the cellar. The sliding wall was closed, but she could hear faint movement below her. She felt a sudden rush of fury. Someone must have broken in!

She yanked at the lever. The wall slid back, revealing a faint pink glow. Only one thing gave off that glow ... Before she'd stopped to think, she was hurtling down the stairs. From below her came several short, sharp barks.

Freya? What was Freya doing here?

"... can't explain it scientifically, Dad, but it's definitely—I mean, there's this new country called Nordlandia, and—"

It was Neil! She took a step forward, shaking with anger. How *dare* he come in here on his own like this! And using the Stone! He didn't know what he was doing. Anything could happen.

"... so me and Freya really really need—I mean, there has to be some way to—"

He hadn't noticed her at all; he was too busy Stone-dwelling. And talking to whatever he saw—what an idiot. As if anyone in the past could hear!

"What do you think you're *doing*?" she called out. "Come back right now!"

Neil blinked, bewildered. Who was talking? A figure in a

night-tunic was merging into his father and out again, the pink glow of the Stone flickering across her bare arms. He fought to hold the scene steady, but his father was wavering, breaking up. He cried out and clutched at the air, and at the same moment Astra grabbed the Stone. "Give me that!"

He felt as if someone were yanking him violently through a narrow tunnel. His insides were squeezed together, he couldn't breathe, he was about to pass out ... The next moment half of him was slammed against the other half, as though he'd met a wall. He staggered backward, tried to regain his balance, and fell hard.

"Serves you right," Astra said. She stood there clutching the Stone, glaring down at him. "How could you be so *stupid*?"

He managed to push himself into a sitting position. He felt bruised and wobbly, the way he had when he'd time-travelled that first time and landed in the desert. Maybe this was what happened when you did it too fast. Freya was whimpering and licking his face.

"I was trying—I thought maybe—" His tongue wasn't working properly. "I thought if I could talk to my dad—"

"You're a stupid, selfish boy. How *dare* you come in here without permission?"

"I thought he'd—he always knows what to do."

"You thought he could *hear* you? But Pappa *told* you it wouldn't—ohhhh!"

Astra had flung her hand up in the air, forgetting she was holding the Stone. It flew out of her grasp and landed with a crack on the floor. She gasped, horrified, and snatched it up. The faint glow had disappeared, and the Stone lay dull and lifeless on her palm.

"Look! Look what you've done!" She held the Stone out toward Neil, quivering. "You've killed it!" Crouching down in tears, she stroked the Stone like a living thing.

Neil slumped against the workbench, sick with despair. How could he have been so reckless? Hallvard would be furious. How would he ever face him? He tried to stand up, but a vast black form spread across his vision—a huge grotesque flying thing with gigantic talons. As it swooped toward him Neil cried out and ducked in terror.

"There, you see?" Astra said crossly through her tears. "You're Stone-locked. I knew it."

Neil looked around fearfully, trembling and sweating. The vast black creature seemed to have disappeared.

"That's when you get images even though you're not Stone-dwelling. Scenes you *don't* want and can't control." She laid the Stone carefully on the workbench in its protective pouch. "That's another reason it's dangerous to use on your own."

The black flying thing had been so *real*. But that was true of everything he'd seen with the Stone. He never wanted to touch it again—not when he might see terrifying things like that.

He forced himself to stand up straight, though he still ached all over. "Well, you won't need to worry about me anymore," he said. "I've decided to leave."

"What do you mean—leave?" Astra stared at him as if he'd just told her he was going to join the Fire Reapers.

"Go away. Leave Ashgård. I'm just creating problems here. For everyone."

"But that's crazy." Her mouth had dropped open, and he took a grim satisfaction in her flabbergasted expression. "Where would you go?"

"I don't know. I just know I can't stay here."

"You'll be captured again, you idiot. You'll just make things worse."

That was one good thing about Astra, Neil thought wryly— you never needed to guess what she was thinking. "I can't imagine why you care," he said bitterly. "After everything I've done."

"That doesn't mean I want them to get you! You don't—"

But whatever Astra might have said next was drowned out by a noise from outside like a million firecrackers. She clapped her hands over her ears and Neil ducked. The next moment they were leaping up the stairs, Freya just ahead of them. Another deafening burst of sound, then another. Astra kicked the sliding door open and they raced across the cellar, took the steps three at a time, and almost fell over each other trying to get into the kitchen.

Fru Berta stood there in her nightgown and an old coat, her white hair sticking straight up. "They're back," was all she said. She was gripping her Kalashnikov, her mouth grim. Outside, flashes of intense blue light were shooting across the village, punctuated with blinding white streaks that gave off a high whistle.

"Tabris," Astra said, so softly that Neil almost didn't hear her, "and Lumini thermal lasers ..." Dark figures were streaming from the direction of the gate, fanning out to the houses across the way. Several of them were running up the hill to Mayor Landholm's.

"Just let them try coming in here!" Fru Berta said between gritted teeth.

"Your weapon's useless against those things, Berta," Hallvard said, surprising everyone. He limped into the kitchen and grabbed her arm. "You know that. Go down to the cellar with the children. I'm going to the Mayor's."

"No, Pappa!" Astra launched herself at her father. "You can't! You mustn't!"

Hallvard gently but firmly unclasped Astra's arms from around his waist. "There's not a minute to lose. Take care of yourself, elskede." He seized a stricken Astra by the shoulders, gave her a quick, fierce kiss on the forehead, and was gone before she could say anything more. She rushed after him and would have been out the door, too, if Freya hadn't leapt in front of her, growling. Fru Berta locked and bolted the door and turned to face them.

"You heard your father. Now off to the cellar, both of you. Here"—she thrust the Kalashnikov at Neil—"I can't approach the trees if I'm touching metal." And then she was gone, too, out the back door, hurrying off down the path toward the orchard.

Astra and Neil stared at each other, appalled. They couldn't go downstairs now—they had to see what happened. They crouched beneath the window, Freya huddled between them, as the battle raged. Neil poked his head up at one point to see old Herr Branhammer and another man advancing toward the troops, clutching their Uzis. A minute later a couple of weapon blasts found their marks and they both lay sprawled in the dust. Astra let out a sob and Neil clenched his fists, feeling sick to his stomach.

Astra peered over the sill and ducked down again. "They've got the councillors!"

Neil, peering out in turn, could just make out Fru Vleinigen, being marched along the road in the midst of a squadron of Fire Reapers. And there, at the back of the group, was Mayor Landholm. "They've got the Mayor, too," he muttered grimly. Astra gripped his hand as the same question formed in both their minds. What had happened to Hallvard?

"There's someone missing," she said, poking her head up again as Neil yanked her back down. "There should be four councillors. And there's only three."

"You're sure?"

"Positive." As the sound of marching feet grew louder, she peered over the sill for a microsecond. "I know who it is, too," she said, crouching back down, her face white. "Herr Grünewald."

"Maybe he got away. Or they shot him."

But Astra shook her head. "That's how they knew you were here. I'm sure of it."

Neil stared at her. "You mean—?"

"—I mean he's a spy." The sound of marching right beneath the window almost drowned her out.

Neil couldn't believe it. Herr *Grünewald*? The man who'd said that *he* was a spy? "But if they knew I was here, why didn't they search harder when they came the first time?"

"I don't know. Maybe they made a mistake. Or maybe"— tears filled her eyes—"maybe they really wanted *Pappa*."

"But why didn't they come a long time ago, then?"

"They must have been waiting for the right time."

The sound of marching was fading away. Neil sat up and stared after them. "They're heading toward the brick kiln," he said. "Maybe they're going to—" But he was interrupted by a volley of rooing from Freya. Someone was coming up the back steps.

They leapt to their feet, Neil clutching the useless Kalashnikov, as the door burst open. It was Fru Berta. She staggered in, blood streaming from her temple. Astra and Neil rushed toward her, but she waved them away and collapsed into a chair. Astra ran to get water and bandages.

"You must go, at once," Fru Berta gasped. "Both of you."

"Go? Go where?" Neil said wildly.

Fru Berta touched her temple, wincing, as her fingers came away wet with blood. "They're rounding up all kinds of people." Her chest heaved with the effort of talking. "You're in great danger."

"But we can't. We can't leave you and Hallvard—"

"Hallvard's been arrested." Astra, coming back with the bandages, let out an anguished cry. Fru Berta lay back and closed her eyes. "And they'll soon find out where the lab is. They'll be here any minute."

"We're not going," Neil said. "We can't leave you like this."

Fru Berta opened her eyes and sat up with an effort. "Now listen to me, both of you. You're to go out by the back gate. Then head northwest, toward the mountains." She paused, her breathing laboured. "Stay away from the travelled places. On the other side of the mountains is the village of Ashheim." Her voice was fading and she lay back. "Once you're there, ask for Áilu. She's a friend of mine, she'll know what to do."

The children stared at each other. Astra's frightened, tear-stained face reflected exactly how Neil himself felt. How could they leave Ashgård and head into the Drear Lands? How would they ever make it on their own? Fru Berta spoke so softly they could hardly hear it. "The Trees tell me you have everything you need. You have each other. And the dog."

Menacing growls were rumbling from Freya's throat. From outside came the sound of hoarse shouting, heavy bootsteps running along the road. A deafening burst of fire shook the house. "Go! Go now!" gasped Fru Berta, and waved her hand weakly.

With a last, desperate glance behind them, Neil and Astra raced toward the back door, Freya leaping ahead of them. Boots were thundering up the front steps; the front door was already splintering. They paused to look back only once. In the curtained windows dark shadows were massing, looming and flickering against the light.

Departure from Ashgård

ust flew up in puffs beneath their heels as they raced away down the path, panting as they ran. Neil had no idea where the back gate was, but instead of taking the lead, Astra faltered and fell back. "Which way do we go?" he said, but she just stood there dazedly. He grabbed her arm. "Come on. It's dangerous to be out here."

"I can't," she said, turning to stare in the direction they'd come from. "I can't leave Pappa."

"What are you talking about?" A rising panic seized him. "You heard what Fru Berta said!"

"Yes, but I can't just—I mean, I have to try—"

"You can't do anything, Astra! We've got to go. Right now!"

He looked about helplessly. It was pitch dark out, except for the faint light of a crescent moon, and all around them was an eerie stillness. Suddenly half-a-dozen figures, black against the blackness, appeared at the end of the path from Fru Berta's. Neil shrank back into the shadows, Freya at his heels, pulling Astra with him. They'd have seen the open back door, of course. They'd be asking Fru Berta all kinds of questions. He hated to think what they might be doing to her.

The soldiers were pointing and arguing among themselves. Abruptly, they split up, half of them heading back into Ashgård, the other half taking the same path as Neil and Astra. Neil gripped Freya's collar. It was risky—horribly risky—but he had to do something.

"Can you find the back gate, Freya?" he whispered as she looked up at him expectantly. He'd have to hope that Linn Forberg had taken her on a walk there, and that she remembered the finding games they'd played back in the Yukon. "Go find!"

She dashed off into the shadows. Neil, his heart in his throat, gripped Astra's arm again. "Where can we hide?" he said urgently. The soldiers, sweeping the sides of the path, were getting closer and closer. But Astra seemed to have turned to stone.

"Astra!" he hissed in her ear. "Fire Reapers!"

That roused her. She pointed to what looked like a shed a short distant away, beside the vegetable garden. A dangerous choice, Neil thought, but she was already running toward it, crouching low, and he ran after her. It wasn't a shed at all but a big wooden bin, full of rotten-smelling compost. Neil looked at it in horror, but there was no time to think. Astra leapt into the bin and he followed, the compost squishing and oozing horribly between his legs. He struggled to stay upright, lost his balance, and fell headlong into the slimy mess.

Seconds later footsteps came pounding up to the garden. "By the First Flame, what a stink!" a male voice grunted. "What else? They're Ash-Gatherers," another said. One of the soldiers plunged his weapon into the bin. Its razorlike bayonet grazed Neil's arm and he gritted his teeth to stop himself crying out.

"They're obviously not here," a sharp female voice said. "Brand, take Drengr and continue the search. Eldgrim and I will report back."

The feet and voices headed off, fading to silence. Neil waited until he was sure they'd gone, then pulled himself out of the ooze. Grimacing, he wiped chicory grounds and old potato peelings off his face. Astra suddenly popped up, an apple core stuck on top of her head, and if things hadn't been so disastrous, Neil would have laughed out loud.

"They're going toward the village," she said, peering between two planks. "Two of them, anyway. I can't see the others."

He hoped the soldiers hadn't caught sight of Freya. And now that he thought about it, why hadn't the code in his ankle been triggered?

"We'd better make a break for it," he said. "Where's the gate from here?"

"It's pretty overgrown," Astra said, biting her lip. "So outsiders couldn't find it."

"Then let's hope Freya does."

They climbed out of the bin, wiping the slime off their faces. There was no sign of the soldiers. Weaving in and out of the shadows, they found a narrow, overgrown track. "It's along here somewhere," Astra muttered. The next moment the bushes parted and Freya bounced out, wagging her tail.

"Good dog!" Neil said in relief. She was already disappearing again into the undergrowth. They struggled after her on a half-vanished path, and at last reached the fence. There was the gate—two rusted Chevy car doors, set one above the other.

Astra grabbed the rusted handle, but it wouldn't turn. Neil tried too, then bent to examine it more closely.

"It's been welded shut," he said.

They stared at each other in horror. The fence was far too high to climb over, and getting to the main gate was out of the question. Freya, whimpering, was digging excitedly at the base of the gate.

"Freya!" Neil hissed at her. She'd give them away if they weren't careful.

"You know what?" Astra was watching intently. "She's right." And she threw herself beside Freya and began scooping earth out with her hands as fast as she could.

It was a crazy idea, but they'd nothing left to lose. Neil flung himself beside Astra as a sharp blast of weapon fire came from somewhere nearby. They scrabbled doggy-fashion at the earth, dirt flying into their hair and night clothes. A thermal laser whistled over their heads, and they gritted their teeth and dug harder.

Freya suddenly flattened her belly to the ground and squirmed under the fence. Without thinking Neil shouted at her, but Astra thrust a dirty hand over his mouth and muttered

"Shut up!" Freya took off into the Drear Lands before he could stop her.

He threw himself into the digging again, sick with fear. She must have been spooked by the loud noises. Another blast, so close he was sure the soldiers had seen them. His arms felt as if they were ready to drop off.

It was Astra's turn to drop to her stomach. "What about you?—I can't—"

"You're smaller. Go on! Go through!"

Astra began squirming through on her elbows as Neil kept digging. Her night-tunic snagged on a strip of rusted metal, but he managed to tear it free. With another wriggle she was through. She stood up on the other side, panting. He could hear soldiers calling to each other.

It was now or never. He was bigger than Astra—it would be a tight fit. Halfway through he got stuck. Astra, half-sobbing, dug frantically on the other side. "Come on, Neil! Come on!"

He managed to work an arm free, then his head. He heard a roar behind him as a tree burst into flame, sending clouds of crackling smoke into the air. He sucked in his breath, making himself as small as he could while Astra pulled on his arm. With a final wrench he was through. He stumbled to his feet, chest heaving, and the two of them ran without stopping into the night.

Tripping over grassy hummocks and dried roots, they ran until they could go no farther. They'd lost all sense of direction. Neil hoped desperately they weren't going in circles. Dazed with shock and tiredness, they finally collapsed beside a withered thorn tree.

Above them the sky was filled with a strange orange glow. Where was it coming from? From the village, Neil realized with horror as he looked behind them. The entire place was ablaze. Flames were shooting into the night sky, blotting out the stars. Even from here they could hear the dull roar of collapsing houses, the hissing of straw roofs catching fire.

His throat seized up. Where was Freya? He'd promised her—he'd *promised* her that they'd never—

Astra suddenly burst into sobs and struggled to her feet. "Pappa! Pappa! I have to go back! I have to!"

"No! No! No!" Neil screamed. He flung his arms round her and hung on for dear life. *Whoever-or-whatever-is-in-charge-of-the-universe, please PLEASE help us, help us, help us* ... He shut his eyes and tightened his arms round Astra's waist until, exhausted, she went limp and slumped against him, her face in her hands.

A sudden huge blast in the distance shot a fountain of flame and sparks into the air. The brick kiln, probably, exploding from the heat.

"Come on," Neil said dully. "It's too dangerous to stay here."

He got to his feet, pulling Astra up, and the two of them stumbled onward. Gradually the sounds of the fire behind them grew fainter, though Astra kept turning to look back. Neil kept his face resolutely forward. It was a relief when they could no longer hear anything except the crack of twigs under their feet and their own ragged breathing.

A sudden rustling in the scrub and thickets nearby. They clutched each other in alarm. A Fire Reaper patrol? Wild animals? If only he had his knife with him, the one his uncle had carved!

And then, very faintly, there came a hoarse *roo roo roo.*

The next moment the bushes parted and a bedraggled Freya stood there, trying to wag her tail.

"Freya! Oh Freya!" Neil could have wept with exhaustion and relief. She looked awful. The fur on her back and legs was singed, she was covered in ash, and she kept lifting her right front paw. She must have gone back to look for them.

"You're alive!" Astra bent to hug her and began sobbing all

over again as Neil dropped to his knees and buried his face in the familiar fur. Freya gave a great sigh and collapsed at their feet.

It was obvious they couldn't go any further that night. Neil found a hollowed-out cavity nearby, screened by a tumble of rocks, and collected twigs and handfuls of dried leaves to spread out as a kind of mattress. Then between them he and Astra carried Freya to the hollow, staggering over the rough ground. She flinched a little but made no sound. He lay down beside her, Astra on the other side, each with an arm flung over her. Her warmth and her doggy smell were comforting, and despite—or perhaps because of—the terrible events of that night, they were soon fast asleep.

When Neil woke up, the sun was shining, and it took him a moment or two to remember where he was. Not in the Yukon. And not in the cellar at Fru Berta's. He was out in the Drear Lands, on the run, with an injured Freya and no food. He heard a bird singing somewhere and sat up. How weird—he'd never heard a bird in Nordlandia before.

Freya was awake and licking at her injured foot. Neil shook Astra and she sat up at once, startled and blinking, as confused as he had been. The two of them scrambled to their feet and listened. There was no sound but the birdsong, stopping and starting again. It was eerie to be out here with no one else around.

"We have to find water," Astra said, and for the first time Neil realized how desperately thirsty he was.

"But where—?"

"You stay here while I go look."

He was about to protest when it occurred to him that, if he went too, Freya would try to follow, and she needed to rest. He almost called after Astra to be careful, and then thought better of that too. No telling who was lurking around here ... He gave a shiver and tightened his arms round Freya. Whatever happened they would face things together.

After what seemed to Neil like a long time (though perhaps it was only a few minutes), Astra returned. She was carrying a rusty can with both hands, being very careful not to spill what was in it. Neil stared. "How did you ever find water?"

"Fru Berta showed me." Astra knelt and offered the water to Freya, who stuck her muzzle in the tin and lapped up the whole thing. "She said I ought to know how, since there's so few water sources now. I looked for a certain kind of plant and then dug down."

"And the can?"

"That's easy. They're all over the place. Wherever there used to be a BGC town. Before the Great Catastrophes."

Neil shivered. Was that all that was left now of the world he knew—piles of old tin cans? Freya was nosing the empty container, looking for more water.

"And I found this." Astra put her hand in her tunic pocket and drew out the green spike of a plant, broken off and oozing liquid. "Aloe vera. It'll help Freya's burns. I'm going to get more water."

Neil examined the wounded paw. A big thorn was embedded in the pad. When he tried to pull it out, it broke off, leaving a piece still buried. He smeared some of the saplike liquid on the pad, which Freya promptly began licking, and the rest on her burns.

This time Astra came back more quickly, carrying two cans of water. While Freya drank from one, she and Neil gulped down the other. It had a slightly bitter taste, but it was cool and wonderfully thirst-quenching.

"I don't know if the aloe vera'll help," Astra said doubtfully when Neil showed her Freya's foot.

"We need something to dig it out with. Which we don't have."

"Maybe I can find some calendula. It's antiseptic, Fru Berta said."

Neil shook his head. "We'd better get going. We're not safe this close to Ashgård."

Astra squinted up at the sun. "Didn't Fru Berta say to go northwest?"

They set off with Freya limping behind them. It soon got hotter, but at least they could stop now and then in the shade of a withered tree—gall oaks, Astra called them—to let her rest. Around midday they came across a small waterhole, and waded through ankle-deep mud to drink thirstily. "'There's bound to be something we can eat around here," Astra said, and went off to have a look. A triumphant cry came up from the other side of a large bush. "Over here, Neil!"

Neil left Freya standing in the water and joined Astra near some spindly vines drooping with small greenish-purple fruit. "Wild grapes," Astra said, and promptly popped one in her mouth.

"You're sure?" Neil asked dubiously. The one he picked tasted sour and unripe, but he was too hungry to care—his stomach had been cramping all morning.

They ate the grapes by the handful and stuffed their pockets, then went back to the waterhole. Freya was lying beside it, in the shade of a bush, and Neil looked at her with concern. She already seemed tired, and she was limping more than ever. If they were ever to get to Ashheim and find this Áilu that Fru Berta had told them about, they needed to keep walking. He held out a grape, but after tasting it she spat it out.

They waited in the shade, half-dozing, until the sun had gone down a little, and then set off again slowly, sometimes stopping for Freya to rest. In the late afternoon they saw a range of bare, rocky hills in the distance, rising into mountains beyond. Neil's stomach was feeling a little queasy—the grapes, he figured.

"There's a path through them, if we can find it," Astra said, shading her eyes to look.

"You've been here before?"

"When we left the City. Only I don't remember much."

"You mean you *walked* all the way to Ashgård?" Neil looked at her in horror.

"We got rides on carts sometimes. And once on muleback."

"How long did it take?"

"Days and days. I don't remember now. It seems such a long time ago."

How long will it take us? Neil thought in despair. Especially with Freya like this. And if all they had to live on were these grapes ...

"Maybe we should stay here for the night," he said, looking at Freya. She was worrying her paw again.

"We should try and get closer to the hills first."

"Well, we can't," he snapped. "Freya's exhausted. And it'll be night by the time we get there." He didn't add that he was feeling pretty sick himself.

Astra opened her mouth as if she was going to say something and then thought better of it. Without speaking, they fell back into their new routine—Astra went off to find water, Neil hunted for somewhere nearby to sleep. Out of sight of Astra, his stomach finally rebelled, and he threw up onto the dry earth.

He was still feeling nauseous and chilled when he found the den, hollowed out of the roots of a burnt tree. It held a faint animal smell and he looked round anxiously, but if it had once been used by wild creatures there was no other sign. Again he made a bed of twigs and leaves and laid handfuls of dry grass over them. Freya was already asleep when Astra reappeared, holding something.

It was a small rectangular metal container, the kind the soldiers had used for their moodfood.

"Wow! Where d'you find—?"

Astra crouched down, whispering. "Beside a fire, or what's left of it. And quite close by. The ashes are still warm."

Neil felt a chill spider through him. So soldiers came through here, and not long ago. Where were they headed?

"They must have left in a hurry. Usually they take all the

ashes with them." Astra glanced round nervously, as though they might still be nearby.

Neil was about to point out that his ankle would be hurting if they were still around when he remembered that the code hadn't been triggered the day before in the village. Had it stopped working? It would have been a useful warning device after all, he thought wryly.

The lid of the container was dissolving in Astra's hand. "I don't know about you," she said, "but I'm starving"—and she stuffed a slice of moodfood in her mouth. He was, too—his stomach was emptier than ever. He grabbed a slice himself. Instantly he could taste hamburger with cheese, and french fries, and his mother's homemade mayonnaise. If he closed his eyes he might almost be at their dining room table in the Yukon, with his mother passing the ketchup and his sister squirming in her chair and—

But he quickly opened his eyes again. Imagining scenes like that was only making things worse. He pretended he had something in his eye so that Astra wouldn't see the tears.

"What does yours taste of?" Astra said, chewing fiercely. "Mine tastes of a soup my mother used to make, with fish and herbs and ..." Her voice faltered and a tear rolled down her cheek.

"We better not think about the past," Neil said quickly, feeling dishonest. "Just about how we're going to make it to Ashheim."

"I can't help it." Astra looked down at the last fragment of moodfood in her hand. "Whenever I get sad, she comes into my mind right away." She held the fragment up, the last light from the setting sun glowing through it. The shape wasn't a leaf after all. It looked like a burning flame.

After a silence Neil said, "What happened to her?"

"I don't remember much about her. She died when I was four. She was very clever, Pappa says—they met when they were studying at the University of Scholars in the City." Astra hesitated. "It was when they were both working at the Institute. They were coming home one day when they heard noises in the distance. Some kind of student demonstration. And then they saw hundreds of students running past. The Elite Guard troops were chasing them." Her voice had dropped so low Neil could barely hear her. "My mother ran to a student, a girl, who'd fallen and was lying unconscious, to pull her out of the way ..." She stopped and swallowed hard. "The troops were using sound-stunners. They temporarily paralyze you with sound waves. But if you use them at close range—well, one of the soldiers shot at my mother, and she fell over. It was only after my father lifted her up that he realized she was dead."

To all this there seemed to be nothing to say.

"After that my Amma came to live with us, to look after me. My mother's mother. But when we left the City, she said she was too old to move. My father argued with her, but she wouldn't budge. She said she'd look after the house till we came back. And it's too risky to write letters, so I don't know what's happened to her."

It was fully dark now and he could no longer see Astra's face. "Here I am," she said, "telling stories when we know they could be around here somewhere." He heard her shiver.

"You said they must have left in a hurry. Maybe they were on their way to the next village." He was suddenly so tired he couldn't keep his eyes open. "We'd better try and get some sleep. We've got a long day tomorrow."

121

The Untravelled Way

The next morning it was raining, a light steady rain that dripped from the branches in front of the den. In all his time in Nordlandia, this was the first time Neil had seen rain. Astra was standing outside, her face turned upward. She spun in a circle, holding her hands out. "We hardly ever see this anymore," she called, laughing, her hair and clothes soaked. "It's beautiful, isn't it?"

Neil, remembering the heavy downpours in Vancouver, thought only that it would make for wet and unpleasant walking, but said nothing. They limited themselves to half a moodfood slice each after Astra pointed out that they'd better ration what remained. Somehow he had to find food for Freya, who lay with her head on her paws. He'd seen no small game so far, but maybe in the hills he could set a snare, the way Uncle Dan had shown him.

The other half of the moodfood container turned out to hold a few matches—no doubt for setting fire to any trees they came across, Neil thought grimly. Oddly low-tech, but he didn't care—he was beyond relieved. While Astra dried herself off with the grass from their bedding, he crammed a few small twigs into the container. If it kept raining like this, they'd need them to start a fire that night—he remembered that from wet hiking trips.

The rain had lightened by the time they reached the hills, though all three of them were already wet through. Close up the hills seemed much higher, a barren range of dark rock that rose into low cloud. Astra, her hair plastered to her head, stared upward, frowning.

"We need to find where the path starts. Why don't you go that way"—she pointed to her left along the bottom of the hills—"and I'll go this."

"Okay. But we'd better not get too far apart."

Freya refused to be left behind and limped along behind Neil. He scrambled over rocks and through bushes, then came to a sheer cliff that fell away into a gully so deep he couldn't see the bottom, though he thought he could hear water gurgling. Wherever the path was, it wasn't here. He turned and made his way back to where they'd separated. Astra was signalling wildly to him from a short distance away.

"Look." She pointed as he came up to her, panting a little. Above her a narrow trail, only faintly visible among the rocks, snaked upward and disappeared. Without a word she turned and began climbing, and Neil, taking a deep breath, followed with Freya. After some time he stopped to look back. The plain below them had vanished beneath the cloud cover. They were climbing into the sky itself.

They kept going for what seemed like hours, stopping every now and again to let Freya rest, or to take a break themselves. The bare rock was wet and treacherous—they both kept slipping in their village sandals—and a swirling grey mist meant they couldn't see more than a few footsteps in front. The only vegetation was the odd tuft of coarse grass or a scrubby bush clinging to crumbling rock. The temperature began dropping, too, and soon Neil was shivering in his pants and thin tunic.

Late in the day it began to clear a little, and they stopped beneath a rock overhang screened by a clump of bushes. Astra's face was white with cold and exhaustion, and Neil had never been so frozen. Even Freya looked miserable and beaten. Neil shook the twigs out of the container and lit one of the matches. He tore down some plant tufts, too, and flung them on the small fire before huddling with Astra and Freya for warmth. The fire wouldn't last long, but it would warm them for a few minutes.

What he wouldn't give for his own cosy home and a steaming mug of hot chocolate!

Well, at least he could have the taste of it. "Let's have some of the moodfood," he said, but Astra shook her head firmly.

"We've hardly any left. We've got to make it last."

"You need more fuel when you're cold, my dad always said. To make energy."

"Oh yes, your dad. Well, he's not here now, is he?"

Her sarcasm annoyed him. "There's no point making it last if we die of hunger!" he said.

"We've got lots more days ahead of us." She was staring at him as though he was crazy. "What if we don't find any other food?"

She was being sensible, of course. Which only made him angry. Besides, his stomach was growling. "Well, *I'm* going to have some," he said. "I'm a boy and I'm taller than you, so I need more energy."

They both lunged for the container at the same time. As Neil seized it triumphantly his foot caught the little pile of blazing twigs, scattering it into the open, where it fizzled and went out.

"Way to go!" Astra glared at him. "Look what you did, you idiot!"

Neil jumped to his feet and walked off up the path without looking back. Of all the stupid arguments ... And now they didn't even have a fire! Why was he stuck with Astra anyway? She was impossible to get along with. He'd be much better off on his own. And once he was in Ashheim, maybe this Áilu, whoever she was, could help him get back to his own time, and this whole horrible nightmare would be over. "Watch out, Charlie," he muttered under his breath. "If I ever find out where you are ..."

At least being angry had warmed him up a little. He stopped and looked back. He couldn't see the overhang anymore, and he felt a momentary pang. He really shouldn't leave her alone—it wasn't safe. On the other hand he wasn't ready to go back yet. Talking was so useless sometimes.

He heard a slithering sound at his feet and jumped, startled. A spotted greenish-blue lizard shot out almost from under him and streaked like blue lightning across the bare rock. He ran after it, slipping, nearly falling, but it vanished into a fissure some distance away.

So there *were* animals around here! But would a snare work with a lizard? Freya hadn't eaten for two days. He'd no idea if she'd eat lizard, but at least it was meat.

He tore a thin branch off the nearest bush, stripped the leaves, and bent it into a loop, tying a slipknot and pulling the other end through. Then he lay down on the rock above the fissure, the loop dangling in front of it, and waited. A long tongue flickered out—so the lizard was still there. He stayed as still as possible, his legs cramping, not daring to move. At last a bluey-green head poked out, and the next moment the lizard had darted forward into the noose. Neil yanked upward, the lizard dangling and thrashing, and pulled the loop as tight as he could.

After some moments the thrashing stopped, and he loosened the knot and released the lifeless body. He felt a brief flare of satisfaction—he'd scored one for Freya!—and then a moment of regret for the death he'd caused. *I'm sorry, lizard. I'm sorry.*

He climbed off the rock and hesitated, not sure which way to go. It was getting dark and he'd left the path behind in running after the lizard. A faint roo-roo-roo sounded below him. He followed it and found Freya on the path, some distance down. "Good girl," he said softly, and ruffled her ears. She sniffed eagerly at the small body in his hands. He longed to give it to her right then and there, but he really ought to get back to Astra.

In the last of the light he made his way back down the path. Astra wasn't under the overhang, and for a moment his heart stopped, but then he saw her a short distance away, pulling plants from another rocky crevice.

"I thought you weren't ever coming back." She was pressing her lips together and he saw she'd been crying.

"Look!" He held up the lizard, proud of himself. But she turned away and went on pulling at the plants. "It's for Freya. Food! Aren't you going to say something?"

She turned then and glared at him. "You're such a *tosk*, Neil. A jerk. You can't even apologize."

He was about to protest, to tell her she might at least congratulate him on his first-ever lizard kill. But he could see in her face that another argument was pointless. Freya came limping round the bend and he held the lizard out to her. She took it from him delicately, dropped it on the ground, sniffed and pawed at it, then held it down with her foot and tore it apart, gulping hungrily. He felt tears of relief coming to his eyes—and a kind of pride, too. They'd changed places, he and Freya. He'd become the hunter, for now.

Silently, they went back to their little hideout and spread out the plants Astra had gathered for bedding. Not much, but it would have to do. At least it was dry. Did he dare risk another fire? No—they only had four matches left. They lay down, Freya squashed between them, still licking lizard bits from her paws. Tired as he was, it took him a long time to get to sleep. His dreams were troubled by the sounds of marching, and shouts and cries in a strange language.

He woke with a start. Something had penetrated his sleep. The clouds had gone and a clear dawn was breaking. There it was: the faintest of jingles, carried on the breeze. He scrambled to his feet. They'd passed a rocky pinnacle the evening before—he ought to be able to see a long way from there.

He ran down the path. Ahead of him the pinnacle loomed against the pinkening light. He climbed as fast as he could to the top. Far below, on the plain, tiny uniformed figures were moving around an encampment. Smoke drifted upward from a fire as the faint sound came to him again. The jingle of harness!

And there, at the edge of the camp—mules, dozens of them. That meant they could travel fast—much faster than he and Astra could.

He ran back to the den. Astra sat up with a start, blinking. "I was having such a nice dream. About Pappa and Mamma, and—"

"Astra! Listen." He fought down panic. "Below us, on the plain. Soldiers."

For a moment she didn't seem to register what he'd said. "Soldiers!" he said again. At once she jumped up, rubbing the sleep out of her eyes.

"Where? Where are they?"

"They're still down below. I don't know if they're coming this way or not, but we'd better not take chances. Here." He opened the container. "It'll give us energy, and we'll need it." When Astra hesitated he handed her a moodfood slice and took one himself. His own tasted of scrambled eggs and toast and his favourite blueberry jam, but he swallowed it in seconds.

"We can't stay on the path. They'll see us."

"But we'll get lost. This is the way me and Pappa—"

"They have mules."

Astra stopped chewing and stared at him, eyes widening, then without a word kicked their bedding apart with a foot. "I'm ready. Let's go."

The sun was already burning off the early-morning mist. They struck off along a track that climbed steeply upward, circling boulders and crossing narrow gullies. At first it wound back and forth across the rock face, but soon they were climbing almost straight up, using tufts of plants as handholds. Freya scrambled up behind them, awkward on her three good legs. She looked much better after her meal the night before—more alert, almost her old self.

"The *Drage Tenner*," Astra said when they stopped briefly, nodding at the peaks above them. "The Dragon's Teeth. That's what Pappa called them." They seemed to rear their humped spines upward into the distance, like the spiked back of some prehistoric animal. Would they be able to find a way over them?

Now and then Astra dislodged a trickle of stones that bounced past Neil. Once he looked down and almost lost his balance. Far below was the path they'd left—and was that mules he could hear, or was he imagining things? He turned back, feeling dizzy, and gritted his teeth. They had to get out of sight of the path as soon as possible.

It was noon when they reached what, from below, had looked like the peak but turned out to be merely a shallow depression in the bare rock. So much for dragon's teeth! This one was a worn-flat molar. They collapsed on the hot stone, panting and thirsty. Beyond them the track wound its way round the side of the mountain, reappearing again in the hazy heat of a little valley below before climbing the next peak.

They stopped only long enough to catch their breath. To Neil's relief the track soon carried them out of sight of the path below and began heading down into the valley. The bare slopes gave way to coarse grasses, then to vegetation so luxuriant Neil wondered for a moment if they'd somehow taken another space-time leap. Great leafy palms towered above their heads, tall flowers exploded in red and yellow and orange blossoms, thick vines coiled round tree trunks. A brightly coloured bird called from a branch, a small glossy snake slid into the undergrowth. The air was steamy with a damp, wilting heat. Astra wrinkled her nose. "Ugh. That smell."

A sickly sweet smell, exactly like rotten eggs. Something tugged at his memory. A pulp mill! Prince George had smelled like that when they'd driven through on their way to the Yukon. His mother had said it was the sulphur they used in making pulp. They soon found the source of the smell—a bubbling, boiling spring, too hot even to touch, surrounded by giant stands of skunk cabbage.

For the rest of the afternoon they made their way through

the tangled landscape. Neil, sticky and hot and sweaty, felt relieved when the path began climbing again, even if they were less protected out in the open.

"They'll just think we're some kind of rolling mud balls," Astra said, giggling to break the tension. It was true. They were covered head to foot in drying muck. It made for uncomfortable walking.

Up ahead was what looked like an avalanche of rock, where a thin stream of water dribbled over the lip of a boulder. They stood underneath, holding their open mouths up to the blissful cold. Freya, after lapping thirstily, spun in giddy circles and chased her tail.

"I could stand here for the rest of the day," Astra murmured, the water dribbling over her head and making runnels in the rock dust on her face. Neil ran his hand across his wet muddy hair and stared uneasily about them. True, they'd travelled a long way from their camp of the night before, but with living spies or whatever it was the Fire Reapers had ... Plus he was starving again.

The afternoon sun was fading. In silent agreement they hunted about for somewhere more sheltered to spend the night. Afterward Astra went off to look for berries while Neil slipped away with his snare. He came back, some time later, with one of the spotted blue lizards and a small greenish-gold salamander hanging limply from a vine slung over his shoulder. Casually he tossed the salamander to Freya, then set about making a fire with twigs he'd collected.

"What are you doing?" Astra said, shading her eyes against the sunset.

"Building a fire. To roast the lizard."

"Yuck." She made a face. "I'll just have these." She held out a handful of white tuberous roots that she'd gathered. Neil tried one, but it was fibrous and tasteless. He gutted the lizard with a sharp stone, skewered it with a stick, and laid it across the fire on two forked branches stuck upright. The smell of the roasting flesh reminded him how famished he was. When it was done, he tore off a piece and offered it to Astra.

"It tastes like it came out of that bog," she said, biting into it gingerly. "That smell." And she tossed the piece to Freya, who wolfed it down. Neil felt hurt—he'd caught the lizard for the three of them. He was helping them survive. Didn't Astra understand that?

"You need meat, you know. Protein. My dad always said—"

"I wish you'd stop quoting him. Besides, these roots have protein, too."

"*You* were the one who was so worried about us having enough food, remember?" He could feel anger rising. "When we rationed the moodfood?"

"Someone had to think ahead," she said tartly, "since you obviously don't. Look what happened with the Memory Stone!"

This was unfair, but Neil immediately felt awful. "I said I was sorry. Anyway, that's beside the point—"

Her eyes blazed. "It's beside the point that the Stone's useless? What happens if Pappa can't make it work? What will they do to him then?"

He hadn't thought of that. In fact it was the last thing he wanted to think about—what might be happening to Hallvard and Fru Berta—so he lashed out. "You're such a know-it-all! Did anyone ever tell you that? Who got you out of Ashgård? Me and Freya, that's who!"

He picked up another lizard hunk and ate with wounded dignity. *All I did was talk about my dad, and she gets all huffy.* Astra blew her nose on her tunic and sat with her arms wrapped round Freya, who was whining softly and licking her face. They sat like that, not looking at each other, until the sun had completely set. It got cold then—too cold to be alone—so they crawled into the nest they'd made earlier, with Freya between them, and fell asleep.

In the Mouth of the Dragon

heir days fell into a pattern: put one foot in front of the other, find food where you can, sleep where there's shelter. Freya had got used to walking on three legs and was in good spirits, but Astra was silent and distant. Neil tried not to think about anything except following the narrow track up and down and around the Dragon's Teeth. Each step, he told himself, got them that much closer to Ashheim, and safety.

On what might have been day five of their journey—Neil had lost count—they were slogging up yet another mountain when a low growling in the distance made them jump. Thunder. The first drops started to fall, heavy and warm, and a flash of lightning zigzagged across the horizon. Another rumble of thunder, closer this time. A wind sprang up as well, bringing a blast of cold, and the whole sky turned a lurid yellow.

"We'd better find somewhere out of the storm," Neil yelled down to Astra. Another flash of lightning, almost on top of them, and rain began bucketing down. Freya pressed herself to the ground, the whites of her eyes showing. In minutes they were soaked. Glancing round wildly, Neil thought he saw a cave or hollow just above them, though what with the rain running into his eyes he couldn't be sure.

"Astra!" he yelled, cupping his hands round his mouth and pointing, but the wind tore his words away. There was a deafening crack, so loud it was as though the mountain itself had split open. The next thing he knew Astra was lying face down on the slope below him, absolutely motionless.

"Astra! Astra!" He scrambled down to her, slipping on the loose wet shale, blown sideways by the wind. Freya was already pushing Astra's shoulder with her nose. Neil shook her, but there was no response. There was a horrible charred smell like that of the roasted lizard.

With an effort he rolled her over. Now he saw the burned-off eyebrows, the scorch marks on her clothing, the face pale as death. *Don't panic. Check the pulse.* He'd seen his dad do that once with a neighbour who'd fallen off a ladder and hit his head. Astra's was faint, but definitely there. He shook her again, roughly, but she still didn't wake up.

What was he going to do? Even if he *had* seen a cave, he couldn't carry her there, and if he dragged her she'd be torn up by the sharp rocks. The rain was still pounding down, the thunder rocking and bouncing off the mountainsides. Freya whined softly and lay down next to her. Helplessly, not knowing what else to do, Neil lay down on the other side, as close to Astra as he could. *Please, storm, blow over. Just blow over and leave us alone.* Would he freeze to death before it did? He counted out loud to keep himself awake, he tried to distract himself by thinking desperately of other things. Like Astra's father. Where was he? What had happened to him? And Fru Berta and the other villagers and ...

Slowly he became aware that the rain was slowing down. He tried to stand up, but his knees buckled and he almost fell. Above him the thunder was rolling away, its growls more distant, and patches of blue sky appeared. He heard a whimper, then a few faint groans. Astra's eyes fluttered open.

"What happened? Where am I?" Her voice was thick, groggy.

"You were hit by lightning, I think." *She's okay, she's going to be okay. Better keep my voice steady.* "Can you sit up? Here, take my hand."

She hung onto him and slowly, awkwardly, let herself be pulled up to a sitting position. "Wow, it hurts. It feels like someone hit me over the head." She moved her neck and shoulders gingerly and winced with pain.

For a few minutes I thought you were dead. "I guess lightning

132

packs quite a punch. Can you get up?" He put his hands under her armpits and lifted her. She staggered a little and went white, as if she was going to be sick. "You okay?"

"My tummy feels—upside down." She was lifting her hands and staring at them. "And my fingers feel numb."

He wouldn't tell her yet about the burned-off eyebrows, or the singed and shredded tunic.

"Think you can climb?" For answer Astra clutched her stomach, bent over and threw up, leaving a little greenish puddle of half-digested roots. But she wiped her mouth with the back of the hand and straightened resolutely. "You go. I'll follow."

"You sure?"

She nodded, still white-faced, and so he turned and began climbing back up the slope. Above them the last of the clouds had rolled away and the sun was already drying their wet clothes. He looked about him uneasily. The storm had been terrible—it had almost killed Astra—but at least it had protected them. Now, with the rain gone and Astra moving so slowly, they were sitting ducks.

By the time they reached the top it was almost dark. Astra was swaying with exhaustion and Neil was on edge, startling at every shadow. Beyond them the last fiery streaks of sunset were slashed across the sky. Fire and rock—there seemed nothing else left in the world. He put his arm round Astra.

"Let's go down the other side. Just a short way. Look for somewhere to sleep."

She was already half-asleep, her head on Neil's shoulder. He found a hollow thick with moss, fed by a tiny brown stream. Astra collapsed while Neil cupped his palms in the water and held them out to her. She drank in small, slow sips. Afterwards he took great gulping mouthfuls, the cold water burning his throat. How he wished he had some of the lizard left!

They lay huddled together on the moss with Freya between them. Neil was kept awake by his growling stomach, and Astra tossed and turned and cried out. At long last morning came, utterly quiet, the clouds tinged with peach and rose. Astra sat up, slowly.

"I feel sort of—I don't know, foggy." She touched her forehead and stared up at him in alarm. "What happened to my eyebrows?"

"They got burned off when you were hit." Neil tried to sound matter-of-fact. And then, because he couldn't help it, he grinned and added, "Makes you look pretty weird."

"Not as weird as I feel."

"You're not awake yet." He stood up and stretched, staring over the range of mountains stretching away on either side. "We're on one of the highest peaks, as far as I can see. With foothills down below us. Maybe we're over the worst."

"That's where Ashheim is. Somewhere on the other side of those hills."

He turned to ask if she knew how far it was, but she was pressing her side and wincing. "Look." She lifted her tunic. Between her ribs was a dark-brown burn, charred and blackened at the edges. Grimacing, Neil stared at it more closely. It looked exactly like a tiny tree, right down to the leaves and branches. A birch tree, like the ones that grew in the Yukon. Weirder and weirder ...

"At least it doesn't hurt. Or not much." Astra pulled her tunic down and stood up, wobbling a little. "There, see? I'm okay. I'm fine."

No, you're not. You're shaky and trembly and you've got terrible burns. And Freya was chewing her injured paw again. The sooner they got to Ashheim the better.

They took it slowly going down the slope of scree and bare rock. As the sun rose and the day got warmer, they found themselves among the beginnings of vegetation again—mats of a tiny heather-like plant, scrubby bushes with pale yellow flowers.

Astra stumbled along like a zombie, saying nothing, her eyes half-closed. They stopped frequently to let her rest and to drink from the can Neil had filled with water from the brown stream. Late in the afternoon he discovered a patch of what looked like tiny wild blueberries and tried them cautiously. Yes, blueberries, though much smaller than the fat ones his mother used for pancakes on Sunday mornings. He held a few out to Astra, who seemed to brighten a little and managed to eat some. Freya, as usual, turned her nose up, but Neil ate hungrily and filled the empty can with more berries. It was a long time since they'd had a decent meal.

Astra fell asleep right where they'd eaten, among the berry bushes. Neil, uneasy, kept dozing and jerking awake. Toward dawn he woke out of a dream of huge winged creatures high above them in the night sky, their great leathery wings flapping slowly. Chilled, he glanced up. Were there shapes there, darker black against the blackness, or was he imagining things? Hadn't he seen such a shape that time he'd got Stone-locked in Hallvard's lab?

He shook off the thought and hastily woke Astra. She seemed a little less dazed, though she complained that her fingers were still numb.

After a breakfast of berries they made their way slowly across a spiny ridge that led westward, away from the rising sun. Neil tried to keep an eye out for prey—rabbits? mice?—but either there weren't any or he was too preoccupied to notice.

At the other end of the ridge was the nearest of the foothills. Searching for the easiest route, he stumbled across an overgrown path of hard-packed earth. It led them around the hill and up the next one. At least the going was easier now than on bare rock, the climb less steep.

They started up the second hill as the sun sank below them into a rosy puddle. Neil reached the crest first, followed by Freya. Below them was a long narrow valley with a silver gleam of river running through it. Its banks were thick with trees, more trees than Neil had seen in all his time in Nordlandia. It all looked so—normal. It reminded him, in fact, of the Yukon—of the river and the valley and the clay cliffs—and he was suddenly, horribly, homesick. Freya lifted her nose and sniffed the air, as though she too was remembering her northern home.

"Is that where Ashheim is?" he said to Astra, who had staggered over the top.

She nodded and sank to the ground. "At the end of the valley." She was breathing hard. "You can't see it from here."

Neil's heart sank. At the rate they were going, it would be long past dark before they got there, which meant another night outdoors. He was suddenly exhausted. And ravenous, too. But Astra was saying something.

"... stayed with a woman there with a funny name. She wanted us to stay longer, but Pappa was in a hurry to get to Ashgård."

"You stayed in Ashheim?"

"It was a long time ago, remember." She wrinkled her forehead as if trying to summon a memory. "Mont-something. She used to work with Pappa at the Institute."

"How come you never said before?"

"Because I forgot." Astra shook her head. "Everything's so foggy since the storm."

"And she used to work with your dad?" For the first time since they'd left Ashgård, Neil felt a spark of hope. Maybe this woman could help him.

"Montserrat," Astra said suddenly. "That was her name. Montserrat Lavallet. She and Pappa worked on the Memory Stone together."

"So why didn't you stay in Ashheim?"

"Because Pappa thought we'd be better off somewhere more isolated." Astra was staring at her fingers and flexing them—they must still be bothering her. "He tried to get her to come with us, but she wouldn't. She said it was safer for them all if they were in different places."

Maybe this woman had a copy of the Memory Stone. Maybe she'd even succeeded in sending people back to the past with it! Instead he said, "What's Ashheim like?"

"It's got a funny reputation. People say it's—well, magic. There's nowhere else in Nordlandia with so many trees. "

"*They* must hate it, then."

"I think they're afraid of it. At least that's what Pappa used to say." There was a shiver in her voice.

"Sounds like *you're* afraid of it, too."

"I don't want anything to happen to it because *we're* there."

A chill seized him. He knew exactly what Astra meant. If the soldiers were hunting for them, he and Astra were putting Ashheim in danger. Suppose the Ashheimers wouldn't let them stay?

A faint rustling came to them from somewhere on the hill below. Not wind—the air was too still. The ridge of fur rose along Freya's back. The rustling came again, a little louder, and Freya gave her low warning *ouf*. Something, or someone, was coming up the hill.

Neil grabbed Freya's collar as he and Astra scrambled behind a nearby pile of rocks. The sound of cracking twigs grew louder, and now there were voices. A patrol, out scouting the countryside? They certainly weren't trying to hide—they were laughing and talking loudly in Nordlandish. Freya gave another low *ouf* and he clapped his hand over her muzzle, hardly daring to breathe.

Between the rocks he caught a glimpse of bodies moving through the scrub. A dozen of them in all, perhaps. They weren't in uniform, but this way they could pass for civilians. Astra's arm was trembling against his own, or was that him? One of them began to sing something loud and rollicking and the rest joined in. Any minute now the patrol would be out of sight, and he and Astra could slip away down the hillside.

A sudden clatter—a weapon striking a stone, perhaps—made him jump. Freya, startled, slipped from his grasp and dashed out, barking. Neil, lunging to grab her, lost his balance and sprawled headlong. Then there were shouts and exclamations and running feet, and a weapon clicked in the air above him. *"Svönnork! Merkka liepskjold drieligenigen!"*

He didn't need a translator to tell him what it meant—he was under arrest. He struggled to his knees, feeling sick, and put his hands in the air. They'd been so close—so close ... Two of the men were holding Freya, who growled and struggled. He fought back a sob. Maybe they wouldn't see Astra in the shadows ...

"Svönnork!" one of the men said again, and jabbed him with the butt of his weapon. The one holding Freya tightened her collar until she whimpered. Please don't hurt her, please don't ...

And then from behind him, to his horror, came Astra's voice, high and defiant and panicked. "You mustn't touch him! *Net bevjeveld ipkönijfor!* He isn't a spy, he isn't! And we need help! Please, please, help us!"

An End and a Beginning

hy, why, why? was all Neil could think in the confusion that followed. Of all the stupid, idiotic, reckless—Why hadn't she just shut up?

And then one of the men lowered his rifle and stared at Astra. "By Thor and Odin, it can't be," he said. To Neil's utter bewilderment, Astra threw herself sobbing into his arms. The others lowered their weapons and crowded round, muttering in astonishment—all except one, a massive man with beefy arms, who kept his gun on Neil.

"And who in the name of Odin might *you* be?" he said in heavily accented English.

"He's a friend," Astra said, pulling herself away from the man who held her. "He saved my life. We've come all the way from Ashgård."

The man who had asked the question stepped forward and shone what looked like an ancient flashlight in Neil's face. "You're not a villager, that's for certain." His eyes narrowed, and he glanced from Neil to Astra and back. "Where are you from?"

"It's all right, Magnus," said the man into whose arms Astra had flung herself. "The girl is telling the truth. Either that or she's not Hallvard Bjarnason's daughter."

"Hallvard Bjarnason?" Magnus said, looking dumbfounded. "Where is he?

Astra burst into tears again. It was Neil who said, "The Fire Reapers arrested him."

There were gasps and muttered exclamations. Several of the men shook their head, and one of them said darkly, "We never speak their name aloud. It brings bad luck."

"Where are they now?" Magnus demanded. "Are they following you?" He looked round in alarm as the others stirred uneasily.

"We saw them a few days ago," Neil said, determined not to be intimidated, " when we came over the mountains."

"They'll be in Ashheim next," someone muttered. "They're bound to be looking for the daughter."

"Or the boy," someone else said. "Maybe he is a spy."

"Of course he isn't!" Astra said hotly, drawing herself up. "They captured him, and he escaped, and he made it to Ashgård, and then they—oh, it's a long story, and we're so hungry and tired ..." Her voice trailed off.

"Here we are asking questions when it's plain as day the two of them are done in," said the man who had recognized her. "Here, Sven"—he addressed a tall, heavily built man—"you carry Hallvard's daughter. And you, lad, can you make it to the bottom? We've mules there, waiting for us."

They must be from Ashheim, Neil decided. That was how they knew Astra. Their patched clothing and laughably elderly weapons made it clear they weren't soldiers, at any rate. He nodded, stepped forward, and promptly collapsed.

"Why, the boy's thin as a rail," said the man, helping him up. "Here, Magnus." And Neil felt himself lifted into the air as if he was a feather and slung like a sack over Magnus's shoulder.

"My dog ... Freya ..." He couldn't talk properly upside-down.

"She'll follow, as long as you're with us. We'll get you all tended to, don't you worry."

They set off down the hill, moving fast and silently. Neil drifted in and out of consciousness. From somewhere came soft whinnying and the stamp of hooves, and then they were travelling swiftly through the night, the river murmuring somewhere nearby. After a long time he saw lights and heard voices and felt hands lifting him in the air. The softness of sheets touched his skin. Then the river rippled over his head, submerging him.

When he woke he was in a room with a sloping ceiling, sunlight slanting through a window. He sat up and looked round. A pitcher of water and a bowl stood on a table. A fresh tunic and a pair of much-patched pants hung over a chair. Where was he? He was sore and bruised and he ached all over with a bone-deep weariness.

He climbed out of bed and examined himself in a mirror. An almost unrecognizable face—burnt brown, scratched and mud-streaked—stared back. He washed himself in the bowl and put on the pants and tunic, which was so big he had to roll back the sleeves.

He opened the door cautiously, wondering where Freya was. From below he could hear the sounds of someone moving about. He made his way slowly down the stairs, where a woman was feeding fuel into a stove where a pot bubbled. Freya, to his relief, lay nearby on a blanket. She didn't get up, but she lifted her head and roo-ed happily when she saw Neil. The woman straightened and turned, smiling.

"You were dead to the world when we put you to bed last night!" She reminded him, with a pang, of his mother—the same red-brown hair, though tied back with a ribbon, the same clear grey eyes. "Now you must be a hungry lad. Here, eat." She spooned some sort of cereal from the bubbling pot and set it on the table.

"Where am I? And where's Astra?"

The woman looked surprised. "Why, in Ashheim, of course. It was Ashheimers rescued you last night, didn't you know? Lucky for you that Markko recognized her."

"Markko?"

"One of the hunters who found you. I'm Inga, by the way." And she brushed his hair with her hand, just the way his mother used to. "Now eat your *brødkorn*, child, and don't worry your head about anything else just yet. I looked in on Astra a short while ago. She's still fast asleep."

First he had to check on Freya. She was nosing at her paw again, ignoring the plate of scraps beside her. The pad was hot and swollen and oozing pus. "Don't worry, girl," he whispered, with more conviction than he felt. "There's bound to be a doctor here or something. We'll get help with that paw of yours very soon."

The cereal was deliciously thick and creamy, but he couldn't manage more than a few mouthfuls. His stomach was tight with anxiety. Now they were finally in Ashheim, what would happen to them? Did the Ashheimers still think he was a spy?

"You just rest easy," Inga said, wiping her hands on her apron, "while I move the goats. You're to stay here as long as you need to." She left the room and Neil gazed about him. Everything was old and shabby and recycled, just like Ashgård. The table itself was a slab of metal mounted on an old bicycle frame.

The door opened again a few minutes later, but it wasn't Inga. It was a tiny woman with a face as brown and creased as an old baseball mitt, her white hair in a braid down her back. "So. You must be the brave lad from Ashgård." Her English was so thick it was difficult to follow. "And where is the *jente*? The girl they say was bitten by the dragon?"

Freya roo-ed impatiently and the woman laughed. "The heroic beast who defended you last night! She tells me her paw hurts." She knelt down beside Freya with surprising agility and examined the pad as Freya struggled. "Yes. Very nasty. We need some calming oil."

Lifting the cloth of the covered basket she carried, she drew out a small bottle and tipped a couple of drops into her palm. Freya sniffed her hand warily, then happily licked up the oil. "It is like moodfood in a way, only better. You know of that terrible stuff? So it tastes to your dog whatever she thinks of."

Probably voles, then. Or maybe macaroni and cheese—she loves that.

"Now, bring me a basin of hot water. Not too hot. We need to remove the last of the thorn and clean out the wound."

Neil hunted around in the cupboards, found a battered tin basin, and filled it with water from the kettle. When he returned the woman was holding Freya's paw in her lap and probing the wound with what looked like a long forked needle. To his astonishment Freya was perfectly still.

"Ah yes, the calming oil. Very effective, don't you think?" The woman looked up at him with a mischievous smile. "There!" And she held up a tiny fragment of thorn on the end of her probe. "Humbling that something so small can cause so much harm, no?" She sponged the paw with the water, then took a jar and a clean bandage from the basket. "Here, you can help. Hold the bandage, like this." Neil held it flat while she spread some sort of salve on the gauze. "There. Now wrap it round her paw. Can you tie the ends? Good. Ask Fru Inga for an old sock when she comes back. If you pull it over the bandage, your friend here can't chew it."

Freya lay down on her side, looking positively beatific, and fell asleep. "I don't know who you are," Neil said, grabbing the woman's hand and shaking it as hard as he could, "but thank you—that was amazing—I mean I—thanks a lot."

The woman laughed and shrugged her shoulders. "I am Eirá. At your service." Then she stood up, placed her hands on Neil's shoulders, and looked into his eyes. "You yourself are not doing so well, either."

"I'm okay. Just a little sore." But as he spoke a deep weariness came over him and he had to struggle to keep his eyes open. Eirá took two vials from the basket, one filled with a pale pink liquid, the other green as sea glass. She tipped a few drops of each into a small beaker and handed it to him. "Drink. You'll feel much better."

The taste was awful, like a mixture of soap and cough medicine. "Not, I'm afraid, like moodfood," said Eirá, "but a powerful potion against grief. And the effects of time travel, too."

"How did you know?" Neil asked, astonished.

"The eyes. For those who can read." She shook her head, as if

saddened by the world's ignorance. "There is a part of your eye
that has special light cells. Those cells change when you travel
through time. It is all very complicated. Now, you'll need rest,
you and Freya, both of you."

"You don't—you can't—?"

"Return you to your own time?" She shook her head again,
gently. "No, my skills are not as advanced as that, I'm afraid.
That knowledge has been lost. That was why Montserrat—" She
seemed to stop herself and changed the subject. "But tell me.
How *did* you travel here from your time?"

Eirá, Neil decided, could be trusted with the truth. So he told
her about Charlie and the smoking woodstove and his arrival
in the desert, and how he'd been taken prisoner and escaped
to Ashgård, where he'd met Hallvard and Astra and been
reunited with Freya. He told her how Charlie had ended up in
Nordlandia, too. "So you see, somehow I have to find Charlie
again and see if he knows how to get us back. My mom must be
pretty frantic by now."

"Hmm. Most interesting. You must talk to my sister. Áilu,
her name is."

Áilu? "That was who—Fru Berta told us to—"

"Ah, Fru Berta! She's an old friend of ours. You must come
this evening. Come for dinner. And now where do I find the girl
bitten by the dragon?"

Another visitor came while Eirá was still upstairs. It was
Markko, who in the bright light of morning turned out to be a
short, sturdy man with a trim grey beard and sharp blue eyes.
With him was Magnus, the man who'd been so suspicious, and
whose massive frame had borne Neil down the hill the night
before. Magnus was intimidating, with his beefy arms and towering presence, and he still looked grim.

Markko, however, greeted Neil cheerfully and asked how

he was feeling. Was Fru Inga looking after them? Had Eirá arrived? And what about Astra? Neil answered the questions as best he could, though he was feeling lightheaded and woozy from the potion.

"We've come to ask you a few questions." Markko drew up a chair and sat down. "About Ashgård and exactly what happened. People here are very worried. We've heard all sorts of rumours."

Neil nodded, hoping he'd sound coherent.

"Astra said last night that you'd been their prisoner at one time," Markko went on. "When did you escape?"

Neil tried to remember. "A few weeks ago, I think. It's all rather fuzzy."

"From where? And why were you arrested?" Magnus asked severely.

"I was in the Drear Lands." He certainly wasn't going to tell these two the truth about how he'd got there. Eirá might believe him, but he wasn't sure anyone else would. "I—um—my father and I were travelling from the VilderRegion—"

"So you're FUAZ," interrupted Magnus.

Neil nodded vaguely. "But we got separated, and I got lost. And then *they* found me. But I managed to escape."

"Quite a feat," Markko said approvingly.

But Magnus was frowning. "Prisoners are imprinted with indelible codes, or so we hear. And there are those who think that those codes communicate with them in some way." He was staring at Neil reproachfully, as if he regretted that they'd found him. "It's happened here before. There was a scientist who—"

"It wasn't because of the codes," Markko said quickly. "She'd never been a prisoner. They must have been tipped off."

Neil's heartbeat quickened. Something had happened to the woman Astra knew, then. She wouldn't be able to help him after all. It was just as he'd feared—as soon as he and Astra were well enough, they'd be sent on their way. He felt tears smarting.

"Don't worry," Markko said quickly, seeing Neil's expression.

"You're safe here. I can vouch for that. I'll guarantee your safety with my own body. Hallvard Bjarnason was a good friend to me and Montserrat ..." He trailed off, his voice full of emotion.

"Let's not let our hearts run away with our heads," Magnus said impatiently. "We still have many questions. Such as why they raided Ashgård when they did, and what happened to Hallvard, and—"

But Neil was saved from answering by Eirá. She came into the room and looked round in surprise. "Why, what are you two doing here? Markko, I'm surprised at you. And you too, Magnus. Leave the poor lad alone, he's been through quite enough."

Markko was already rising guiltily to his feet, and even Magnus looked sheepish. "We came to see how they were both doing," Markko said hurriedly. "How's the child?"

"Her wounds are serious," Eirá said, looking grave. "But I gave her a strong sleeping potion. Rest is a great healer, perhaps the best. Now, off with you." She shepherded Markko and Magnus out the door, turning at the last minute. "And you, Neil"—she wagged a strong brown finger at him—"you're to have dinner with Áilu and me this evening at sundown. Don't be late."

Just before the door closed, she looked back and gave Neil a wink. If Áilu was half as powerful as her sister, he and Astra were in good hands.

Áilu the Wise

ilu and Eirá lived at the other end of the village in a tiny crumbling ash-brick cottage. Neil walked there that evening through the golden light of late autumn. It was hard to see why Ashheim had the special reputation Astra described. True, there was the river lined with trees, the vibrant green of the valley. But the village itself looked as poor and rundown as Ashgård—perhaps poorer. And what did people live on here? There was no brick kiln, no evidence of any other industry, and none of the large vegetable plots he'd seen in Ashgård. Perhaps Astra had been wrong.

It was Eirá who opened the door and led him along a low passageway not much higher than Neil's head. At the far end they came out into a small cluttered room filled with books and charts and various strange instruments. An old woman, even older and more wrinkled than Eirá, sat in an armchair peering through a magnifying glass at a parchment scroll. When she saw Neil she let the glass fall—it was fastened round her neck by a cord—and waved him to a low stool nearby. "Eirá, fetch the last of the *sima*, there's a dear. Oh, he can't have *sima*?" She shook her head. "Eirá says it'll counteract the potion, and we can't have that, can we? Then it'll have to be cranberry cider. Have you ever had cranberry cider?"

He hadn't, but it turned out to be delicious. This time, he decided as he sipped it, he was going to be the one asking questions. But Áilu got there first.

"Now, you're an odd specimen." She was examining Neil through the magnifying glass. "From another age, Eirá tells me. How long ago?"

"Well, I—I don't know exactly," Neil stammered. "But we had wolves, and polar bears, and cell phones, and where I come from was called the Yukon."

"*That* long ago?" A large golden lizard suddenly crawled out from a corner and began clambering up Áilu's chair. "It must have taken a lot of energy to get you here." The lizard climbed into Áilu's lap, and she stroked it like a cat as it flickered its scarlet eyelids at Neil.

"It was an accident, really," Neil said.

But Áilu waved her hand dismissively. "No such things as accidents, child." She frowned at him as though he'd said something rude. "You were summoned."

"But it could have been anyone," Neil said, his exasperation growing. "I mean, I only came because Freya jumped—"

"Of course Freya jumped," Áilu said severely. "Animals are much more intelligent than humans. *She* knew. Besides, the Trees foretold it."

That was what Fru Berta had told him, too. He decided not to argue. There was something much more important he needed to ask. "Your sister says you can't help me get back to my time," he said, "and my mom must be really worried." He broke off, swallowing hard.

"Time, as you know, is simultaneous," Áilu said, more gently this time. "It's possible your mother hasn't even noticed."

This struck Neil as nonsense, but he changed the subject. "I have to find this guy called Charlie," he said. "The blacksmith told us he'd seen him in the City. So that's where I have to go, if you can tell me where it is."

Áilu and Eirá exchanged glances, and Eirá coughed. "You don't know what you ask," Áilu said softly, and the hand stroking the lizard stilled. "There are many dangers between here and the City—and you bear one of their codes. You would be seized in no time."

Neil felt his heart sinking. Didn't they understand? "You

148

mean—I'm just supposed to sit here and do nothing? There must be *someone* who can take me there."

"I told you he was feisty, Áilu," Eirá said, and they both laughed.

"And a good thing, too," Áilu said, looking at Neil. "Because you're going to be tested—more than you realize."

He'd had quite enough of tests, thank you very much. Hadn't he been tested already, just getting here with Astra, not to mention his escape from the Fire Reapers?

"We're going to find out what comes next," Áilu went on. "Fetch me my drum, Eirá."

Eirá went to a cupboard in the corner and took out a drum made of skin stretched over a frame and decorated with mysterious curved symbols. Áilu began beating it softly in a steady rhythm with the flat of her palm, eyes shut. After a few moments she and Eirá began a kind of breathy guttural singsong low in their throats. Neil stared at them, baffled. How was this going to give them any answers?

All at once the walls of the cottage swung open and he found himself standing in what looked like a Yukon birch forest in summer, the sunlight shimmering through the leaves. A breeze came up, and for a moment he could have sworn that the leaves were speaking, though he couldn't make out what they said. How wonderful it was to be back home with the sunlight on his face!

And then he saw a man approaching through the forest. A tall man, taller than anyone Neil had ever seen, dressed all in black, his face averted so that Neil couldn't see it. As he came, each tree he passed withered and died, leaving a leafless trunk. Neil wanted to cry out, but when he opened his mouth no sound came. He flung his arms protectively round the nearest tree, but the man laughed and pulled him away. His touch was like ice, yet it burned like fire, and Neil felt his own arm wither under it. "How is a child like you going to defy me?" the man said, and his voice was deep and unearthly and full of contempt. And then he raised his hand again—

149

"Child? Are you all right?"

Neil opened his eyes. Somehow he was lying on the floor of the cottage and Eirá was bending over him, a look of concern on her face.

"You must have had a powerful vision," Áilu said. She was leaning forward, watching him intently. "Can you tell us what happened?"

After he finished there was a long silence. At last Áilu said, "Yes, I thought so. A great task has been laid upon you, child from the past. A task that involves facing those who are trying to destroy us."

Neil swallowed hard and shook his head. "I really only came to find Freya. And now I've got her, I need to go back."

"The only way back," Áilu said slowly, "is through. Together with the girl and the dog. They were also in the forest in your vision, though you could not see them. I cannot tell you what will happen—my knowledge does not extend so far. But I can tell you how to begin, and I can give you what help I can."

"I'm not the right person for this job," Neil said weakly. "Really. I just want to go home." Maybe if he closed his eyes Áilu and Eirá would disappear. Maybe this whole thing was some weird dream, and he'd find himself back in his bedroom in the Yukon.

But when he opened his eyes Áilu and Eirá were still sitting there, watching him. Eirá's face was gentle, Áilu's stern. "No one can refuse their task," Áilu said. "Not without destroying themselves. But you will have help on this journey, because it is vital for all of us that you succeed. Not just for the Ash-Gatherer villages, but for all the Bi-Souls."

"Who are they?" Neil said, feeling quite overwhelmed.

"You will meet them in due time. You will meet the Aqua Libere, too."

He remembered *that* name—the soldiers who'd captured him had accused him of being one of them. It was all getting horribly confusing.

"Your task is a necessary one for all the Realms and Nations," Áilu continued. "Indeed for the entire planet. Remember that you have succeeded in one task already—you came through the Dragon's Teeth and lived to tell about it." She stood up briskly, and the golden lizard slithered to the floor. "Now, let us have our meal, and afterward you must leave us. There are things I must do to help you prepare for your journey."

Over the next few days Neil was left largely on his own. He spent one morning with Markko and Magnus and other members of the village council, telling them what had happened in Ashgård. His answers seemed to satisfy them, and the word "spy" wasn't mentioned again. Extra watches were stationed round Ashheim at night, but then word came from other villages that Fire Reaper troops had been seen returning to headquarters. For the time being, it seemed, there would be no more raids.

Astra continued to sleep, getting up only in the evenings to join them for dinner. She was uncharacteristically quiet, but the colour was returning to her face and her eyebrows were just beginning to grow back. Eirá, who came daily to check on her, reported that her wounds were healing nicely, though the peculiar tree-shaped mark on her side remained. "The Tree Elders were watching over your journey," Eirá told Neil, "and they probably saved Astra's life. They stood between her and the dragon's fire, and left their sign."

"Is that why the Fire Reapers didn't find us when we hid in the compost?" Neil asked, light dawning. "Was that because of the Elders, too?"

"Very likely." Eirá nodded. "If you were hiding in vegetative matter, you were under the Elders' protection."

Neil himself had felt much better ever since drinking that awful-tasting potion. For the first time the parts of him that had been left behind in the past seemed to have caught up with him. As for Freya, the deep cut in her paw was sealing shut and was almost as good as new.

He tried not to think about what might be happening to Hallvard or Fru Berta. Eirá assured him that such thoughts would do no good, and in fact could do harm. So instead he roamed the village with Freya, swam in the cool clear river, and went rabbit hunting with Markko and the other men. The rabbits, it turned out, lived in colonies throughout the valley, and the villagers traded their fur and meat for items that the other Ash-Gatherer villages produced, such as the ash bricks from Ashgård or the metal cooking pots from Ashpolten.

Once he asked Eirá why the village was so poor. In the past, she explained, their wealth had attracted many raids—not only by the Fire Reapers, but also by the Útlagi, the bands of outlaws that roamed the various hinterlands outside the City. "Our safety lies in our poverty," she told Neil. "And then there are the rumours that witches live in Ashheim—which Áilu and I do nothing to discourage." She smiled mischievously again.

"*Are* you witches?" Neil wanted to know. He'd never actually met a real witch.

"If by 'witch' you mean knowing the languages of the other Realms and Nations, then yes, we are witches," Eirá answered softly. "But once upon a time all of humankind knew those languages, too." She looked at Neil with those disconcerting bright eyes that seemed to know him inside out. "Plants, for example. Did you know each plant has its own song? To make the calming potion that I used for Freya, for example, I had to learn the songs of several plants."

This seemed ridiculous. It certainly wasn't scientific. But then he thought of the murmurous distant singing of the Memory Stone, and how he'd had to learn to tune into that. Was that the same thing Eirá was talking about?

"There are many languages, and one cannot learn them all," Eirá went on. "I speak those of a few of the plants, but Áilu knows many more. She knows the speech of the forests and the lakes and the mountains. She will ask the mountain passes and the trees and the rivers to be kind to you and Astra when you travel through."

Neil shivered. He didn't want another journey. He especially didn't want a journey where the mountains had to be spoken to. If he couldn't go home, he wanted only to stay in Ashheim with Fru Inga and Markko and Áilu and Eirá. Suppose he just said no?

At the end of the week Áilu sent word that she wanted to see Neil and Astra, along with Freya. She was sitting in her chair as before, the golden lizard perched on its back. Freya lay down at their feet, keeping an alert eye on the lizard. Áilu picked up her magnifying glass and examined Astra with curiosity.

"Eirá tells me that you are nearly well again, child." Áilu let the glass drop and leaned back, folding her wrinkled hands.

"I'm much better, thank you," Astra said, nodding, though her face clouded. Her eyebrows were growing back, slowly, which meant her face still looked weird. "But I keep thinking about Pappa. Maybe we should have stayed—"

Áilu shook her head firmly. "You could have done nothing. You are far better placed to help him here."

"Neil says you know about the future. Can you tell me what's happened to him?"

But Áilu shook her head again. "My knowledge is not unlimited. I have no information about your father. But perhaps Neil has told you that, according to my informants, you are to undertake a task of great importance. Great importance."

"I have to find Pappa first. Maybe after that—"

"There are no maybes, Astra," Áilu said rather sharply. "You have both been summoned to the task, you and Neil, and the dog Freya, who led the way. A task of such magnitude that children from two different time fields must unite their powers to complete it. And there's no time—so to speak—to lose."

Astra flushed deep red, her lower lip quivering. "But I didn't ask—"

"No one *asks* for such tasks." Áilu sat up straighter; it almost seemed she'd grown taller. "They are too daunting. I can tell you, however, that the only way to reach your father is to undertake this one."

Astra glared at Neil, as if it was all his fault. I didn't choose this either, he mouthed at her. But Áilu was speaking.

"—must both listen very carefully. The beings in the Many Realms tell me that the first stage of your journey will take you to the Valley of the Slaves."

Astra gasped. "What's the Valley of the Slaves?" Neil asked, dismayed.

"It is where they develop and manufacture their weapons," Áilu said slowly. "Using slave labour, as the name suggests." She said the words as though she had a bitter taste in her mouth.

"Why us?" Astra blurted out. "We're just a couple of kids."

"Exactly." Áilu nodded as though it was all perfectly clear. "You are far less threatening than adults."

"And what are we supposed to do there?" Neil asked.

"That will be revealed in due course. What I can tell you is that a network of—let us call them freedom fighters, though they would call them terrorists—will guide you there. You needn't worry about travelling alone."

That was the least of their worries, thought Neil. It was all very well for Áilu to sit there, calm as you please, and tell them that this was what they had to do. She wasn't going on any dangerous journey.

"Will I find Pappa there?" Astra leaned forward eagerly.

But Áilu shook her head. "I do not know." She was stroking the lizard again; Freya, watching, gave a short, sharp bark. "What I do know is that your journey will begin bright and early tomorrow morning."

Neil and Astra exchanged looks of despair. "Couldn't you—I mean, wouldn't it be better to send someone else?" Astra said feebly.

"I've asked Markko to provide you with two of his best mules," Áilu continued calmly. "And there is another ally for each of you. Eirá, bring me my chest."

Eirá went to the corner cupboard and took out a small wooden chest, bound with metal bands and fastened with a heavy bronze hasp. Áilu undid the hasp and lifted the lid. The object she drew out and handed to Neil made him gasp. It was the size of a ballpoint pen, fashioned out of some shimmering black metal, and light as a feather.

"It was found by one of our villagers after a skirmish with a group of their soldiers," Áilu said. "It is called a SerraTube, is controlled by thought, and it can cut through anything. However, I must warn you that it is powered by energy stolen from the living. Every time it is used, some part of a living thing dies."

Neil stared at the device with repugnance. "Then I won't use it. Ever."

"You may be placed in a situation where you have no choice. I give it to you because it is their own magic, and therefore can be used against them."

Áilu bent over her chest again and lifted out what looked like a tiny silver flute. "This," she said, handing it to Astra, "is an Etheric Sensor. It allows you to see beyond the material level into the energetic one. And to communicate by means of it, too, once you are skilled enough."

Astra lifted the little flute to her mouth and blew through it, but no sound emerged. She ran her fingers over the finger holes, puzzled. "But how do you do that?"

"I'm afraid I cannot tell you. It belonged to a woman scientist who was doing research here. She managed to smuggle it to me just before they took her away."

"Montserrat Lavallet!" cried Neil.

Áilu and Eirá stared at him in surprise, and Astra glanced from one face to the next. "Montserrat? Pappa's friend? But she isn't—" She broke off, light dawning. "They captured her? She's a prisoner, too?"

"I'm afraid so, my dear." It was Eirá who spoke, taking Astra's hands in hers. "Almost a year ago now."

Astra's eyes filled with tears. "She was so kind to us when we stayed here. Pappa wanted her to come with us."

"She'd made a home here by then," Eirá said gently. "She and Markko were very much in love."

So that explained why Markko had found it so difficult to talk about her.

"It's only a prototype," cautioned Áilu. "Montserrat felt she was on the verge of a breakthrough when—when she was taken. There was no time to explain how it worked. I also suspect that it will not work inside any Fire Reaper structures. But I feel she would have wanted you to have it." She closed the lid of the chest and handed it back to Eirá. "You must go to bed early," she told them. "You need to conserve your strength. You're going to need every bit of it."

Áilu stood up then—Neil hadn't realized till now quite how tiny she was—and held her hands out, squeezing each of theirs in turn. Freya growled softly, as though she was aware of the dangers that lay ahead, and the golden lizard blinked its scarlet eyelids.

"My blessings on you, children," Eirá whispered at the door, hugging them. "If you need help, call on the beings of the Many Realms, and we will try to provide it."

Neil wasn't sure how they were supposed to do that, but a growl from Freya distracted him. The golden lizard was clinging to the wall just above them, flickering its long tongue. As Freya leapt at it, Neil grabbed her collar just in time and pulled her back.

Holy crap! he thought shakily. It would have been terrible to start their journey with the murder of Áilu's pet.

Encounter with the Bestia

e woke to a bright copper dawn and Fru Inga gently shaking him awake. He must have slept, though it seemed only moments since he'd gone to bed. Laid out on a chair were a pair of lightweight leggings, sturdy leather riding boots, and a rabbit-fur jacket for cold nights. They all fitted perfectly, and he was glad to have the new clothes. Astra joined him on the stairs, her face a mix of excitement and apprehension. She had new leggings and boots, too, and a tunic the colour of river water under her fur jacket.

Outside the morning air was chill, a relief after the intense heat of the past few days. Markko was supervising the saddling of two mules—a sorrel mare and a grey gelding—while Fru Inga and others came and went with food, bedding, additional clothing. Freya dashed back and forth among them, ears pricked, energized by all the commotion. But she sat quiet and alert when Neil strapped on the special dog pack that had been made for her, as though she too recognized the gravity of the occasion.

"If anyone asks," Markko told them, "you're Fru Inga's niece and nephew, and you're returning to Ashfjord with medicine for your ill mother." A couple of jars of one of Eirá's healing potions had been placed in their saddlebags. At last all was ready, and Markko held each mule in turn as the children mounted.

"This is Gísil," he told Neil, who was on the mare. "Her name means 'arrow-shaft.' She's a great tracker, and she's strong and resilient. And this," he said, turning to Astra, "is Arnbi, whose full name is Arnbjörn, which means 'eagle bear.' He has a big heart, he's brave, and he'll follow Gísil anywhere. Keep them as long as you need them, and send them home when you're done." Then he leaned forward and pressed an envelope into Neil's hand. "That's for Montserrat. If you find her." He looked away quickly so that Neil couldn't see his face.

"Safe journey, lad," Fru Inga said, squeezing Neil's arm. "We'll be praying for you." He'd hardly had time to thank her for looking after them when Eirá came hurrying up.

"Áilu has a last message for you," she said in a low, urgent voice. "You must head north until you see a clump of gorse bushes beside a dry streambed. Wait there for your first guide." She touched each of them in turn, her fingers held in a circle—for their protection, Neil supposed. "One last thing. You must not discuss your task with anyone. Anyone at all." She looked fiercely at each of them, looking for once as fierce as her sister, and Neil and Astra nodded solemnly in return. Then she stepped back and nodded at Markko. He struck Gísil on the rump and the mare leapt forward, with Arnbi following.

As they rode out of the village, Neil turned to look back. Only Eirá stood there, her hand lifted in farewell, or blessing. Everyone else had disappeared. Out of fear? Neil wondered. He and Astra really were on their own.

They followed a winding path along the river that dwindled into an overgrown track as it left the fields and trees behind. Neil gazed around him, conscious of a chill at his neck that wasn't just the fall air. Once or twice he glanced back at Astra. Her face was serious and preoccupied, reflecting his own feelings.

He'd been nervous about the journey by muleback—he'd only ridden a horse a couple of times—but Gísil had settled into a comfortable gait that made riding her easier than he'd expected. Freya, who'd been spooked by her at first, now trotted steadily alongside, ears swivelling to catch the slightest sounds.

The sun was climbing higher in the sky and Neil had long

since taken off his jacket. He was getting hungrier by the minute; their morning cereal seemed a long way away. They were crossing a bare rocky plain that stretched away on either side of them, broken here and there by low ranges of hills. There were still no signs of life—no birds, no animals, not even insects. Nothing but silence, except for the rustling of the coarse grasses in the breeze.

Astra spurred Arnbi forward so she could ride side by side with Neil. "It creeps me out out here. And there's nowhere to hide, if we had to."

The same thought had occurred to Neil. "I guess we have to hope that first guide turns up. Anyway, Freya and the mules'll give us warning about any danger."

"I wish I'd had more time to figure out the Etheric Sensor." Astra sighed. "I don't feel prepared at all."

"Me neither," Neil said forlornly. He hadn't felt prepared for any of these journeys—not when he'd jumped through the smoke and flames after Freya, not when they'd had to flee from Ashgård, and not now. His father would have been appalled. They'd always planned for any possibility when they went camping—always took extra clothing, flares, bear spray. Though even his father would have had a hard time planning for what had happened since the night Neil found the unlit stove smoking.

It was the mules who were in charge this time. Gísil seemed to know exactly where she was going, and Neil had long given up on any attempt to direct her. He was drooping from the heat when, as they rounded the nearest of the hills, the first traces of a dried-up stream appeared. Some distance along was a cleft in the rock where yellow-flowering gorse bushes clustered. Neil and Astra gazed wearily about them, but there was no sign of anyone.

They slid off their mules, so sore and tired they could hardly stand. Gísil and Arnbi dropped their heads and began to graze on the sparse grass, while Freya flopped down in the shade of the bushes, panting. Astra, groaning, dug her water bottle out of her saddlebag. "I hope whoever this guide is gets here soon. And that we don't have to ride much farther."

Neil rubbed his backside, hard, and shook out his legs, which felt as if they were permanently curved in the shape of a mule's belly. The guide's absence was adding to the uneasiness he'd felt ever since leaving the village. They'd need to find water for the mules soon, too. He drank deeply from his own bottle and was about to gingerly sit down when Freya leapt up. She oufed in warning, staring at the gorse bushes, which were swaying though there was no wind. Astra stepped closer to Neil and clutched his arm.

The bushes swayed harder, and Freya erupted into barking. Then they parted, and there stood—well, a being of a sort Neil had never seen in his life. It had the head and antlers and athletic haunches of a stag, but a human torso and hands that were part hoof. Around its waist it wore a belt with a spear slung from it, and its antlers were tipped with sharp metal points.

The mules brayed, Astra let out a scream, and Neil took a step backward, his legs wobbling. But the being had dropped to all fours and was shaking its great head as though to reassure them. And then it opened its mouth and spoke in a deep rumble. "Greetings, human children. I am Hreinn-Sál of the Bestian Nation, and I am to be your guide for this leg of your journey."

It was Astra who found her voice first. "You must be—my father told me—he said that—"

"Ah yes," Hreinn-Sál said, nodding. "Your admirable father. One of the wiser humans. It saddened us greatly when we heard that he had been captured by the enemy."

"But what *are* you?" said Neil wonderingly. "You talk like a human, yet you look—"

"We live far from human habitation," Hreinn-Sál said, "and we take many shapes. Those few who catch sight of us speak, later, of dreams and nightmares. But we have contact with those who are able to accept our kind." Hreinn-Sál slowly rose to his full height, and Neil was glad he was a friend and not an enemy. "And now we must waste no time in talking, which humans are far too prone to do. There will be time, later, to explain further. Here, drink. Give some to the mules and the dog, too."

He took a slim flask from his belt and handed it to Astra. Even a mouthful of the drink—it tasted, Neil thought, like a grassy meadow—was refreshing, and he felt his soreness melting away. "And now," said Hreinn-Sál, "we must be on our way. The Fire Reapers are afraid of the Bestia—they think we are some sorcerer's evil spell." And if a half-stag half-man could be said to grin, he grinned. "But we need to make shelter by nightfall."

With that he turned and began cantering along the stream bed as it rose up the slope of the hill. Neil and Astra mounted as quickly as they could and set out after him. Sometimes they could barely keep Hreinn-Sál in sight, and then they'd find him waiting for them round the next corner. The stream bed deepened into a narrow, dark ravine, almost shutting out the sky overhead. Its black walls—basalt, Neil guessed—radiated heat so that sweat poured from his body, trickling down his back and neck. The mules moved as if swimming through molasses, heads hanging, while Freya panted heavily beside them.

Just when Neil thought he couldn't bear it any longer, the ravine began to widen. They'd come out on the opposite side of the hill above another great plain, shimmering in the heat and covered with giant boulders that looked as if they'd been heaved there by some angry god. Hreinn-Sál scanned the landscape, ears pricked, nose quivering.

"We must cross that by nightfall," he said. "The heat, especially for those who have not adapted to our altered climate, is very intense." Here he looked hard at Neil, who privately vowed he wasn't going to utter a word of complaint. "Fortunately there's a spring not far from here where we can obtain water." There was nothing for it but to follow him down the hill, and Neil urged Gísil forward. At least Astra looked as uncomfortable as he felt, her face bright pink and running with sweat.

The plain was baking. Neil looked at Freya with concern; she was lifting her paws from the hot sandy ground and panting so hard he worried about heatstroke. "How far is the spring?" he called out to Hreinn-Sál, but the Bestia was too far ahead to hear him. Gísil stumbled on a rock, and when Neil patted her shoulder to steady her, his hand came away soaked in her sweat.

A kilometre or so farther on he saw two huge boulders up ahead, a dark V of shadow between them. Gísil flung up her head, nostrils flaring, and broke into a trot. As they neared the boulders Neil could hear the trickle of water that the mules had already smelled. Suddenly they were plunging into the shadow, where a tiny spring bubbled up out of the ground. Freya and the mules waded in, drinking deeply. Neil and Astra half-climbed, half-fell off, soaking themselves from head to foot. How good it felt to wash the sweat and dust off! Hreinn-Sál waited until the others were finished and then lowered himself in, rolling on his back in the water. When he got out he shook himself, spraying everyone, his wet hide gleaming in a stray band of sunlight.

"Now, onward," he said. "We will keep as much as we can to the shade of the larger boulders. If the dog tires, I can always carry her." He gave a couple of low growls that made Freya turn her head to stare at him, then stand up and walk away, as if in a huff. Hreinn-Sál smiled. "I see I've offended her with my offer. Good. She has courage."

The blast of heat beyond the nearest boulders was like opening the door of an oven. They hadn't gone very far when they heard strange whistling sounds, high and piercing, that seemed to come from all around them. Arnbi skittered sideways, flicking his ears, as Astra tried to soothe him. Neil glanced up, expecting to see a flock of birds, but there was nothing.

"It *sounds* like it's coming from the sand," Astra said in a puzzled voice. As she spoke the sound disappeared and then erupted again, for all the world like thousands of tiny birds calling to each other. Neil was just about to ask how sand could

162

possibly whistle when Hreinn-Sál, who was some distance ahead, came trotting back.

"The Great Dunes," he said when he reached them, pointing toward an undulating row of hills in the distance. "That's where we are headed. And that is where the whistling comes from. It's the noise the wind makes, flowing over the sand."

The noise grew louder as they approached, ebbing and flowing with the breeze. But despite the wind, it was no cooler, and there were no more boulders to shade them. They began plodding up the side of a dune, the mules sinking in the deep sand. Neil closed his eyes and told himself that, if he ever got home, he would never, ever complain about heat again. Even in Vancouver, in summer, it had never been even close to this. They reached the top of the dune and plunged over the edge, the mules half-sliding down the sandy slope. The whistling noise rose to a shriek, subsided, then rose again. The mules laboured up another dune, and then another. Just when Neil had decided that, at the top of the next dune, he was going to roll to the bottom and lie there forever, Hreinn-Sál pointed to what looked like a tumble of volcanic rocks in the near distance.

"That is our destination. It is not much farther now. There will be rest there, and food. Be of good cheer." And he plunged down the slope, his huge antlers casting long shadows in the late afternoon sun.

A whole herd of strange creatures came forward to greet them. Lion-like beings with the heads of men, a woman with the wings of an eagle, another with the glowing green carapace of an insect, still others with fins or spines or claws. There were some like Hreinn-Sál, too, with antlers and hooves, and even a half-human wolf-being with fierce golden eyes, just like the one he'd seen during his forced march through the desert.

He must be seeing things, Neil decided. His eyelids were crusted with salt and he was almost falling from the saddle.

"Welcome to our home," said a woman with the mane and tail of a horse. She bowed low and gave a series of whinnies that made Gísil and Arnbi whinny back in excitement. "I am Hästsjäl. We are honoured to have you as our guests."

Neil dismounted clumsily and would have fallen if the horse-woman hadn't caught him. "Come," she said, taking him and Astra by the hand. "You need food and rest." The mules, already unsaddled, were walking away with several horse-beings, deep in conversation. Freya was sniffing noses and tails with wolf- and fox-beings and rooing happily.

Astra and Neil stared at each other, dumbstruck. Was it all some sort of desert hallucination? Hreinn-Sál cantered up to them, grinning again. "All this will be very strange to you, human children. But you are in good hooves and paws. Come and see what has been prepared for you."

They were led along a rocky passageway that opened out into a huge, cool cave with a natural pool at one end. After they'd bathed, drying themselves with large palm leaves, Hästsjäl and several other beings brought stone bowls of goat's milk and cheese and prickly pear. Neil ate ravenously, almost embarrassed by his hunger. When he and Astra couldn't eat any more, they were taken to the back of the cave, where fragrant hay bedding had been laid out for them.

"The caves are cold at night," Hästsjäl said. "You'll be glad of the hay. And now, sleep well. You are safe here."

After the horse-woman left, Neil and Astra stared at each other in the gloom.

"Pinch me," Astra said. "This can't be real."

"No one back home would ever believe me." Neil shook his head, marvelling. Humans who were part-animal and could talk to other animals—or maybe they were animals who were part-human? Whatever they were, it was all pretty amazing.

"Pappa told me about the Bestia once," Astra said

thoughtfully. "He said there was a Bestian scientist who worked at the Institute, before his time. I thought he was just making up stories to amuse me."

Neil tried to imagine what Mr. Boyd, his science teacher, would have to say. He'd say it wasn't possible for such different species as a horse and a human to cross-breed. And Neil would explain that, in the distant future, it was possible, somehow ... But before he could think of an explanation, he fell asleep.

"You're right, of course. It's not possible."

They were sitting, Neil and Astra, with Hreinn-Sál the following evening, drinking a delicious fruit mixture before their evening meal. They'd slept most of the day, exhausted, until Hästsjäl came to say that they were to join some of the Bestia for dinner. Hreinn-Sál was there, and one of the eagle-beings, and a woman who appeared to be part-lizard, among others. Neil noticed, with some repugnance, that the lizard-woman was eating flies from a small plate, delicately licking them up with her tongue.

"It isn't possible for humans and, say, reindeer to mate," Hreinn-Sál went on, "but that's not how we came into being. Late in the twenty-first century, some scientists and artists decided that the only way to prevent the extinction of more species was to increase their status among humans. They wanted to demonstrate that, in fact, we were all animals, that we were all equal."

"And so they began experimenting on themselves," broke in the lizard-woman eagerly. "They perfected a form of gene grafting that allowed humans to acquire animal characteristics. They lived among animals and learned animal languages. They took great risks by devoting themselves to the future well-being of all life. Some of them, later, even undertook to acquire plant and mineral characteristics, and formed their own nations."

"The results were, perhaps, not entirely unexpected," Hreinn-Sál said quietly, "especially when it was shown that these new beings could produce offspring with acquired characteristics. A new form of miscegenation, people called it—interbreeding between members of different species. They were afraid of us. They drove us out of the world's Cities."

Neil looked around and wondered how anyone could be afraid of these gentle beings who had been so kind to him and Astra. No one *here* had accused him of being a spy, or talked about him behind his back, like they had in Ashgård.

"The name Bestia was given to us by the Fire Reapers," Hreinn-Sál added, and Neil noticed that several of the other guests shuddered. "We call ourselves the *Tweir-Sál*—the Two-Souled Ones, or Bi-Souls. We communicate in UL and Old Nordlandish as our common languages, but each of us also speaks an animal language—sometimes more than one. Hästsjäl, for example"—he nodded toward her—"speaks several animal languages from the Hot Zones as well as Horse. And I learned Wolf so that I might communicate with my companion." Here he indicated a delicate-looking being with the head and paws of a wolf, thick lustrous black fur, and a curved wolvish tail.

"I'd like to learn Mule," Astra said eagerly, "so I can talk to Arnbi. Can someone teach me?"

"And I'd like to learn Dog," Neil said. "I mean, I already know a little—" He gave one of Freya's roo-roo-roos, which made several of the wolf-beings laugh.

"Perhaps Ulvsjäl here can teach you some basic vocabulary," Hreinn-Sál said, smiling, and one of the wolf-beings nodded his head. "He knows several Dog dialects."

Suddenly there were swivelling ears and whiffling noses, and a young zebra-being clattered into the cave. Hreinn-Sál acknowledged him with a toss of his antlers. The zebra-being blurted something in Old Nordlandish, then switched to what Neil supposed was Zebra.

"The South Tower watch has just sighted a platoon of Fire

Reapers at twelve fenlongs' distance," Hästsjäl translated in a low voice.

A clamour of voices broke out. Hreinn-Sál lifted a hoof for silence, frowning. "Tell Fjellgeit to place the troops on high alert," he said sharply to the zebra-being, who nodded hastily and clattered out again. "We rarely see Fire Reapers so close to the Caves," he went on, looking gravely at Neil and Astra. "You are to go with Hästsjäl at once."

Neil and Astra scrambled after the horse-being, who guided them through a series of tunnels to a cavern filled with stalagmites. At the base of one of the stalagmites was an opening in the cave floor. "Climb in," Hästsjäl said, motioning them inside. "And stay here till I come for you." And she galloped off.

"Ugh," said Astra as they felt their way down. It was a short drop to the bottom, which was lined with dried grass. "This reminds me of the cellar in Ashgård. Except much smaller."

Neil said nothing. He was worrying about Freya and hoping she was safely with the wolf-beings.

"I *hate* this," Astra said suddenly. "I hate having to hide. I hate that they have so much power." She fell silent again, and then burst out: "Sometimes I almost *hope* they find us."

"Believe me," Neil muttered, "you don't. You wouldn't want to be taken prisoner by them."

"Maybe they'd lock us up with Pappa and at least I'd know what happened to him. We're almost prisoners anyway."

But before Neil could ask her what she meant, he felt a flicker of pain round his ankle. He clenched his jaw, all his muscles tensing. The Fire Reapers—they must be getting closer ... The pain flared up his leg and into his torso. Whoever or whatever had protected him up till now was obviously no longer working.

For the first time since they'd fled from Ashgård, pure fear engulfed him, a kind of fear that left him helpless and ashamed. He fought back, silently, tears filling his eyes. Astra must have sensed it, because she said, "What's the matter, Neil? What's happening?"

There ... there just in front of him ... could it really be his father? It was his father as he'd last seen him, lying in his bedroom, his face pale and gaunt. He was turning his head to Neil and saying, "Remember I'll always be with you, son." And then the scene shifted, and in place of his father Flame-Protector Arngrim stood there, staring straight at him. His flaming cape flowed round him as he lifted the weapon from his shoulder and levelled it at Neil's forehead—

"No!" Neil shouted, trembling. "No! Never!" And he tried to stand up, though his left leg buckled beneath him.

Astra grabbed his arm. "Are you crazy? They'll hear—"

"Flame-Protector Arngrim!" His arm was shaking so badly he could hardly lift it. "He's right there, look! He can see us!"

"No, he isn't." Astra shook him, hard. "He isn't there at all. You're getting Stone Lock." And she pulled him down beside her and held on to him.

Flame-Protector Arngrim still stood there, as large as life, but he was beginning to fade. Neil watched, sweating and trembling, gritting his teeth against the pain.

"It happened to me once, too. Getting a memory I didn't want ..." Astra shook her head. "It was horrible. I don't even want to think about it."

They sat huddled silently together for what seemed like an age. The pain gradually ebbed away, leaving Neil shaken and chilled. At last they heard hoofsteps and Hästsjäl's face peered over the edge of the opening. "It's quite safe," she said cheerfully. "You can come out. They came within a couple of fenlongs and then turned off."

Astra and Neil clambered up into the cavern one at a time, blinking. Neil rubbed his left leg, which felt weak and crampy.

"You're quite sure they've gone?" Astra asked cautiously.

"You poor things," Hästsjäl said. "Yes, they're gone. Now you're to join us in the main cave again. Hreinn-Sál wants to talk to you."

Some of the Bi-Souls were bringing in platters of food, but neither Neil nor Astra felt hungry. Hreinn-Sál motioned them to sit beside him and gazed gravely at them. "It's most unusual for them to come so close," he said at last. "Normally they keep their distance from our quarters. The only conclusion I can come to is that they know you're here. Their spies must be watching closely."

A murmuring in different languages ran round the circle of Bí-Souls. A woman with the head and torso of a lion but human hands leaned forward. "We've driven them off before, Hreinn-Sál," she said, in a deep growl. "We can do so again, if need be."

"Indeed." One of the wolf-beings nodded a shaggy head. "Now is not the time to succumb to fear. We've never done so before."

"Our job," Hreinn-Sál said slowly, "is to protect the children. At all costs." He fell silent and let the import of his words sink in. "The Fire Reapers likely do not want to risk an all-out assault. But the children cannot stay here indefinitely. It seems to me best that they travel onward as soon as possible—perhaps when they are not expecting it."

"Then let's send them with our Leopard Squadron!" cried a young leopard-being. "That'll keep them at bay!"

But Hreinn-Sál and one or two of the others shook their heads. "They must travel as unobtrusively as possible," Hreinn-Sál said. "The other Assembly members and I will consult as to who might be the best guide." He turned to the children, smiling gently at them. "For now, I urge you to rest, if you can. Meanwhile we will prepare for the next stage of your journey. The sooner you reach the Valley of the Slaves, the better."

Neil glanced quickly at Astra, his heart sinking. Her face showed she was feeling the same way. But with Hreinn-Sál looking straight at them, he was determined to show bravery, so he sat up and squared his shoulders.

"We're ready," he said.

Journey to the Moving Mountains

"A t least it'll be cooler," Astra said hopefully.

The sun had just risen, a dull grey disk in a grey sky, and she and Neil were standing in the shelter of the main cave, watching packs being loaded onto Gísil and Arnbi. Neil, yawning for at least the twentieth time, rubbed his eyes and tried to shake the fog out of his head. Hästsjäl had woken them with the moon a pale crescent in the east. "Hreinn-Sál and the Assembly think it best for you to leave right away," she'd whispered, "while their troops are resting."

Neil felt as though an icy hand had just gripped his stomach and squeezed, but Hästsjäl was still talking. "... will guide you as far as the Moving Mountains. From there you will travel to the Valley with another guide, one who knows that terrain." And with that she left them to fumble into their clothing and make their way outside.

Now Hreinn-Sál himself was walking toward them, accompanied by a Bi-Soul quite unlike any they'd yet seen. She wore a long white belted tunic and had gold-feathered wings like— what was that small golden falcon his mother had taught him to identify back in the Yukon? A kestrel, that was it. The wings were tucked neatly against her sides above vestigial arms, and golden feathers flowed back from her forehead.

"Neil and Astra, this is Tårnfalk," Hreinn-Sál said as the bird-being held out her hand. "You'll be in good hands—or perhaps I should say wings." And he laughed loudly at his own joke, as if trying to dispel the gloomy mood.

"Good day to you both," Tårnfalk said. Her English was harsh and guttural. "I have not had the pleasure of meeting human children before. Some day, perhaps, you will meet my own fledglings."

"Oh, Hreinn-Sál, couldn't we stay longer?" Astra looked appealingly at him. "There's so much we want to see and learn."

Hreinn-Sál shook his head gently and laid a great hoof on her head. "Someday, human child, when this is all over, we will invite you to return, I promise. But these are evil days." And a look of such sorrow crossed his face that Neil felt that icy hand in his stomach again.

Before anyone could say anything else, Hästsjäl came hurrying up to tell them that all was ready. At that moment an anguished roo-roo-roo came from the other side of the cave. Freya had arrived, accompanied by several dog and wolf Bi-Souls, and it was obvious she didn't want to go any more than the children did. The mules were escorted by several horse-beings, who helped the children mount. It seemed as though every Bi-Soul in the place had come to see them off. Neil and Astra each leaned down in turn to shake Hreinn-Sál's hoof and thank him for guiding them safely.

"I am grateful to have had the privilege," Hreinn-Sál said, and bowed his great head. "May the beings in the Many Realms be with you."

As they rode out of the cave, Neil with a lump in his throat and Astra near tears, they turned to look back. Hreinn-Sál raised his hoof, and several of the wolf-beings threw back their heads and howled. Freya immediately howled back. Neil would have howled, too, if he could, but instead he wiped his eyes with the back of his hand and tightened his grip on Gísil's reins.

Tårnfalk flew just ahead of them, guiding them along a sandy path through the tumble of volcanic rock. After a few minutes they emerged onto the lip of a cliff. Beyond them, stretching to the horizon, was a wide plain of tussocky dead grass and cracked earth. "We call this the Domain of the Beetles," Tårnfalk explained as the children looked round in dismay. "It was once a wetland, full of geese and ducks and swans. But now ..."

"How long will it take us to get to the mountains?" asked Neil, hoping they'd be spending as little time as possible in this barren landscape. "And why are they called the Moving Mountains?" Mountains moved, of course, but only over millions of years.

"Two days' travel, if we meet no obstacles. I will fly ahead to patrol, but I will keep you in my sights. As for the name, you will see for yourselves."

They rode all morning across the baked, claylike earth, seeing nothing except insects—spiders large as dinner plates, fat glistening beetles, scorpions with hairy legs as long as Neil's fingers. They scuttled into the fissures as the mules approached, or disappeared under rocks. Tårnfalk regarded them all as a moving feast, and frequently darted down to scoop up a wriggling insect in her beak.

"Ugh!" said Astra. "I'm glad we don't have to eat them."

"Have you ever tried them?" Tårnfalk snapped up a particularly juicy-looking beetle and crunched it happily. "Quite delicious. Much better than moodfood, I assure you."

Fortunately, the mules seemed unperturbed by the scorpions, either avoiding them or crushing them with their hooves. Freya gave them a wary berth, though she played pouncing games with the beetles. At noon Tårnfalk called a halt—not, she said, because *she* needed it, but because non-Bi-Souls needed to rest. As the mules cropped the coarse grass, Astra and Neil shook out their stiffness and helped themselves to food from the packs. Tårnfalk perched on a nearby rock and told them stories about her ancestors.

"They say that my great-great-wingfather came from this area," she said, turning from time to time to stare up at the sky. "That's what we call our bird ancestors. I'm told I take after him in my feather colouration." She seized a scorpion, popped it in her beak, and crunched. "And my great-great—I don't know how many greats—grandmother was one of the original scientists in the Bi-Soul experiments. She helped to develop a writing system for Kestrel. A very difficult language—much more difficult than Mule or Wolf." She gave a harsh guttural shrawk to demonstrate, making everyone jump. "To give you an example, in Kestrel there are no nouns. So the word 'kestrel,' in our language, is translated as 'feathering-moving-dazzling.'"

"And how do you say 'human'?" Astra wanted to know.

"'Heavy-lumpish-stupid,'" said Tårnfalk promptly.

"But that's not true!" Astra protested. "I mean, there's lots of humans who aren't like that at all."

"Just kidding." Tårnfalk gave a kestrel grin and shrugged her wings airily. "All I can say is, I'm glad *I* can fly. It must be so dull not to be able to. Now we'd better get going." And with that she launched herself into the air and was soon a distant, circling speck.

Later all Neil could remember was the endless plain under endless grey sky, the wind that blew loose soil into their faces, the heat that seemed to suck all the moisture from his body despite the cloud cover. More than once he thought longingly of the pool they'd bathed in the night before. It had been so cooling, so soothing. Perhaps they'd added something special to the water.

By late afternoon Freya was panting heavily, her belly sagging. Neil was just about to suggest they look for somewhere to make camp when Tårnfalk, who had been patrolling the skies above them, came winging down at great speed. "A Fire Reaper patrol," she hissed at them, fluttering just above Gísil's head. "The 'shrivelled-dead-empty.' To the south-south-east, three fenlongs or so. Follow me!"

Abruptly she wheeled in the opposite direction. Astra and Neil spurred their tired mules. A few minutes later they saw ahead of them the scorched walls and collapsed roofs of a ruined village. The orchard was a heap of charred wood and ash. Tårnfalk flew down and perched on a crumbling wall. "Hide here wherever you can," she hissed again. "Make sure the mules are hidden, too. I'll come back when it's safe." She rose in the air, circled above them, and flew off.

173

They found a house with a more-or-less intact roof and managed to get the mules inside. Then they spread out their jackets and extra clothing in the lee of one wall to make a bed. The wind had died down and the shadows were lengthening.

"I hope Tårnfalk's all right," Astra said. Neil peered out through the crumbling bricks. Still no sign of the patrol, or of Tårnfalk, either.

"They can't touch her if she stays out of range," he said, hoping this was true.

They must have slept, because when they woke it was fully dark. Overhead the moon had risen, a pale sliver like a fingernail paring. Freya lay asleep beside them. The only sound was that of the mules, black shapes in the darkness, flicking their tails.

"What do we do if she doesn't come back?" Astra said in a small voice.

"Of course she'll come back," Neil said, irritated. He'd been thinking exactly the same thing but didn't want to admit it. "She's not going to leave us here."

"I'm hungry. I'm going to see what else Hästsjäl gave us." Astra rummaged in the packs and came back with two oranges and a handful of nuts. The stars wheeled in the heavens as they ate, but still Tårnfalk didn't return.

"Maybe the mules know their way back to the caves."

"We can't go back, Astra. We've got to get to that Valley somehow."

"I know what we're *supposed* to do." It was Astra's turn to sound irritated. "But we can't get there without a guide. Hreinn-Sál said so."

"You can go back if you want. I'll take Freya and keep going."

Even in the darkness he could feel Astra's glare. "D'you *always* have to pretend you're the brave one? That's the stupidest thing I ever—"

But what Astra felt about the stupidest thing ever went unsaid, because a voice—a high, shrill, accusing voice—spoke out of the darkness.

"Who are you?"

They scrambled to their feet. A bent figure in the doorway shuffled forward, leaning on a staff. His clothes hung from him and a long straggly beard brushed his chest. He stopped a few metres away, staring. "Who are you?" he repeated. "I haven't seen human children in years."

"Who are *you*?" said Neil, his voice wobbling.

"My name's Dýri," said the man. "Or at least it was. No one's called me by my name since they left."

"Since who left?"

"The people who lived here," said Dýri impatiently, and waved a thin arm at the ruins. "This was a village, once. Vindstille, we called it. Just a tiny place. But those devils"—he shook his staff at the sky—"those devils came and burned us out. They took everyone away except me, because I was too old. Expected me to die, I suppose. Except I didn't." He gave a bitter chuckle. "I'm a tough old nut."

"Where did they take everyone?" Astra asked, looking round uneasily.

"Ah, you don't want to know that. It's not a story for children." He lifted his head and sniffed noisily. "I can smell oranges," he said. "Have you got oranges?"

When Astra handed him one, he began eating at once, not even bothering to peel it, slurping and smacking his lips. After a moment he paused and stared at them suspiciously. "You aren't *Fire Reaper* children, are you?"

"No!" Neil and Astra said together, loudly.

"Then what are you doing here?"

"It's a long story," Neil said, "but we're on our way to the Valley of the Slaves." Astra dug her fingers in his ribs, and too late he remembered that they weren't supposed to tell anyone.

"The Valley!" Dýri stopped eating and looked at them in horror. "You mustn't go there. It's no place for children. No place for anyone. No one who goes there ever comes back." He finished the orange and wiped his mouth on a ragged sleeve. "That's where *these* people ended up—as slave labour." He looked at them pityingly, shook his head again, and disappeared into the darkness.

"Wow," said Neil after a moment. "Maybe he's crazy."

"Except something happened to the people here." Astra looked round uneasily again.

"Well, Áilu warned us, didn't she?" Neil said lamely. "She said it would be dangerous."

Astra wrapped her arms round herself in the chill air. "I wish Tårnfalk would come back."

"Me too."

They lay down again, but it was impossible to sleep, and they startled at every sound. It felt like hours later when they heard a flapping of wings and a soft shrawk, and Tårnfalk seemed to fall out of the air beside them. She was having difficulty balancing. One of her wings was drooping and badly torn, and many of her neck and head feathers were broken or missing.

"Tårnfalk! What happened?"

It took a while before Tårnfalk could speak. She breathed heavily, eyes closed, and when she spoke her words were laboured. "I hadn't expected ... I can handle Tabris and Luminis, I can dive and swerve ..." She paused again, her chest heaving. "But they have a new weapon." She opened her eyes with difficulty. "I was attacked. In the air. By hybrid beings that are part-human and part—" She shuddered. "I don't know. Horrible black-winged things."

Horrible black-winged things. He'd seen them that time he'd used the Memory Stone on his own, and again when they crossed the Dragon's Teeth. Nightmares, he'd thought. Except now they were real.

Tårnfalk stretched out her torn wing, wincing in pain. Blood still streamed from several deep bite wounds. "Eirá's potion!" Astra exclaimed, and ran to pull a jar from Arnbi's pack. Tårnfalk shuddered as Astra spread the salve very gently on her feathers, then gave a great sigh and let the wounded wing droop.

"You've quite possibly saved my life, child."

"Now you need to rest," Neil said. "We'll stay here till you're better."

But Tårnfalk shook her head. "No. It's not safe." She glanced up through the shattered roof at the darkened sky, and Neil and Astra anxiously followed her gaze. "They've been driven off for now. I killed at least one of them. But they're sure to return. They report to that patrol, and they know I'm wounded. And they almost certainly know who I'm guiding."

"But we can't leave you behind," Astra protested.

"The journey is much too important to be abandoned," Tårnfalk said quietly. "Now, listen carefully ..."

Not long afterward they rode out from the ruined walls of Vindstille in the greying light. Gísil and Arnbi were edgy, snorting and stamping their feet, but there was no sign of the Fire Reapers. Neil took the SerraTube that Áilu had given him from his belt, studying it anxiously. Áilu had said it was controlled by thought, but how? What would happen if he needed to use it?

They were to keep the paling moon in sight, Tårnfalk told them, and by daylight they'd see the Moving Mountains in the distance. "Just before you reach the mountains you will see a salt pan—the remains of an old lake. Turn westward round the pan, and you will come to the Black Pillars. You must wait there for your guide. On no account attempt to enter the mountains on your own." And with that she huddled amid the rubble of the wall, folded her head under her wing, and went to sleep.

The first ranges of the Moving Mountains came into view soon after sunrise, so high their peaks vanished into cloud. They were a curious purple colour, though maybe that was because of the red-and-purple sky. Neil and Astra rode steadily toward them all morning across the dry plain. The mountains were still purple, with deeper purple folds, but they seemed no closer.

They stopped just long enough to feed and water the animals and themselves, then forged on into the furnace of the afternoon. Neil found himself drooping in the saddle, then jerking awake. Had they ever had a life before this one, this endless crawling journey? He'd long ago let Gísil have her head, and Arnbi plodded dutifully behind. Ahead of him the mountains loomed suddenly nearer, as if they'd moved after all. They seemed way taller than the Rockies, which he'd seen once on a trip to Banff. Had they been formed after his own time? Was that even possible?

As a crimson sunset cast long shadows across the plain, he and Astra shared out the last of the water with the mules and Freya. They'd better be able to find more in the mountains. In the sunset glow the plain turned red, and Astra's face and arms, and his own skin. They hadn't gone far when all of a sudden Gísil broke into a trot, her nostrils flaring. What was that up ahead? It looks like a vast pool of blood ...

No, it was a trick of the light. Up close the expanse turned white and crystalline, and Gísil's hooves crunched along the edge. The salt pan, at last! Gísil turned and began trotting westward, head held high. Neil turned and gave a thumbs-up sign to Astra, who spurred Arnbi up alongside.

"See?" she said. "I knew we'd be okay." She's developed this annoying habit of taking credit for everything, Neil thought. "The beings of the Many Realms must have come through after all."

Neil figured it was probably thanks to Gísil and Arnbi rather than any mysterious beings. Still, at least they hadn't encountered any roving patrols. And judging by his ankle, there weren't any nearby, either. Now to keep an eye out for those Black Pillars ...

The sun was sinking below the mountains, staining the sky with long crimson streaks. Neil leaned forward, straining his eyes. It was hard to make out anything. Beside him Freya stiffened and oufed, and he looked around uneasily. Had she heard something, or was she just on edge in the growing darkness?

But then Gísil let out a snort and skittered sideways, tossing her head. Now he could hear something too—a strange kind of creaking, like hundreds of windmills. He looked up, and what he saw froze his blood: huge winged creatures high above them in the night sky, their great leathery wings slowly flapping.

Behind him Astra shouted something he couldn't hear. Gísil broke into a gallop, with a trembling and skittering Arnbi close behind. But the mules were tired, and soon slowed to a trot. Neil frantically banged his heels on Gísil's sides, but it was no use. The winged creatures dropped lower, shrieking and crying. Freya slunk under Gísil's belly, panting with fear.

We're doomed, Neil thought. Gísil, with a last surge of energy, leapt forward, but it was too late. A dozen or more of the creatures swooped toward them. Fanged mouths, flattened snouts, huge jointed wings with clawed elbows—gargoyles from some cathedral come to life.

Arnbi screamed behind him, a high bloodcurdling scream, and Neil swung round. One of the gargoyles had landed on the mule and was clawing at his rump. Arnbi screamed again and reared up as a terrified Astra hung on for dear life. The gargoyle wrapped its wings round Astra, opened its fanged mouth ...

Okay, tube! Neil yanked the SerraTube from his belt, shaking so badly he could barely hold it. *Do whatever it is you do.* He held it out with one hand, clinging to Gísil with the other, and concentrated as hard as he could. Nothing. *Please ... oh please ...*

A sudden beam of brilliant white light shot out from the tube and struck the gargoyle. Its wing crumpled into smoking ribbons and the creature twisted away, writhing and howling. Neil aimed the tube at another creature, then another as the smell of scorched flesh grew. The rest of the pack rose upward, hissing and screeching.

"Come on!" Neil yelled to Astra. "Let's go!"

179

The mules galloped for their lives, Freya hurtling alongside. Neil, glancing behind them, saw the creatures fall back, still screeching in anger and frustration. They rose and faded in the night sky, carrying their wounded companions with them. He gave a half-sob and urged Gísil onward. The mules flew past the edge of the salt pan toward the mountains.

Two enormous towers of black rock stood just ahead of them, silhouetted against the last streaks of sunset. At the base of the towers the mules came to a shuddering halt, their flanks lathered and heaving. Neil and Astra collapsed in their saddles, Freya sank to the ground, and for a while no one moved.

Astra dismounted first. She was reaching shakily for her water bottle when she gave a cry. "Neil! Look!"

The little finger on her left hand had withered and turned completely white.

Under Mountain, Under Stone

he first rays of sun, glancing off the pillars, shone directly into Neil's eyes and woke him up. He'd spent most of the night drifting in and out of nightmares where he was fighting the gargoyles again, and he leapt to his feet, grabbing the SerraTube.

But everything seemed quiet. A short distance away, Gísil and Arnbi were cropping the coarse thistly plants for all the world as if they hadn't spent the previous evening in a life-and-death encounter. Freya lay nearby, calmly licking her paws. Astra rolled over beside him, gave a groan, and opened her eyes.

"Is it morning already?"

"'Fraid so."

She sat up among the rumpled clothing they'd spread between the pillars and stared at her little finger. It was even more withered and deformed than the night before, a shrivelled white grub.

"It looks awful, doesn't it?" Her face was stricken.

"If I hadn't—" Neil stopped and swallowed hard. He hoped fervently he'd never have to use the weapon again. "I feel terrible."

"Why? It's not *your* fault. You had to use it. What would have happened if you hadn't?" She grimaced. "Besides, it doesn't hurt. Much."

Neil fetched Eirá's salve and wrapped the finger with a strip torn off an extra tunic. It felt a bit better, Astra said, though he wasn't sure whether to believe her.

"Now we need to find water," she said, getting up.

"We need to leave soon, too," Neil said. "We can't stay here." In the blinding light from the pillars they were visible to anyone. But where was their guide?

He stared up at the towers soaring into the sky above them. They weren't natural rock formations after all. They were beautifully chiselled out of some hard black stone—obsidian, maybe? Who put them here, and why?

Astra was examining a nearby bush. She stripped one of its long, strange leaves and tipped a droplet of dew into her mouth. "Here." She held another leaf out to Neil. "It's not much, but it's better than nothing."

Yes, it was, though after a dozen or so leaves the amount of water wouldn't have filled a thimble. Neil tried tipping a leaf into Freya's mouth, but she merely nibbled at it and turned her head away.

"And now I'm going to try and figure out that Etheric Sensor." Astra pulled it from her pack and sat down. "While we're waiting."

"Not here, Astra. We can't stay here. We're not safe."

"Well, what do you suggest?" She shaded her eyes and stared at Neil. "You heard what Tårnfalk said. That on no account were we to—"

"I *know* what she said." Neil frowned at her. "But maybe the guide got held up. Or didn't get the message. Who knows? All I know is, staying here is asking for trouble."

"*You* go, then. No one's stopping you. I'm busy." And she bent her head over the Etheric Sensor again.

Neil gave a nearby stone a vigorous kick, sending it flying against one of the pillars. Of all the times to try figuring out that thing! Were they just going to sit here all day?

He strode past Astra, fetched Gísil and saddled her, then whistled to Freya. Above him he could just make out a broken rocky path, more like an animal track than a real trail, winding upward round the mountainside. Tricky, perhaps, but sure-footed Gísil would have no trouble with it. From the top he could check out the area. If their guide didn't arrive, they'd have to discover their own route through the mountains.

Gísil, however, was reluctant to set foot on the trail. "Come on, girl!" he said with irritation, urging her forward. Freya, too, refused to go—in fact she went and sat down beside Astra—and for a moment their fear made him afraid. Then he remembered one of his father's favourite sayings: *Courage is fear that has said its prayers.* He used his knees and his heels on Gísil, hard. She tossed her head, as if to tell him what she really thought, and stepped forward.

Once started, they moved slowly but steadily up the narrow trail. It was treacherously crumbly and so steep that Neil had to lean low over the mule's head to keep his balance. At the first bend he stopped to look down. They'd climbed so high already! The pillars, far below, looked like stubby pencils, while Astra and Arnbi and Freya were mere dots. Feeling dizzy, he turned away and urged Gísil upward.

They'd gone only a short distance when he heard a distant rumble. A rock slide? He glanced up the slope but could see nothing. Now he heard it again—a deep growling that seemed to come from inside the mountain itself. Gísil suddenly stumbled in the loose shale, recovered herself, then went down on her knees. Neil shot forward over her head and landed, dazed, at the side of the trail. Another few centimetres and he would have gone over the edge.

He picked himself up slowly. His knees and elbows were nicked and scratched, but otherwise he seemed okay. Gísil had struggled to her feet and stood twitching and blowing air through her nostrils. She tossed her head at him and nipped at his neck when he picked up the fallen reins.

"Okay, Gísil. I was wrong to make you come up here. I admit it."

And then he noticed the deep gash on her left foreleg. Heart sinking, he bent to examine the cut more closely as Gísil pulled her leg away.

"Now," said a strange, rumbling, peremptory voice, "you see what happens to people who don't follow warnings."

Holy crap. Neil spun round, but couldn't see anyone.

"Over here," said the voice. "Look down. Near your foot."

Neil looked down at the trail. The voice seemed to be coming from—but that was absurd.

"The animate are always so *blind*. Yes, it's me who's speaking. Down *here*."

There was no mistaking it this time. The voice—imperious, clear, precise—was coming from a fist-sized rock a metre or so away. Neil stared at it, unable to believe his eyes.

"Did you just—?"

The rock sighed. "It's so tedious always having to explain. Not all of us have mouths, you know."

"Well," Neil said, struggling to find his own voice, "back where I live, rocks don't talk."

"Oh yes they do. You just don't *listen*. We may not be able to move, but we're quite capable of *thinking*."

Neil sat down hard, torn between amazement and irritation. "Well, it's very weird. It's just not something I'm used to."

The rock sighed again. "Oh, you don't need to remind me, I assure you. It's an endless struggle against ignorance."

"Do all of you—?" Neil glanced round. "I mean, there's millions of you, and—"

"Yes, is the short answer. But not all of us speak UL. I, however, am Piedra of the Kärna, at your service."

At his service? How? The rock must have guessed what he was thinking, because it said, with exaggerated care, "I'm to be your guide on the journey ahead."

Their guide? This was really too much. How were they going to be guided by a lump of rock? "I don't want to be rude," Neil said, "but—well, you are kind of stuck here, aren't you?"

"I would have thought it was *obvious* that I can travel in your pocket," Piedra said. "But as usual I'm guilty of overestimating human capabilities."

Piedra didn't seem guilty of any such thing, but Neil let it pass. "Then how come you're up here, on the trail? I mean, if you're our guide, why weren't you down at the Pillars where you were supposed to be?"

"An unfortunate accident, I'm afraid. A passing patrol carried me up here."

"A patrol?" Neil looked round in alarm.

"Oh, they've gone," said Piedra offhandedly. "They were here two suns ago. Thank heavens they dropped me, otherwise I'd have ended up in a Firepit Circle."

This was so disturbing that Neil didn't pursue the question further. "And you know how to get us through the mountains?"

"I've travelled quite a bit in my day," Piedra said, bristling. "It's hardly a new experience. And *through* is hardly the word. Which is why you need *me*. Now, if you'll be so kind as to pick me up, we can return to the Pillars—the sooner the better."

With a pang, Neil remembered that he'd gone and left Astra by herself again. He reluctantly bent down, lifted the rock up, and slid it into his pocket.

"I'm upside down, you idiot!" Piedra shouted.

Neil hastily pulled him out again. "Can't you see?" Piedra asked huffily. "No, obviously, you can't. My upside is where that streak of copper is, across what you would call my forehead."

Yes, there was the vein, very thin, almost unnoticeable. Neil carefully put Piedra back in his pocket the right way up and made his way slowly down the trail, leading Gísil by the reins. Astra came running to meet them, her face white. "I thought something had happened when you took so long—Oh, Gísil! Your leg!" She glared at Neil. "So, Mr. Wilderness Expert. Way to go."

"As a matter of fact," Neil said hotly, "it's a good thing I went. Because I met our guide."

"Oh?" Astra crossed her arms and glanced round. "And just who might that be?"

Feeling foolish, Neil took the rock from his pocket and held it out. Astra stared at it, then burst out laughing.

185

"You *can't* mean—"

"Here we go again," Piedra said loudly in an offended voice. "I've already explained it all to the boy."

Astra gaped, open-mouthed. Then she gave a snort. "Is this some kind of joke? Come on, Neil, admit it. You're using ventriloquism, aren't you?"

"Of course he isn't," said Piedra sharply.

"Neil, this isn't funny. Gísil's hurt, thanks to you."

By way of answer Neil handed the rock to her and walked away. "I must say you're a *very* poorly designed life form," Piedra said haughtily from Astra's palm. "You can't even trust the evidence of your own senses."

Astra's eyes widened. "And you," she said, stung, "are a very *rude* life form. Why are you even bothering with us?"

"Because I gave my word," Piedra said, even more haughtily. "I'm honour-bound to protect you. The fate of the world depends on *you*. Though why they chose you two I can't think."

"Here," said Astra, tossing Piedra back to Neil. "I'm going to bandage Gísil's leg. It's ridiculous arguing with a stone."

"You had a narrow escape," Piedra told Neil reprovingly as he repacked the saddlebags. "The Moving Mountains are so named for a reason. No one who knows them ever travels through them."

"But what about that Fire Reaper patrol?" said Neil. "They went over the mountains, didn't they?"

"Ah yes," said Piedra, and gave a grim chuckle. "And by now they will have understood why everyone for miles around avoids these ranges." He dropped his voice to a whisper. "They crush those who enter without permission."

That must explain the grinding and rumbling he'd heard. Neil looked up at the mountains with a new mixture of foreboding and respect.

"Which is why," Piedra continued, "you need a guide who has permission to pass through the Gateway—the Black Pillars."

Astra had wandered over and was listening skeptically. "You mean we say 'Zim-zam-zoom' and a big hole opens up?"

Neil shot her a warning look, but it was too late. "I've a good mind," Piedra said huffily, "to leave you to the mercies of the Vampyriae. Hideous black flying things," he added when Neil and Astra looked blank.

So that was what they were called. Neil shuddered at the memory and glanced up at the sky. "They were created at the Fortress," Piedra said darkly, "in their Biological Weapons Unit." The Fortress—that place where Neil had almost ended up as a prisoner! "They lack souls and are without mercy. So let us move quickly."

They were to stand, Piedra said, between the Pillars. Neil and a suitably abashed Astra led the mules, followed by Freya, while Piedra rode in Neil's pocket. It was a tight fit getting all of them in place—every piece of them, Piedra cautioned, with no stray body parts sticking out.

"And now what happens?" Neil asked, hoping he sounded suitably humble.

"We wait," Piedra said, "for the correct alignment between the sun's rays and the tops of the Pillars. Meanwhile we are safe from any attacks here."

And then what happens? Neil wanted to know, but didn't dare ask. They sat and waited, watching the sun's rays creep up the towers. The mules stamped their feet and swished their tails impatiently.

"The Pillars were placed here years ago by the Guardians who dwell under the mountains," Piedra explained. "By my own people, the Kärna, and the Loode Sterren, and the Fell-Náttúra who were imprisoned after a battle long ago." Piedra sighed. "But that is a long story—too long to go into here. All you need to know is that even the Fire Reapers have not succeeded in discovering the key." And he gave another grim chuckle.

187

Freya caught sight of a beetle and leapt out from between the Pillars to pounce on it. Neil ran to grab her by the collar and haul her back inside. At that moment, a gust of breeze brought a faint but terrifying sound—the flapping of great wings. There they were, dozens of dark specks on the far side of the salt pan, small as mosquitoes but growing steadily larger. The streak of copper on Piedra's forehead turned pale. "The Vampyriae!" he said, and for the first time his voice seemed to tremble.

Arnbi was skittish and Astra was having a hard time holding him. Neil tied Gísil's reins to Freya's collar and grabbed Arnbi's bridle as the shrieks and cries of the Vampyriae came echoing across the sky.

"They're interfering with the signal," Piedra muttered, glancing up at the sun. Arnbi suddenly kicked up his heels, striking the Pillars with his hooves. He reared back, breaking Neil and Astra's hold, and galloped off.

"Arnbi!" Astra yelled, and darted out from the Pillars before Neil could grab her. The first Vampyriae were arriving, circling and screeching above the towers. Neil felt sick to his stomach. His hand went to the SerraTube on his belt as two or three of them swooped after Astra, shrawking in triumph.

"No!" shouted Piedra, his copper vein blazing. "It's dark techno—it'll stop the Gateway opening!"

But I have to ... I have to save Astra ... The mule, terrified, had jerked to a halt, and Astra managed to scramble on his back as the Vampyriae circled her.

Far below them, a sudden grinding and rumbling filled the air. Gísil brayed and struggled, and it was all Neil could do to hold onto the bridle. Then a huge cloud of dust boiled up, blotting out the sun. The rumbling grew deafening, the dust cloud so thick Neil couldn't breathe.

The Pillars were moving!

A massive slab of granite in the earth opened inward, shimmering round its edges. He felt as if he were being sucked toward it. In the confusion he dropped Piedra, but he didn't dare let go of Gísil. He fought against the sucking, but his body seemed paralyzed. Gísil snorted and stamped as Arnbi galloped into place, almost knocking Neil over. The flapping of leathern wings rushed over them, bringing a hideous rotting smell, and were gone. Then the dust and the shimmering swallowed them up.

They seemed to be in a vast, high cavern. Water dripped steadily somewhere, reminding Neil how thirsty he was. He lay there panting, trying to recover his breath. The walls gleamed wetly, though he could see no source of light. His arm throbbed painfully; he must have banged it against something.

"That was a close call!" said a familiar sarcastic voice. "Considerably closer than I like—and believe me, I've had a few in my time."

Well, at least he's safe, even if I did drop him, Neil thought.

"Where are we?" It was Astra, sounding scared. "What happened?" Gísil and Arnbi gave whinnying snorts, as if to express their opinion of the situation, and Freya let out a howl. *So we're all safe,* Neil thought to himself, almost giddily.

Freya suddenly began barking furiously. In the dim light, the strangest being Neil had ever seen—even stranger than the Bestia—shuffled into view. He was tall and skeletal, and his face and body were embedded with red carbuncles and black onyxes that seemed to grow out of his flesh. Lumps of coal and granite bulged from his scalp, and his eyes were pale blue quartz.

"Ah, Melchior." It was Piedra again, sounding relieved. "May I say how glad I am to see you. A very close call, as I was just telling the children."

"They're getting bolder, sir," Melchior said, in a voice like the grinding of two stones. "At one time they'd never have dared to come so close." He bent his lumpy head and looked closely at Neil and then at Astra, who stared back at him in amazement. "So these are the children who were expected."

"*Un*expected, if you ask me," said Piedra grumpily. "I hadn't realized human children could be so difficult. Mark my words, Melchior—"

"Oh, do let's get on with it," Astra said with sudden exasperation. "You've already told us what you think of us. But you've got us, so what are you going to do with us?"

There was a shocked silence, in which Neil hid a smile. Piedra, it seemed, had met his match. Melchior turned without a word and shuffled off down the cavern. The others followed, Neil feeling distinctly small and intimidated in the cavern's vastness. Melchior turned into another cavern, smaller than the first, its ceiling so low that he had to bend almost double, then another and another. Strange phosphorescent stalactites hung from the ceilings, bands of copper and gold shone in the walls. They passed caverns filled with strange noises, caverns shaped like amoebas with tunnels running off in all directions. The twists and turns were dizzying.

At last they entered a high, narrow tunnel where hundreds of thin gold filaments branched off along the walls and ceiling in all directions—like a golden spiderweb, Neil thought. The walls were hung with red and gold banners, each embroidered with four interlocked symbols: a paw, a leaf, a ruby, and a human hand. The banners seemed to be woven of the finest tissue, and moved as if in a faint breeze. "The antechamber of the Mínera," said Melchior, turning to Neil and Astra for the first time on this odd journey. "And these banners bear the coat of arms of the Four Nations."

Ahead of them a vast opening streamed with light, and the sound of voices and laughter echoed from it. As they reached the entrance Neil stood there blinking, dazzled, trying to take it all in. They were in a cavern so immense it seemed as if the whole interior of a mountain had been hollowed out. Great jewelled lamps hung on enormous chains from the ceiling, and the cave walls pulsed with luminescence. A massive table had been hewn from a block of granite, and round it, on chairs of elaborately carved white marble, sat a motley collection of beings who made Neil's jaw drop. Some were like the carbuncled Melchior, each with different gemstones growing from their flesh, and some were coloured lumps of granite like Piedra, only much larger, while still others seemed made entirely of agate or slate or some other mineral. At the head of the table, facing Neil, was a being with emerald hair, her body veined with gold and her hands and fingernails studded with tiny rubies.

"Welcome, human children," she said, and her voice had an after-ring to it like a tuning fork. "I am Guldsterre. We have been expecting you for a long time." She held out her ruby hands, indicating an empty chair on either side of her. "You must sit beside me. With the dog-being, of course."

Gísil and Arnbi were led away by two young women who seemed half-sapphire. With Freya between them, Neil and Astra walked round the table to take their places, Neil acutely conscious of his damp, grubby clothing. As they sat down, a dozen or more beings like Melchior came into the chamber carrying steaming tureens and dishes and platters made of transparent crystal. One of the beings carried a huge flagon and filled Neil's goblet with a pale golden liquid. He drank it down at once. It was sparkly and bubbly and deliciously thirst-quenching, though he couldn't have said whether it tasted more like lemonade or more like honey or more like butter melting on popcorn.

Then Guldsterre stood up and lifted her goblet to propose a toast. "It is a great privilege," she began, "to have these two children in our midst today. Those of us who dwell in Mínera time have waited many eons for this day to arrive. We are deeply honoured, human children, to be able to assist you in your task."

A roo-roo-roo echoed round the chamber. Freya was reminding everyone that she was a bearer of the task, too. The beings all laughed—a strange mixture of booming and tinkling. Guldsterre bowed her head toward Freya, then drank deeply from her goblet and set it down.

"Millions of years before your time," she said, her face grave, "the Earth passed through another terrible era. A race of Giant Beings evolved and came to power, and their reign culminated in a mighty battle, when many were captured and enslaved." A hush fell over the assembly. "So we have more than a passing interest in the outcome of your task, human children," Guldsterre went on. "It has been given to us to provide an escort for your journey to the Valley, and to assist in any way we can. Your sojourn with us will be short, but we will do our utmost to make it a pleasant one."

With that she sat down and everyone turned to the meal, laughing and chattering. Neil couldn't identify any of the dishes, but each was more delicious than the last, and he and Astra ate till they were stuffed. At last everyone was finished, the empty plates were removed, and a group of gemstone-beings came into the hall carrying instruments of a kind Neil had never seen—lyres made of silver, flutes of translucent pearl, others he couldn't name. As they began to play, he was reminded of something, some melody he'd heard once, perhaps in a dream. Or was it the sound made by the Memory Stone? Only now he thought he could make out words in some indecipherable language: *Om ma am or om ma am or ...*

As suddenly as it had begun, the music stopped. He felt as if he were floating, and the pain in his arm had floated away, too. His eyelids drooped. He couldn't have moved if his life had depended on it. Strong arms lifted him in the air and carried him, and he was laid in what felt like a nest of feathers. And then he was sound asleep.

"Welcome, human children and canine-being, to our little gathering," Guldsterre said, smiling. "I trust all three of you slept well."

She sat at a round table in a smaller cavern hung with tapestries, a vast map spread out in front of her. On one side of her stood an older being, his hair white, his temples and ears studded with silver-white crystals, wearing a gold breastplate and shin armour. On the other side, also armoured, stood a younger being with a brilliant tiger's eye stone in his forehead and the same gold-veined body as Guldsterre. Behind them, half in shadow, was a Mínera elder with a braid of silver wound round her head, rubies erupting from her neck like a collar.

"My mother, Silfra the Learned." Guldsterre held out her hand as the older being inclined her head. "And my generals—Rhodium and my brother Chalcedon." Both generals bowed, and Neil, feeling self-conscious and awkward, bowed back. Astra, with great presence of mind, held out her hand, and each general in turn took it and kissed it.

Guldsterre turned to the map, studded with many twinkling pins of different colours. "As you can see," she said, "we are studying a map of Terrania—the planet you know as Earth."

Neil and Astra leaned over the table. It was recognizably a map of their planet, except that a lot of it was different. There seemed to be islands in places Neil didn't remember, and others missing in places that he did—Great Britain, for example, had become a series of tiny islets. On the western edge of Canada, the Alaskan Panhandle had disappeared and the Yukon was much closer to the sea than he remembered. Vancouver Island had all but vanished, while much of the Lower Mainland, where Vancouver once stood, had disappeared altogether. Was this *really* what would happen in the future?

"This map must seem strange to you," Guldsterre said to Neil. "The oceans have risen so much since your time, as the stories of the older ones remind us." She looked at her mother, who nodded, and Neil noticed for the first time how sad Silfra's expression was. "Many earlier records," Guldsterre went on, "have been deliberately altered or destroyed by the Fire Reapers and their allies, including the United Chinese Empire and the various GalactiCorps. One of our tasks here, in the Timeless Caverns, is to preserve as much of the old knowledge as we can."

She waved a hand round the cavern. Neil saw that it led into other caverns filled floor to ceiling with shelves containing scrolls, manuscripts, ancient leather volumes. "My mother, as the Guardian of Wisdom, is in charge of this task," Guldsterre explained, "as female Mínera have been since we first came into existence."

"But even I," broke in Silfra for the first time, in a voice so deep it seemed to come from somewhere far beneath them, "can know only a fraction of all that is contained here. And now that so much is being falsified, it becomes ever more difficult to tell fact from fiction."

There was a heavy silence. Astra leaned over the map again. "There's no trees anywhere!" she exclaimed. "It all looks like desert."

"It is the mission of the Fire Reapers, as you may know, to destroy forests all over the world," Guldsterre began slowly. "Once all the trees are destroyed, the Fire Reapers say the world will return to its pure beginning state—to fire—and a new world will emerge from the ashes of the old."

"My father told me something about it," Astra said in a small voice, "but I didn't know—I thought they'd be stopped. Somehow."

Guldsterre pointed to the pins. "These mark the places where the Fire Reapers are carrying out their campaigns. They are working in a pattern. From south and west and east upward to the far northern reaches of Nordlandia, where the very last of the great boreal forests grow." Her voice quivered, then steadied again. "Those last stands are here, on the island of Finnmark." She pressed a ruby fingernail on a green sliver of land. "There are those who are secretly working with us. But the Fire Reapers are many and we are few, and we have been unable to challenge them. Until now." Her green eyes suddenly blazed with fire, and Neil thought that he wouldn't like to be on her wrong side.

"But our task has been made much harder," said Rhodium, and his voice was like stones being tumbled along the bed of a river. "One of our own—one of the Mínera Beings—has joined their side." Guldsterre stiffened, her brother Chalcedon's knuckles turned white, and Silfra the Learned clenched the arms of her chair. "He was one of the Three Generals of the Caverns," Rhodium went on, "together with Chalcedon and myself. Some say he fell in love with a Fire Reaper officer, others that he was bewitched by the flames of the burning trees. Whatever the truth, he left on a journey three years ago and never returned. Now, so we are told, he has risen to be their second-in-command, reporting to the Archons themselves." Rhodium absently touched one of the silvery crystals at his temple. "You will know him, if you meet him, by the gemstone in his forehead—the sardonyx that gives him his name, with its bands of red, white, and black."

"He has immense power," Guldsterre added softly, "because he took with him many of the secrets entrusted to us by the Mínera Nation. He is a formidable enemy. And it is he who now commands the Fortress of Villieldr—the Fortress of Flame—in the Valley of the Slaves."

"Is it true what we heard? That no one ever comes back from the Valley?" faltered Astra. Neil glanced at her, feeling equally helpless. *It's no place for children ... You've been cursed ...* That was what the old man in the ruined village had said.

"You will be able to enter the Fortress much more easily than any of the Bi-Souls," Guldsterre said gently, "or adult humans, for that matter."

"You mean—we're going to be *spies*?" Astra said, her face white.

Guldsterre laid her ruby fingers on Astra's arm. "Trust that you have more allies than you know, who will augment your own abilities."

"Wouldn't it make more sense to get an army together and fight them?" Neil asked.

"We are not yet ready." Guldsterre shook her head firmly. "We must strike when the time is ripe—not before. And we must hope that the Fire Reapers do not move first." She clapped her hands and a young Mínera Being entered, bearing on a cushion a scroll tied with a gold ribbon. *"A laissez-passer,"* said Guldsterre, handing the scroll to Astra. "It will allow you to pass unmolested as far as the Valley. My brother and his troops will escort you there, guided by Piedra."

Astra and Neil looked at each other, each thinking the same thing. They were being guided to the very mouth of hell and then abandoned. Guldsterre must have guessed, because she said, "I believe Áilu gave both of you gifts. You must use the protection they offer you."

"But I don't know how to use mine," Astra protested, pulling it from her belt.

"Let me see." Silfra the Learned leaned forward eagerly, holding her hand out, and examined the silver tube with great interest. "A most intriguing device. And made of lissium from the Asteroid Belt, which is twenty times lighter than titanium. In which case ..." She turned it over, then nodded. "It must be charged with bioluminescence in order to function."

She placed the tube on a small tablet on the table. Slowly at first, increasing in intensity, the tube began to glow with the same luminescence that pulsed from the cave walls. Neil and Astra stared until the glow became too blinding to look at.

"There!" She handed the tube back to Astra, who took it wonderingly. "The glow will fade but the charge will last a long time. The rest is up to you. You must practise patience."

"And now," Guldsterre said, "the night turns late, and you must get what sleep you can. Sapphiria will guide you back to your room. You leave at first light."

The Valley of the Slaves

eil, hands jammed in his armpits, jumped up and down to keep warm. For the hundredth time he wished he was going home to the Yukon, to his mother and sister, to the house on Golddust Avenue. He'd had quite enough of adventures, thank you very much. They were exciting when you read about them in books, but in real life—well, that was something else altogether.

Freya, at least, was happy about all the commotion—she was racing back and forth, shoving her nose against his hand impatiently. Astra, meanwhile, was still trying to get the Etheric Sensor to work. She'd spent a good part of the night blowing through it and playing the finger holes. Now she was grumpy from lack of both sleep and success.

"It's no use." She held the tube out to Neil with an expression of disgust. "Bioluminescence or no bioluminescence, it just doesn't do anything."

Neil tried blowing through it, too, but nothing happened. Perhaps it had been damaged somehow. Or, more likely, only Montserrat Lavallet knew how to make it work.

"There's not much point in—" Astra began, and broke off. Guldsterre had entered the outer cavern with two other Mínera beings. They were carrying gold breastplates and shin armour that turned out to fit Neil and Astra perfectly.

"Our spies report," Guldsterre said in a low voice, "that Fire Reaper troops have been sighted to the north of the village of Ashfalten, which lies on your planned route to the Valley." Her expression was so grave that Neil's heart skipped. "My brother and his officers have been mapping out a different route for you."

As she spoke Chalcedon trotted up on his magnificent chest-nut mule, his cloak draped over her rump. Behind him was Melchior, leading Gísil and Arnbi, and beyond them twenty or so Mínera troops, bearing strange translucent spears and daggers and scimitars. At their head a soldier carried a banner bearing the coat of arms, which was also carved on each shield.

Chalcedon greeted his sister by raising his arms and clasping his hands sideways, and Guldsterre did the same. Once Neil and Astra were mounted, she turned to her guests. "Go well, children," she said, placing a hand on Gísil's and Arnbi's necks in turn. "You travel with much guidance and attention. Do not forget that." Then she turned to Astra, who sat astride Arnbi with the still faintly glowing tube at her belt. "You, child, have been illumined by our bioenergy. Remember that it will not last forever. You must use it wisely."

She stepped back and raised her hands again in the clasped gesture, lifting them to her forehead. Then the little cavalcade moved forward out of the cavern, along a ledge of rock that wound dizzyingly upward. When Neil looked back, Guldsterre and the cavern and all its inhabitants had disappeared from sight.

"I myself have actually been *in* the Valley," Piedra said with dignity as they rode along. "Which is more than I can say about anyone else here."

"Did you tell Chalcedon?" asked Neil.

"I tried. Of course he ignored me. The Loode Sterren always think *they* know best."

"I'm sure he's picked the route he thinks is safest," Neil said cautiously. Piedra promptly retreated in a huff and went to sleep in Neil's saddlebag.

Apart from the clatter of hooves on rock and the jingle of harness, they rode in silence. For all Piedra's highhandedness,

Neil missed his conversation. Chalcedon seemed preoccupied; he spoke only to his second-in-command, a tall lieutenant with shiny gray cubic crystals along his jawline. Behind him Astra was once again fiddling with the Sensor, letting Arnbi pick his own way forward.

They stopped for the night among slabs of concrete—slabs from a long-gone freeway, Neil realized with shock, but cracked and pitted from erosion. They'd spent hours travelling through a monotonous rocky landscape, broken here and there with stands of burnt trees and piles of ash. "The closer we get to the Valley," one of the soldiers told him, "the more devastated it is. The Fire Reapers have been very active round here."

"Hmph," Piedra said in a muffled voice from the saddlebag. "He calls this devastation? This is nothing."

Neil climbed down from Gísil, slowly, his body aching. "How did you end up in the Valley?" he asked Piedra.

"I was born there." Piedra sighed as if all the weight of the world sat on his shoulders. "My brothers and sisters and I came into being during a volcanic eruption, when I also acquired the copper vein in my forehead. You animate beings have no idea what we stones have had to go through. Or what we've witnessed in our long—"

The conversation was cut short by a soldier directing Neil and Astra to tie up their mules. Some of the troops began unloading supplies; others built a fire in the lee of one of the concrete slabs; still others began cooking a meal. Neil and Astra, wrapped in the cloaks of mercury thread that Guldsterre had given them, ate their stew and listened to the jokes and laughter of the soldiers. It made Neil lonelier, shut out from the conversation in different languages, and he wriggled closer to Astra.

Off to one side Chalcedon and his senior officers pored over a map, talking in low voices. Presently Chalcedon motioned to Neil and Astra to join him. He looked more relaxed now, the firelight striking the tiger's eye in his forehead so that it glowed in bands of cinnamon and gold. "Perhaps you'd like to take a look at our route," he said, pointing to the well-worn map spread out on the ground. "Tomorrow will take us into the VándrLanden, where we must keep sharp watch for any bands of Útlagi. The next day should bring us to the edge of the Valley itself. From there—" he nodded at his second-in-command "—Lieutenant Galena says we can see the Gribbhålla Gate. He says it's the most fearsome thing he's ever seen."

It occurred to Neil that Chalcedon was rather enjoying terrifying them. Still, he was treating them like adults—unlike a lot of people they knew, as Astra pointed out later when they were curled in blankets beside the fire with Freya and Piedra between them.

"Hmph!" said Piedra rather loudly. "He's a mere child. He can't have been around longer than a few hundred years or so."

"You're just mad," said Astra tactlessly, "because he's using a map instead of relying on you."

"And if he'd asked me I'd have told him my plan for getting into the Valley," Piedra said, ignoring her. "But now I won't. Let's see how *he* handles it."

"Wouldn't it be better to at least discuss it?" Neil said, alarmed.

"I made a solemn promise," Piedra said haughtily, "to protect and guide the two of *you*, not to mention the dog-being. A vow, I might add, which I have so far kept, as you might have noticed. I made no such vow about Chalcedon."

"Of course we've noticed," said Neil soothingly, "and we're very grateful, Piedra."

Astra rolled her eyes but said nothing. Instead she lay on her stomach and took the Etheric Sensor from under the blanket. "I just realized something," she remarked after a few minutes. "These finger holes—I don't think it's a musical instrument after all."

"Look," said Neil. "It's pulsing."

Indeed it was. The faint glow had returned to the Sensor, brightening and dimming in intensity. Astra, watching it

200

closely, said, "You know, the pattern of pulses keeps repeating. Sort of the way the Memory Stone did."

"Maybe it operates on energy signatures," Neil suggested. An idea suddenly struck him. "Why don't you try looking through it instead? And use the finger holes to adjust it?"

Astra gave him a dubious glance, but she lifted it to her eye and peered through. "Nothing. It's just—oh, wait a minute." She tapped the finger holes. "There's a sort of—I don't know ... a pattern, with changing shapes ..." She sat up, excited. "Some of the shapes—they're people, a lot of people, dressed in rags— and they're chained together!—they're so thin, Neil!—and—oh, I can't look anymore." She lowered the tube and covered her eyes. "I think it was the Valley, Neil. I think I saw some of the slaves."

"Are you sure? You weren't imagining it?"

"Look again," said Piedra quietly, "and see if you see the Gribbhålla Gate."

Astra lifted the tube to her eye once more. "I can see ... there *is* a gate, it looks like it's woven out of strips of black iron. And there's Fire Reaper troops just inside it. It's very high, I can't see—" She moved her fingers along the finger holes experimentally. "Now I can ... there's something on the top ..." She shuddered and dropped the tube, looking as if she was going to be sick.

Neil grabbed her arm. "What? What did you see?"

"It was horrible." She made a face. "A horrible—I don't know, a sort of monster...."

"The Gribbhålla Gate." Piedra nodded grimly. "It's the Valley, all right."

"And those slaves—did you see anyone you recognized?" Neil asked—he was thinking of Hallvard and Fru Berta—but Astra shook her head and stared at the Sensor with revulsion.

"I hate it. I don't ever want to touch it again."

"Trade you for the SerraTube, then," Neil said promptly.

"You will do no such thing," said Piedra firmly. "Interfering with higher plans brings only disaster, as you have seen. Of all

the idiotic suggestions. Some people think life should be *easy.*"
And as Astra and Neil stared, abashed, the gleam of Piedra's
copper vein dimmed. He had settled himself to sleep.

By midmorning they found themselves in another desert,
utterly different from the one they'd crossed with Hreinn-
Sál. It was studded with hoodoos—tall sand pillars banded in
reds and ochres, some of them ten storeys high. The heat was
intense, and a plague of biting insects, so tiny you couldn't see
them, drove the mules and Freya crazy. They even found their
way under the golden armour, biting necks and torsos. What
with the heat and the insects and the gritty sand seeping into
everything, it made for a horribly uncomfortable ride. Astra,
half-asleep, was swaying on her mule, and Neil watched her
worriedly. Every time he woke during the night, she'd been fiddling with the Etheric Sensor. He wondered if, like the Memory
Stone, it was possible to get addicted to it.

The company stopped at noon to rest the animals and eat a
hurried meal, a rising wind lifting the sand into tiny tornadoes.
By the time they pressed on under a darkening sky, the blow-
ing sand was so thick they could see only a few metres ahead.
"Remember what I said about a poorly designed life form?"
Piedra said smugly from inside the saddlebag. "I rest my case.
Personally, I've always found sand rather beautiful."

"Oh, shut up," said Neil, trying to scratch a particularly
difficult-to-reach itch. Up ahead, Chalcedon's mule was whinnying and rearing as dark shapes emerged out of the blowing
sand, travelling at great speed. "Útlagi!" came the shout from
the troops. The shapes resolved into small dark wiry men riding desert ponies and carrying ancient weapons—rifles and
machine guns. They were dressed in a motley collection of
clothing and head coverings against the sun, and they were
covered in scars and tattoos.

Their leader pulled his pony to a halt and shouted something to Chalcedon in a language Neil didn't recognize. Chalcedon turned to one of his officers, who translated, and Astra was asked to produce the *laissez-passer* that Guldsterre had given them. The Útlagi leader took it, frowning, and pretended to study it—at least, Neil thought, he didn't seem to be really reading it. Then he looked up and stared at the children. The other Útlagi, also staring, began talking among one another and pointing.

"They've never seen anyone as beautiful as you, girl child," Piedra said from the saddlebag. "Their leader's very taken with you."

Astra reddened and turned away on Arnbi. "You speak Útlagian?" Neil asked Piedra in surprise.

"My boy, when you have thousands of years, you have time to learn many languages. They're offering Chalcedon a dozen desert ponies for her." And indeed two or three of the Útlagi had approached Chalcedon and were talking to him through his translator, pointing frequently to Astra.

"How dare they!" said Astra indignantly. "I'm a human being, not a cow."

The leader took a ragged scarf from round his neck, rode forward, and presented it formally to Astra. She was about to refuse it when Piedra said hurriedly, "For heaven's sake, accept it! They'll try to carry you off if you don't."

Astra reached out reluctantly and took the dirty scarf. The leader grinned and nodded and swung his pony round in circles of triumph, but not before staring closely at Neil with a mixture of reverence and fear. He conferred with his men again, and they began pointing at Neil and gesticulating.

"They don't known what to make of you," Piedra said. "They know you don't belong here. They think perhaps you're an interloper from a distant tribe." He snorted. "Or that you might be magic of some sort. Even a kind of god. I'm afraid they're a most credulous life form."

Well, I did get here by magic. And the SerraTube was definitely magic, though of an evil kind. Neil couldn't help grinning to himself.

"You know what, Piedra? If I'm a god, you'd better start paying me more respect from now on."

"And if I'd known it was going to go to your head like that, believe me, I—"

The Útlagi leader suddenly shook his head, frowning, and spat on the ground three times. The negotiations with Chalcedon had evidently reached a stalemate. Then he raised his arm, shouted a command, and the ragged group turned their ponies and thundered away through the hoodoos. They seemed to melt into the distance, as if swallowed up by the sand itself.

The company camped within hearing distance of the Svær Fossefalls—the Great Waterfalls, Piedra told Astra and Neil. Even from a couple of kilometres away, its faint thunder filled the air. The falls spilled over a kilometre down a sheer cliff face, Piedra said, after an earthquake two hundred years ago that had diverted the Svær River. "Which isn't big at all, compared to what it used to be," Piedra said, "but it's one of the few rivers in Nordlandia that are still flowing."

How awful, Neil thought. Suppose the Yukon River disappeared like those Nordlandian rivers, with its salmon and its grayling, its terns and mergansers, the swallows that swooped low over the water to catch insects on summer evenings? But if the glaciers all disappeared in the future, then the Yukon River, fed from the Choda glacier at the southern end of Atlin Lake, would vanish, too. The glossy green Yukon that flowed all the way to the Bering Sea! He swallowed hard, thinking of those bike rides to the dam, his walks with Freya.

"There's a cult of worshippers that's grown up around the

Fossefalls," Piedra said, "because water's so scarce now. They make sacrifices to keep it flowing."

"What kind of sacrifices?" asked Astra.

"Chickens, mostly. The odd goat or two."

"But that's—that's barbaric!" Astra and Neil looked at each other in disgust.

"Barbarism," said Piedra, "co-exists with advanced technology—as it did in your time, Neil. It's the great tragedy of the human race, I'm afraid. With us stones, half of our body faces the earth and half the sky, so we're the most balanced of life forms. But then, as I've said before, humans are a very poorly designed—"

"Life form," said Astra wearily. "We know."

"Everything else," said Piedra condescendingly, "functions beautifully. Humans have only themselves to blame."

But before the argument turned nasty, rumours came of a change of route. Instead of going the long way round and crossing the Svær fifty kilometres upstream by the Svær Bridge, they would ford the river at first light, directly above the Falls. Piedra sucked in his breath.

"The Fossefallen will be very angry," he said in a low voice. "It's bad luck to interfere with the river."

"Who's being superstitious now?" said Neil loftily. But Piedra only continued to mutter to himself, a muttering he kept up the next morning while they broke camp. Chalcedon had sent his lieutenant and two other officers ahead to determine the best point at which to cross. The pack mules had been led through successfully; now the officers would cross, followed by Neil and Astra and then the troops.

As they rode toward it, the sound of the waterfall grew deafening—though at least it shut out Piedra's grumbling. The crossing place was at a point where the river widened and slowed, a hundred metres or so above the Falls. One of the officers urged his mule in. It stepped in reluctantly, lost its footing, and plunged beneath the water. Astra gasped, and Gísil, who didn't like water, tossed her head and stamped her feet. But the mule surfaced, struggling, the drenched officer still on its back, and swam steadily to the other side.

"It's deeper than I thought," Neil whispered as they sat side by side on their mules. How would Gísil handle it? And what about Freya? She was a strong swimmer, but the current was fast. Chalcedon must have already thought of it, because another officer rode up with a length of rope, which he showed Neil how to knot under Freya's front legs and round her body. Neil fastened the other end to his saddle pommel.

Now it was their turn. Astra was to go first, since Arnbi was unfazed by rivers. He sauntered in as if he did this every day and launched himself into the water, Astra clinging to his mane for dear life. Gísil, upset about being separated from Arnbi, reared and whinnied. She put her front hooves in the water, then pulled back. At last she danced in sideways, flinging her head up, and swam after Arnbi. Freya dog-paddled behind, swinging out sideways in the current but held firmly by the rope.

At last both mules scrambled up the bank, water streaming from their flanks. "Really," came Piedra's loud voice, "that was most unpleasant. I've experienced *falling* into water before, and rolling along a river bed. But moving *through* it—really, it's most unnatural."

"Why, Piedra," Neil said, in mock surprise. "You mean, in your long life, you haven't gone *swimming* before?"

But before Piedra could reply, the sound of wailing and keening came to them on the breeze. Approaching them through the rocky terrain was a group of men and women dressed in long blue robes with scalloped edges. Two women at the front carried a small statue between them, while another clutched a struggling and squawking chicken. It was a good thing that Freya was still tied to Neil's saddle or the chicken would have suffered a premature end.

"What did I tell you?" muttered Piedra. "The Fossefallen with their water goddess Atla. She was one of the Waves, the

206

nine beautiful daughters of Aegir, Lord of the Sea. It's a bad omen—a *very* bad omen." The group knelt in a circle a short distance downstream, where the spray from the Falls shimmered in the air, and began praying. Several of the soldiers lifted their steepled fingers in the Fire Reapers' sign, and even those who hadn't looked round nervously, as if expecting the Fossefallen to attack.

"Are they afraid of those people?" whispered Neil. Surely not—there were only a few of them.

"They're afraid the Aqua Libere might turn up," said Piedra in a low voice. "They protect the Fossefallen."

Astra and Neil exchanged glances. Had they evaded one set of enemies only to encounter another?

"The Aqua Libere fight to protect the remaining sources of water all over Terrania," Piedra went on. "They won't be pleased we contaminated a water source."

They turned their mules north along the riverbank into a landscape of boulders and thornbushes, with no sign of the Aqua Libere or anyone else. In the afternoon the skies darkened to match the company's mood. Thunder echoed above them, and lightning flashed across the horizon. Astra turned white and crouched lower on her mule, her hand unconsciously going to the exit wound at her side. Then the rain came, driving sideways in solid sheets. By the time they managed to outride the storm, everyone was drenched and bedraggled. Chalcedon ordered a halt and a large fire was built, despite the fact it advertised their position in the open terrain. But even its warmth didn't seem to cheer anyone.

"We're supposed to reach the Valley this evening," muttered Piedra, "though what Chalcedon plans to do once we get there I can't imagine." Neil felt bleaker than he had in a long time. What would happen with the code in his ankle once they got to the Valley? As for Astra, her hair plastered to her head, she looked equally miserable. Once they reached the Valley they'd be on their own. And after her vision of the Gribbhålla Gate ...

They soon rode on, into a cloudy and starless evening. After an hour or so they saw the outlines of high needle-shaped mountains far in the distance, like fangs round a mouth. A tortuous narrow track took them up a rocky slope, which fell away in sheer cliffs that dropped hundreds of metres. Neil and Astra reined in their mules at the lip, their eyes widening. Far below was a vast and barren plain on which nothing moved. The Valley of the Slaves! In the middle was the Fortress of Flame itself, the size of a small city, rearing up out of the earth, its massive grey walls studded with watchtowers. How were they ever going to enter it? Or cross that vast expanse unnoticed?

Chalcedon motioned Neil and Astra alongside him. "Our task was to bring you safely to the Valley. But now that we are here—" He paused and shook his head, looking troubled. "The Fortress looks much more impregnable than our spies reported. No doubt the Fire Reapers have been busy increasing their fortifications, and their surveillance."

Good, thought Neil. Let's drop this whole dumb idea. Let's go back and get an army together instead of tackling this thing on our own.

"We'll make camp and await further instructions." Chalcedon wheeled his mule around, signalled to his lieutenant, and galloped off, leaving the children to stare after him.

"No instructions. Another bad sign," muttered Piedra. "Oh, do take me out of this infernal saddlebag. A stone can't breathe in here."

Neil lifted him out, and the three of them stared at the Valley. "A thoroughly nasty place," said Piedra. "And they've probably used paralysis mines in the approaches, too."

"*Paralysis* mines?" said Astra faintly.

"When you step on them they detonate soundlessly," Piedra said cheerfully, "and then they paralyze you. Not forever, though. Just a couple of hundred years."

"Well, that's a comfort," Neil said. "For a minute there, you had me worried."

"Or perhaps they've used sonar reassemblers instead," Piedra said, ignoring him. "They disassemble you, atom by atom, using sound waves, and reassemble you somewhere else. Of course they might have even newer weapons I haven't—"

"But this is ridiculous!" Neil burst out. "We *are* cursed. Just like that man in the ruined village said!"

"You're succumbing to the Fire Reapers' power," Piedra said severely. "To their rule by fear. How about using the Etheric Sensor to check the Fortress?"

Astra quickly pulled the Sensor from her belt and lifted it to her eye, then shook her head. "All I get is those patterns."

"Maybe the frequency's changed," suggested Neil.

"Or maybe there's some sort of interference," Piedra said, frowning. "Try again."

Astra placed the tube at her eye again and fiddled with the finger holes. "No, still noth—just a minute." She pressed a fingerhole, twice. "There, that's better." She gulped. "If you can call it better. There's a bar of red light all the way round the Fortress. Is it some kind of force field? And I can see the Gate now. It's *huge!*" A long silence. "And there's dozens of those Vampyriae. They're hovering above the Gate. And Fire Reaper troops by the hundreds—they're in a kind of parade square, they're marching. And on the top of the Gate itself"—her voice quivered—"is that *thing*. It must be ten feet tall. And it has *three heads*—a huge lizard one, and a giant snake's, and I think the third is a vulture's. And it has scaly wings, and a long scaly tail, and *human* arms and legs." She shuddered and lowered the Sensor, her face white. "It's the most horrible thing I've ever seen."

Piedra nodded grimly. "It's a female Gribbhålla. The Fire Reapers have tried all kinds of biological experiments. They produced a brood of these beings."

"You mean—there's *more* of them?"

"I'm afraid so—though not all in the Fortress. The one at the Gate is an early prototype. It can hardly fly."

"That's really reassuring," Neil said gloomily. "Maybe it'll just open the Gate for us and let us in."

Astra stared at him for a minute. "You know, Neil, that may be the most brilliant thing you've ever said."

Neil stared at her in disbelief.

"No, I'm serious. If we look like we belong there ..."

"But how—I mean, how would we—?"

"We disguise ourselves as slaves," Astra said.

Oh brother, Neil thought. Aloud he said, "So we disguise ourselves as slaves. Then what?"

"We wait until there's a delivery of new slaves," Astra said eagerly. "They must get them all the time. No one could work like that, in those conditions, for very long. We'll hide ourselves among the newcomers and slip in when the Gate opens."

"You know, I may just have to revise my opinion of human beings," Piedra said, his copper vein positively twinkling. "That's a most inspired plan, child—even better than mine."

"And what was that?" Neil wanted to know.

"I was going to have you offer me to the Fire Reapers as a magic weapon. Now before you say anything, you must admit they'd be intrigued, to say the least, by a speaking stone."

"But Piedra, they might have done something awful to you!" Astra's eyes were wide.

"Yes, that was a chance I'd have had to take. But if I could be of some small help to the cause ..."

"Meanwhile," Neil said to Astra, frowning, "there's a couple of things you haven't thought of. What about Freya? And that code in my ankle?"

At that moment a young soldier came galloping up, reining in his mule beside them. "Chalcedon wants to see you right away."

210

Chalcedon's Plan

ou may remember," Chalcedon said, "our discussion in the Timeless Caverns about the general who defected to the Fire Reapers?" He had been sprawled on his cot when they arrived; now he sat up eagerly and leaned forward. "The one who's become their second-in-command—General Sardonyx?"

Neil and Astra nodded, still flushed and out of breath after their gallop to the encampment. A brazier filled with twigs and branches burned nearby, its flames flickering across Chalcedon's face. He paused, staring into the flames, biting his lip, and Astra thought she had never seen someone so impassioned, so aflame with his ideas.

"I'm going to send him a message," Chalcedon said, "telling him that I want to join him. Join the Fire Reapers, I mean."

Neil and Astra looked at him in horror, and Chalcedon hastily raised his hand. "No, no, no. It's a ruse, that's all."

Neil and Astra gave audible sighs of relief. "But how do you know he'll go for it?" asked Astra.

"General Sardonyx and I were once very close—in fact we played together as boys. We trained in the Mínera Beings' army together and rose swiftly through the officer ranks." Chalcedon shook his head sadly. "So I'm convinced he'll be overjoyed by my decision."

"And—what about us?" Astra wanted to know.

"If he agrees," Chalcedon said, "you'll go with me as my cadets. Along with Lieutenant Galena, of course."

"And Freya," said Neil. *And Piedra*—but he wouldn't say anything about that to Chalcedon. Especially not now, when faint harrumphs were coming from his saddlebag.

211

Chalcedon looked as if he was going to say no, and then changed his mind. "Of course, Freya. But we must keep our travelling party small. We're taking a risk." He stood up, dismissing them. "As soon as I hear from General Sardonyx, I'll send word."

"If you want *my* opinion," Piedra said grumpily as they walked the mules back, "I think Chalcedon should do as he's told. Wait for those instructions instead of coming up with his own ideas."

"But something must have happened," Neil pointed out. "After all, look what happened to you at the Pillars."

"Oh, I don't mean a guide," Piedra said. "There was no mention of that. But I'm sure there'll be guidance of some kind."

This all seemed bafflingly vague to Neil. How were they to receive this guidance? Besides, wasn't it better to have Chalcedon's help than try to enter the Fortress on their own?

"Maybe having Chalcedon guide us *is* what's supposed to happen," Astra said. "The more I think about our plan, the crazier I think it is."

"Astra's right," said Neil, with more firmness than he felt. "Going with Chalcedon gives us some protection."

Piedra snorted. "*If* the Fire Reapers believe his story. Suppose they don't? Suppose they think it's a trick?"

There was a long silence.

"Not to mention that the task has been laid on the two of you alone," Piedra added. "Another presence may create danger you cannot foresee."

"But *you're* another presence," Astra pointed out. "Surely we're allowed to have *some* help."

"I've said all I'm going to say," Piedra said with finality. "I suggest you slip away at once, on your own, and use the Sensor to keep an eye on things."

Neil and Astra stared at each other in alarm. Was Piedra right?

Footsteps sounded behind them, and the cubic features of Lieutenant Galena loomed out of the darkness. His weapon was slung over his shoulder, and his face was alight with the same determination as Chalcedon's. "General Sardonyx has responded favourably—more than favourably," he said. "Come. General Chalcedon awaits you."

Chalcedon held a lightstone above him as they picked their way down the cliff face in the dark. Lieutenant Galena had given each of them a tabard, a long vest with the Mínera Beings' crest, to be worn over their tunics, but advised against the golden armour. "We are going as new recruits," he told them. "We must appear to be friendly."

"You're taking me with you, of course?" Piedra said to Neil while they were fastening the tabards in place.

"You keep saying the task is mine and Astra's," said Neil severely. "So you have to promise to stop telling us what to do."

"I'm only offering advice for your own protection," Piedra said meekly.

"Then don't interrupt when Chalcedon is talking," added Astra. "It's very annoying."

All the same, as he slipped Piedra into his pocket, Neil was glad of his company. Piedra even managed to contain himself— if only barely—when Astra told Chalcedon about the red bar of light around the Fortress, and how it might be a dangerous force field.

"And how," said Chalcedon, "do you know that?"

Muffled squeaking came from Neil's pocket, but there was no help for it now. Reluctantly, Astra drew out the Sensor and handed it to Chalcedon, who examined it with great interest. "As a matter of fact, the field will present no difficulty," he said, handing the Sensor back. "They will, of course, disable it before our arrival."

"How *did* you get in touch with the General?" asked Neil.

Chalcedon held out a tiny glowing red pebble, no larger than a fingernail paring. "The General is a Mínera Being and has access to our technologies," he explained. "When charged with bioluminescence, this chip of garnet infused with yttrium transmits information." He smiled ruefully. "If we had more time I could show you how it works. But the General and his officers will be awaiting us at the Gate."

Neil felt his heart beating faster, and he and Astra exchanged an apprehensive glance.

"I expect," Chalcedon went on, "that the General will want to discuss the terms of my supposed defection. As part of those terms, I will ask him to show us the Fortress so you can determine the lay of the land."

Even so, thought Neil, how would he and Astra know what to do next? They'd have to trust that things would be made clear somehow. Perhaps Áilu and the Many Beings would get a message to them.

Climbing down the cliff, he and Astra had to concentrate hard to keep their footing on the slippery shale. At the bottom of the cliff they paused, panting, and surveyed their surroundings. A vast sandy waste stretched away into the distance. On the far horizon the fanglike mountains looked even higher and more menacing. The massive sprawl of the Fortress cast a long threatening shadow that seemed to leak toward them.

After they'd all had a quick drink from their water containers, Chalcedon and Lieutenant Galena set off briskly. Neil and Astra exchanged alarmed glances. Were they expected to keep up? It was hot and oppressive here in the Valley, without a breath of wind. Perhaps Mínera Beings didn't tire like ordinary humans.

For what seemed like forever they slogged on through the sand. They were both feeling more and more worried, but neither wanted to admit it to the other. At least they hadn't encountered any paralysis mines or sonar reassemblers—or could the Fire Reapers control them at a distance, too?

It was almost dawn by the time they reached the Fortress. Above them the clouds had scudded away, revealing an almost-full moon. They were hot and exhausted, and Freya was panting heavily. The massive stone walls, hundreds of metres high, towered above them, with no windows or openings visible anywhere. What was weird, now they were so close, was how eerily silent it was. How was it possible for a place the size of a city to be so soundless? A spasm of fear seized Neil's stomach. And then—though maybe it was just his imagination—a faint pain flickered in his ankle.

Chalcedon and Lieutenant Galena were waiting for them at the base of the nearest guard tower. "Don't touch the walls," Chalcedon cautioned as they approached. "The Fire Reapers have converted a kind of algae into a toxic weapon."

Neil grabbed Freya's collar and looked at the walls with distaste. They were coated with a kind of thin slime that seemed to quiver and contract. And now he heard a sound after all, a peculiar, piercing humming. "The walls give off that noise," Chalcedon said, as Neil looked for the source. "It normally operates at a much higher frequency, which you wouldn't be able to hear. It deters any living thing from approaching by mentally disorienting them. Of course, if they do ..." He shrugged. "The algae finishes them off. The Fire Reapers have a *most* effective defensive weapons system."

It was a good thing that Chalcedon had guided them, thought Neil with relief—they'd have been toast otherwise. The two Mínera Beings turned and walked onward. Neil and Astra and Freya stumbled after them, beyond tired. Images of an icy glass of root beer kept surfacing in Neil's head. If a Fire Reaper handed him a cold drink right now, he thought, he'd go straight over to their side.

Another step, and another, and another ... At last they reached the corner. And stopped dead.

"It's just how I saw it!" Astra cried.

There, just ahead of them, was the Gate, its twisted bars of black iron patterned with red metal flames soaring into the sky. A flock of Vampyriae circled and screeched around it. And perched on the very top, its heads tucked under a wing, was the Gribbhålla, like a unique and grotesque decoration. At the sight of Neil and Astra, the Gribbhålla stirred, lifting each of its three gigantic heads slowly. It stretched its wings, so vast they seemed to reach the opposite walls, and writhed its heads toward them. Freya, barking courageously, threw herself in front of them as the Gribbhålla's massive lizard head swung low, tongue flickering.

A sudden grinding sound made the Gribbhålla rear back. The great black Gate was swinging open. Beyond it stood massed phalanxes of Fire Reaper troops, a dozen or so officers at their head, their flame-emblazoned cloaks swirling round them. As the little group passed through the Gate, the Gribbhålla bent its enormous heads again, its three mouths yawning, its red and blue and purple tongues flickering dangerously close. One of the officers gave it some sort of command and it reared back, hissing.

The officer turned to the group and bowed low. As he straightened, his hood fell back, revealing the glowing banded gemstone in his forehead. The General himself! His black eyes glittered, and black diamonds veined his hands and jaw.

"I am pleased," he said, "to welcome you, on behalf of the First Flame and the Archons, to the Fortress." He made the sign of the flame to his visitors, lifting his steepled fingers in the air.

"We thank you, General Sardonyx," Chalcedon replied, and made the sign of the flame in return. It was chilling to watch. "These two are my cadets," he added, indicating Neil and Astra. "Two youngsters from one of the Ash-Gatherer villages. You must excuse their village manners. They have joined my entourage only recently."

"You may be assured that, as our guests, your stay here will be a pleasant one," the General said. He swung his black gaze in their direction and smiled, revealing teeth like mottled pebbles, chipped and uneven. Neil had never seen such a terrifying smile.

But Astra drew herself to her full height and met his gaze. "Thank you, sir," she said. "We would expect no less."

The Gribbhålla began to laugh, its shrieks and cackles echoing round the walls from its three mouths.

The Fortress of Flame

The General led the way with Chalcedon beside him, the ranks of soldiers parting to let them pass. The Gate clanged shut behind them. As they moved forward through the phalanx of troops, Neil trembled with fear. Would any of the soldiers recognize him? Would his code give him away?

Abruptly the old searing pain flickered in his ankle and leapt up his leg. Astra caught him just as it buckled under him.

"You've got to fight it!" she whispered, her voice shaking. "Don't let them see!"

Neil pulled himself upright with what felt like superhuman effort and took a step forward. It was agonizing, like walking on knives. He clenched his teeth and focused all his attention on trying to walk normally.

On the opposite side of the vast courtyard was a high stone archway that buzzed with crackling light. The General tapped something on his belt and the crackling ceased. "Chalcedon has requested," he said, giving another of his terrifying smiles, "that I show you round the Fortress. No doubt, General"—he bowed again to Chalcedon—"you will want to see the scale of our production facilities."

"Indeed, yes." Chalcedon gave a curt nod, and the little group stepped through the archway into a wide stone corridor that branched off dizzyingly into others. Soldiers in their flame-marked uniforms erupted round corners and hurried past in both directions, glancing covertly at the strangers. With the General once more leading the way, the group walked along corridors and up and down stairways until Neil and Astra were completely disoriented. At one point, with the General and Chalcedon far ahead of them, Neil suddenly stopped and leaned against the wall.

"I can't go on," he muttered. "I can't do it anymore."

"But you have to." Astra looked anxiously at his face, white and beaded with sweat. "You have to, Neil." Freya whined softly and nudged him with her nose. "Freya's telling you the same thing. We can't let them—"

"*There* you are!" It was Lieutenant Galena, coming back down the hall, his irritated expression changing to surprise. "Are you all right?" he asked. For Neil, still leaning against the wall, was bending over and clutching his leg and mumbling to himself.

"He's just—it's all been a little too much for him," said Astra hastily. "So many things have happened since we left our village, and—well, it's just caught up with us." Which had the benefit of being at least partly the truth.

Lieutenant Galena nodded. "Very well. I'll send for assistance." The next thing they knew, a floating chair appeared, made of some incredibly light metal and steered by a young soldier. Neil, still clutching his leg, was helped onto it.

"Take him to the officers' quarters," the lieutenant commanded. "And bring him to the Temple when he's feeling better." The soldier snapped to attention and made the sign of the flame.

"Freya and I have to go with him," Astra said firmly. "He won't get better otherwise."

Lieutenant Galena hesitated, then nodded. They soon found themselves in a brightly lit clinic, where a smiling young woman in a flame-coloured lab coat handed Neil two orange pills and a glass of water. "These will soothe and give energy," she told him. Neil drank them down obediently. Almost immediately the colour began returning to his face, and he lifted his head and actually smiled.

"You look so much better," Astra said, relieved, as Freya licked Neil's hand. "Are you sure you don't need to lie down for a while?" Neil had climbed out of the floating chair and stood there looking round wonderingly.

"These pills," said the woman condescendingly, "are instantaneous. Not like your village remedies."

"I feel fine," Neil said to Astra. "Fantastic. Really." The searing pain had completely gone, and the seasick feeling in his stomach.

The young soldier led them along a corridor where a narrow tube-like opening rose up through the floors of the building. When he touched something on his belt, a large transparent bubble floated down the opening and hovered near the floor. Neil and Astra watched in astonishment as the soldier reached out and poked the bubble. It dimpled like a balloon and then split open.

"Please, enter the CloudTube," the soldier said in strongly accented English.

After a moment's hesitation, Astra stepped in, amazed to find it bore her weight. But Freya rooed loudly and wouldn't budge.

"Come on, silly girl," said Neil. "Don't tell me you're afraid!" He had to lift her in. She cowered between his legs, her ears flat against her skull.

At once the opening sealed over and the CloudTube began rising up through the column of air. It travelled almost to the top of the Fortress in mere seconds, coming to rest at the edge of a platform. The three of them stepped out into a vast empty room, its marble floor stretching away before them. Thousands of shelves lined the walls from floor to ceiling, each crammed with tiny glass vials. In the centre of the floor was a gigantic bowl-shaped hollow, and beside it a massive altar of black onyx and rubies.

Neil and Astra stared around them in awe, trying to take it all in. "Where is everyone?" Astra said aloud, puzzled.

"And why did they bring us up here?" Neil wanted to know. He'd barely spoken when a door at the far end of the room opened. The General, followed by Chalcedon and Lieutenant Galena, strode toward them.

"I see our treatments have had their effect," the General said to Neil, looking at him closely and smiling that mottled smile.

"Those pills are amazing." I'll have to be careful not to give anything away, Neil thought. "They made me feel better at once."

"We've made some of the greatest advances in knowledge in the history of humankind," the General said expansively. "Not only in medicine, but in other fields, such as transportation, as you saw with the CloudTube. To develop that we partnered with CloudCorp. It's the corporation that now owns the clouds."

Neil shuddered. Owning the clouds! It was absurd. But the General, barely pausing, swept his hand grandly round the room. "This is our Temple. The second of our temples—the first is in the City, where the First Flame and the Archons preside." He pointed to the bowl-shaped hollow in the floor. "And here is where we light our ceremonial fires from the Flame of Truth, which burns day and night. Please, go closer. Take a look."

A small flame flickered in the very centre of the bowl. As Neil and Astra approached it, the General crossed to the nearest shelf and lifted down a vial. "Here is also where we keep the Archives of Fire-Reaped Tree Species—the evidence of our labours," he said proudly. "They are duplicates of those stored at the First Temple."

"But—it just looks like ash," said Astra, as the General approached and handed her the vial.

"Indeed." The General nodded with satisfaction. "This ash was taken from the burning of the Black Forest in Tysklandia, as the label states. We have vials from various parts of Nordlandia, too. Including"—he glanced casually at Neil—"the area known as Beaufortia."

Neil stared at the back of the General's neck as he turned to look reverently at the walls of vials. Could he have found out—? No. It wasn't possible. Was it? Neil felt a chill. He didn't dare look at Astra, in case he let on that he'd noticed.

"Each vial represents one of our redemptions throughout the planet of Terrania," the General went on. "We have very early samples of forest-burning from the Drear Lands, which are now, of course, uninhabited. We were assisted there, of course, by the planetary redemption already underway—what you would call 'climate change.'"

"It's certainly a—a remarkable collection," Astra said bravely, handing the vial back. It had been all she could do to hold onto it without throwing up. So it was really true, what they were up to. She hadn't quite believed it before. They really were burning forests all over the world. She'd held the proof—the residue of tree corpses—in her hand. It was insane. Yet the man in front of them didn't look insane. He looked vain and proud and rather pleased with himself.

"Remarkable indeed," Chalcedon broke in, nodding. He took down one of the vials himself and studied it closely. He's doing a very good job of acting, thought Astra approvingly.

"Shall we continue our tour?" the General said, and turned toward the ceremonial fire pit, his black eyes glittering. Astra, who was closest, saw the tiny flame flickering in them for a moment. "Now what would you like to see first? Our Weapons Research Laboratories? Or what about"—and he spun round, his face a grinning mask—"our hidden Weapons Production Facility, two kilometres underground, from which no one has ever yet escaped?"

All at once—the General must have given some signal—hidden doors in the walls burst open. Dozens of Fire Reaper troops stormed into the room, brandishing their weapons. Freya, barking furiously, charged toward the soldiers, and Neil grabbed his SerraTube. But it was too late. The troops seized him and Astra and handcuffed them. They chained Freya to the wall while Chalcedon stood and watched with Lieutenant Galena, a satisfied smile on his face.

"You planned this all along!" Astra spat out, glaring at Chalcedon. "You *traitor!*"

222

"You needed all these soldiers for two kids and a dog?" Neil said, though his voice trembled.

Chalcedon turned to the General, still with that maddening smile. "It seems rather cowardly, don't you think, Sardonyx," he said, "to send mere children to do their dirty work?"

The General crossed his arms and gazed at them with contempt. "You should be pleased to have such an impressive escort to your new quarters," he said, and gave a long, chilling laugh that had echoes of the Gribbhålla's laughter in it.

"How could you?" Astra shouted at Chalcedon. "How could you go over to their side? How could—?" But that was as far as she got, because a soldier clapped a hand over her mouth and began dragging her away. She struggled and fought, but it was no use. They were dragging a shouting Neil away, too. The last thing he heard was Freya's yelping and howling as he was carried, still struggling, through a doorway.

He came to in darkness. He was lying on damp ground somewhere, and from a distance came the whine of metal on metal, the shriek and clang of machinery. His head was splitting; they must have hit him, or given him something that knocked him out. Slowly he became aware of another noise—that piercing, humming sound they'd first heard outside the Fortress, only louder and closer. And to top it all off there was a horrible smell of sulphur and burnt rubber and other things he couldn't identify.

He pushed himself into a sitting position. His handcuffs had been removed, but his wrists were scraped and bruised and he felt battered all over. He must be in some sort of jail cell. The General's last words slowly surfaced in his throbbing head. *Our hidden Weapons Production Facility, two kilometres underground, from which no one has ever yet escaped ...*

That might explain the horrible smell and the machinery noises. He must be somewhere far below the earth, trapped along with the thousands of slaves who were forced to work in this place. Was Astra here somewhere, too? And Freya? He felt a rush of bleak despair.

He began crawling forward slowly on his hands and knees. The uneven ground was muddy and runnelled with water. Something ran past him, squeaking, and disappeared. Mice, or rats. His skin crawled. All of a sudden his shoulder made contact with metal. He felt along it until he came to an edge, then stood and let his fingers travel upward to a corner. Yes—a door. He pounded on it with his fists, knowing it was useless.

"Well, you *have* got yourself in a pickle, haven't you?"

Piedra! In the horror of the last hours he'd forgotten him. "Am I ever glad to see you!" he said with feeling, fishing in his pocket for the familiar grainy stone.

"I got jostled around thoroughly while they searched you, let me tell you," Piedra said, and Neil could have sworn that his copper vein was sending out angry sparks. "Needless to say, they attached no importance to a mere *stone*."

Neil felt for his belt and gave a cry of alarm. It was gone— and the SerraTube with it.

"You didn't expect them to let you keep it, did you?" sniffed Piedra. "They took the Etheric Sensor, too, of course. Chalcedon was able to tell them all about it, I'm sorry to say."

Neil swallowed hard. "What's happened to Astra? And Freya?"

Piedra gave one of his operatic, long-suffering sighs. "They took the girl child and Freya off to the Weapons Research Laboratories. Or so they said. And then they threw you in this cell."

Neil's blood ran cold. The Research Laboratories! What kinds of things did they do there? He clenched his fists, feeling sick and helpless.

"I *could* say I told you so," said Piedra. "However, I'll refrain. As you made quite clear, the task was yours and Astra's. I was hardly going to interfere with unwanted advice."

"Thanks a lot," Neil said sarcastically. "You might have 'interfered' when we got in trouble."

"And when, exactly, would that have been? I seem to recall telling you not to go along with Chalcedon's plan. Of course neither of you wanted to listen."

Neil was about to reply angrily when he remembered that he, too, had felt less than certain about the plan. "None of us could have guessed what Chalcedon was *really* up to," he said gloomily, by way of reassuring himself.

"I think we might say," said Piedra, "that we've jumped out of the frying pan into the fire. The *fire*, get it?" And he gave a hollow laugh.

"It isn't funny, Piedra."

"You don't need to tell *me*, my boy. Believe me, I've been in tight spots before, but this time I'm squeaking."

"Then what are we going to do?"

"I'm afraid, at the moment, I don't know. As Guldsterre told you, the General is a formidable enemy. And now he has a formidable ally."

"But how could Chalcedon have done that, Piedra? How could he betray his own sister? And all the other Mínera Beings? And everyone who's fighting against—?"

"Yes, yes, yes, child. You've come up against true evil for the first time, I'm afraid. Or perhaps I should say the absence of light, for where there is fear and ignorance, light cannot enter."

At that moment they heard heavy bootsteps coming toward the door and a grating being opened. A strange red light flooded in and a hand thrust a dish through the opening.

"Hey! Aqua Libere spy! Here's your slop!"

"I'm not a spy!" Neil shouted angrily, jumping up to grab the plate. But the grating had already slammed shut and the guard was striding away. Neil sat down miserably. He couldn't see the food, but it smelled revoltingly like boiled spinach.

"Now you must eat, even if it's terrible," Piedra said firmly. "Humans cannot function without fuel."

If he says one more thing about being a poorly designed life form, I'm going to—I don't know, stand him on his head. But Piedra held his tongue for once, and Neil began picking at the food. It was impossible to tell what it was, and he pushed his plate away.

"We need a plan, Piedra." He changed position to ease his aching ribs. "Is there any way we can get in touch with Áilu and the Many Beings?"

"From inside a Fire Reaper building, no—their powers are too strong."

"I know!" Neil sat up straighter. "I'll see if I can roll you under the door, and you can check things out."

"Now that," Piedra said crossly, "is the most ridiculous suggestion I've ever heard. In the first place, you're not rolling me anywhere. You *need* me. And in the second place, it won't work. Even if it were possible, you'd probably set off an alarm. Not to mention," he added in a lower voice, "the fact that they are no doubt listening to our conversation somewhere."

Neil sagged in defeat. He'd been clinging tightly to his last shreds of courage, but this was too much.

"Now let me think, and don't interrupt," Piedra said sharply. "I have no intention of spending my last several thousand years in a Fire Reaper prison."

Astra, too, had woken an hour or so before, but not in darkness. She was lying on some sort of table, her arms and legs strapped down, in a room so brilliantly lit she could hardly open her eyes. Her skull was pounding—had they hit her over the head?—and she felt woozy and sick to her stomach. She yanked at the straps, but they refused to yield. Panic rose in her chest and she forced herself to breathe.

Where was she? And what were they going to do with her?

She lifted her head as high as she could and strained to look round. Against the far wall were cages containing white rats, several tiny orange monkeys, a pacing lynx, and a large falcon that stared at her with its fierce golden eyes. And there, in the farthest corner, was Freya, lying with her head on her paws.

"Freya! Freya girl!" she called, softly, eagerly. Freya lifted her head, sat up, her eyes fixed on Astra's face, and rooed. Then she pawed at the mesh and began pacing, whining softly.

"We'll find a way to get out of here, Freya," said Astra, with a determination she was a long way from feeling. "Just as soon as I can think of something." But what that something might be she had no idea.

The door opened and several people in white lab coats hurried in, the Fire Reaper emblem on their sleeves. None of them even so much as looked at Astra. "Hey!" she called. "Come and let me up, at least!" But they quickly disappeared into different parts of the lab. Astra was left to stare at the ceiling for what seemed like ages, her limbs stiffening in the straps, trying not to worry about what might happen. Or where Neil was.

Much, much later the door opened again. More people in lab coats, followed by several Fire Reaper officers and guards. Last of all came the General himself, sweeping in with his flame-emblazoned cloak billowing behind him. He stood beside the table, the sardonyx in his forehead glittering in the lights, an amused look on his face.

"Where am I?" Astra gave another yank to the straps. "Why am I tied down like this?"

"I see you've lost none of your feistiness, my dear. I'm glad our little *contretemps* has had so little effect."

"You're not going to win, you know. There's too many—"

But the General's chilling laugh broke in. "Very prettily said. But alas, there are many forces arrayed against you. And more importantly, we have the Truth on our side." He leaned toward her, his breath smelling like pond scum. "Our victory is not in question. And it may be sooner than you think."

"Where's Neil? What have you done with Neil?" She was trembling and the metallic fabric of the straps bit into her arms.

"He's quite safe and unharmed. There's no need to distress yourself." The General paused and folded his arms. "I have a little proposal to make."

"Let me up first."

The General raised his eyebrows, then gave one of his mottled smiles and gave an order to two of the lab workers. Once unfastened, Astra sat up slowly, rubbing her chafed wrists. Her head still throbbed and the room was spinning dizzily.

"Suppose," said the General, "I were to offer you a way of seeing your father?"

Her *father*? Her mind whirled. "Where is he? Is he here?"

"Not here in the Fortress. He's assisting us with our research elsewhere."

"You're lying. He'd *never* do that. Ever!"

The General gave a low chuckle and looked round at his officers, who grinned. "Your loyalty and courage are admirable. But you are also a child. You haven't yet grasped that everyone"—he leaned very close, his foul breath in her face again—"has a price."

"You're wrong," Astra said. "My father doesn't."

The General straightened and his smile disappeared. "Your father understands that if he wishes no harm to come to you, it is in his best interests to cooperate."

"NO!" shouted Astra, leaping off the table as two of the officers seized her. One clapped his gloved hand over her mouth as she struggled.

"Do keep your voice down," the General said mildly. "Your shouting upsets the animals." And indeed the monkeys were gibbering and Freya was howling. Astra was forced to sit, and as the room quietened, the General said, "Now, perhaps you'd like to hear my proposal." He fixed her with his glittering black-diamond eyes. "As you may or may not know, you are presently in the Research Laboratories. Our scientists here are responsible, among other things, for the development of new warrior beings. The first Gribbhållas were bred here, and the early prototypes of the Vampyriae."

He began to pace with excitement. "We are now engaged in a new and much more ambitious project, one with far-reaching implications. We need your assistance. Assistance that only you, as Hallvard's daughter, can provide."

"I'm not helping you with anything," Astra said, though her voice quavered.

The General folded his arms and regarded her evenly. "I give you my word that, if you agree to assist us, you'll be permitted to see your father. If not ..." The General sighed. "I'm afraid it may make your father's situation more difficult."

An icy finger traced Astra's spine. "My father hasn't done anything wrong!"

"He is a prisoner," the General said curtly. "As—may I remind you—are you."

Could she play for time? Pretend she'd go along with them? Her breath was coming in shallow spurts. "What do you want me to do?" she said slowly.

"We understand," the General said, "that you were your father's apprentice in his research work. We know, moreover, that you were particularly adept at using the device you call the Memory Stone—which is now, of course, in our possession." He paused as if to wait for his statement to sink in. "We would like your assistance in continuing that work."

"I just did what my father told me," Astra said, a little unsteadily. *Where* is *the Stone? Maybe they don't know it needs pixillite* ... "Besides, I thought you said he—"

"He is assisting us. But we will progress more rapidly with your help. We want to achieve manifestation from the past as rapidly as possible."

"We don't know how to do that."

"I realize," the General said a little sharply, "that you are not there yet. That is why we would like your help." He stared past her, his eyes glittering. "Our goal is to be able to manifest that most beautiful of all beings—fire."

Astra felt her heart beat faster. "Fire?"

"If we can manifest all the fire that has ever existed in the world"—the General was still staring past her, his eyes fierce—"then we can achieve our goals quickly. You can be part of our noble plan. The sooner this world is destroyed, the sooner a newer and better one can rise from the ashes."

A little burst of clapping broke out from the assembled officers. Astra shuddered. *They're* all *insane. Completely, totally insane.*

"In return," the General said, his gaze returning to her, "you will be allowed to spend time with your father."

It was all Astra could do to keep her voice level. "Where is he? And why should I trust you anyway?"

"I can produce your father tomorrow if you wish. He's been taken to our headquarters in the City." The General gave a little chuckle. "I'm told he finds our beliefs compelling. He's taking instruction from the First Flame himself. General Chalcedon is—how shall I put it?—assisting him."

"I don't believe it!" shouted Astra, quite forgetting about disturbing the animals. "I don't believe any of it! You're a *monster*! You're horrible and cruel and evil and—"

The General drew back his gloved hand and slapped her, hard, across the face. Tears of anger and pain pricked her eyes.

"I'm surprised," the General said, straightening his jacket, "at your manners. Really, what do these *intellectuals*"—he spat out the word—"teach their children?" Astra shrank back as he loomed over her. "You're lucky I'm a forgiving being. However, you'll remain here until we decide what to do with you." He paused at the door, a look of contempt on his face. "In the meantime you and the dog object can commune with each other."

He strode out, followed by his men, and the lock clicked shut behind them.

Astra Makes a Discovery

They came for him, or so Neil thought, in the early hours of the morning, though it was impossible to tell what time it was. They clapped handcuffs on him and dragged him out of the cell and up stairs and along passageways. He vomited once, whether out of fear or lack of food—he still wasn't eating what they brought—he didn't know. And then he was hauled into a small, brightly lit room where a heavyset officer with a shaved head and pale eyelashes sat at a desk, watching impassively. The guards pushed him into a chair in front of the desk. The officer consulted some papers, and without looking at him said, "Nee-ill. Nee-ill Grez-koo. That is your name?"

Neil nodded, blinking. The lights hurt his eyes after the long hours of darkness and he couldn't think properly.

"Speak up!" the officer said sharply.

"Yes," said Neil, clearing his throat. "Actually, it's pronounced—"

"We have information, Grezkoo, that you are a spy for the Aqua Libere. Is this true?"

"No," Neil said firmly. "I don't even know who the Aqua Libere are. I mean, I've never met them."

"We have information," the officer said, his lip curling, "that you were seen in the company of the Fossefallen, who are protected by the Aqua Libere, on the banks of the Svaer River."

Information that could only have come from Chalcedon, of course. A bad omen, the soldiers had said when they'd seen the Fossefallen. "They showed up after we crossed the river," Neil protested. "They were angry with us because—"

But the officer cut him off again. "Misleading the interrogator will only lead to further punishment. Were you or were you not resident in the Ash-Gatherer village known as Ashgård, where the populace regarded you as a spy?"

"Yes, but—"

"And do you or do you not bear an ankle code that marks you as a former prisoner of the Fire Reapers of Planetary Redemption?"

"Yes, but—"

"And did you or did you not escape custody when you were a prisoner, thereby proving that you are in fact a child spy of the Aqua Libere?"

"No!" shouted Neil. "I mean, yes, I escaped, but—"

The officer waved a dismissive hand. "Take him away and arrange for his transfer."

"But you're wrong! It's all wrong! It's not true!" The guards had already seized his arms and were dragging him away. "Look, I can prove it! I'm not from Nordlandia at all! I've come from the past, I don't know anything about—"

The officer looked up from his papers wearily. "Don't waste your breath with that preposterous story, Grezkoo. We know the truth. Hallvard's daughter told us everything."

It was very late in the evening when the janitor came in, as he usually did, to clean the lab and feed and water the animals. He was a stocky, elderly man from the Custodial Unit, made up of slaves who were too old or worn out to work on the weapons production lines. Cleaning the lab was his favourite task—though he'd made sure no one guessed—because it meant he could talk to and touch the animals. They reminded him a little of freedom, and his homeland, and what life had been like before he was captured.

He was astonished, this evening, to discover a child fast asleep on the lab floor. The delicate features, and the hair cut short in female Nordlandian fashion, suggested a girl. Who was she, and what on earth was she doing here? She wore some sort of vest with a strange symbol on it and Ash-Gatherer clothes underneath. And she was curled up beside a cage containing a new arrival—a golden dog.

His heart lightened at the sight of the dog. He pressed his fingers against the mesh, and the animal tentatively wagged its tail and licked his hand. Then he bent over the child. There were traces of tears on her face. She must have cried herself to sleep. Best to let her stay asleep, then. He fetched a thermocover from a cupboard and spread it over her.

But in turning to his tasks he knocked over a flask on the counter. The child sat up, blinking in the light. When she saw him in his Fire Reaper slave uniform—orange, with red and yellow flames licking at the legs and sleeves—she cowered against the cage.

"Don't worry," he said, in the New Nordlandish he'd pains-takingly learned. "I won't hurt you. I'm just here to clean up." Oddly, she didn't seem to understand him, so he repeated what he'd said in UL. It felt strange to speak his own language; many of the slaves spoke no UL, and most of the guards spoke only Nordlandish. "Who are you?" he said. "And how did you end up in here?"

But she only backed even closer to the cage, her fingers wound through the mesh. She must be with the dog. Perhaps it had been captured with her. An awful thought struck him. "Listen, kid. They're not using you in one of their experiments, are they?"

She still didn't answer. Perhaps she didn't understand UL either. He squatted down near her. "See, I'm not a Fire Reaper," he said softly. "I'm a slave. This here's the slave uniform. But if you tell me who you are—well, maybe I can help."

She stared at him, her eyes troubled. The dog rooed softly and pawed at the mesh, and he reached through so it could lick his fingers again. Its strong shoulders and alert expression reminded him of a long-ago dog of his own.

"I came here because of a special task," she said suddenly—maybe because the dog had trusted him. So she understood him after all. "It's too complicated to explain."

He shook his head, even more puzzled about where this child had come from. "What's your name?"

"Astra. And this is Freya." She indicated the dog. "What's yours?"

"Charlie. Back home they call me Tombstone Charlie."

Tombstone Charlie? What a strange name! Though she'd heard it somewhere before, she thought.

"Where are *you* from?" she asked. "Your accent—it's different."

The man called Tombstone Charlie gave a rueful grin. "I'm from what you call Beaufortia. But if I told you how I got here, you wouldn't believe me."

Beaufortia ... Tombstone Charlie ... Of course! "Neil told me all about you," she said, suddenly animated. "He told us about the tunnel in the smoke and how he got here from the past and how maybe you were here too. And you are!"

He was staring at her, baffled. Of course, Astra thought—he can't possibly know about Neil being here or how I met him. So she explained as best she could how Neil and Freya had arrived in Ashgård, and how some people suspected he was a spy, and how the three of them had escaped after the village was attacked by Fire Reaper troops.

A growing light seemed to illumine Charlie's face. "Well, whaddaya know," he said. "I never thought ... Boy, was I careless. Shoulda closed down that tunnel, I guess. Except I didn't know how."

"But you're the one who found it, aren't you?" Astra said, confused.

"It was an accident," Charlie admitted. "I'd been readin' about time travel and tryin' out all kinds of things. Alchemy, quantum physics, you name it. And then one night—kazoom!—I find myself in Nordlandia. In the City."

234

"In the City!" Astra breathed. "What happened?"

"Well, no one believed my story about comin' from the past, for a start. I thought time travel would be no big deal by now." Charlie shook his head ruefully. "Which was why I came to the future in the first place. I figured there'd be a lot to learn."

"That's what my father was working on—time travel," Astra said eagerly. "He's a famous research scientist."

"Holy moly!" Charlie rubbed a hand wonderingly over his close-cropped head. "I sure hit paydirt when I met you. So much stuff went arsey-turvey after I came through that—well, I figured I'd really screwed up." He gave a wry smile and shook his head again as if to clear it, then grew serious. "So where's this Neil now?"

"He's a prisoner, like me. Here in the Fortress somewhere." She decided not to say anything more about their special mission. Áilu had warned her not to, and then she'd gone and told Chalcedon about the Etheric Sensor, and look where that had got her.

"Then we gotta find him," Charlie said sombrely. "If they think he's a spy, and he escaped from them once before, he's in real danger."

Astra's heart flipped over. "I know. But what can we do?"

"You leave it to me. We gotta come up with some skookum plan. Just you try and make sure they don't take you someplace else in the meantime."

He was a strange man, she reflected after he'd gone. She'd never heard words like skookum and paydirt before. Olden-day words from the distant past. Still, she had a gut feeling about Tombstone Charlie that reassured her. After all, Freya had rooed at him and wagged her tail.

Neil stood at the end of his chain and peered through the thick, acrid smoke on Line 54, trying to make out faces. It seemed too much to hope that Hallvard or Fru Berta might be here. But some of the other captives from Ashgård might have ended up in this vast underground weapons factory—Dr. Forberg, perhaps, or Mayor Landholm, or one of the councillors. Perhaps they were mere metres away, chained like him to their particular cauldron. It would be some relief, in this horrible place, to know he wasn't completely alone. He didn't even have Piedra anymore—though he could imagine what Piedra might have thought about finding himself here.

"Get moving, you piece of vermin!" an overseer yelled, striding toward him with his whip raised. Neil shuffled once more toward the massive cauldron, where the disgusting-smelling sludge they called tirillium was bubbling away. The smell—the same one he'd noticed in his jail cell, only a thousand times stronger—made him sick to his stomach. And there was that awful humming again, too. It seemed to crawl inside his head, like some dreadful itch he couldn't scratch.

Together with the other slaves, he began hauling on the giant levers that raised the cauldron from the fire pit to the transport rails high above them. Suddenly it tipped and some of the molten liquid splashed a slave on the other side. He screamed and dropped his lever, and as the overseers shouted and yelled and applied their whips, it was all the rest of them could do to steady the rocking pot. At last it reached the rails, where other slaves began clamping it in place for its journey to another part of the factory. Still others were guiding a new cauldron onto the fire pit.

Neil slumped back, exhausted. Already it felt as though he'd never known any other life than this stinking, belching inferno. His orange slave uniform was crusted with dirt and sweat, and he had a livid welt on one arm from standing too close to the fire pit. He'd have been better off in the Truth Chamber after all. That was where they'd taken him after the interview with the officer who said he was lying. They'd taken away all his clothes, too, including his tunic, though he'd begged them for it. Poor Piedra! What was he going to do without him?

Afterward they'd strapped him down on a narrow metal table and angled a blinding light into his eyes and taken turns asking him questions. Always the same questions, though there were many different questioners. *Tell us about the Aqua Libere's plans to attack Fire Reaper facilities. Give us the names of your leaders. Explain exactly how you are allied with the Arbolé and the Bestia and the Mínera Beings.* They'd threatened him with worse treatment when he couldn't give them the answers they wanted. "We specialize in fire," one of the interrogators told him softly. "We'll leave you to imagine how we might use it to make you talk."

Then they changed their tack. Other interrogators came in and began asking him about Hallvard and his work as a research scientist and why he'd been in Ashgård. They said that Astra had already told them everything, and they simply wanted to confirm her information. Neil was sure they were lying. But as time wore on, and the light made him nauseous and dizzy, and he couldn't think properly, he decided she must have cracked. He moved past hunger and thirst and became a hollow, empty shell, so fragile that a breath could have blown him away. They kept telling him they knew all about the Memory Stone, that Astra had told them how it worked, that it was pointless to protect her. They told him that Hallvard was now in the City, assisting them with their research. He found himself in despair, then resentful, then furious. Why had they given in when he hadn't?

And then, all of a sudden, the interrogation stopped. They unstrapped him from the table and allowed him to use the bathroom and gave him a meal—moodfood, but he didn't care, he was ravenous. He overheard one interrogator telling another something about orders from high up and how it was obvious he was a low-value suspect. And then they placed him in some sort of elevator that went down, down, down, and handed him over to the guards on Line 54.

He wiped the dripping black sweat from his forehead and bent wearily, unthinkingly, to the lever.

It was late the next day before anyone came into the lab. Astra's stomach was growling with hunger, and Freya lay listlessly in her cage. Only the monkeys periodically shrieked and gibbered, as if trying to attract attention. To distract herself, Astra paced up and down, trying to prepare herself for whatever might happen next. Maybe, if she agreed to cooperate—at least for now—they'd let her stay exactly where she was. That way she could keep an eye on Freya and talk to Charlie on his next round. She tried not to think about Neil, or what might be happening to him.

But how long was she to be left here? Were they going to let her starve? She closed her eyes and tried to summon a memory of her mother, the way she always saw her when she was Stone-dwelling. But the memory was pale and faded, like the old photographs her grandmother had hidden away under the floor coverings in their house. That was the problem with Stone memories; they were so vivid they erased the originals. Her father sometimes said the Stone "owned" the memories it summoned.

So instead she thought about her grandmother, her firm, no-nonsense Amma, with her strong, competent hands and her soft skin. It was Amma who'd first told her stories about the olden days, the stories that were now called myths. Such as the one about white stuff that fell out of the sky. Amma claimed that her own great-great-great-grandmother—Astra couldn't remember how many greats—had *seen* the white stuff, had even worn wooden sticks on her feet to walk on it! Astra hadn't believed her. And it was Amma who'd made Astra swear to tell no one, not even her father, about the old-style books and photographs she kept hidden. It was a criminal offence to keep private records of any kind. Only those issued by the Department of Memory were permitted.

She was jolted out of her thoughts by the sound of the door

being unlocked. To her surprise, it wasn't the General who stood there but two women, one of them in the uniform of a Fire Reaper officer. She was tall and blonde, and her upper sleeve bore the word *Flamme-Véurr* and four stylized flames. The other woman, shorter and darker, appeared to be from the United Chinese Empire. She wore the clothing of a City businesswoman—the short high-collared jacket and flowing pants made from expensive tildein, a material far beyond the pocketbook of the average City dweller. Tildein, so Astra's father had explained, was made from an indestructible alloy of several non-Terranian metals, kept the wearer cool no matter the heat outside, could be changed to a different colour through thought, and was self-cleaning.

The Fire Reaper officer stepped forward. She radiated quiet power without any of the General's cruel hauteur. "You are probably very hungry," she said, in a gentle voice. "We have ordered you a meal. I am Flame-Protector Vígdís of the 56th Lumini Regiment, and this is Corporatist Sirikit Thonkorn. She is the Chief Executive Officer of the GalaxTec Mining Corporation."

Corporatist Thonkorn, smiling, held out her hand, and Astra shook it cautiously. She had no idea why the head of the GalaxTec Mining Corporation should be introduced to her, but it seemed prudent to be polite. She tried to keep her mind light and clear and focused.

"GalaxTec," went on Flame-Protector Vígdís, "has signed a contract with us to be the sole supplier of the mineral pixillite, which, as you know, is found only on the asteroid Antikleia."

Pixillite? Why were they telling her about pixillite? Her knees trembled and she pressed them together to make them stop.

"Flame-Protector Vígdís negotiated the agreement with us on behalf of her people," Corporatist Thonkorn said. She placed her hands together in prayer position and bowed slightly to the officer, her almond eyes lustrous and soft. "It has been a most productive relationship."

"And since our contract specifies exclusive access," the

Flame-Protector added, nodding at Corporatist Thonkorn, "we've made certain it won't fall into the wrong hands."

They must have found out that pixillite was needed to power the Memory Stone—but how? The Stone's pixillite level had been almost flat after Neil used it. Had her father been forced to tell them? If only she and Neil had thought to grab the Stone before they'd raced upstairs the day of the attack! She felt her throat clog up.

"You may be wondering," Flame-Protector Vígdís was saying smoothly, "why we are telling you all this." She paused for effect. "Once we recharged the pixillite level of the Memory Stone, we expected to be able to operate it with any trained user. Unfortunately, that has not been the case."

So either her father had refused to help them, or whoever he'd been forced to train couldn't get the Stone to work.

"That is why we are turning to you," Flame-Protector Vígdís continued. "We know you are an expert, and the Stone can be recharged whenever necessary."

So now they're trying to flatter me and bully me at the same time. Astra took a deep breath. "Okay, I'll help you," she said, a little unsteadily. "On two conditions."

Corporatist Thonkorn gasped. "Really, you are not in a position to bargain," Flame-Protector Vígdís said, looking displeased. "Besides, this is your opportunity to redeem yourself, despite your friendship with an Aqua Libere spy."

"He's not a spy!" said Astra vehemently. "He doesn't even belong in our world. He got here by accident—"

"Ah yes." Flame-Protector Vígdís steepled her fingers together and smiled, as if at a private joke. "That ridiculous story about being from the past."

"He is from the past," Astra blurted out, adding impulsively, "We materialized him." As soon as she'd said it she regretted it, but it was too late. Flame-Protector Vígdís and Corporatist Thonkorn exchanged glances, and Flame-Protector Vígdís's left eyebrow rose slightly.

"I see. We understood that you had not yet achieved that stage."

"Well, it was sort of an—an accident," Astra said, trying desperately to backtrack. "I mean, we weren't able to duplicate it."

"Nevertheless, you apparently succeeded in the permanent materialization of a human." Flame-Protector Vígdís's eyes narrowed. "Or am I to understand you are lying?"

Uh oh. Now she'd done it. *You watch that impulsive tongue of yours*—how often had Fru Berta said that to her?

"No. I mean yes. I mean—"

"If I may make a suggestion, Flame-Protector Vígdís." Corporatist Thonkorn stepped forward, her eyes no longer lustrous but steely. "Perhaps the child could give us a demonstration? That would leave no doubt about her ability to assist us."

A small smile flickered around Flame-Protector Vígdís's lips. "A most apt suggestion, Corporatist Thonkorn. We will arrange to have the Stone brought here at once. How soon can the next shipment of pixillite be delivered?"

"By eight hundred hours." Corporatist Thonkorn bowed her head, her hands once more in prayer position. "I will send thought immediately." She took a devcom from her breast pocket and held it to her temple, letting her thoughts enter it for transmission.

"I won't be able to work," Astra said quickly, "if I'm worrying about Neil. You have to agree not to harm him."

Flame-Protector Vígdís frowned and folded her arms. "I need hardly state how inappropriate your request is. Whatever the origin of the boy, he is an enemy of the state. He must be kept under the closest surveillance." She gave Astra a long, appraising look. "I am not authorized to make such an agreement."

"And I have to stay here in the lab to do my work," added Astra. "With Freya"—she pointed to the cage—"right beside me instead of in there." Her heart was hammering so hard she was sure they could hear it.

Corporatist Thonkorn looked horrified. Flame-Protector

Vígdís's jaw tightened, and she tapped her foot. "I make that three conditions altogether. The boy, the location, and the dog object. Perhaps you were never taught to count." She stared coldly at Astra. "I will take your requests to the appropriate authorities. In return, you must agree to assist us for as long as we need you."

"And one more thing," Astra said, her heart in her throat. "The General told me I'd see my father if I helped you. I need to know he's okay."

Flame-Protector Vígdís looked as if she was going to explode. "You rejected the General's generous offer," she said icily. "I am not in a position—"

There was a knock at the door. A young soldier entered, guiding a floating tray laden with delicious-smelling dishes, and Astra remembered how hungry she was.

"Ah, your meal," said Flame-Protector Vígdís, turning her steely gaze on Astra. "We will leave you to enjoy it." She turned at the door with a contemptuous glance in Freya's direction. "No doubt you will want to share it with the dog object."

The Janitor Uses His Head

stra wolfed down the meal with both hands, pushing pieces through the mesh for Freya, who gulped them down ravenously. It wasn't moodfood but the kind of food she'd had only a few times in her life. There was some kind of fish, for example. Even in the City, fish was for special occasions only—you went to the Dietary Proteins Bondegård where you could buy small frozen chunks for an astronomical sum.

It crossed her mind that they could have drugged the meal, but she was too hungry to care. Besides, if they wanted her help, they were unlikely to do anything that might fog her brain.

She'd almost finished when a technician came to open Freya's cage. So they were going to agree to her conditions! As the door swung open, Freya practically leapt into her arms, rooing in excitement and licking her all over. "Freya Beya! Oh, Freya!" Astra said, laughing and crying and hugging Freya tight. Even the technician had to smile as Freya rooed again and then did a mad dash round the lab.

After the technician wheeled a cot in and placed it in a corner, a wave of exhaustion washed over her. So much had happened over the last couple of days—no wonder she was overspent, as Fru Berta would have said. But even lying on the cot with Freya curled in her arms, sleep eluded her. All she could think about was that stupid lie she'd told about Neil. She'd said it to protect him, to convince them that he really was from the past, but instead she'd made things worse. Much worse. How soon would they guess she was bluffing?

And where was Charlie? It was getting very late. Maybe he'd

had second thoughts about helping her—though that didn't explain why he hadn't come to do his chores. Had someone overheard them the night before? She glanced round the lab nervously, wondering if it was bugged.

Two of the monkeys in the nearest cage were picking lice off each other. The lynx lay with its magnificent head on its paws, its eyes half-closed. She'd noticed earlier how thin it looked. Perhaps it was refusing to eat. She got up to look for animal feed, but all the cupboards were locked. Why hadn't she shared her food with it?

She lay back down, feeling more miserable than ever.

They've got even more slaves down here, Charlie thought to himself as he maneuvered his way down the production lines. Many were from the Drear Lands, as before, but there were others from the Scattered Isles, from the VilderRegion, even—judging by appearances—from Antarctica and other Resettlement Areas. Though of course you couldn't always be certain. There'd been large-scale migration in the wake of the Great Catastrophes, or so he'd been told. Whole populations moving toward the Earth's—Terrania's—poles, while a wide belt that stretched round the middle of the planet was nothing but scorched desert, with temperatures so extreme that nothing could live there except a few drought-resistant plants.

He eased his way past a knot of overseers, but one turned and grabbed him by the arm. "Your ID," he barked in Old Nordlandish. Charlie, who'd long ago learned the basic Old Nordlandish commands, stood still as the guard held his ControlReader to the back of Charlie's skull. It gave off a series of beeps and barks. The guard glanced at the reader, grunted, then looked at Charlie with suspicion and back at the reader again. Something was fishy. Still, he let Charlie continue on his way.

The slaves had always found ways to take out or alter the earlier embedded microchips, but now that the codes were imprinted on a thin layer of skin, they were impossible to remove. Still, on slow nights when his chores didn't fill up his time, Charlie used a Coder he'd found forgotten in a washroom to figure out how to alter codes. The day before he'd been able to overprint his own code with a new one that allowed him access to the production lines.

He was pretty sure Neil was down here somewhere. He'd checked first in the holding cells in the Dungeon, and then in the various Truth Chambers on Floor 11, but had turned up nothing. Well, not quite nothing. Neil had certainly been interrogated in one of the Truth Chambers, some days before. Charlie had found some scraps of clothing in one of the Analysis Ports, glowing with radiation. He'd known it was Neil's because it looked like Astra's tunic, though all that was left of it was the collar and part of the inner lining. He searched the lining pocket. They wouldn't have missed anything, but still ... Nothing but a plain chunk of granite, just the kind of thing he'd have carried in his own pockets as a boy. He was about to put it back, but on second thought he tucked it in his uniform. Pointless, really, but he liked defying the Fire Reapers in small ways whenever he could.

He'd also checked with fellow slaves who worked at the Dematerialization Unit and whom he knew he could trust. No twelve-year-old boy had been delivered in the last few days. If the Fire Reapers suspected Neil of being a spy, he was too valuable to simply eliminate. No doubt they'd bring him back for more interrogation, just as they had Charlie. Besides, here was a boy who'd turned up claiming—just like Charlie had, three years ago—to be from the past. They'd be suspicious—and intrigued. Now that he came to think of it, maybe they'd want to question *him* again, too ...

In the intense heat of the production lines, the sweat was pouring off him, staining his uniform black. He'd forgotten just how bad it was down here. How had he ever lasted two-plus years in this hellhole of stinking smoke and back-breaking work? Not to mention that infernal white noise that prevented anyone from having a thought in their heads. It was a wonder more people didn't go mad. He'd only got out himself because he'd been badly burned in an accident when a pot cracked, and when he recovered they'd sent him to the Custodial Unit. He'd been lucky, really. He hoped Jean-Paul would remember to feed the lab animals when he finished his own shift. His fellow janitor could keep his mouth shut, but he was sometimes forgetful.

Charlie bent to pick up a piece of solidified tirillium from the floor. It was strangely attractive when it was solid—a shimmering blue. He stuck it in his pocket, with some vague idea of showing it to Astra to prove where he'd been in his search for Neil. To tell the truth, he wasn't sure why the Fire Reapers were keeping him around. They certainly had no compunction about getting rid of people. Maybe they had some idea that he might turn out to be useful after all. He'd been foolish enough to tell them where he came from when he'd been rescued from that Breathing Hole in the City's dome, which was where he'd landed after the smoke tunnel. They hadn't believed him, of course. So they'd clapped him in the City dungeons. When he managed to escape by bribing a guard, he knew it would be only a matter of time before he was recaptured, what with , with his odd clothing and the embedded code. The citizens of the City were far too frightened to help prisoners.

To think he'd made his way to the future, only to discover that the inhabitants knew even less than he did! They might be more technologically advanced in some ways, but they were barbarians. How had he ever dreamed up the idea, back in the Yukon, that they might have something to teach him?

There, on the next pot—wasn't that a child slave? But when he got close, he realized it was a Drear Lands child, his black skin ash-coloured from the dust and smoke. Charlie's heart sank. Over the last two days he'd worked his way, one by one, through the worst lines, the ones where slaves were sent first, and he was coming to the end of them. If Neil wasn't here ...

"Charlie!" He whirled at the sound of his name. A slave he knew from his days down here was signalling him urgently. "You are looking for a boy, no?" Karim whispered, his gaze darting round to make sure no overseer was in sight.

Charlie couldn't help smiling to himself. He ought to have counted on the slave grapevine sooner. "You know where he is?"

"Next line over—54. Pot number fifteen." Karim's gaze darted round again. "They are afraid of him, the guards. They call him *Tíð Sveinn*—Time Boy. Is it really true he's from the Golden Age, like you?"

The boy was right where Karim had said he'd be, a small, thin figure covered in ash and grime. Charlie's heart went out to him. The poor kid. And all because of his own foolishness in experimenting with powers beyond his control! He hadn't exactly planned to end up in some future world run by maniacs who worshipped fire.

He lurked in the shadow of one of the rail line's pillars, waiting for the overseers' shift change, then hurried forward. "You don't know me," he said in a whisper, as the boy turned in surprise, "but I'm here to help you." An overseer wandered past, and Charlie grabbed the nearest lever and pretended to pull on it. "Name's Charlie. Hotter down here'n old Sam McGee, eh?"

If an angel or an astronaut had suddenly appeared at his side, Neil couldn't have been more astounded. He simply stared at the man, mouth open. The overseer, after a glance at the pot crew, continued up the line. Charlie dropped his hold on the lever and squeezed the boy's arm. "Astra and Freya are okay. Chin up, kid. I'll be back."

And then he disappeared into the shadows again.

It seemed like only minutes later when heavy footsteps sounded in the hallway outside the lab. Was it really morning already? Astra sprang up, and Freya rooed in alarm. The door swung open to reveal an officer she hadn't seen before—a Flame-Defender, judging by the three flames on his shoulder—and two soldiers, one of whom carried a small silver box. They strode into the lab, where the Flame-Defender clicked his heels and presented Astra with a sheaf of papers. The soldier carrying the box set it down reverently on a table and stood staring at it, as if it might come to life.

"You have been granted an honorary commission in the Fire Reapers of Planetary Redemption," the Flame-Defender said crisply. He was short and dark and spoke UL with an accent; Astra wondered where he was from. "As such you have the authority to requisition any materials or slaves needed for your work. The dog object has also been reclassified from Subservient Life Form—its status in the Warrior Creation Program—to *Flamme-Sveitungr*, 3rd class."

Well, that's a relief, thought Astra, though if the man hadn't been so serious she would have burst out laughing at the absurdity of it all. The Flame-Defender clicked his heels again and strode out, followed by his soldiers. Astra moved eagerly toward the box and lifted the lid. There was the little silk pouch, emitting its soft glow. And inside—she drew it out with trembling fingers—was the Memory Stone, still its pink quartz self! There, inside, was the Wheel, spinning and shimmering as it always had. She felt flooded with joy and sadness and fear, all mixed up. Would she still be able to enter the Stone? Could she tune herself to its vibrations in this dreadful place? And if she could ... did she want to? The last thing she wanted was to help the Fire Reapers. Suppose she just told them the Stone wouldn't operate in the Fortress? But perhaps they'd already discovered that it *did* ...

Freya rooed softly, as if she understood Astra's problem. Astra held the Stone tightly in both hands, closed her eyes, and focused. Almost at once memories began racing past, rippling slightly as though they were underwater, but the usual scene—the one of her mother in the sleeproom—didn't come. There, instead, was her old home in the City, there was the learningpod she'd attended a few streets away! And there was her favourite teacher, Herr Kainulainen, who wasn't of pure Nordlandish stock because his father was Finnish and who'd therefore been slightly suspect.

Abruptly the scene went blank, and the next moment it was as if the Stone had decided to suck her into itself. Some powerful force seemed to be bearing down on her body, squeezing her from all sides. What was happening? Had they done something to the Stone? And now a wind rose, tearing at her clothes, scouring her face. She tried to cry out, but the wind tore her voice away.

It was some sort of trick. The Fire Reapers had rigged the Stone so it would devour her. She struggled helplessly, flailing her arms, trying to push back. Just when she was sure she couldn't bear it a moment longer, the wind dropped and the pressure disappeared. Murky colours swirled about her, finally settling into—what? Where was she?

She was in the garden of their City home, standing near the jasmine bushes her mother had planted. Only the bushes were much smaller, so it was a long time ago. Her vision sharpened. There, hanging from one of the orange trees, was the cuddleswing she'd found once in a storage room at the back of the house. And there—why, it was her parents, large as life, walking toward her, holding the hands of a tiny girl of about two. It was her! Her father's smile was tender and happy in a way she'd never seen before; her mother was laughing and barefoot in a long blue dress. She could hear every sound—the crush of the grass under their feet, the rustle of her own dress. What was that smell? She saw the faint perspiration on her mother's upper lip, the dampness at her neck. Yes, now she remembered. The perfume her mother always wore—White Lilac.

"Mamma!" she cried out, "Mamma!" They continued walking toward her, looking down at the child between them, swinging her by the arms. This was unbearable! She called again—she was face to face with them now, she could have reached out and touched them—but instead they walked right past her as though she wasn't there. She whirled round to watch them go. They grew smaller, turning into dark, two-dimensional silhouettes in the early-summer sunshine. And then they disappeared through the open door of the house.

She couldn't remember, later, how she found herself back in the lab, only that she was sobbing so hard she couldn't breathe. Why had this scene come now, in the Fortress of all places? Why had she seen her parents and her younger self, happy and safe, with no knowledge of what was to come? What was the point of the Stone if it caused so much pain? Physical pain, too—that familiar wave flooded her head and she pressed her fingers to her temples. Only it was worse this time, travelling down her arms to her fingertips and back again, and she found herself gasping. She sat gritting her teeth while Freya licked her face and whined softly. Was the greater pain somehow connected with the unfamiliar memory?

Slowly the pain and her hiccuping sobs subsided, and she looked around. Present-day reality had never seemed so dreamlike, as though it were some sort of screen between her and another, realer world. Freya was whining and pawing at her and she automatically rubbed the dog's ears. What was she going to do now? The Stone did work here, after all, though it seemed to operate differently, beyond her control. The memory seemed to have chosen her, rather than the other way round. And the entrance to the Stone had been terrifying.

What on earth was she going to tell the Fire Reapers?

She sat silent, thinking, for a long time.

Charlie?

Tombstone Charlie?

From the Yukon?

It wasn't possible. It was—well, it was beyond incredible that Charlie was here in the Fortress, too. And not only that, but he'd somehow found Neil and knew who he was.

But who else would have mentioned Sam McGee? They'd read the poem in his English class, a hilarious tall tale about a man from Tennessee who, before he froze to death during a bitter Yukon winter, asked a friend to be sure to cremate him so he'd finally be warm. Neil even remembered a couple of lines. *"The Northern Lights have seen queer sights, But the queerest they ever did see, Was that night on the marge of Lake Lebarge I cremated Sam McGee."*

He might have stared after Charlie forever, mouth agape, if the new overseer hadn't given him a cuff on the head and ordered him to get back to work. But for the rest of his shift he barely noticed the heat and the grime and the weight of the cauldron. After all this time, here was the very man who'd got him into this mess in the first place! And now he was offering to help? Who was he kidding?

On the other hand, Charlie wasn't chained to a fire pit and seemed free to move about. Did he work somewhere else in the Fortress? He also claimed to know about Astra and Freya. Neil could have kicked himself for not thinking to ask questions. Now he'd have to curb his impatience till Charlie came back— if he did. He felt a sudden rush of fear that Charlie wouldn't return, and then almost immediately a surge of anger. Hadn't Charlie screwed things up enough already? Why should he trust him?

The Stone Intensifies

"I see," said Flame-Protector Vígdís late the next day. She wore a uniform so crisp it could have cut through steel, and her blonde hair was pulled tightly back from her face. Around her in the lab were half a dozen other Fire Reaper officers. They all looked at Astra as though she was some particularly distasteful insect.

"You mean to tell me," Flame-Protector Vígdís went on, "that even though it received three additional pixillite baths, and as a result is twenty times more powerful than the old Stone, it produces no results?"

"N-no. I'm afraid not." Astra was standing as tall as she could, but she still felt very small next to Flame-Protector Vígdís. Freya stood protectively beside her, the ridge of fur on her back raised. "I've tried several times. I don't seem to be able to do anything with it."

"You really don't expect me to believe that, do you?" said Flame-Protector Vígdís softly. "After all, you told us you had materialized the boy who is now a spy."

"That—that wasn't true," stammered Astra. "We couldn't—I mean, my father hadn't—that is, with the old Stone we weren't able to—"

An older officer with a sharply angled face broke in. "Is it possible we underestimated the time the child requires?" Astra shot him a grateful look.

"I deliberately arranged for the Stone to be delivered yesterday morning, Flame-Protector Brynjólfr," said Flame-Protector Vígdís sharply, "so that the child would have time to familiarize herself with it. Surely, after thirty-six hours—"

"On the contrary, I suspect we've been too lenient." An officer with several gleaming medals on her jacket looked coolly at Flame-Protector Vígdís. "Perhaps withholding food would sharpen her concentration."

"Or removing the dog object," another officer said.

"I have to have Freya with me while I work," Astra said quickly. "That was one of my conditions."

The officer with the medals raised her eyebrows. "And who are you, a mere child—and an Ash-Gatherer child at that—to impose conditions?"

"I agreed to the presence of the dog object in order to stimulate her performance," Flame-Protector Vígdís said, looking round the circle of officers. "It appears, however, that even under optimum conditions she is unable to produce the results we require."

"May I suggest," said the angle-faced officer, "that we allow her another day or two? We know from our studies that the Stone's operations are complex, and that a user requires considerable time before even—"

"Her father *invented* the Stone! And she was the primary operator!" exclaimed the medalled officer. "One would have thought that, given those circumstances—"

Another officer broke in, a slender young man with white-blond hair and a beautiful, cold face. "Time is of the utmost," he said in a low, urgent voice, "now that the Mínera Beings and the Bestia are reported to be on the move, not to mention—"

But Flame-Protector Vígdís cut him off with an icy glare. "This is not a matter for discussion here, Flame-Defender Varghöss," she said, her voice angrier than Astra had ever heard. "In the meantime I'm inclined to agree with Flame-Protector Brynjólfr. We will allow her another twenty-four hours, and then we will ask her to demonstrate."

Twenty-four hours! How could she learn enough about the Stone's new powers in twenty-four hours to prevent them—*if* she could prevent them—learning what it could do? She hadn't dared approach it again. The materialized memory had been wonderful, overwhelming, but it was far too painful to live through twice. Besides, what would happen the next time she entered it?

"Perhaps it's a matter for the Archons?" said the medalled officer.

"Flame-Protector Vígdís has spoken," said Flame-Protector Brynjólfr, quietly but authoritatively. "We will assemble here again at seventeen hundred hours tomorrow."

"And Neil?" Astra asked, her heart thumping. "What about Neil? You said you'd take my request to the highest level."

"Did I?" Flame-Protector Vígdís's expression was cool and emotionless. "Perhaps you misunderstood. We require—no, we *demand*—results. If you perform well tomorrow, we will give your request serious consideration."

For the second time in as many days, Charlie found Astra curled up fast asleep beside Freya, traces of tears on her cheeks. He shook her gently and she leapt up in terror. "I can't, I can't—oh, Charlie! I'm so glad to see you!" And she threw her arms round him.

"What's up, kid? They didn't do anything to you, did they?" More than ever, after seeing Neil, he felt responsible for these two. This little girl wouldn't be here either if it hadn't been for his own meddling. How could he ever have thought that, in the future, human nature would somehow be different?

"No, but I have to make the Stone work or they'll—they'll—I don't know what, but it'll be horrible, and I can't, Charlie, I *can't* let them find out!"

"You're getting way ahead of me here, kid. What stone? What are you talking about?"

For answer Astra drew a small silken pouch from under her pillow and took out a chunk of rock. She handed it over to

Charlie, who stared at it, baffled. "It's just quartz. Pink quartz. What's so special about it?"

"It's—well, it's a Memory Stone, and my father invented it, but the Fire Reapers stole it and then they—oh, it's *so* hard to explain ..." But bit by bit, she did, as Charlie listened and stroked his chin.

"So they claim they've made it more powerful," he said when she'd finished. "Have you tried it out already?"

"Yes. And I got this memory about my parents—" Astra buried her face in her hands before looking up again. "And it was wonderful, but it was awful, too. Because we were all so happy. I could hear sounds, I could smell Mamma's perfume ..." She gulped back tears. "And I don't know how it came. I was always in control before. But now it's like the Stone decides ..." She shook her head, still gulping. "I'm scared, Charlie. I don't know what it'll do the next time I try it. And the last thing I want is to help *them*." She couldn't hold back the tears any longer, and flung herself into Charlie's arms again.

"Seems to me you got the heebie-jeebies more'n you need to right now," Charlie said reflectively, stroking her hair. "The thing is, you don't know *what* it can do. Maybe you can still control it. Maybe you just need practice."

Astra raised her head and looked at him doubtfully. "But it was all different. How it felt when I entered it, and the memory, and the pain afterward ..."

"I think you gotta give it another try. Only way forward, I figure."

Astra bit her lip and shook her head. "I don't want to."

"You gotta tell the Frippers *somethin'* about how it works. Best to be honest when you can, in my experience. Unless you're a real good liar."

"The Frippers?"

Charlie grinned. "It's what I call 'em. Fire Reapers of Planetary Redemption—FRPR. Get it? Hard to take 'em quite so seriously when they're called that, I figure."

Astra stared at the Stone lying inert on the pillow beside her. "If you're sure ..." she said, still doubtful.

"I'm sure. Now, how about I stick around while you try? That way you got me and Freya keepin' an eye on you."

Astra picked up the Stone and closed her eyes. Almost at once she felt that strange, terrifying force again, the one that seemed to be making her smaller, sucking her backward into the past. Once again she held on for dear life, and once again a wind—stronger even than before—tore at her clothes and seemed to lift her bodily upward. She could no longer see Charlie or Freya or even the room. She seemed to be travelling down a funnel of mist, with the wind howling in her ears and a whirling in her head.

At last the wind began to die down and the swirling colours spun round her. There, in the distance ... Where was she? Somewhere she'd never been before, that was for sure. The edge of a vast plain dotted with strange pointed trees, in the foot-hills of high mountains with white paint on their peaks. Not far away, hidden in bushes, were a group of beings she recognized as human, but shorter and darker and stockier, dressed in ani-mal skins and holding rough spears with chiselled stone points. A smell of woodsmoke filled her nostrils. Then they raised their spears and began creeping forward.

Beyond them, at the foot of the hills, was a vast herd of ani-mals, animals with great branching antlers and delicate hooves. She'd seen pictures of them on the imagebank. Reindeer! How beautiful these live ones were! Abruptly they flung up their heads, shifting nervously, and stampeded for the hillsides. Not all of them, though—a few broke away in panic. The humans began to run, yelling in some strange language, driving those few toward a narrow cleft between two hills. There, hemmed in, the animals were trapped by a fence of woven branches at one end and the band of humans at the other. As Astra watched in horror, some of the humans threw their spears and two or three of the animals went down, their flanks streaming with blood. One of the hunters seized a fallen reindeer by its antlers and lifted a knife to its throat.

Sick rose in her throat, and with a great effort she turned her head away and closed her eyes. Almost immediately she was flung forward, and she thrust her arms out to try and stop herself from falling. Someone was saying, "Astra? Astra!" A face came swimming into focus, wavery and underwater—a man's face with weathered skin and bright blue eyes ...

"Holy moly!" Charlie said. "What happened?"

She stared at him, dazed and blinking, not quite registering what he was saying. "I—I don't know. It was weird. It was—it wasn't a memory. It was something I'd never seen before."

"I heard all this shouting, I thought maybe you were in danger." Charlie shook his head, perplexed. "And drumming hooves, like a whole herd of caribou on the run."

"You did? You heard it?"

"It was too loud to miss. And Freya here was barking her head off. She musta heard it, too."

"Oh, Charlie! D'you know what this means?" She leaned toward him, her eyes shining. "It's *real*! They're really real! The Stone—it manifested sound! Except ..." She leaned back, perturbed. "I don't know how I did it. I mean, I didn't *do* anything."

"So what did ya see, exactly?" Charlie folded his arms and listened intently.

"Humans, sort of, in animal skins." She shuddered. "Hunting reindeer in some place I'd never seen before. They had spears, they drove some of the reindeer into a trap."

"Triple holy moly!" Charlie let out a long, slow whistle. "You saw something from thousands of years ago. Something that musta once happened all over what you call Nordlandia."

"But I don't get it. I mean, if it wasn't *my* memory, where did it come from?"

Charlie shook his head. "Seems you can go way back with this new version of the Stone. Maybe you were tapping into memories from some long-ago ancestor of yours."

"My father spent years trying to do that. Trying to manifest memories from the past." Astra stared at Charlie as a wave of sadness swept over her. "He made prototype after prototype. And now ..."

"Well, it's got a ways to go yet, kid. I mean, you're the only one who can see these memories. And they don't stick around."

"Except the Fire Reapers think they do." Astra gave a deep sigh of unhappiness. "I did something really stupid, Charlie. I told them we'd materialized Neil. You see," she added quickly, before Charlie could say anything, "They think he's a spy, they don't believe he came from the past, so—well, the words came out of my mouth before I could stop them."

"Hoo boy." Charlie let out another slow whistle. "You let the cat outta the bag before you even knew you had a cat, so to speak."

"But what am I going to do now? Now it turns out the Stone has these new powers?"

A flicker of uncertainty crossed Charlie's face. "When are the Frippers coming back?"

"This afternoon. Seventeen hundred hours." Astra stared at him pleadingly. "You said you were going to come up with a plan."

"Well, first I had to find Neil. And now I know where he is—"

"You do?" Astra jumped to her feet, startling Freya, who was lying beside her. "Where is he? Is he okay? Why didn't you *tell* me?"

"Whoa, whoa, whoa!" Charlie held up his hands protestingly. "You were just a tad worked up about the Stone thing when I got here, remember? Yeah, he's okay. They got him working in Weapons Produc—"

But he didn't finish his sentence, because Astra was swaying woozily back and forth, her face ashen. Charlie managed to catch her just in time.

"Hey, kid." He slung her arm round his shoulder and helped her over to the cot as Freya trotted anxiously alongside. "Maybe you overdid it with that memory stuff. Here, better lie down for a bit."

It was true. She felt limp, exhausted, as though all the blood had drained from her body. "So he's okay?" she murmured, her eyes shut, grateful for Charlie's solid presence. "Where is he?"

"He's fine. He's—well, he's working, sort of like me." *Better not to give her any details just yet, seein' the state she's in.* "Now you just rest, okay, kid? You gotta look after yourself."

"But they're going to come and ask me to ... ask me to ..." Her voice trailed off and her eyes closed. Already she was fast asleep. He pulled the blanket over her and tucked her in. Best thing for her, the poor kid. Meanwhile, he had to think of something, and fast. But what?

He cleaned the cages and fed the animals automatically, his mind racing. He was locking up the lab, after checking one last time on Astra, when it came to him. It was the slimmest of chances, and it might not work. But that was a chance they'd have to take. Better than sitting here like ducks in a shooting gallery.

Meanwhile, if the Frippers even suspected that what Astra had said was true, they'd definitely want to interrogate Neil again. Maybe even carry out experiments on him. And that meant only one thing. It meant that Neil was in danger.

He began to run.

Astra's Demonstration

It was a much larger group who arrived for the demonstration that afternoon. General Sardonyx himself strode in first, his black diamond eyes flashing, with Flame-Protector Vígdís close behind. A dozen or so other officers followed in his wake, along with Corporatist Thonkorn. Watching him enter, Astra felt her heart shrink to a tiny hammering pinprick. Only Freya, pressed firmly against her leg, gave her courage.

"Well, Hallvard's daughter," the General said as he came to a halt in front of her. He squeezed his gloved hands together and smiled his cold, pebbled smile. "May I say how much I've been looking forward to this afternoon. I'm most gratified that you've decided to cooperate with us."

If I was Tårnfalk, Astra thought to herself, I'd rush forward and claw your eyes out. Instead, hoping her voice sounded steadier than she felt, she said, "I don't really have a choice."

The General laughed—that horrible sound like rattling stones—and looked expansively round at the others. "We always have choices in this world, my dear girl." Some of the officers nodded; Flame-Protector Vígdís watched Astra like a hawk. "You made a choice to come here, did you not? Unfortunately for you, it was the wrong one." And he laughed again, as though it was the funniest joke in the world.

Flame-Protector Vígdís stepped forward, her fierce gaze still on Astra, and touched something at her belt. The door opened and a lab worker, dressed all in clinical white, entered. *He isn't human*, Astra thought as she stared at him. His eyes were gold metal balls without pupils, and his nails and teeth were made of shiny greyish metal.

260

"This," said Flame-Protector Vígdís proudly, "is one of the first generation of human-metal hybrids, made by combining the molecules of human cells with milicronium molecules. Milicrons, we call them. Milicron BN942 worked on the latest prototype of the Stone and is here to assist you with its operation, if necessary."

The Milicron saluted, and then there was an expectant silence. Astra took the Stone from the pouch, hands trembling. So much for any plan of Charlie's. He hadn't been any help at all. She held the Stone in both hands and closed her eyes. *Oh, beings of the Many Realms, if you can hear me, please help.* What would happen this time? What kind of memory would come?

A sudden idea came to her. Suppose she tried focusing on a particularly harmless memory? A memory that would give nothing away ... An image of the Ashgård vegetable garden came into her mind. Almost at once she felt that sensation of being sucked into the past, that horrible squeezing pressure, the roaring wind. She was whirled topsy-turvy down the funnel of mist. And then, as the mist evaporated, there—there was the garden! There was Fru Berta, weeding the eggplant and perspiring under her kerchief. Astra saw herself kneeling among the rows of yams, digging them up and throwing them in a basket. She could smell the rich earth, feel on her skin the intense, baking heat. What a little paradise it had been! If only she'd been able to stay forever. She could even taste the stew they'd be having for supper that evening.

Tears came to her eyes. She felt herself being pulled away and tried to hang onto the basket, but the mist was already swirling round her. The vegetable garden grew smaller and smaller, as if she was looking through the wrong end of a telescope, and then it vanished. Abruptly she found herself back in the lab, holding the Stone. General Sardonyx and the others didn't look very pleased, to say the least. The General was scowling, Corporatist Thonkorn looked terrified, and Flame-Protector Vígdís was red-faced and fidgeting like a child.

"Hardly a success, Flame-Protector Vígdís." The General raised an eyebrow and looked coldly round the room at the others. "The child's being granted more time seems to have made no difference whatsoever." He pointed to something lying on the floor a short distance away.

Astra stared at it in amazement. It was a yam—a small, thin, dirt-covered yam! She was so astonished she barely heard what the General was saying.

"... told us she materialized an entire human being. Instead, she first of all produces nothing, and now"—his eyebrows rose in derision—"she gives us a dirty little vegetable, of all things."

Astra stared at the yam again. She'd actually brought a memory to life! She'd finally achieved what her father had set out, so long ago, to do. The Fire Reapers had no idea how impressive the yam really was. She wanted desperately to pick it up, to prove its reality, but she didn't dare. She kept glancing at it, sure it would fade, but it looked remarkably solid.

"I had high hopes," the General went on, "that using the child would make a difference, but it hasn't. Such a pity. Especially after all the time and expense involved. These experiments are becoming remarkably tedious."

That must mean, Astra thought, that, unlike Charlie, they hadn't heard the sounds that accompanied the scene—the chink of the trowel, Fru Berta muttering to herself, the laughter of children in the distance. But before she could puzzle over this, Flame-Protector Vígdís broke in. "Perhaps, General," she said, and her teeth were gritted, "we could ask Corporatist Thonkorn to guarantee that the pixillite was free of impurities." She turned to the Corporatist, who was visibly trembling. "I'm sure you remember that the last shipment we received was found to be contaminated with traces of thionisium."

Corporatist Thonkorn bowed so low that it seemed her head would touch the floor. "We traced the source of the contamination immediately," she whispered, straightening and placing her hands together, "and those responsible were dematerialized as a lesson to others. I can assure you, my esteemed General, Flame-Protector Vígdís—"

"I'm sure contamination isn't the issue here," the General said impatiently. "Vígdís, you held overall responsibility for the project. Regrettably, you have failed to achieve results." He turned his back on her and addressed Flame-Protector Brynjólfr. "Brynjólfr, you will take over this project immediately. I am promoting you to the rank of Flame-Shielder. You will report to me daily." Brynjólfr saluted, his face impassive. "You, Vígdís, will return to the Dematerialization Research Station—with better results this time, we hope." Flame-Protector Vígdís saluted, too, though a spasm of rage crossed her face.

"And as for you ..." He turned to Astra, all pretence of friendliness gone. "I'm convinced you are capable of more. Much more. You are, after all, Hallvard's daughter, you worked beside him. And your father is one of the finest scientists Nordlandia has produced."

Trying to quell the terror flickering through her, Astra stood her ground, Freya glued to her side. "Perhaps," the General said, and his eyes seemed to cut through her with the hardness of diamond, "it would help you to know about your good friend the spy. Given your lack of success here, we have no other option but to investigate your claim that he is a materialization."

Astra took a step forward, her voice quivering. "You promised not to harm him. What are you going to do?"

Freya gave a short, sharp bark and the General glared at her, too. "We will soon know whether you've been telling the truth. And if you haven't ..." A cold gleam came into his eyes. "Why, then, we'll demote both you and the dog object to experimental status and transfer you to the Warrior Creation Program, as spare parts."

"You promised!" Astra shouted, flinging herself at the soldiers, but they were already striding out of the lab after the General. As the door closed in her face, Flame-Protector Vígdís shot her a look of pure hatred.

She slumped to the floor. Scenes and images from her earlier Stone-dwelling journey were flooding back—the humans with their spears, the cries and shouts of the hunt, the hunter lifting his knife to the reindeer's throat. She shut her eyes and held her hands over her ears, but nothing drowned out the vividly replayed scenes. This was Stone-lock, worse than she'd ever had it. Now the blood was pouring into a hollowed piece of horn held by one of the hunters, who raised the horn to his lips ...

Dimly she became aware of Freya, whimpering and licking her face. She tightened her arms round her, pressing her face into the fur to block out the images of death.

Charlie hurried past the lines in the stinking heat, past the thousands toiling at the pots filled with bubbling tirillium. Several times he had to duck behind a pillar or into the shadows when he saw an overseer coming. He'd been in such a hurry he'd forgotten to check the codes again and alter his own. What a stupid risk!

He rounded the corner onto Line 54. Sweat was pouring down his face, trickling under his clothes. No guards in sight, thank the gods—whoever they were. Pot number four, five, six ... His heart seemed to hammer out the sequence. Twelve, thirteen, fourteen ... Here, with its dozen slaves shackled to the fire pit underneath, was pot number fifteen. But where was Neil?

He raced back to the previous line, almost colliding with a guard on the way. "Tirillium spill on Line 52," he managed to stammer out. "I couldn't find a spill slave." The guard hurried off, emergency transmitter flashing at his belt, and Charlie came to a screeching halt at pot number 27 on Line 53.

"Where is he?" he said, breathing hard, as Karim looked up dully.

"They came for him an hour or two ago." Karim's face was sombre, his eyes dead. "Huang over there"—he jerked his head—"says they took him to the Truth Chamber. But I heard something else." He dropped his voice so low that Charlie could barely hear him. "I heard they took him to the *Brjóta Líkami*. The Dematerialization Research Station."

Despite the stifling heat, Charlie felt his whole body turn to ice. But what Karim said next almost made his heart stop beating. "You had better watch out. I hear you are next."

When the blindfold was taken off, Neil blinked, dazzled. He was in a big white room, brilliantly lit and filled with clinical but menacing-looking equipment—drills that might have been for filling teeth, an array of what appeared to be scalpels, a giant wheel with saw-like edges. It looks like a dentist's office, Neil thought, only a hundred times worse. At that moment a dentist's office seemed like the better alternative. He'd have cheerfully undergone any number of fillings if it meant he could get out of this predicament.

"Stay put on that chair," the guard who'd removed his blindfold said brusquely, "or I'll have to handcuff you." And he went out.

What were they going to do with him? Why had they brought him here? It was so silent! No more of that horrible white noise drilling into your skull day and night. But now he found himself straining his ears, trying to hear who—or what—was coming. The not knowing, the waiting, was almost worse than anything else. He was sure it was deliberate.

Suddenly the door opened on a group of soldiers dragging in another slave who wasn't being cooperative. He was struggling and swearing, and getting kicked and cuffed for his efforts. The soldiers didn't so much as glance at Neil. They threw the slave to the ground and, after a last kick or two, slammed the door behind them.

Neil stood up cautiously. The slave was an older man with

a scrubby beard who lay as if unconscious. His face was badly bruised and his eyes were swollen, but he managed to open them as Neil bent over him. The eyes opened wider.

"Doggone if it ain't you, kid ..."

"Charlie! Are you okay?"

"Damned if I don't keep gettin' you in all kinds of trouble," Charlie muttered, clutching Neil's arm and managing to sit up. Still leaning on Neil he stumbled to a chair, his other arm holding his bruised ribs. "Those brutes did a good job on me, let me tell you. Not for the first time, neither."

"If you're asking me to feel sorry for you, you can save your breath," Neil said, suddenly angry. "It's your fault I'm here in the first place."

Charlie nodded slowly as he eased himself into the chair. "You're right there, kid. I don't blame you for being mad." He sighed and shook his head. "I meant well, but I guess that don't count much in the end."

"Why'd they bring you here anyway?"

"Search me. Maybe 'cause they saw me talkin' to you. Though logic isn't the Fire Reapers' strong point."

"Great. So now we're both here in this—in this ...." He couldn't bring himself to say "torture chamber," because it was too frightening to admit the possibility even to himself. He trailed off, swallowing hard. If he was angry at Charlie, he was even angrier at himself for very nearly crying.

"At least it ain't the Truth Chamber," Charlie said, trying to sound cheerful.

"It's probably worse," said Neil, looking round at the instruments. "I spent time in the Truth Chamber, in case you didn't know."

"I *do* know," said Charlie quietly. "And I'm sorrier'n I can say, kid, that you got put through that. That reminds me—I found somethin' of yours there." He put his hand in his pocket and pulled out the rock he'd found, holding it out apologetically. "I know it ain't worth much—"

"Piedra!" To Charlie's astonishment Neil leapt straight out of his chair. "I thought I'd lost you forever!"

"Oh please," said a weary voice as Neil cradled the rock in his palm. "As if my ears haven't suffered enough. Do keep your voice down."

"Did I hear—?" Charlie said slowly, staring first at the rock and then at Neil.

"Of course you did," said Piedra tartly. "Really, it amazes me why you humans think you're superior. You can't even trust your senses."

Good old Piedra! "I'm so glad you're here," Neil said with feeling. "I never thought I'd see you again."

But Charlie looked hurt. "I know all about Immortal Soul and non-human intelligences," he said. "Though I never made the acquaintance of a rock before. Leastways, not one that could talk."

"Well, it was certainly touch and go there for a while," Piedra said to Neil, ignoring Charlie's comment. "But never mind that now. Where are we?"

"The Dematerialization Research Lab," said Charlie quietly. "Nobody knows much about it, except—well, no one who ends up here ever comes back."

Neil shot Charlie a frightened glance while Piedra sat silent, considering. "I see," Piedra said at last. "Out of the frying pan into the fire *again*. Only worse. Someone remind me why I took on this assignment."

This was hardly reassuring. "Piedra," said Neil, "why didn't you talk to Charlie when you were in his pocket? Maybe the two of you could have got help."

Piedra sniffed. "You really think he'd have listened? You heard what he said. Besides, I was assigned to you and the girl child, not to him."

"Then can't we do something now? With the three of us, maybe we'd have enough power to send out a message to Áilu. Or the Mínera Beings."

"Perhaps," said Piedra doubtfully. "With Chalcedon's betrayal, however, I'm afraid I can no longer trust even my own people. Who knows who else is secretly supporting him?"

But they were left with no time to talk further. The door opened and a tall Fire Reaper officer entered, a woman with blonde hair and rigid bearing. Neil hastily shoved Piedra into a corner of the chair. The officer was accompanied by a fleshy-faced, thick-lipped man in a lab coat and a peculiar human-like being with metallic eyes and nails. Behind them were half a dozen soldiers.

"I am Dr. Zamorin," the man in the lab coat said, smiling charmingly, hands in pockets, as if he'd just dropped in for tea. "I am the director of this research station. I can assure you you have no reason for alarm. We merely wish to clear up a certain— misunderstanding, let us call it—about your origins. Your coop-eration will also augment our current scientific knowledge—"

"Never trust a fella using ten-dollar words," Charlie mut-tered, half to himself.

"Silence!" The Fire Reaper officer, standing there with her arms folded, glared at Charlie. "How dare you interrupt?"

"Perhaps, Flame-Protector Vígdís, I might make things clearer," the doctor said smoothly, and smiled again at Charlie and Neil. "We would like to find out whether you are both, as you claim, from the past. It seems to us most—shall we say, intriguing?—that some considerable time after your own arrival"—he nodded at Charlie—"this boy turns up, also claim-ing to be from an earlier time. An odd coincidence, no?" His eyes gleamed with zeal. "We felt it was prudent to investigate."

"Not to mention," Flame-Protector Vígdís added coldly, "the additional information given to us by Hallvard's daughter."

There it was again, Neil thought. Astra had broken under questioning and told them—what? Just as rage flared up in him—*Astra! How could you?*—Flame-Protector Vígdís gestured curtly to Charlie. "Let us begin with Slave 3964."

Charlie stood up as the soldiers moved toward him, wincing and clutching his ribs. "Tell those thugs of yours to keep their hands off," he said. "I don't need no help. Just don't touch the boy."

Neil felt a wave of shame and gratitude. *Even though I was angry with him, he's trying to protect me.* As Charlie was shepherded across the room, the metallic being withdrew a tiny tubelike device from the back of its hand and inserted it into the wall. Immediately the wall dissolved, revealing an inner chamber that glowed with acid-green light. Charlie was half-pushed into it, and the wall sealed over as though the opening had never existed.

Beads of sweat broke out on Neil's forehead. Was he imagining things, or was the wall pulsing? Dr. Zamorin and Flame-Protector Vígdís paid no attention to him; they were watching the being, who was transmitting waves of the acid-green light. Minutes passed. Neil felt sick with dread. He tried not to think about what might be happening to Charlie, or what would happen when his own turn came.

At last the metallic being took the device out of the wall and handed it to Dr. Zamorin, who studied it intently. Moments later, the wall unsealed itself, and out stumbled Charlie. He was breathing hard, and as he came toward Neil he gave off a faint greenish glow. He sat down in the chair, slumped back, and closed his eyes. Neil stared at him in horror.

"And now," said Dr. Zamorin soothingly, turning to Neil, "it's your turn." He thought he heard Piedra whisper something, but he couldn't tell what it was. He got up at once and walked resolutely toward the wall. Better to walk with dignity on one's own, like Charlie, than be dragged by the soldiers.

Once again the wall dissolved as the metallic being inserted the tube, once again the chamber with its acid-green light appeared. Neil swallowed hard and muttered Áilu's name. As he stepped into the chamber, he could see her, a wrinkled walnut with blazing eyes. For just a moment he thought he could feel her hand in his again—a remarkable hand, smooth and unlined. Then the wall sealed shut behind him.

The light intensified and began to pulse, slowly at first, then faster. The walls moulded themselves around his body, pressing against him on all sides so that he could barely breathe. It felt like a live thing, moving as he moved. And now he could hear, faintly at first, then louder and louder, a rhythmic beat, though whether it was outside him or the beating of his own heart he couldn't tell.

Thousands of tiny sticky hairs, like caterpillar feet, began travelling all over his body and face. He shut his eyes and mouth and tried to curl into himself, to protect himself from what felt like the explorations of a giant insect. And now the chamber began to spin, slowly at first, in one dimension, horizontally, and then in circles and ovals and figure eights, like an out-of-control midway ride. He felt as if someone had hold of his arms and legs and was pulling in opposite directions. He was splitting apart into tiny fragments and flying to the corners of the room. And meanwhile the giant insect was probing, scouring, sucking on his very insides, even his thoughts, digesting them and spitting them out.

Centuries later the spinning slowed, and the walls that had held him in their sticky embrace peeled away. The light dimmed. Suddenly another light, white and blinding, burst upon him, and there was the Fire Reaper officer and the doctor and the metallic being, all staring at him. But he couldn't quite get them in focus, nor could he seem to remember how to walk. He wobbled forward uncertainly and threw up.

The metallic being gripped his arm and escorted him to a chair, where he sat with his head between his knees. He felt someone squeeze his shoulder. Charlie. When at last he raised his head, Charlie gave him a glance of fierce sympathy, then glared at the others. "There's nothin' you won't stop at, is there? Other life forms are all fair game. Even kids."

"Perhaps," said Flame-Protector Vígdís haughtily, "you forget that we are human, too, like you and the boy. Though considerably less deluded." She turned to the doctor, nostrils flaring. "A most interesting set of results, Dr. Zamorin. Most interesting."

"Indeed." Dr. Zamorin nodded, and his voice quivered with excitement. "The molecular structures in certain parts of their bodies have changed in shape and orbital rotation. Our theories of time travel predicted this."

"The angularity of the H_2O molecule has been reduced by .0004E," said the metallic being in a melodic female voice, "and the carbon molecule—"

"Thank you, DL015, but there's no need to bore our subjects with trivial details," Flame-Protector Vígdís cut in crisply. "They need only know that we are indeed fortunate to live in an era when science can provide us with such exact and incontrovertible results." She turned back to the prisoners and addressed Neil. "These results," she said icily, "confirm what Hallvard's daughter told us—that she succeeded in materializing you during one of her father's experiments."

"She can't have told you that," Neil said, though his mind was fuzzy and he was having difficulty forming thoughts. "It isn't true." *Oh, Astra, what have you done?*

"Continuing to lie," Flame-Protector Vígdís said, her voice like a knife, "is really not in your best interests, Grezkoo. We know, of course, that you became a spy for one of her father's allies, the Aqua Libere. And we all know what happens to spies who are caught, don't we, DL015?" She looked with satisfaction at the metallic being, who gave a peculiar tinny laugh.

"Now, as for you, 3964"—she turned to Charlie—"we suspect that you are from the same time period as the boy, and that Astra and her father materialized both of you." Her eyes glittered. "You can tell us the truth yourselves, or we can resort to other means of fine-tuning the results. I assure you those methods are considerably more unpleasant than the Dissolution Analyzer."

"I ain't tellin' you nothin'," said Charlie thickly. He looked like some strange new being himself, thought Neil, with his white hair sticking straight up and that green tinge to his skin. "You're a bunch of barbarians. You're a disgrace to humanity."

The officer's face darkened, as if black blood ran through her veins. "Very well." She took a deep breath and stood, if possible, even taller. "Then you leave me no option. You will both be delivered to the Plane of Oblivion until we are ready for the next stage of analysis."

Neil grabbed Piedra just in time. The floor beneath their chairs thinned and dissolved, and they plummeted down through black space.

The Plane of Oblivion

Astra had never felt such pain. It pulsed through her entire body, and she remained shivering on the floor, trying to shut out the flood of images. What she'd have given for Fru Berta's cloudberry cordial! Flashing lights went off inside her head, and if she opened her eyes the lights blurred and dazzled, as though she was looking at them through rain. From time to time they crackled like static, making her jump. The exit wound in her side throbbed painfully.

At last, hours later, like a slowly passing thunderstorm, the Stone-lock faded. Astra crawled to her cot and fell onto it, Freya beside her. She was limp with relief, but a new terror seized her. The General was furious with her, and she'd made a new enemy in Flame-Protector Vígdís. What would they do with her now?

She didn't have to wait long to find out. She was drifting in and out of uneasy sleep when she heard footsteps, faint at first, then coming closer and closer. She sat up, clutching Freya. As the door opened, light flooded into the room, and there stood the lab worker Milicron. Or was it? A dozen or more identical Milicrons were trooping into the room. One of them stepped forward and spoke in a voice a mile deep.

"You are to come with us," it said. Astra stood up, still hanging on tightly to Freya.

"The dog object stays here," said another, and they all nodded, their metallic eyeballs clicking.

Astra took a deep breath, her fingers tightly wound in Freya's collar. She had to think quickly. "Perhaps you didn't know," she said, trying to control her shaking, "that whenever I use the

Stone, some bits of me get left behind in the past. I need animal molecules to fill me up again."

The Milicrons clicked and fidgeted, apparently uncertain what to do. A couple of them actually bent down and examined the girl and the dog.

"Indeed," one of them said with distaste, "they are connected by their skin coverings. The child's arm has fused with the dog object's fur."

The entire group looked at Astra with repugnance, as if she were covered in germs. Several of them even took a few steps backward. "Good idea," Astra said to them, and made shooing motions with her hand. "Better keep your distance. You never know what you might catch."

One of them—was it the original Milicron?—said softly, "As human-milicronium hybrids, we have no immunity whatsoever. If we catch so much as a cold ..." A murmuring tinged with sadness rippled through the entire group, and for the first time Astra actually felt sorry for them.

"We must, however, fulfill our orders," said another Milicron firmly, and at once the group surrounded her and Freya, though they kept their distance.

"Where are you taking me?" Astra said, taking care to still appear to be welded to Freya.

"We were created to serve the Stone," the same Milicron said. "As you are a necessary component of the Stone, we must protect you."

Was that all she was here—just a piece of the Stone? That must be how the Milicrons thought of themselves. Still, this was no time for quibbles. "From what?" said Astra suspiciously.

Another Milicron, turning to the one who had spoken, said something sharp in a series of clicks and buzzes. The other Milicron replied, equally sharply, and suddenly all the Milicrons were arguing among themselves in their strange metallic language, gesturing and pointing at Astra, who stood watching uneasily. Her fate, and Freya's, depended on who won, she was sure. She half-turned toward the open doorway, trying to calculate how fast she could run. But even if she could get away from the Milicrons, where would she go?

A high-pitched metallic scream made her whirl. One of the Milicrons was collapsing, folding in on itself, disintegrating into a pile of blackened metal and wire and ashes. As Astra stared in horror, another Milicron stepped forward, its gilded eyes glistening with moisture. "Milicron AX315 did not understand," it said, "that our orders were defective. Unlike most of our masters, we are hybrid beings. We therefore understand, as they do not, the need for your integrity." As Astra looked puzzled, another Milicron added, "The separation of you and the dog object would result in your own dematerialization. Our masters would be most displeased."

"And you were going to—?" Astra couldn't bring herself to finish the sentence.

The Milicrons nodded. "The dog was to be dematerialized in the Dematerialization Research Station," said the first Milicron, speaking so softly that Astra could hardly hear it. "Your own fate is in the hands of the First Flame and the Archons. Until their decision is made, you are to be consigned to the Plane of Oblivion."

"And where is that?" Astra said, alarmed.

The Milicrons gave a tinny laugh. "It is an invisible dimension, so it cannot be described in human terms. You will not be harmed. Please, step this way."

One of the Milicrons pointed to a spot on the floor a short distance away. She moved toward it uncertainly, still holding Freya. The floor suddenly gave way, and the two of them were falling, falling endlessly through a black and soundless void.

At first she could see only blackness. Were the Milicrons sending her to her death after all? As she spun slowly, dizzyingly, she became aware of Freya's howling, a lost and lonely sound in infinite space. The howling disappeared in the void and still they fell, as though some hole in the earth had opened up and they were plunging to the planet's core. She tried to scream, but the air rushing past tore the sound away.

At last the sensation of falling slowed and stopped, though she hadn't landed anywhere. Instead she seemed to be floating in some vast nighttime region where all sound had vanished. She felt fur brush her arm and realized, to her immense relief, that a whimpering Freya was floating beside her. She hung onto the dog's fur and strained to make out something, anything.

Tiny sparks like fireflies appeared in the distance, flickering on and off. Sounds came to her, too, distant murmurings and whisperings that seemed, at times, to resemble voices. If only she still had the Etheric Sensor! "Is anyone there?" she called, her voice thin and high and frightened. "Is anybody there?"

Nothing. Only—after the longest time—the echo of her own voice, as if she'd spoken inside some vast, hollow cave. What a horrible fate—to be left to float through some vast lightless region of interstellar space.

At last the distant murmurings and whisperings came back, and after a while she made out words. "We are here," a collective voice said, faint and far away, in a strangely accented UL. "Who are you?"

So she wasn't completely alone! She could have wept with relief. "I'm Astra," she called back excitedly. "Astra Bjarnason of Ashgård village. With my dog Freya." And at the sound of her name, Freya let out a long, heartbroken roo.

She waited, but no further response came. Maybe she'd imagined the words. Maybe all she was hearing was the background radiation of the universe, the great cosmic hum her father had told her about.

"Who are *you*?" she called in desperation. After a long time the voice came again, the voice that seemed to be made up of many other voices. "The Arbolé," the voice said, in a long sighing that sounded like wind through the branches on a stormy day.

The Arbolé! The living half-trees that could move and talk, or so the villagers said. Astra hadn't believed they really existed. Fru Berta claimed that her son Toivo had joined them, but Astra had been sure that was just to make herself feel better after Toivo disappeared. The tree-like murmurings made Astra think of sunlight and grass and earth, and she felt comforted.

But how could trees survive here without light and water? Perhaps it was a trap. Perhaps whoever had answered was really a spy for the Fire Reapers and would pass on any information she let slip. For that matter, how were she and Freya going to survive here? She clutched Freya more tightly and repeated the same thing over and over in her head. *We need your help, beings of the Many Realms. We need your help, beings of the Many Realms. We need your help ...*

"Out of the frying pan into the fire," Piedra said. "Again."

Neil clutched Piedra more tightly and stared about him in the appalling darkness. His freefall had come to an abrupt halt, as though his parachute straps had suddenly tightened and he hung there, dangling. He could see nothing, not even the gleam of Piedra's copper vein. He'd never been anywhere so lightless.

"I really must stop saying that," Piedra went on, "because every time I do, something worse happens. You'd think a billion-year-old life form would learn to keep quiet."

"I don't know why you're so calm," Neil muttered. "And where's Charlie?"

"Oh, he'll have fallen *much* farther," Piedra said airily. "With that enormous belly of his—"

"Hey! You watch your mouth!" It was Charlie, somewhere close by. "You'd think a billion-year-old life form would have learned to be *politer*."

"Politeness," said Piedra witheringly, "is greatly overrated. What use is politeness in our present predicament?"

"About as much use as a mouthy chunk of granite," Charlie retorted.

"Okay, you two," Neil said hastily before Piedra could reply. "Stop bickering." Which was exactly what his mother was always saying to him and his sister, and a pang of longing went through him. "We need to put our heads together and think. What's that over there?"

For off in the distance was what looked like a filament of light, so thin it might have been woven from spiders' silk, fading in and out. It disappeared into the vast depths of the void below him and rose above him out of sight.

"Your eyes are better'n mine, kid," Charlie said. "I can't see a thing."

But Piedra said, "Now that is interesting. *Very* interesting. That is a LightWire. Though installed, I suspect, by someone who is not fully familiar with the technology. And not functioning very well, either."

"A what?" said Neil and Charlie together.

"You remember that web of fine gold wires in the Caverns of the Mínera Beings, child?"

Yes, Neil did, vaguely—there'd been so much that was new it was overwhelming.

"The Mínera use light to capture and transmit energetic information from living beings," Piedra explained. "Thoughts, feelings, intuitions, desires, for example. LightWires function as a kind of antennae for those of us below ground. My own people, the Kärna, invented them by transforming solid gold into light," he added proudly.

"You did?" Charlie exclaimed. "Like the old alchemy texts say?"

"The Kärna," Piedra said sniffily, "are light-years—if you'll pardon the pun—ahead of any other beings. We have, after all, had many thousands of years—"

"So it's transmitting information," Charlie said thoughtfully. "From someone, and to someone. But who?"

Nobody had an answer to that question. The pulses from the LightWire brightened, or perhaps their eyes had adjusted to the darkness.

"I'm sure those flashes are coming in some sort of pattern," Charlie said after a minute or two. "Maybe it's like the Morse code we used, back in my Merchant Marine days."

"Morse code is a very primitive—" Piedra said, and broke off. "Oh. Wait a minute." After a long pause he said, "It *is* a pattern." And after another pause—"It must be one of the languages in the Tree language family that use sound or light."

"A *language*?" Neil and Charlie fairly shouted together. "What's it saying?"

"As I told you, the LightWire's faulty," said Piedra huffily. "But if you'll keep quiet I might be able to translate."

Far off the intermittent sparkings continued, changing colour now from gold to luminous green to orange and back again.

"The roots ..." Piedra paused, as though struggling for the right words "... may trip us, but the—oh, what's the UL word?— the canopy, that's it! The canopy will open out in the end."

"What's that supposed to mean?" said Neil, baffled.

"Is that it?" Charlie wanted to know. "Isn't there anything else?"

"Whoever is transmitting is wary of us," Piedra said slowly. "And also, perhaps, of any communication falling into the wrong hands. But I'm fairly certain it's the Arbolé."

"The Arbolé?" said Charlie wonderingly. "I thought they were a myth. You know, made up."

"The *Arbolé*!" breathed Neil. Those tree beings that Fru Berta had talked to, and Toivo had joined!

"Hot doggety!" Charlie said. "So how do we reassure them?"

The LightWire suddenly flickered rapidly, and a sound like faint humming reverberated round them.

"They've picked up on your presence," Piedra said to Charlie, "and they're puzzled by it. They know no humans who have such a strong affinity for gold, unless they are Mínera Beings."

Charlie laughed. "Tell 'em I'm an honorary Mínera Being." And then, more somberly: "Tell 'em we're prisoners in this dimension."

"So are they," Piedra said as the LightWire continued to flicker, "and they say their powers are much depleted, now they're no longer in contact with the natural world." Piedra paused again. "They are tree hybrids, and like all trees they must harvest light in order to live. Without more light, they say, they will not be able to communicate with us further." Even as he spoke, the LightWire gave a crackle and faded out. "There, you see? They exhausted themselves talking to us."

"Isn't there some way we can fix it?" Neil asked.

"I'm afraid," Piedra said gloomily, "I can be of no assistance. Some of the Kärna specialize in metals transformation, but I am not among them."

"Shoot," said Charlie, sounding crestfallen. "And here I was figurin' you could tell us the secret." The Kärna must have been working at the molecular level, perhaps altering electron orbits, though of course he didn't know exactly how they'd done it.

"The Tree Elders ..." said Neil, and faltered. Surely they could help the Arbolé? But he didn't have Fru Berta's skills, which probably wouldn't work on the Plane of Oblivion anyway.

"Fire!" said Charlie suddenly. "If we could make fire ... It's what the old alchemists used to re-energize gold."

"And how, exactly," said Piedra in the same gloomy tone, "are we going to do that?"

"I dunno," Charlie admitted.

"We could rub two sticks together," Neil said, remembering his camping trips. "If we had sticks," he added sheepishly.

"Or two stones," said Piedra after a pause.

"But we don't have—" Neil began, and stopped. "Piedra, you aren't suggesting—?"

"There's a tiny fault line," Piedra went on, "just above the copper vein that runs through me. A hairline crack. I believe that, with enough pressure—"

"But we can't do that to you!" Neil exclaimed.

"Oh, I'll still be the same Piedra," the rock said, though Neil fancied that his voice trembled a little. "I'll just lose a tiny part of me, that's all."

"Hot doggety!" Charlie said again. "You just gave me an idea!" And before either of the others could say anything, he fished the little piece of tirillium from his pocket, the one he'd picked up on the weapons production lines. "We can rub this against Piedra instead!"

"Oh, we can, can we?" Piedra said, his copper vein flashing dangerously.

"All we need's a spark," said Charlie soothingly. "That oughta allow us to re-energize the gold and restore the LightWire. Leastways, if things work the way I think they will."

"And if they don't?" Neil asked in dismay.

"Energizing the gold molecules may make the LightWire unstable. And if that happens"- Charlie hesitated—"there could be—unpredictable effects."

Piedra gave a heavy sigh. "The story of my life. Well, I don't suppose there's an alternative. Hand me over, Neil."

"Okay. Here goes." Charlie took hold of Piedra and began rubbing the tirillium against him. "You all right, buddy?"

"If you call boiling hot and being rubbed to bits all right," grumbled Piedra, "then yes, I am." Which meant that he really *was* all right, Neil thought happily.

When he got tired, Neil took over while Charlie flexed his aching wrists. "Now," Charlie said firmly, taking a turn again, "we gotta all think of light, okay? It'll help send 'em the spark when we get it."

"*If* we get it," Piedra added, though his copper vein began to glow, as if he was thinking hard.

Neil shut his eyes and concentrated as fiercely as he could. The golden wires in the Timeless Caverns, illuminating the darkness ... cloudless sunny days from last summer in the Yukon ... Astra with her red-gold hair, and golden Freya with her gleaming fur (this last image with a lump in his throat).

Minutes later Charlie let out a shout as a spark leapt into the air between his fingers. Almost imperceptibly, the LightWire began to glow.

The Hall of Judgement

stra wasn't sure at first. Maybe she was just imagining—no. It was definitely there. The distant hummings and whisperings had started up again. And now the flickerings of light began, resolving into a steady glow, not that intermittent staticky crackle. She stared, transfixed. Even Freya, in the brightening glow, seemed mesmerized.

Whatever it was was growing steadily stronger. Soon the light was so dazzling she couldn't look at it. It was filling the darkness, eradicating it bit by bit. She stared about, astonished. It was like watching the sun rise. She felt weepy and shaky and overjoyed all at once. *Something was erasing the Plane of Oblivion!*

She felt a sudden jerk, as though whatever held her up was loosening. A brief, heartstopping moment, then another jerk. And then she was plummeting downward, tumbling and turning, falling endlessly through space again, blinded now by light. A roaring in her ears grew louder and louder ...

GROUUUMPHHH! She landed, hard, all the breath knocked out of her. The air was filled with choking smoke, making her splutter. Whimpering a little, dazed and bruised, she managed to push herself upright.

She was beside some sort of gigantic furnace. The roaring came from towers of flame, orange and scarlet and blue, that leapt hundreds of metres into the air above her head. Black figures, barely visible through the dense smoke, prodded at the flames with long pokers. Where was she? She felt sick with horror.

Something was lying on the ground a short distance away. A human figure, its head to one side, arms flung out. Could it be—? Astra crawled over to it. Charlie! He was breathing—*thankgodthankgodthankgod*—but he didn't stir. She shook him, hard.

"Astra! Over here!"

She whirled just in time to see Neil, covered in soot and ash, stumbling out from behind some piece of machinery.

"Neil!" She ran toward him. "You're okay!" She could have wept with relief. "What happened—where are we—?"

"Charlie was fixing the LightWire, only ..." He stared at her in disbelief. "What are you doing here?"

"I don't know." She shrugged helplessly. "Charlie's hurt."

They took turns trying to bring him round. "Where's Freya?" Neil asked suddenly. "Was she with you?" Astra spread her hands helplessly. And where was Piedra? They looked at each other in growing alarm.

Abruptly they felt a whoosh of fresh air, almost immediately cut off. The hundreds of black figures at the furnace began rushing to and fro, and through the roar of flame they heard another sound, gradually growing louder—the tramp of marching feet.

"We've got to hide," Neil muttered. He grabbed Charlie's legs, Astra grabbed his arms, and between the two of them they managed to pull him further into the shadows. The marching feet halted, followed by the magnified bellow of a familiar pebbled voice. "Lower the flame level, you fools!"

Astra and Neil couldn't make out the General's features in the smoky gloom, only the faint gleam of the jewel in his forehead. He scanned the shadows with his lightstone and strode toward them, his red and black cape sheathing him like a flame.

"Flame-Protector Vígdís brought the disturbance on the Plane of Oblivion to my attention," he said. He sounded almost amused, as though they were playing some elaborate game. "And here we are in the Tree Incineration Chambers. We meet in the oddest places, don't you think?"

A sudden volley of barking erupted. Freya, covered in soot, burst from a corner and rushed bravely at General Sardonyx.

284

"Shut that dog object up!" the General shouted. Two of his troops chased after her. Others, at a sign from the General, seized Astra and Neil and bound their arms behind them. They trussed up Charlie, too, who still lay inert.

"Since you are so eager to return to this plane," the General said, "we will proceed at once with your trial." Behind him a captured Freya, struggling and biting, was being dragged back. "You will, of course, be given a fair hearing. No one can accuse us of subverting justice."

He motioned to Flame-Protector Vígdís, whose eyes glittered as she stepped forward.

"I can report the decision of the First Flame and the Archons with respect to the three criminal unbelievers," she said, and her voice was triumphant. "You, Grezkoo. You will be charged with spying for the Aqua Libere, as well as perjury and insubordination. Slave 3964"—her eyes flicked downward at Charlie with contempt—"will be charged with assisting traitors to the state, as well as insubordination and dereliction of duty. And you, daughter of Hallvard"—she glared with pure hatred at Astra—"are to be charged with high treason for your sabotage of our foremost military research program."

They've won, Astra thought despairingly. They've really won. She staggered a little and would have fallen if the soldiers hadn't caught her.

"Tomorrow," went on Flame-Protector Vígdís, "you will be tried for your crimes in the High Court of Nordlandia, along with your fellow terrorists."

Terrorists? What terrorists? But there was no time to ask, because a distant commotion and the sound of quarrelling voices interrupted them. A man was hurrying forward, pursued by soldiers. From one of the Ash-Gatherer villages, judging by his appearance, his clothing bedraggled and dirty. He straightened and saluted the General, panting heavily.

"Begging your pardon for interrupting, Your Honour, but I brought an urgent message."

There was something familiar about his voice. Astra peered closely at him.

"It's not good news, Your Honour, I'm sorry to say. They're approaching from the east and the southwest—there's reports that the Bestia have joined the alliance, too—even the Aqua Libere are arming, people say ..." He broke off at an angry gesture from the General, fished a metal wafer from his pocket, and handed it over.

Councillor Grünewald! So he *was* a spy for the Fire Reapers, just as she'd suspected. He must have been feeding them information all along ...

The General had illumined the wafer and was reading it, his face darkening. He tightened his fist round it and stared into the distance, breathing heavily. "You may go, Grünewald," he said curtly as the man backed away, cringing. Then he swung round and strode off, his cape swirling round him, his officers hurrying to keep pace.

"March the prisoners to their cells!" Flame-Protector Vígdís shouted. The soldiers prodded them forward roughly. Dazed and bruised as she was, Astra felt a tiny glimmer of hope. The Bi-Souls had risen against the Fire Reapers after all! But how many were they? And how long would it take them to get here?

The soldiers shoved her and Neil forward again so that she stumbled and almost fell. Above them the flames were leaping upward once more, their roar deafening. Black figures darted round them, prodding hundreds of tree trunks into the furnace.

They came for her early the next morning, after a wretched night on a cold stone floor somewhere in the Fortress. She was taken along a dizzying network of corridors and stairs and tunnels, and finally through a doorway into a vast, high-ceilinged hall. The Temple—the very place where Chalcedon had betrayed them! Where was he now? Was he really in the City with her father, like General Sardonyx had said?

Her guards led her past the thousands of shelves with their tree corpse samples. A transparent box as tall as a person, with a low bench inside it, had been placed at one end of the room. A cage, she realized with a shock. As her captors pushed her through the opening, her shoulder touched it and a jolt of electricity shot through her, making her knees buckle.

She sat down on the bench, trembling. At the other end of the room was a high dais, with seven elaborately decorated chairs arranged in a half-circle. Above the dais a black canopy patterned with flames glittered in orange and gold and scarlet. Guards—special ones, judging by their flame-topped helmets—stood on the dais and at each of the many doors.

Moments later Charlie and Neil were led in, their ankles shackled. Charlie looked as if he'd aged twenty years overnight. He shuffled forward, his shoulders slumped, his face battered and swollen. Neil, too, had changed—he stared straight ahead, unseeing, even when he was pushed roughly into the cage beside her. Astra looked at him in horror. She tried to take his hand, but it fell limply out of hers.

A deafening blast of martial music erupted from hidden loudspeakers, and the huge imposing door behind the dais swung slowly open. As the guards snapped to attention, six people wearing flowing robes and strange tri-corner hats filed slowly into the hall. They were followed by a seventh, a man considerably older but commandingly tall, with cropped white hair. His robe was red and he wore a band of shining dark metal round his forehead, bearing a tiny flame that flickered like a candle. Astra couldn't take her eyes off it.

"Behold!" one of the ceremonial guards announced in a ringing voice. "The Archons and the First Flame of the Fire Reapers of Planetary Redemption! All bow!"

The guards raised their hands in the sign of the Flame, then touched their foreheads. The Archons seated themselves as the older man in the red robe moved to the edge of the dais. He faced the transparent cage and addressed the prisoners.

"I am Vígeldgeirr, First Flame of the Fire Reapers of Planetary Redemption," he said, in a voice so clear and pleasant that, for a brief, mad moment, Astra thought he might be a kindly person after all. "The Archons and I guide the spiritual and moral direction of the Fire Reapers. Each of the Archons"—he indicated the people in the chairs with a sweep of his hand—"is responsible for a sector of Terrania. Our role is to keep our original vision as pure and unwavering as flame."

He folded his hands and gazed at the prisoners sadly. "I have been deeply troubled by your refusal to comprehend the truth of our beliefs, after our hospitality here in the Fortress. I must confess to being deeply baffled by your continuing resistance. What do you gain by it?" He shook his head and held his hands out to them. "There is still time for you to repent. The Fire Reapers have moved beyond truth, beyond vision, beyond understanding, to the Absolute. 'For now we see through a glass, darkly, but then face to face.' "

He's mad, Astra thought to herself. He's completely insane.

But to her horror Neil stood up and, in a kind of robotic monotone, said, "Oh great Flame, forgive us, for we know not what we do."

Astra stared at him. What on earth was he saying? She half-rose, but Charlie nudged her and shook his head almost imperceptibly.

"Great Flame," Neil went on, "I have seen the error of my ways. I beg for the mercy of this Court. I wish only to be given the opportunity to serve the Fire Reapers. I wish to become a living flame, to be consumed as you are by your immense task."

They must have drugged him, Astra decided. There was no other way Neil would ever have said what he'd just said. But why hadn't they drugged her, too?

Vígeldgeirr nodded gravely as the Archons leaned toward one another, whispering. "A wise decision, my child," he said.

"Very wise indeed. We will be delighted to re-educate you in Fire Reaper ways. Guards"—and he waved a hand at the soldiers—"take him away."

Astra could no longer contain herself. "This isn't a trial!" she shouted. "This was supposed to be a trial! Besides, he's innocent, he hasn't done anything!" She could feel Charlie tugging at her tunic, but she plunged on. "The world you're creating is horrible! I never, ever want to live in your world! And millions of others feel the same way!"

But it was as if she hadn't spoken. Vígeldgeirr and the Archons ignored her, glancing at their illumined wafers or at the Countdown to Redemption clock on the wall as Neil was led unprotestingly away. She watched in anguish until the door shut behind him. Only then did the Archons turn their attention, not to Astra, but to Charlie.

"You, Slave 3964," said an Archon at the edge of the half-circle. "Stand up."

Charlie heaved himself painfully to his feet and stood there, head bowed. Where was the brave and defiant Charlie she knew? Had he been drugged, too?

"You are charged with insubordination, renegade-ism, subversion, and—the most serious charge of all—providing assistance to traitors to the State. How do you plead?"

Charlie swayed back and forth, eyes half-closed, and for an agonizing moment Astra thought he was going to begin saying the same awful things Neil had. But at last, mumbling slowly and with effort, he said, "Not guilty. Not that it makes any difference."

"Speak up," another Archon said. "We cannot hear you."

"Not guilty!" Charlie snapped, and for a moment his eyes blazed. He pulled himself up to his full height and stared at his judges. "You can destroy me if you want. I don't matter. But I guarantee we'll win out in the end. The world wants light—not the light of your infernal fires, but the light of understanding and love and tolerance. And one day we'll have it. One day—"

"Remove him!" shouted one of the Archons, a beautiful middle-aged woman, leaping to her feet. "Remove him at once!"

"Before he corrupts anyone else!" shouted another, an older man, shaking a fist.

"Kill him! Kill him!" shrieked a third, a toad-like man with rubbery lips. "His words are blasphemy! Take him away and destroy him!"

The guards swung round and pointed their weapons at Charlie. Astra clutched the hem of his tunic, terrified. Vígeldgeirr watched the two of them with a slow, contemptuous smile.

"Alas," he said, "my fellow Archons have spoken. I would have counselled patience, perhaps even one more chance at reform. But, as you have heard, they believe that poison leaks from your soul, and that you must be stopped—at once."

Two of the guards opened the cage and dragged Charlie out. "Leave him alone!" screamed Astra, throwing herself on the nearest guard and pummelling him with her fists. "He's done nothing! You mustn't touch him! He's a good man! He's—"

But the guard gave her a shove that threw her to the floor. By the time she got to her feet they were dragging a struggling Charlie across the room and out the nearest door. Astra found herself alone in the courtroom, facing the Archons. Vígeldgeirr gazed at her with a smile so tender that she could have cheerfully plunged a knife into his heart then and there.

"Daughter of Hallvard." He stood with his hands folded under his sleeves, looking solemn. "It grieves us greatly that you, of all people, have failed to see the truth of the Great Flame. Like your father, you possess great gifts—gifts that should be offered to us." He shook his head, and Astra could have sworn she saw tears in his eyes.

"I don't believe in your truth," Astra said. "Anyway, there's no point in my saying anything. You'll just twist it into something horrible and untrue." It suddenly struck her that the whole thing was a joke—some absurd, nonsensical joke—and she laughed out loud.

The tenderness vanished from Vígeldgeirr's face. "Perhaps you have failed to understand," he said softly, "that we hold the power of life and death over you."

"Oh, I know," Astra said almost flippantly. "But you still can't make me say what you want me to say, or do what you want me to do. You think you can control people, but you don't at all."

If the guards had suddenly broken out into a dance routine, the Archons could not have looked more dumbfounded. They stared at the First Flame and each other in consternation. Vígeldgeirr, his whole body shaking, raised his arm and pointed a quivering finger at her.

"You are hereby charged," he said, his voice trembling with rage, "with high treason, insubordination, subversion, and sabotage. How do you plead?"

"Oh, guilty, of course," said Astra cheerfully. She felt a giddy freedom. It didn't matter what she said, so she might as well say anything. "You've already decided I'm guilty. Who cares what I say? Certainly not you."

Murmurs of shock and outrage from the Archons. "You will remain in this courtroom," Vígeldgeirr said hoarsely, "as witness to the trials of your fellow terrorists. Perhaps that, at least, will teach you a lesson."

The wall to Astra's left dissolved, revealing another transparent cage as large as a small room. Within it stood an array of beings, dozens and dozens of them—Mínera Beings who shimmered in different gemlike colours; Bestia with horns and hooves and claws; a handful of Aqua Libere priestesses in their blue robes. There were Ash-Gatherer villagers, too, men and women and children, standing silently and fearfully. She couldn't see her father among them, but there, quivering behind the Aqua Libere women, was Fru Berta! Her face was lined and shrunken, her eyes downcast. Astra's heart went out to her. She focused her attention on her as hard as she could, but Fru Berta had withdrawn into a world of her own.

A guard touched the wall to the right, revealing another

room-sized cage. Astra gasped. Here, visible to her at last, were the Arbolé. They were dressed in many shades of green and brown and beige, and a different kind of leaf grew from each forehead and down their backs. Their skin resembled bark, and the sinews of their arms and hands and feet were like tree roots. But they all looked ill, their eyes dull, their chests sunken. Something took hold of Astra's heart and squeezed.

One of the Arbolé stepped forward and turned toward the Archons. He was tall and slender, with clothing—or perhaps it was his skin—like the bark of a paper birch. "I am Bjarkansál of the Arbolé," he said, in not much more than a whisper. "I speak on behalf of our leader, Arduinna, equal among equals. She is very ill and requires immediate medical attention."

He gestured with his hand and the group of Arbolé parted. In their middle, half-lying in their arms, was a tall, willowy woman with long copper-coloured hair. Around her neck was a garland woven of willow withes and oak leaves, and on her head was a circlet of pine cones. But the leaves in her hair had withered and her skin was deathly pale. She lay with her eyes closed, barely breathing. She was, Astra thought, wilting to death.

"You are prisoners and enemies of the state," Vígeldgeirr snapped. "You are not permitted to make demands." His upper lip was curled in a sneer, and Astra couldn't imagine how she'd ever thought he might be kindly and benevolent. "Through our generous intervention you were provided with the necessities of life, including light. If your mongrel origins make you a weak life form, that is your affair."

Vígeldgeirr continued speaking, but Astra barely heard what he said. The radiance of the Arbolé, even in their depleted state, filled the courtroom. It even seemed to intimidate the Archons, who crouched in their chairs, watching Bjarkansál with a mixture of fear and loathing.

"... sentenced to the Plane of Eternal Night," Vígeldgeirr was saying, his voice dripping with revulsion. "It is a plane that lies in a spatial dimension beyond the outer reaches of the most distant galaxies, and it is a place of no return—ever." He turned his black gaze on the cage across the way, and finally on Astra. "You, too, will be sent to the Plane of Eternal Night. And like them you will drift beyond the stars, alone forever among the frozen reaches of outer space."

She was being sentenced, then, to eternal exile. Yet for the moment she felt nothing. Instead she gazed at the Arbolé leader, lying so still among her fellow Arbolé. Bjarkansál turned back toward the Archons, his face grave.

"Once again I draw the attention of this court to the urgency of medical—"

Vígeldgeirr, ignoring him, motioned to the guards stationed at the massive door behind the dais. It opened slowly to admit two Milicrons, each holding a heavy chain. At the other end of the chains was Freya. Her tail was tucked between her legs, and she was whimpering.

"So now she's on trial, too?" Astra shouted, leaping to her feet again. "She can't even defend herself! Of all the horrible—"

"The Varg-Minne Project—perhaps you've heard of it?" interrupted Vígeldgeirr coldly. "It's our newest research project in the Warrior Generation Laboratories. The Varg-Minne are part-human, part-Gribbhålla, and part wolf, with an element of dog to make them obedient. We expect them to be our most efficient and lethal warriors yet. That, daughter of Hallvard, is our sentence for the dog object."

But Astra barely heard the last of what Vígeldgeirr said. There was the sound of a distant, dull explosion, and shouts, and running feet. The Temple was suddenly plunged into darkness.

Out and In Again

From somewhere nearby came the noise of running feet and shouts in UL and Nordlandish. Astra sat up slowly, rubbing her head where she'd banged it. She was still in the cage, but her guards had disappeared, and the vast hall was still in darkness. Where was everyone? What was happening?

She got to her feet unsteadily and touched the cage wall. This time it didn't shock her, but the wall was as solid as ever. A raw welt, oozing blood, had formed on her scalp. She licked her fingers and rubbed saliva over the wound.

More running feet, more shouts, and a door nearby burst open. Fire Reaper soldiers, evidently, yelling at each other in New Nordlandish. One of them took out his lightstone and flashed it round the room. The light passed over her, paused, flashed back. Blinded by the beam, she shielded her eyes and heard bootsteps rapidly approaching.

"You," one of them said, his voice slurred, the lightstone in his hand wavering. "Who are you?"

"She's a prisoner, stupid," said another, giving his colleague a shove. "A terror—whaddaya call 'em?—terrorist." He hiccuped and stumbled forward, swaying drunkenly in front of the cage.

Uh oh. They'd been drinking the notorious *ófriðr-mjǫðr*, the war-mead they gave soldiers before battle. Astra thought quickly. "I'm the daughter of—of a famous scientist who's helping your leaders," she said, swallowing hard. "The Memory Stone Project—have you heard of that?"

"Yeah?" one of the others said cynically. "Then how come you're a prisoner?"

294

"They, uh, they're keeping me safe here. Your leaders, I mean." She licked her lips and hurried on. "If the terrorists—the Arbolé and the others—get hold of me ... well, who knows what they'll do?"

It sounded ridiculous even as she said it, but the soldiers seemed to believe her. They stared jumpily at the shadows round them as if the terrorists were lurking there.

"That's what Eldjárn said," the first soldier said in a loud whisper. "Him and Úlfrún, they said there was Bestia regiments besieging the east wall—"

"Shut up, you idiot!" This came from an older man at the back who pushed his way forward. "Rumours, that's all they are, rumours!"

"Then how come our officers took off?" demanded the cynical one, rounding on him as another burst of yelling broke out. They were about to come to blows, Astra was sure.

"You've got to get me out of here," she said urgently.

"And how are we supposed to do that?" the cynical one said in his unpleasant nasal voice. "You think we know the codes? We're just grunts."

"There'll be a reward if you save me. A big reward," Astra added hurriedly.

The first soldier lifted his Tabri from his shoulder and aimed it drunkenly at the cage. Astra cried out and ducked just in time. A blinding beam hit the cage with a sound like fat sizzling in a frying pan, and the front wall melted away.

"Where's my reward?" he said as Astra darted past the smoking and dripping edges of the cage.

"Forget it, Bayani, we gotta get out of here!" yelled another. From somewhere far off came the faint but unmistakable whistle of Lumini flares, the eerie whine of Tabris, then the horrible shrieking of the Gribbhålla.

The cynical one prodded Astra with his weapon. "You. We're not leaving you here." He pushed her in front of him toward the empty dais, the others close behind him with their weapons raised. The older man was shining a lightstone along the floor, searching for something.

"There. There it is."

Buried in the floor behind the dais was a tiny glowing flame, no bigger than a pinpoint. The soldier knelt and pressed it with his finger. A narrow section of floor slid open, revealing a flight of stairs, going down. At once there was a scramble for the opening. The last thing Astra wanted was to go down into that dark hole, but she didn't dare resist. The rest of the soldiers clambered in behind her and her captor, and the floor slid back over their heads, leaving them in total darkness.

In the holding cells far underground, Neil and Charlie heard nothing but the dull roar from Weapons Production on the next level up. The roar drowned out the approach of thousands of marching feet, the first exchanges of Tabri and Lumini fire, the screeching of hundreds of bird-Bestia squadrons clashing with the Vampyriae. Even the release of several dozen half-finished Varg-Minne, their wolf-Gribbhålla howls shattering enough to split eardrums, didn't penetrate.

But the blast in the east wall—the result of Disintegrons strapped to the bodies of mole-Bestia troops who dug into the foundations—shook the whole Fortress. Neil, still dulled by the drug the Fire Reapers had given him, heard only a loud and baffling noise, but Charlie struggled to his feet and stood gripping the bars, his heart beating wildly. They'd given him another good beating before throwing him in the cell—they'd broken his nose this time, he was pretty sure, and one of his legs didn't work properly—and he didn't dare hope, not really. He strained his ears to listen, glancing upward in alarm as the ceiling showered dust around him.

And then he heard something else—faint shouting and cheering, growing rapidly closer. Half a dozen slaves in soot-covered uniforms ran past his cell, whooping and punching the air. What was going on? Now more were dashing past, frenzied with joy, not stopping even when Charlie shouted at them. Guards and overseers were running past, too, in twos and threes, their faces terrified.

"Hey! You! Get me out of here!" Charlie rattled the bars frantically, but he might as well have been invisible. He shouted until his voice was hoarse, until the tears were streaming down his face. And then he saw someone he actually knew—his old friend Karim.

"Charlie? It is really you?"

"Yes, goldarn it, it's me! Ya gotta get me outta here pronto!"

"But I cannot—I do not have—"

"Grab one of them guards!"

Karim seized the nearest one and yanked him to a halt. The man, blubbering, fell to his knees. "I was only following orders, honest—I couldn't help it—"

"Shut up," Charlie said succinctly. "Now get his MoleculeCoder."

The guard at once thrust it at Karim. "Today it's *Flamme-sjau-fimm-níu-tveir-tveir-fjórir*," he whispered. Karim punched in the code. A few agonizing moments later, the cell doors swung open, and hundreds of shouting and cheering prisoners poured out. As the terrified guard scuttled off, Charlie flung his arms round Karim and grinned at his startled and blackened face.

"Time Boy," Charlie said. "We gotta find him."

Neil was at the far end of the last cell block, huddled in a corner, asleep. Charlie shook him roughly. The boy woke and stared uncomprehendingly up at him, the pupils of his eyes still cloudy. Charlie and Karim heaved him to his feet. Then the three of them stumbled toward the daylight leaking through the gaping hole in the east wall.

"Whose idea was this, anyway?" muttered the cynical soldier.

The tunnel had turned out to be slimy with damp and

infested with cockroaches, and the effects of the drink were wearing off, leaving them ill-tempered. "Fire's blood!" the soldier cursed, and hit out at the cockroaches with the butt of his Tabri. They simply fell to the ground, crunching under their feet. Astra, shuddering, gritted her teeth and offered silent apologies for destroying so many of them. After all, if a stone was a being, then certainly cockroaches were.

"Gyorig's! It was Gyorig's idea!" said the first soldier. "Good old Gyorig, from that sunken little island off the Pacific DeadSea!"

This was apparently some sort of insult, because the others guffawed as Gyorig said angrily, "Just shut up, all of you! You'd be dead by now if it wasn't for me!"

"Dead, he says!" sneered the first one in a high grating voice. "Me and Broidic here are crack shots, Gyorig. Not like you, you little fire-pisser!"

"And you, you dumb Nordlandian, you can't even speak UL!" A fist connected with a face as Gyorig lashed out at the speaker. The speaker hit back, his fist landing with a crack on Gyorig's jaw. The soldier named Broidic tried to push between them, yelling, "Break it up, you two!" But Gyorig shoved him out of the way and he fell heavily, landing just centimetres from where Astra was crouched, trembling, against the wall. The lightstone he'd held went out, plunging them all into darkness.

The body on the ground lay absolutely still. "By the balls of the First Flame," muttered Gyorig's opponent, and the next minute a fist landed with the sound of a cantaloupe dropped from a height, followed by an "Unnnnnhhh!" Astra pressed herself even more tightly against the wall, crushing dozens more cockroaches in the process.

"Ash-licker!" shouted Gyorig, panting heavily, and the two of them went down, punching and struggling as the others cheered and shouted. Holding her breath, Astra edged her way slowly past the body. The groans and heavings faded behind her as she groped her way down the tunnel.

Outside the Fortress, Hreinn-Sál and a regiment of Bestia were positioned behind a low hill beyond the east wall, re-checking their weapons. There was a lull in the battle—perhaps the Fire Reapers were rethinking their strategy. Just as well, Hreinn-Sál thought grimly. His troops were exhausted from the day's fighting, after being on the march for the last week. He was resharpening his antlers when a call came from the lookout: "Humans approaching!"

Hreinn-Sál peered out from behind the rise of the hill. Like his reindeer ancestors, he had weak eyesight, and his eyes hadn't yet fully changed their colour from summer yellow to winter blue. Slaves had been pouring out of that hole they'd blasted in the east wall all day, but this little group was making straight for them—two orange-suited slaves, dragging the body of a younger human. What on Terrania were they doing?

Hreinn-Sál motioned to his lieutenants, tightened his grip on his weapon, and stepped out from behind the hill. "Who goes there?" he bellowed, raising himself to his full height and tossing his antlers.

Charlie, who had Neil's left arm slung over his shoulder, stared in terror and amazement. Who was this creature with the antlers and hooves of a stag and the body of a human?

"Seize them!" the stag-like creature shouted. The next thing Charlie knew, two other animal beings—one an eagle-human, the other part mountain goat—had grabbed him by the arms, while two more grabbed Karim.

"The boy needs help, he's sick!" Charlie shouted. But the beings holding him paid no attention. Maybe they think he's dead, Charlie thought, and I killed him.

"Hey!" he shouted again. "Just a cotton-pickin' minute! I'm a friend, see?"

The stag-being regarded Charlie suspiciously. "So why did you capture the boy child?" He gestured to his lieutenants, who were lifting Neil tenderly onto the back of a half-horse.

"We didn't. We rescued him. We got hold of a guard and a MoleculeCoder—"

"And what have you done with the girl child?"

"Nothing." Charlie swallowed hard. "See, we were all in the Hall of Judgement, we were prisoners, and then me and Neil were dragged away—"

"And who is *this* human?" The stag-being motioned to Karim, who'd been listening fearfully.

"He's a friend. He was a slave, like me. Look, I'm tellin' ya—"

The stag-being frowned, and stared at the Fortress in the distance, and sniffed the air. "Your smell is—strange. Not of this world."

"I come from another time," Charlie said hesitantly. Would these beings believe him? "Same as Neil does. In fact, you could say I brought him here."

The stag-being regarded him with suspicion again. "The boy child was sent on a special mission, as was the girl. Or so Áilu told us. What part do you play?"

Damned if I know, Charlie thought wearily. Out of the fryin' pan into the fire—that seemed to be the story of his life ever since he'd arrived in Nordlandia. When all this was over—if it was ever over—he'd have to write a book. Though no one would believe a word of it.

"Let's just say an experiment I did went kinda wrong," Charlie said lamely. "And I been regrettin' it ever since."

The stag-being stared at Charlie and then at his hooves, considering. "We will have to hold you until we can verify your story," he said at last, as Charlie felt the blood drain from his face. "Our first concern must be for the boy." He motioned to those who held Charlie and Karim. "Take them away. But do not harm them."

The tunnel seemed endless. Here and there a supporting beam had collapsed, and Astra had to crawl over it under the dangerously caved-in ceiling. Either the tunnel had been built in haste, or the Fire Reapers hadn't bothered repairing it. Perhaps they'd believed they'd never have to use it. Even worse, side tunnels branched off in all directions, and Astra was never sure which one to take. From time to time she lifted her head and flared her nostrils for the tell-tale smell of fresh air, but nothing came.

It was unbearably hot, and she was desperate for a drink of water. She barely noticed the cockroaches anymore. Or the patches of slime, or the stink of decay, or the looping spider-webs that she clawed at without thinking when they clung to her face. She'd almost given up hope of ever finding her way out. And then, turning a corner, she saw far above her a tiny fissure of light. She scrabbled toward it over another fallen beam.

Below it a series of crumbling steps had been cut into the earth walls. She dug in her fingers and hauled herself up step by step. At last, with a final heave, she was directly below the fissure in the tunnel roof. She reached up a hand and pushed. Clods of sandy earth collapsed around her, showering her with dirt, and—oh the joy!—fresh air rushed through. She managed to grab hold of a withered-looking bush, and with the last of her strength pulled herself through.

The sun was setting, and its brilliant reddening rays blinded her as she staggered out. She was outside the Fortress, at last! She took in great lungsful of air and stood unsteadily, trying to get her bearings. In the distance dozens of figures were pouring out of a jagged hole in the foundations, whooping and shouting. Among them were Fire Reaper guards in twos and threes, skulking off along the walls and trying to look invisible. She scanned the crowd anxiously—had Charlie and Neil managed to escape, too?—but could see no sign of them.

She stared about her, shielding her eyes. There, out on the plain as far as the eye could see, were the scattered encampments of the besieging armies—Mínera Beings with their bright banners, regiments of Arbolé with gleaming arrow-shaped weapons, Bestia troops in furred and feathered squadrons. The Fortress itself was surrounded by Fire Reaper soldiers, their wedge-shaped phalanx penetrating into the plain. But retreating Fire Reaper troops were fleeing right past her, their uniforms stained with dust and blood, faces grey with fatigue. Other Fire Reaper troops rushed past with floating stretchers, carrying the bodies of wounded or dead comrades. She edged away from the battlefield, looking for a crevice or hillock where she might hide.

A fearful screech erupted above her head and she instinctively flattened herself. A Vampyrion! It dropped like a stone, hissing and shrieking. She curled up in a ball and threw her arms round her head, expecting the worst. Instead, the Vampyrion veered away at the last minute, still screeching, followed by a volley of deafening shrieks and *kak-kak-kaks* high above her.

Astra uncurled and stared upward in astonishment. A battalion of Bird-Bestia! They were attacking a flock of Vampyriae with bloodcurdling cries and screams. Broken tail-feathers and bits of leathery wing dropped out of the sky. At last the Vampyriae were driven off, still screeching. A blur of golden plumage detached itself from the Bird-Bestia and plummeted downwards.

"Tårnfalk!" Astra shouted. The falcon-being braked to a halt, and Astra flung her arms round her feathery neck and burst into tears. Tårnfalk wrapped a wing round her and gently nibbled her ear. "There, there. You're quite safe."

"I thought you were dead ... I thought I'd never see you again ..."

"Oh, we Raptor-Humans are tougher than that," Tårnfalk said cheerfully. "I'm perfectly well, as you see." She grinned, her beak opened wide. "We made quite a meal of those Vampyriae, my troops and I." And she preened her feathers as if she'd personally finished them off.

"You can't imagine how glad I am to see you," Astra said fervently. "It's been so awful, and I don't know where anyone is, and ..." She burst into tears again.

"Now, now, child. All is not lost. You and I, at least, have found each other."

"But Neil and Freya and Charlie—we were all prisoners, but I got out, and now I—" She broke off, exhausted. Tears trickled down her cheeks, tracing more runnels through the mixture of dust and cockroach juice. "I have to find them, I *have* to. Piedra, too."

"Now just who are Charlie and Piedra?" Tårnfalk asked, cocking her head on one side. But before Astra could answer, the distant whistle of Lumini lasers broke out, followed by the high whine of Tabris, the shriek and chatter of other weapons. A vast and distant noise came to her—the faint but rising tread of thousands of feet, the GRAWP! GRAWP! of dematerialization devices, a massive confusion of shouting and cries. She could just make out, through a boiling cloud of dust, the red flashes of the Tabris, the eerie luminescence of the light-based weapons. She turned away, shaking violently, and clapped her hands over her ears. Tårnfalk pulled at her urgently with her beak, half-dragging her toward the safety of a nearby rock outcrop.

An advance party of Arbolé had reached the Fortress, where some of them were launching ladders of living vines to scale the walls. A handful of Mínera Beings were lobbing Disintegrons over the ramparts, and from inside came the sound of vast explosions. Astra stared in dull horror, then, before Tårnfalk could stop her, pulled herself away and began running toward them. "Stop!" she shrieked, waving her arms frantically. "Stop! There are friendly beings inside!"

Tårnfalk flew after her. "Are you out of your mind?" she hissed, seizing Astra by her tunic.

"I have to! I have to!" Astra lashed out at Tårnfalk, trying to wriggle out of her beak. "Let me go!"

Hreinn-Sál, moving his troops forward in a flanking movement, could see almost nothing through the boil of dust and smoke, but he clearly heard Astra's voice and smelled her distinctive smell. The girl child! What was she doing here? He flung up a hoof to halt his troops. The next minute a small figure came running toward him, still waving her arms, Tårnfalk in hot pursuit. A Fire Reaper soldier took aim at her, but Tårnfalk swooped down and knocked the weapon from his hand with her talons. The next moment Astra had run blindly into Hreinn-Sál's embrace, sobbing her heart out. Hreinn-Sál enfolded her with his hooves, relief flooding him.

"That was madness, child, running into the line of fire ..."

"Hreinn-Sál, you mustn't, you mustn't!" She was gulping, almost incoherent. "They're still in there—Neil and Charlie and—you mustn't blow it up, you mustn't—"

"But they aren't, child. The boy is in our field hospital, recovering. The human you call Charlie rescued him, or so he says."

Astra's eyes widened. "Neil's safe? He's okay?"

"He will be, once we find the antidote to the drug—"

"And Charlie? Charlie's okay, too?"

"Yes. Now you must stay with Tårnfalk—"

"But Freya—" Astra looked imploringly at him. "She's still in there somewhere. And Piedra, too!"

At that moment a dematerialization device whinged over Astra's head, barely missing her. Hreinn-Sál pushed her, none too gently, toward Tårnfalk. "Go. At once. Now!"

There was no defying Hreinn-Sál. She let Tårnfalk lead her to a safe zone behind battle lines, ringed by heavy Bestia troops—hippo-, elephant-, and bison-beings. Several Bi-Souls were poring over topographical maps and battle plans. Guldsterre was among them, though Astra barely recognized her in her helmet and armour. She gasped out loud when she saw Astra.

"Have you materialized out of thin air, dear heart?" She put her arm round Astra's shoulder and drew her close, her face lined with sadness. "It broke my own heart when word of my brother's betrayal and your imprisonment came back to us." Rhodium and his lieutenants gathered round, exclaiming in surprise and relief, and then a tall Arbolé, pine cones erupting from his knuckles, came forward.

"I am Furu-Sál, at your service," he said, and inclined his pine-cone-laden head. "May I ask," he said, and his face was weary, "whether you have word of Arduinna?"

304

"I saw her, but she's—she's very ill," Astra blurted out. "The others, too. We have to help them. And Freya and Piedra and—"

"Piedra?" said Guldsterre sharply. "His descendants were among the founding members of the Mínera Beings. We must rescue him at once. Rhodium." She turned to her general. "What are the reports coming back from the advance parties?"

Rhodium touched a miniature LightWire wound round his ear. "They've cleared the lower two levels. They're working their way upward. They think that's where the leadership have retreated."

"Then we must enter immediately," Guldsterre said. She turned, frowning, to Furu-Sál. "Do I have your agreement to put together a rescue party?"

Furu-Sál turned to two or three other Arbolé standing near, and they spoke in low tones. "Yes," he said, turning and looking straight at Guldsterre. "We are in agreement."

"Each of the Nations will nominate two officers," Guldsterre declared. "And you, child, must lead the way. No one else knows the Fortress as you do."

But I don't, thought Astra. I only ever saw the labs and the Temple. And it's so big and confusing and—

"There's no one else," Furu-Sál said grimly. "Your friends are ill or injured."

"And no one else will recognize the dog-being," added Guldsterre.

I can't, I can't, Astra thought in desperation. I can't go back inside! I barely got out alive!

"You will have help," Guldsterre said gently. "You will not be alone. Those with you have many powers."

Astra looked at Guldsterre, her face sombre and blood-smeared under her golden helmet, and wiped the dirt and sweat from her own face. "Okay," she said, trying to stand up straighter. "Okay."

The Fortress Redux

he last of the slaves—the weakest and sickest—were still leaving through the gaping hole in the Fortress. Many of them stumbled along, leaning on others and paying no attention to the little band of Bi-Souls who slipped past them. Fjellgeit, Hreinn-Sál's adjutant, had been appointed to take charge of the rescue mission, accompanied by two eager younger Bestia troops. Behind him and Astra came Picea and Álmveig of the Arbolé, and Zircon of the Mínera Beings along with young Amethyst, Rhodium's daughter, and a quartz-pale young soldier named Melke.

In the vast warren of holding cells on the bottom level of the Fortress, all the doors stood open. Astra stared in horror at these tiny lightless boxes, the floors filthy and damp, the odd rat or mouse flicking past. Wherever she'd been held, the night before their so-called trial, it wasn't here. There was a vile smell of burning chemicals from somewhere, too.

"This awful air," Álmveig said heavily, and shook her sweating, autumn-coloured leaves as she adjusted the Chlorophyllider at her hip. "I've never transpired so much in my life."

Not a single Fire Reaper soldier or guard passed them; either they'd all fled already or they'd retreated to the upper floors. The group made their way carefully over the rubble of a stairwell to the next level, where the burning smell was overpowering. Astra gasped at the vast black expanse that stretched away before them, the size of a small city, devoid of life except for the flames still flickering under the smelting pots.

"What a horrible place," Astra whispered to no one in particular, feeling sick to her stomach. Fjellgeit, who was standing beside her, wrinkled his goat nose. "I've never smelled evil before," he said sombrely, "but this is it." And he shook his horned head as if trying to dislodge the odour.

They moved on past the long lines of cauldrons, looking for an exit to the upper floors. Astra tried to orient herself. Where had she and the others landed when they'd plunged out of the Plane of Oblivion? Was that vast tree-burning furnace somewhere on this level? And where was Piedra? Somewhere in their descent he must have fallen out of Neil's tunic and ended up—where? How, in all this vastness, would they ever find him?

A sudden scuffling made them all whirl, but it was only a rat, leaping from rung to rung on the platform above them. Fjellgeit, whose hoof had gone to his Chromobact, relaxed and smiled grimly. "The Fire Reapers have behaved like rats, too," he said. "Abandoning a sinking ship."

"Except their leaders," said Picea, whose spruce-needle aroma was welcome in the poisonous air. "*They* fled to the upper decks, the cowards. What's there, Astra, that they'd guard above all?"

Astra considered. There was the Temple, with its massive Archive—surely they'd want to protect that. But there were also the Warrior Generation Laboratories, their most important research program. The place Freya had been condemned to.

"The laboratories," she said. "That's where Freya is. Unless they've moved her."

"Then we'll split up," Fjellgeit said, "into six teams. Each team will reconnoitre an exit leading to the upper floors."

The exits on the south and east sides had been destroyed by the original blast or by later Disintegrons. But they soon discovered that the stairs and CloudTubes on the north and west sides had been blocked or damaged, too—"possibly deliberately sabotaged," Zircon said grimly.

Fjellgeit, nimble and surefooted, scaled one of the damaged staircases, only to discover that the door at the top had been sealed shut from the inside. "It proves that some of them, at least, moved to the upper levels," he said when he clattered back down. "We need a platoon of Mole sappers to blast a hole."

"And it'll bring the whole place down around our ears!" retorted Picea. "Not to mention give us away."

"Then it seems to me," Zircon said, "that you need our expertise." And he took from his belt a tiny curved blade, no bigger than a fingernail paring, that glinted with sparkling dust. Lifting his arm, he flung it at the door. The blade lodged itself in the metal, which flew apart under it.

"How did you do that?" Astra said, staring in amazement.

"Our Dhilalia, as we call them—our crescent moons—consume arnostium molecules, among other things," Zircon said casually. "Careless of them not to have replaced the doors with some newer alloy."

Already the two younger Bestia were hurrying up the damaged staircase and through the new opening. "Discipline's not what it was in my day," Fjellgeit said, shaking his head at them. He bent down so that Astra could scramble onto his back before climbing the staircase once more, followed by the others. The Fortress's gleaming hallways stretched away before them in several directions, eerily empty.

"By the Bi-Souled!" a young wolverine-Bestia named Jarfr-Sál said, his weapon at the ready, glancing round disappointedly. "I was looking forward to a little skirmish, myself."

Fjellgeit glared at him. "You could have got yourself killed, advancing recklessly like that! Have you forgotten everything you learned at school?" And turning his back on the abashed young Bestia, he said to Astra, "Now, where are the laboratories from here?"

The illuminated icon in the lab had read Flame-Level 9, or so she remembered, but where were they now? "We're on Flame-Level 1," Amethyst reported, coming back from a reconnoitre with another young Mínera soldier. "Eight levels to go."

Astra regarded her admiringly. Amethyst looked so young, not more than sixteen or so, with a dazzling purple eruption of her Mínera self shimmering through her hair. Yet she was so brave and competent in her armour, her weapon over her shoulder. Perhaps she could be just like Amethyst when she grew up.

They avoided the too-visible CloudTubes and used only the few intact stairways. But the place seemed utterly deserted, and they moved unhindered from floor to floor. Astra, terrified of running into a Fire Reaper officer, or even General Sardonyx himself, felt increasingly uneasy about the silence. She pressed a little closer to Fjellgeit, grateful for his sharp hooves and horns as well as his weapon.

"You don't suppose they've mined the lower floors with paralysis mines, do you?" she whispered.

"Paralysis mines are far too unstable to use in an enclosed area," Fjellgeit reassured her.

From somewhere nearby came the sound of voices and of something heavy being dragged. The group scattered quickly into doorways or corners, Amethyst pulling Astra with her. Moments later six Fire Reaper soldiers came hurrying round a corner, followed by two Milicrons dragging an enormous flame-coloured sack.

"Divided six ways there'll still be plenty to last us," panted the shortest and fattest soldier, who was having trouble keeping up.

"Come on, move it!" snapped another, turning to give the nearest Milicron a cuff on the head. But the cuff never landed, because Fjellgeit stepped out into the hallway. The Fire Reapers started back in surprise, bumping into one another as the other Bi-Souls emerged. One of the Fire Reapers spun on his heel and took off down the hall, but he was brought to ground by a blast from Picea's Chlorophyllider. As he writhed on the floor, Fjellgeit confronted the others.

"Looting the place, are you?" he said darkly as the Milicrons shrank back in alarm.

"We were saving—"

"—guarding the valuables—"

"—Temple items, they're sacred, we couldn't let them fall into unbeliever hands—"

Fjellgeit jerked his Chromobact at them, motioning them against the nearest wall, where Jarfr-Sál and Picea began cheerfully confiscating weapons. Then he waved his weapon at the Milicrons. "Open it," he commanded.

The Milicrons fumbled in terror at the knots of the sack, which turned out to be a Fire Reaper cloak. It was stuffed with a treasure-trove of objects—gold candlesticks, plates and goblets carved from crystal, tiny silver ash-sample boxes—all marked with the familiar flame icon.

"Guarding them, huh?" said Fjellgeit sarcastically, poking among the pile with his weapon. "Planning to sell them off, you mean, and save your necks." He glared at the line-up of soldiers. "You're a disgrace, the lot of you. If I was your commanding officer, I'd have you shot."

"*They* didn't stay," one of them said sullenly. "They just abandoned us."

"And *you* didn't have the courage of your convictions?" Zircon demanded. No one answered.

Something familiar in the middle of the pile caught Astra's eye—a slender silver tube with tiny finger holes. "My Sensor!" she exclaimed, darting forward and seizing it. Apart from a few nicks and scratches it seemed unharmed. She tucked it in her pocket, relief flooding through her. Meanwhile, Fjellgeit paced back and forth in front of the soldiers.

"Things will go easier for you," he said, "if you cooperate. First things first. Where are the Archons? And General Sardonyx?"

"We don't know about the Archons," one of them said at last, after some hesitation.

"But General Sardonyx—he took a crack battalion out to the battlefield," another said proudly. "He knows what the Prophecies say about the End Times. He wants to be part of it."

Fjellgeit and the others exchanged glances. Were they

310

telling the truth? "Take them away," Fjellgeit said, motioning to Jarfr-Sál and his young Bestia colleague, "and report back to Guldsterre and the others on what we've been told. If Sardonyx is out there ..." He shook his bearded head slightly. As the prisoners were marched off, Jarfr-Sál snapping at their heels, he turned to the Milicrons.

"And who—or what—are you?"

"I am Milicron BN942, sir," one of them answered in his deep metallic singsong, though his voice trembled. "We are human-metal hybrids."

"I know him!" Astra blurted out, staring at him. "He's the one who saved Freya! He went against orders, he risked his life!"

Fjellgeit regarded Astra, considering, and then back at the Milicron. "He's just a piece of animate machinery. How could he possibly think for himself?"

"We learned otherwise," the Milicron said, "that day with the girl human." Something flickered in the depths of his pupil-less eyes, something that hadn't been there before. "That is why, only hours ago"—his voice broke and steadied again—"we chose not to obey, Milicron RJ731 and I, when we were ordered to sacrifice ourselves in the destruction of the exits." He glanced at his colleague with what, in a human, might have been called tender concern. "Many of our other colleagues now lie among the rubble."

"Then why were you helping the looters?" Fjellgeit stood with his hooves folded, his face severe.

"They promised to lead us to the Outside. We have never been there. We only know of it through rumours." Again something flickered in those eyes—a deep, weary sadness.

"Well, that's unfortunate, because you're under arrest," Fjellgeit said decisively.

"Oh, please, Fjellgeit." Astra stepped forward impulsively. "Can't you give them a chance?" Fjellgeit's upper lip lifted from his teeth in anger, but she rushed on. "They saved our lives, mine and Freya's. And they've turned against the Fire Reapers. They're on our side now."

"They were still helping the looters," Álmveig pointed out.

"We had no choice," Milicron BN942 said steadily. "After we turned against our masters, they would have destroyed us. We had to find a way out."

Fjellgeit and his lieutenants exchanged glances again, and Fjellgeit looked guardedly at the Milicrons. "How do we know we can trust you?"

"We can guide you," Milicron BN942 said, "wherever you wish to go." He held out his palm, with its array of icons. "If you will take us with you when you leave."

Fjellgeit stared at them. "Very well," he said at last. "You must guide us to the Warrior Generation Laboratories. And then to your masters—wherever they're hiding."

The Milicrons looked terrified, and Milicron RJ731 clutched his colleague's arm. Milicron BN942 nodded slowly. "We will do as you wish," he said softly. "At least we will be together." And he linked his own metallic digits with his companion's.

"Then lead the way," Fjellgeit said, and his voice was deep and grave. "There is no time to lose."

On Flame-Level 9, all was in darkness. The Bi-Soul band followed the Milicrons down a series of corridors and past door after door, finally stopping at one where Milicron BN942 tapped his palm. The door swung open, and Milicron RJ731 swiftly drew a finger up the wall. As the room leapt into light, Astra looked round, apprehensive. There was the metal table she'd been strapped to; there was the cot where she'd slept. But the cages that had once been full of monkeys and falcons and other animals were empty. The place gave her the creeps.

"What did they do with the animals that were here?" She hated asking the question because she wasn't sure she wanted to hear the answer.

"The normal practice," said Milicron RJ731 softly, "was to take them to the Central Operations Unit as needed."

As needed? What did that mean? Another chill shot through Astra. "We're wasting time," Fjellgeit said impatiently. "How do we get there?"

The Milicrons turned and led them through room after room, each accessible only by Milicron touch, and each filled with more terrifying-looking equipment than the last—things that looked like gigantic dentists' drills, others shaped like claws or knives or insects' eyes, still others that seemed alive and moved their parts as the little group passed them. They came at last to a long, low tunnel that looked for all the world like a City thought-tube station.

"No, not by thought," said Milicron BN942 when Astra asked. "That, in fact, is a pretence, in the City too. Our masters have not yet discovered how to harness thought—or at least, not human thought. It operates by Milicron circuitry."

The Milicrons did nothing that Astra could see, but the next minute a series of transparent capsules floated into view, each containing a single reclined seat. "This is our Inter-Laboratory Transport, with an oxygenized interior atmosphere to counteract the lack of air pressure," Milicron BN942 explained. "Now, if you will each enter a capsule, we can be on our way."

"How do we know," Zircon asked, "that you're not just delivering us to the Fire Reaper leaders?"

"They would destroy us," said Milicron RJ731 simply, "because we have revealed to you one of their technological secrets."

The little group regarded one another, looking troubled. It was Astra who said, "I think they're telling the truth."

"We do not know how vegetal tissues will react to such an atmosphere," Picea said firmly. "I can't risk it."

"We're all living cells of some kind or another," Zircon pointed out. "Ours move more slowly, that's all."

"Very well," said Fjellgeit, a little impatiently. "The Arbolé will remain behind to protect against possible sabotage."

As the Arbolé took up guard positions at the entrance of the tunnel, the others each climbed into a capsule through an opening in its top. The openings immediately sealed over, leaving Astra panicking. But a mere second or two later, the lids opened automatically in an identical station. Had they moved at all?

As they stepped out onto the platform, there came such a shrieking and a howling and a braying that Astra had to clap her hands over her ears. They were in a long white room that contained hundreds of cages—eagles, tigers, cougars, boa constrictors, wild boars, even a crocodile in a tank. As Fjellgeit and the others moved forward, weapons drawn, Astra slipped away and hurried down the ranks of cages. In each a pair of golden or brown or piercing blue eyes stared back at her. "Where's Freya?" she implored of a regal-looking greyhound that came forward and sniffed at her eagerly. But the greyhound was a dog, not a Bestia, and lacked the power of human speech. She hurried on.

It was a dizzying place. Walls appeared suddenly in front of her or faded to one side. A kind of pulsating corridor that made strange sucking and moaning sounds stood just ahead, its sides undulating in and out as though it was alive. At the far end was a door that seemed to be made out of live flames, and she hesitated.

The Etheric Sensor! Why hadn't she thought of it before? Maybe it wouldn't work here in the Fortress. She yanked it from her pocket. It took several minutes before she could see anything except whirling, blurry shapes, but at last the scene steadied and held. There were the terrifying flames, up close now, leaping and growling ...

And then she laughed. The fire was nothing but mist! A sort of orangey-red mist-and-sound show. Very effective, but nothing to be afraid of. And beyond the mist ... She could see, as though she were looking through the wrong end of a telescope, a tiny group of white-coated lab technicians around a table. One of them was holding a sort of razorlike scoop, narrow and elongated. She strained her eyes and adjusted the Sensor, but

314

the picture was already fading and she couldn't make out anything more.

She took a deep breath, pushed her way along the pulsating corridor, and plunged through the fiery mist. At the far end of the room was the group of technicians, crowded round the table. Along the walls were dozens of cages holding what she thought must be wolves, black and grey and white and brown and mottled. They caught her scent and began pacing and howling. One or two of the technicians turned at the noise, frowning, and Astra ducked behind an insect-eyed machine.

The technician she'd seen holding the scoop plunged it downward and lifted it up again. As another tech held out a beaker, the first one dropped the contents into it, dripping blood. Then she stepped back to remove her gloves, and for the first time Astra saw what was on the table. Unearthly screaming—from who?—filled the air ...

When she came to, she was dimly aware of the sharp commands of the Bi-Souls and of a blur of white coats against a wall. It was Fjellgeit who told her, much later, that her screaming had brought them running, and that the Milicrons led the way through the fire-mist even though it had turned their elbow hinges to rust. And then Fjellgeit himself was walking across the room toward her, cradling a limp golden body in his arms.

"The dog-being is alive," he said gently, kneeling down beside Astra. "They must have used some sort of soporific on her."

Astra bent over the familiar golden head with its velvet ears, her hot tears spilling onto Freya's muzzle. "I can find no evidence of harm," Fjellgeit went on, "other than a small patch where they must have extracted tissue."

Freya's eyes fluttered open, and she struggled to rise. "It's okay, Freya girl," Astra murmured, stroking her. "It's okay." And Freya, hearing the familiar voice, smelling the familiar smell, relaxed and gave a great sigh and fell asleep again.

"Two of the Arbolé will take care of her," Fjellgeit said gruffly, though he was smiling with relief too, "and will return her to your companions. Meanwhile, I'm afraid we cannot linger. We must make for the Temple at once, and we need your assistance. You are the only witness to the events in the Hall of Judgement."

A Bargain Is Negotiated

he CloudTube that led to the Temple had been damaged beyond repair. Fjellgeit stared up at the shattered cylinder that dangled inside the shaft far above them.

"More Fire Reaper devilry," he muttered to himself, and
turned to the Milicrons. "Is there any other way to get up there?"

But the Milicrons shook their heads. The Temple had been
accessible only to a chosen few.

"There's nowhere else they'd be holed up, is there? What do
you think, Astra?"

Astra shook her head uncertainly. The Milicrons were more
decisive. "They cannot leave the Flame of Truth," Milicron
BN942 said firmly. "They would rather die with it."

"Then perhaps," Álmveig said calmly, "I can be of assistance."
She unwound a length of vine from her waist and tossed it into
the bottom of the shaft. At once it began sending out young
green tendrils that moved steadily upward, seeking light. In a
matter of seconds a thick, jungle-like liana hung there. As Astra
stared, astounded, Álmveig leapt lightly into the air, caught
hold of the vine, and climbed up hand over hand. A few minutes later they heard the sound of her feet on the platform and
a whispered injunction: "Come on! Follow me!"

Zircon was next, climbing slowly but steadily, followed
by Picea and Amethyst. Then it was Astra's turn. I can't, she
thought helplessly. I don't have the strength. For the first time
she realized how exhausted she was.

But Fjellgeit was already hoisting her up. She grabbed the
vine and felt herself being lifted higher, very gently, as though
the vine itself was helping her. Fjellgeit followed her and then

the Milicrons, who examined the vine with startled metallic clicks before jerkily climbing. The vine was already rolling up behind them, detaching its tendrils from the shaft's walls.

And not a moment too soon. A motley group had appeared in the hallway below them—a half-dozen or so Fire Reaper soldiers, glancing up angrily, a couple of badly damaged Milicrons, and a few slave overseers, still in their orange uniforms. The soldiers yelled insults and levelled their weapons at the platform, but either they were too afraid to shoot or the platform itself was shielded in some way.

"Fear and revenge make for strange bedfellows," said Fjellgeit, glancing down at them. "Come. We must hurry."

But it proved impossible to move beyond the platform. A clammy, filmy substance filled the air, clinging to their bodies. It was like trying to move through gigantic spiderwebs. The Milicrons came to a complete halt. Fjellgeit and Zircon slashed at it with their weapons, but the substance simply reformed, swirling over them, wrapping its clammy strands around them.

"I believe," murmured Melke, the quartz-pale Mínera Being, "we must observe the principle of non-resistance."

"You call yourself a soldier?" Fjellgeit snapped, trying to claw the substance from his face. "Of all the—"

"He's from one of our regiments where the oldest stones lead," Zircon explained apologetically. "They fight their battles differently there."

Melke dropped to the floor on his stomach, disappearing from sight beneath the swirling substance. "There's a thin layer of open air beneath," he called softly. "I think we can get through."

The others followed him, even Fjellgeit, who lowered himself awkwardly to his back legs, looking very uncomfortable. Astra, who'd practised just such a maneuver when she was younger, playing at Fire Reapers-and-Villagers with the Ashgård children, wriggled forward easily beside Melke. He smiled at her and touched her hand, and she felt a strange glowing warmth—the same feeling she'd had all those years ago when she'd been a small girl in the City and her mother had bent over her in the sleeproom.

And now, for the first time, she could see shapes emerging as the substance thinned. Here was the vast dim hall, here the transparent cage she'd escaped from, pockmarked with Tabri holes. There was the dais where the Archons had presided. But there was no sign of anyone. The hall was empty.

"They *must* be here somewhere," Fjellgeit growled, getting to his feet, weapon at the ready. The last shreds of the substance drifted away, leaving their little group standing there edgily. Abruptly a door on the far side opened and a group of slaves came in hauling rickety wheeled carts filled with logs. Astra had time only to wonder, momentarily, what they were doing and why they were using such primitive technology when the slaves saw them. Terror-struck, they dropped their hauling ropes and leapt back.

"Move so much as an eyebrow," said Fjellgeit, in a growl so deep even Astra was startled, "and you'll find your molecules feeding my Chromobact." The slaves clung to each other, eyes wide. Álmveig unleashed her liana, which circled round the group, tendrilling over them and binding them tight.

"Now," said Fjellgeit, cradling his weapon, "perhaps you'd be so kind as to tell us just what you're—"

But he got no farther. A sound like thousands of bolts of lightning crackled through the hall, leaving them all momentarily deafened. Astra clutched at Melke, who had turned even paler. Flickering shapes—human shapes—were appearing on the dais, brightening and then fading. It took her a few moments to distinguish the familiar fire-red robes.

The Archons!

As they came into full three-dimensionality, the cones at Picea's temples turned from dark brown to pale beige. Even Fjellgeit stood with his mouth open. The Archons stood in a half-circle, facing them, with Vígeldgeirr at their head, wearing the shining band of dark metal lit by a tongue of fire. He smiled—a slow, contemptuous smile—and stepped forward.

"Did you really believe," he said, and his voice dripped sarcasm, "that by destroying the Fortress you could destroy us? You are no match for our technology, any of you—misshapen beings that you are."

A low murmur of anger rippled through the troops. Picea's cones turned bright orange, and Zircon and Amethyst raised their weapons.

"Your Chromobacts and Chlorophylliders are powerless against us." Vígeldgeirr waved his hand dismissively. "We do not share your dimension. We address you from the Plane of Forms."

"So that was the terrible sound we heard," Melke murmured. "The fabric of space-time tearing ..."

"We have manifested ourselves," Vígeldgeirr said, and his voice was filled with anger and disgust, "because unbelievers have violated our most sacred space. No one has ever done so before without our consent. We are here to return what is sacred to the sacred."

"Sacred?" It was Fjellgeit's turn to step forward. He was trembling with rage, his upper lip lifted from his teeth. "How dare you speak of sacred when you treat other beings like objects? When you build an entire society on the backs of those you enslave?"

"Perhaps," said Vígeldgeirr, his voice icy, "you do not know to whom you speak. I am Vígeldgeirr, First Flame of the Fire Reapers of Planetary Redemption, Guardian and Interpreter of the Flame of Truth." He held his hands aloft as if to encompass the hall. "This temple is dedicated to Fire, that most Sacred Presence, and to the punishment of those who deny the truth."

"And I," Fjellgeit said, and his voice was clear and steady, "am Fjellgeit of the Tweir-Sál, also known as the Bi-Souls—one of those misshapen beings. Unlike you, we believe in freedom and equality for all. We believe no one has the right to impose their beliefs on others."

320

Vígeldgeirr gave Fjellgeit a pitying smile. "What a pretty speech. Unfortunately for you, the Prophecies have already spoken." His eyes flashed. "It is written in our Prophecies that we, the Fire Reapers of Planetary Redemption, will reclaim the planet from the infidels. At the end of the Great Work, the Prophecies say, a new world will rise from the ash, a world we will rule until the end of time."

"But your Prophecies also say something else." It was Picea, transpiring heavily. "They say that when the Temple falls, the City will follow."

"You are quoting out of context." Vígeldgeirr was smiling contemptuously again. "The actual sentence is: 'When the Temple falls, the City will follow, and at the Last Stand the final flames shall devour them.' It is you, as the Prophecies make clear, who will be devoured. You and your deluded followers."

"The Fortress is surrounded, Vígeldgeirr." Fjellgeit adjusted his hold on his weapon. "Most of your troops have fled. They preferred their lives to dying for an insane cause. You will be leaders with no one to lead."

There was a sudden agitated murmuring from the Archons, and Vígeldgeirr's face darkened. "We do not wish to waste further time with those who pollute the Temple," he said sharply, and pressed some sort of device at his belt. Almost at once other shapes flickered into being beside the dais—two large rectangular shapes, solidifying into three dimensions. The prisoners' cages!

Astra gasped. There was Fru Berta, along with other Ash-Gatherers and Mínera and Bestia; and there, in the other cage, were the Arbolé, all of them ashen and drawn. Arduinna, especially, looked as though she was barely alive. She lay curled up on the floor of the cage like a shrivelled plant.

Fjellgeit and Picea and the others started forward, but Vígeldgeirr raised a hand. "Remember they are in a dimension you cannot reach. If you persist, I assure you that the Temple, and all of you with it, will be instantly destroyed."

"Isn't that what you want?" shouted Fjellgeit, and lowered his head as if he intended to rush forward and butt the Archons with his goat horns.

"We would prefer that to having the Temple overrun with unbelievers, yes."

He looks so calm! thought Astra. He sounds so logical, so sensible. Yet he's insane.

"But we are willing to strike a bargain, if you wish. We are prepared to negotiate the release of these prisoners."

"Hostages, you mean." Fjellgeit raised himself to his full height. "We refuse to negotiate with evil incarnate."

But the prisoners in the cages, their faces anguished, raised their hands, imploring silently for help. Picea leaned forward and murmured something, an agitated something, in Fjellgeit's ear. Astra overheard snatches: "—*must* save them ... cannot abandon them ... no choice ..."

Fjellgeit turned, frowning, as a vehement argument broke out among the rescue party. It was Álmveig who had the final word. "They have killed so many of our kin," she said softly, "all over the world. None of you have suffered as much as we have. We cannot allow them another victory."

Fjellgeit looked searchingly from face to face. Zircon shook his head, but the others nodded or glanced away, looking defeated.

"Very well," Fjellgeit said slowly, turning toward Vígeldgeirr. "We are prepared to bargain. But we demand the immediate release of all the prisoners, with no further harm done to them."

Vígeldgeirr smirked triumphantly. "Of course. It shall be done at once if you agree to our demand. We have only one."

"What is it?"

"Leave the girl child with us."

There was a moment of stunned silence, and then gasps and angry murmurs from the Bi-Souls. Fjellgeit raised his head, his horns proudly upright. "You know perfectly well we could never agree to such an outrageous proposal."

Astra felt sick. Had they walked into a trap? A crafty smile was spreading over Vígeldgeirr's face.

"Of course, if you reject our offer"—he paused dramatically—"you will never see these prisoners again. The sentence reached at their trial will be carried out." He flung out a pointing finger, as if already banishing them. "They will be exiled to the Plane of Eternal Night, where they will drift among the stars forever."

And indeed the cages were already beginning to fade. Their occupants were clawing at the walls, mouths open in soundless shrieks. Astra stared at them in horror. She'd saved herself, but she hadn't been able to save *them*. How could she let this happen? Especially to Fru Berta. Fru Berta had saved *her*—her and her poor father, wherever he was—by giving them refuge in Ashgård. And it was Fru Berta who'd saved her a second time that terrible night of the attack on the village.

She stood as straight as she could, though she was trembling so hard she could barely speak. "I accept the bargain," she said.

Another stunned silence, followed by a babble of Bi-Soul voices. Fjellgeit seized her arm. "Don't be a fool!" he hissed, glaring at her. "You don't know what you're doing. I won't allow it."

"I'm not a child," Astra said firmly. She wrenched her arm free and faced him. "I've had to make a lot of grown-up decisions." Her voice quavered and she rushed on. "I'm sorry, Fjellgeit, but I have to do this."

She really had no right, she knew, to be speaking that way to a senior Bestia leader. It was Melke who spoke into the shocked stillness, his voice soft but clear. "The child has become wise beyond her years," he said. "She is learning to move with events rather than against them. To surrender rather than to oppose."

"I suppose this is another of your different ways of fighting battles," Fjellgeit said to Melke, his voice as sarcastic as Vígeldgeirr's had been. "I was instructed to protect the child on pain of death, and I don't intend to stop now."

He lifted his hand as a signal, but Astra had already guessed his intention. She dropped to her stomach and wriggled through their legs toward the Archons, gaining by surprise. As she reached the dais and stood up, she gasped. Fjellgeit and the others had turned into dim, flickering shapes that brightened and faded and sometimes disappeared altogether. Somehow, somewhere, she had wriggled across the barrier that lay between the dimensions.

She turned toward Vígeldgeirr, who was watching in triumph. "You see?" He raised his voice, pointing. "The child has chosen. She is, as your colleague pointed out, wise beyond her years."

Whatever Fjellgeit said in return was too muted for Astra to make out, though his shadow-form paced back and forth while the others milled around him in agitation. "And now you must keep your part of the bargain," she said levelly to Vígeldgeirr, forcing down her terror.

"Indeed," said Vígeldgeirr, with that false, ingratiating smile. "We always conduct ourselves with honour." He pressed the device at his belt. The cages shivered for a moment, solidified again, then dissolved into mist and faded away. The prisoners stood staring about them, unable to comprehend what had happened.

"Fru Berta!" Astra rushed forward and flung her arms round the older woman. She was thinner and she looked older, but recognition was slowly dawning on her face.

"Why, it's Astra!" She bent over her and pressed her close. "I never imagined I'd—oh, it was so dark where we were, so dark. No light at all." She shuddered. "But I told myself I'd soon see my Toivo and my husband again, if I was lucky."

It was dawning on the other prisoners that they were finally free. In groups of twos and threes, ecstatic, crying, they were stumbling toward the Bi-Souls. They shimmered briefly for a moment before crossing that invisible barrier and fading into pale shadows of themselves. A few of them, before passing through, glanced gratefully at Astra, while others hurried on regardless. Only Arduinna, leaning on Bjarkansál and several other Arbolé, let her gaze linger on Astra, with an expression of tenderness. Then she, too, was gone into shadowhood.

Astra gently disengaged herself from Fru Berta's arms. "Go on, Fru Berta. Go and join them."

Fru Berta looked bewildered, and Astra gave her a gentle push. Tears welled in her eyes as Fru Berta nodded obediently and shuffled slowly away, fading into shadow like all the others.

"Come, child," Vígeldgeirr said behind her. "I'm delighted you've chosen to assist us." Astra dragged her eyes from Fru Berta, the horror of what she'd done slowly dawning on her. "But first we will see that you are well fed and rested. You have had—shall we say—a most eventful journey."

She heard a rumbling behind her and turned. The slaves were once again dragging their carts toward the bowl in the floor where the Flame of Truth burned. "The Flame must be fed," she heard Vígeldgeirr say. "Behold our Living God!"

Beyond the carts were those shadowy figures, merging and blending, growing smaller as they moved away. Then the smoke from the smouldering pit swirled across her line of sight and the shadows disappeared.

Neil Faces a Choice

eil was sitting with Hreinn-Sál and the other Bestia round their fire, wrapped in a blanket, when the first members of the rescue party stumbled wearily into camp. Picea and Álmveig were jubilant—they'd rescued the Arbolé!—but Zircon and Amethyst, their faces grim, told some bizarre tale about Astra having volunteered to take the prisoners' place. A ridiculous story, Neil thought. Then Fjellgeit arrived, and in a low, troubled voice, swaying from exhaustion, he described what had happened in the Fortress and how Astra herself had accepted Vígeldgeirr's terrible bargain.

Neil didn't know who to be angrier with—Fjellgeit for abandoning Astra, or Hreinn-Sál for allowing her to go in the first place. Not to mention that they hadn't found Piedra, either. He still felt dizzy from whatever drug the Fire Reapers had given him, but the dose of potentiated gold he'd received in the field hospital was helping to clear his head. He staggered into the centre of the circle, where he pointed a shaking finger at Fjellgeit. "How could you? How could you come back without her? And what about Piedra?"

"And who gave you permission to speak?" demanded Hreinn-Sál, raising his antlered head and glaring at Neil. He lifted a hoof and motioned to him to sit down. "No being hears properly with his fists clenched," he said quietly. "Your anger will get us nowhere. Fjellgeit has given us a clear account of what happened. A most regrettable development—but one, it appears, that the girl child initiated herself."

"He's lying," Neil muttered, still standing where he was. "I know he is. Astra wouldn't do that." But two of the largest

326

Bestia—an elk- and a bison-being—picked him up between them and deposited him back in his place in the circle. Neil shook off their grip and sat clutching his blanket, feeling furious and helpless.

"I share the boy's desperation and rage, though I choose not to act on it," Hreinn-Sál said heavily, with a glance at Neil. He looked round the circle. "We have received some very disturbing reports from other sources," he said, his tone grave. "We must call a meeting of the Assembly. While the returned prisoners are being cared for, we must decide what to do."

At the meeting that night, each Bi-Soul Nation was represented by its leader and two or three senior officers. Picea, Álmveig, and Bjarkansál represented the Arbolé. Arduinna, still very ill, had been sent to recuperate in the Timeless Caverns under the care of Silfra the Learned. Guldsterre was there with Rhodium and his daughter Amethyst on behalf of the Mínera Beings, while Hreinn-Sál, Hästsjäl, and an eagle Bi-Soul named Ørn-Sál spoke for the Bestia. Fjellgeit was there, too, no doubt to answer any questions.

Finally there was Neil, feeling desperate and alone, who'd been invited to attend by Hreinn-Sál. Charlie was still in the hospital along with Freya, though at least he'd been able to see both of them. He hadn't seen Freya since the dreadful day they'd been imprisoned in the Fortress. She thumped her tail weakly at him, lying there with bandages round her belly, and he buried tears of relief in her fur. As for Charlie, he'd been fast asleep on his cot, his injured leg elevated and dressed with bandages, another thick bandage across his nose. Dear old Charlie, who'd dragged him out of that cell to safety! He watched him for a few minutes, a lump in his throat, and then tiptoed out.

But Astra—Astra was gone. He'd been in the hospital when she'd made it out of the Fortress, and then when she'd gone back in with the rescue party. That was the worst—that he hadn't even had a chance to see her. He still couldn't believe she'd willingly gone back to the Fire Reapers.

"Let us dispense with formalities and begin our meeting at once," began Hreinn-Sál. "Fjellgeit, give us your assessment of the situation inside the Fortress."

Fjellgeit stood up, looking old and tired. "The Fortress has been largely abandoned," he said in his gruff voice. "We encountered no resistance. Most of the guards and other troops have fled. The Archons have transferred themselves to another dimension, by what means we do not know." He paused and went on. "There may be pockets of resistance here and there—senior officers, perhaps, who have holed up rather than fleeing. We were told that General Sardonyx had joined the fighting, but I've been informed that he has not been sighted. I recommend a mopping-up operation, to commence at first light. And a thorough search for our colleague Piedra."

"Very well." Hreinn-Sál nodded gravely and turned to Guldsterre. "I will ask you to appoint one of your officers to take charge of such an operation."

Guldsterre inclined her head, her emerald hair glittering in the torchlight.

"And Álmveig"—Hreinn-Sál turned toward her—"may I ask you and your fellow Arbolé to take charge of organizing the care and return of the escaped slaves. The Fossefallen have said they will provide activated water to assist with the emotional trauma."

Álmveig glanced at Picea and Bjarkansál before turning to a sapling-like Arbolé nearby and giving swift orders in an undertone.

"Now, are we to understand, Fjellgeit," continued Hreinn-Sál, in that same grave tone, "that any military operation against the Archons to rescue the girl child would be futile?"

"I believe so, yes." Fjellgeit was drumming a nervous hoof on the ground. "We have seen—indeed, experienced—their ability to enter different dimensions at will. We saw the girl child fade into a shadow form when she entered their plane." He swallowed hard and paused before he could go on. "However, the Fortress must be kept under guard against any refortification by fresh troops."

"Can I have permission to speak?" Neil said nervously, standing up. Hreinn-Sál frowned and nodded. "I think—I mean, we have to find a way to rescue Astra somehow. She'll be expecting us to." He pointedly avoided looking at Fjellgeit, whose leadership abilities were obviously non-existent. "We can't just give up now."

"The only way to rescue the girl child," said Hreinn-Sál tartly, "is to defeat the Fire Reapers." As Neil sat down again, feeling deflated and angry, Hreinn-Sál continued, "I will ask you, Fjellgeit, to take charge of strategic planning for the mopping-up operation, since you and your team are familiar with the Fortress's layout."

Oh, great. Reward him for losing Astra! Neil thought disgustedly.

Fjellgeit inclined his goat head and sat down, and Hreinn-Sál motioned to someone standing just outside the circle of light. A young woman with the lithe body of an athlete stepped forward. She wore high blue-grey boots and her head was wrapped in a length of blue cloth, one loose end pulled across her lower face. Now she flung it back, revealing gleaming dark skin and black curls.

"Identify yourself for the gathering," said Hreinn-Sál.

"I'm Mesi of the Aqua Libere," said the young woman. "Or at least that's my nom-de-guerre." And she grinned insouciantly, as if she was having a good time.

"Tell us what you saw."

"A few days ago I was travelling through the Skapraun Mountains north of here." Her voice was nervous and eager. "I was on my way to reconnoitre with other members. We'd heard there was a water source that needed protection."

329

"Yes, yes," said Hreinn-Sál impatiently. "I understand you saw troop movements?"

"Regiments of United Chinese Empire troops, travelling northward. They were in the valley below us, they didn't see us. But there must have been at least ten thousand of them."

Around the circle there were muttered exclamations in several languages. Guldsterre, her eyes intense, leaned forward. "Why? Why would they be travelling that way?"

Mesi grinned again. "That's what we wondered. So we decided to follow them. They headed through the Sigr-Bruni Pass. We kept them in sight for almost a day, but after that we had our own work to do, so we turned back."

"But why? There's nothing beyond the Pass but the odd Ash-Gatherer village." It was Hästsjäl who spoke, for the first time.

"And the forests of Finnmark," said Guldsterre softly. "If they're joining the Fire Reapers there ..."

"We have another report to consider that bears on this one," Hreinn-Sál said. "Thank you, Mesi. You and your fellow Libere are to be commended." Mesi nodded and grinned again and strode off, and Hreinn-Sál motioned to two Bestia soldiers standing some distance away. They dragged forward what turned out to be a Fire Reaper soldier, a low-level *Flamme-Sveitungr*, his uniform blackened and torn, his wrists bound behind him.

"Unbind him," commanded Hreinn-Sál. As the soldier stood rubbing his sore wrists, Hreinn-Sál said severely, "We understand you have some information for us. Mind you tell us the truth. We have ways of finding out if you don't."

"Why should we believe anything he says?" said Ørn-Sál, his white-feathered head lifted suspiciously. "He'll tell us what he thinks is in his interests."

"Because I deserted, that's why," the soldier said, almost belligerently. He rubbed his hands nervously along his jacket and looked pleadingly at Hreinn-Sál. "I never wanted to be a Fire Reaper, see? They came recruiting in our village, they said we'd have three squares a day and a good wage. We were all starving. The crops had failed because of the heat and hailstorms."

Ørn-Sál made a shrill whistling sound. "But you still joined. You knew who they were and what they were doing."

"You try sticking to your beliefs on an empty belly," the soldier retorted, and then seemed abashed by his own insolence. "That—creature there, whatever he is"—he pointed at Fjellgeit— "found me and my mates looting the Fortress. He can vouch for me."

Fjellgeit nodded slowly, and the soldier, encouraged, hurried on. "Day before yesterday, it was. Me and my mates, we overheard some of the officers. They were talking about the Prophecies." The soldier paused and licked his lips. "Some place called Bjarkaney. The Island of Birches, in UL. I'd never heard of it. But one of them said word had come down from higher up, that that was where the Last Stand would be. I remember that phrase clearly, the Last Stand." He stopped again and shook his head. "I don't know if it's worth anything. But maybe you, sir"— he nodded at Hreinn-Sál—"can make something of it."

"The leader of the Archons used that phrase," Fjellgeit said slowly. "He said, 'When the Temple falls, the City will follow, and at the Last Stand the final flames shall devour them.' "

"Where's Bjarkaney?" asked Amethyst.

"My great-great-Tree-Uncle came from there—Bjørkøy, it used to be called," said Bjarkansál softly. "It was once part of Finnmark. It's the only northern island that survived the Great Drowning." He stopped and looked down, and when he spoke again there were tears in his eyes. "The last of the virgin boreal forests grows there."

The Assembly stared round at each other in growing alarm. It was Guldsterre who said aloud what everyone was thinking. "So the Last Stand—the last, great battle—is to take place in the last stand of boreal forest." She shivered and fell silent. No one else spoke.

At last Hreinn-Sál roused himself. "You've done well to tell us," he said, looking at the prisoner. "Give him a meal," he added, and motioned to the guards to take him away.

"They must be intent on fulfilling the Prophecies as fast as possible," Rhodium said. He stood up, his hand going instinctively to his weapon. "I think it almost certain they've begun destroying the City themselves."

More sharp intakes of breath. Neil, quite forgetting how annoyed Hreinn-Sál had been with him the last time he spoke, leapt to his feet. "We've got to stop them! That's where Astra's father is!"

Hreinn-Sál, frowning, turned to look at him. "How do you know?"

"The Fire Reapers said he was in the City. They said he was helping them with their research, but *I* think they were lying."

Hreinn-Sál stared at Neil, then shook his head. "The battle in the North will demand all our resources. The Fire Reapers have a vast network of allies. And we're already stretched far too thin."

"Astra sacrificed herself to save a lot of beings, didn't she?" Neil tried to look resolute, though he felt horribly close to tears. "We owe it to her. Besides, it's thanks to her I got Freya back."

"The boy has a point," said Hästsjäl quietly.

"We owe Arduinna's life to the girl child," added Picea sharply. "Not to mention Bjarkansál here and the other Arbolé leaders."

There was a long silence. At last Hreinn-Sál said heavily, "The deciding battle is upon us. Far sooner than any of us imagined. We have no choice but to direct all our energies there." He paused and looked round intently at the Assembly. "Do I have your support?"

No one spoke for at least fifteen seconds. Then, one by one, each being raised a paw or a twig-entwined or gem-crusted hand. Neil clenched his fists so hard that the nails bit into his palms.

"You're wrong!" he burst out. "You're wrong, all of you!

You're *so* wrong!" And before anyone could say anything, he burst out of the circle and ran off into the night.

It was Guldsterre who found him, half an hour later, curled up under a scrubby bush some distance from the camp. He was punching angry holes in the sand and occasionally kicking the bush for good measure. Approaching on silent feet, she bent over him and touched his shoulder, and he jumped.

"You've every right to be angry, Neil," she said, crouching down beside him. "Your loyalty is admirable. Unfortunately, things don't always work out the way we want."

"But it's not fair!" Neil burst out again. "How can we just— just *abandon* her? And Hallvard?"

"It may feel that way. But in reality, with every blow we strike against the Fire Reapers, we're helping your friend. Fjellgeit made it clear that we cannot reach her."

"I still think we should try," he said stubbornly. "Maybe Fjellgeit's wrong. Maybe there *is* a way."

"Why don't you join my personal troops? You're a brave boy. I'd be glad to have you."

To be invited by one of the Bi-Soul leaders was immensely flattering. Neil hesitated, but only for a moment. "I'd better stay with Freya and Charlie," he said. "They need me here."

"If you reconsider, let me know. We leave tomorrow at first light." She stood up and strode off into the darkness, her gems glinting in the moonlight. Neil watched her go, feeling torn and regretful. At the same time a new resolve was forming in his mind. Maybe there *was* a way. He had no idea if it would work, but he felt the same way Hreinn-Sál did—he had no other choice.

First, though, he had to talk to Charlie.

He waited outside the hospital tent until one of the guards went off to piss. He ducked inside and hid behind a curtain until a couple of nurses had passed by. Then he crept between the cots to the far side of the tent.

"Who's there?" Charlie called sharply. He was lying propped up with his arms behind his head.

"It's me," Neil whispered.

"Time Boy! You're okay after all!" Charlie was grinning, which definitely meant *he* was okay, too. "I'm still kinda jumpy," he added ruefully. "If I was back in the Yukon I'd have yanked my rifle out right quick."

"Charlie, I have to talk to you." He glanced around, but the nearest patients were asleep and there were no nurses in sight.

"In the middle of the night?"

"Something terrible's happened. To Astra."

Charlie stared, his face sombre. "You don't mean she's—?"

"No, no. She's alive. But—well, she was with this rescue party, but the Archons said they'd only hand over the prisoners if she—"

"Wait, wait, wait. What rescue party? What are you talking about?"

Of course—Charlie didn't even know Astra had escaped the first time! After Neil had explained it all—"You mean she's a prisoner again?" Charlie said, horrified.

"And what's even worse, she's in another dimension. Or that's what Fjellgeit says."

Charlie stared at Neil as if he'd lost his mind. "But that's crazy! Why didn't someone stop her?"

"I don't know." Neil shook his head miserably. "Anyway, there's this big battle coming up and Hreinn-Sál and the others are leaving in the morning and Hreinn-Sál says—"

"A battle?" Charlie sat up as far as his elevated leg allowed him. "With the Frippers?"

"Your leg's still injured," Neil pointed out as Charlie tried to stand. "You can't go."

"They had me up walking today. I'm fine." Charlie lay back down, looking disgusted. "Sounds like the Frippers set a trap. They knew damn well your friends'd try a rescue. They had the perfect bait—Arduinna."

That's all water under the bridge now, Neil thought, remembering an expression of his mother's. A hot coal burned in his throat. Would he ever see her again?

"Fjellgeit says Astra's in some dimension called the Plane of Forms. Can you get us in, too?"

"You're askin' a heck of a lot." Charlie shook his head. "My alchemy powers ain't what they used to be. And I never even heard of the Plane of Forms."

"But we have to try. Or at least find out where she is." Neil's voice shook from exhaustion. Here he was asking Charlie for help, when it was Charlie who'd messed things up in the first place!

Perhaps Charlie was thinking that, too, because he gave a wry grin and ruffled Neil's hair. "You up to a little thievin'?"

Startled, Neil nodded.

"Then here's what I need. Repeat after me. A pinch of antimony sulphide, a bottle of clove oil ..."

It took him a couple of hours to get everything. Most of it was in the hospital dispensary, though a few items came from the desert itself, including the leaves of a particular shrub—easier to find by night because of its intense odour. In the camp kitchen he found a lightstone, two small pots, some dried fruit, and two large water bottles, which he filled with water. Then, his arms laden and his pockets bulging, he crept back to the hospital tent and tapped their pre-arranged signal on the outside wall next to Charlie's cot.

It seemed like forever, but it was probably only minutes later that Charlie joined him in the shadows. He'd cut his left pant leg off so he could get his pants over the heavy bandages. "I'm fine, I'm fine," he muttered, brushing off Neil's anxious queries. "Let's head over there, away from the camp."

Apart from the dozens of scattered campfires in the distance, all was quiet. Most of the Fire Reapers had fled, it seemed, and Bi-Soul troops patrolled the perimeter of the Fortress. That was a relief. Still, Neil was sure it was just a matter of time before they sent reinforcements from the City—and then what? Would the Bi-Souls' remaining troops be able to hold the Fortress?

A few minutes later they were hunkered down in the lee of a dune. Charlie sent Neil off to look for large stones and busied himself measuring ingredients into a pot. When Neil returned, panting under the weight he was carrying, they arranged the stones in a small circle and built a fire with twigs.

"I figure a couple of hours or so," Charlie said, "though without the proper equipment, not to mention the wrong day of the month ..." He shook his head and sat down awkwardly in the sand with his injured leg stretched out.

"Then I'm going to go get Freya," Neil said. He didn't add, *Because I don't know where we'll end up, and I don't know if we'll ever get back.*

Charlie nodded. "Only you gotta keep her quiet."

Of course she'll be quiet! Neil thought indignantly as he hurried off. She's a very intelligent dog. She knows what to do.

Getting Freya out of her cage proved to be the easy part. She thumped her tail and rooed at him softly, but she was still very weak and he had to lift her down. She walked haltingly, stopping often, panting. Neil looked at her with concern. Maybe taking her along wasn't such a good idea after all. And Charlie's injury wasn't healed, either. Maybe this whole plan was totally stupid. What kind of match were they for the Fire Reapers? And how were they going to find Astra anyway?

He stared up into the dark, starry sky, feeling both desperate and foolish. "Áilu," he said aloud, softly, "if you're listening, we could use your help here. And the beings of the Many Realms, too. I mean, I don't know if they exist, but if they do—"

No, that wasn't right. He tried again. "What I mean is, if you're around and not too busy, beings of the Many Realms, could you give us a hand?" That sounded weird, because he didn't know if the Many Beings *had* hands. Maybe they had paws, or hooves, or—nothing.

"Look, guys," he added hastily, "we really need help here. It's really important," he added for good measure. And then, because he didn't fully trust Charlie, "And if we get into another dimension, could you please make sure it's the same one Astra's in?"

Beside him Freya lifted her head and gave two short, sharp barks. He'd never heard that particular variation before and looked at her in surprise. No doubt she was adding her two cents' worth. He hoped the beings of the Many Realms had heard them.

"I thought maybe somethin' had happened to ya," Charlie said, squinting in the glow of the fire as Neil and Freya approached. "Or you changed your mind."

Neil shook his head. "Freya can't move very fast. How's the mixture doing?"

"Gettin' there." Charlie peered into the basin and stirred it with a stick. "I gotta reduce it—boil it down. Several times over. And then we drink it."

Drink it? Neil shuddered. Given the ingredients, it was sure to taste awful.

"And then what happens?"

"I'm hopin' it'll let us tune in to Astra's energetic field. So we can find out where she is."

But if Astra had become a shadow on a plane of shadows ...

"Energy fields don't change," Charlie explained, "no matter what dimension we're in. That's what quantchemy's about—transmutin' our consciousness so it can function on different levels."

It all sounded very dubious, except that enough had happened in the last few weeks that Neil wasn't certain about anything anymore. His father's lab—it seemed such a small place now! And then he felt guilty, because he still loved his dad and missed him terribly and hadn't thought about him in ages.

Charlie was decanting the mixture from one pot to the other and back again. "To cool it," he told Neil. Then he set the mixture over the fire again and sat there watching, deep in concentration. Neil lay down on the sand, Freya's head resting on his stomach, and stared up at the stars. The world was a bigger place than he'd ever realized. And the Yukon—the Yukon was farther away than ever.

The Palace of the Archons

stra herself didn't feel like a shadow. Standing on the dais beside the Archons, she felt utterly real. The world she'd just left, the one where Fjellgeit and the others were now dim shapes, was the shadowy one. But she barely had time to think about it, because Vígeldgeirr was speaking to her. "My dear, you must be tired and hungry. Let us travel to where you can have a meal, and a bed."

"Not back to the lab," Astra said with revulsion. She never ever wanted to go there again.

"Oh no, no." Vígeldgeirr seemed to find this suggestion amusing. "I'm afraid the Fortress is quite beyond repair."

"Are we going to use the secret tunnels?"

At this Vígeldgeirr laughed outright. "Our abilities have evolved far beyond such primitive means, my dear. No, we will translate ourselves somewhere else entirely."

What on earth does he mean? thought Astra. Even as she wondered, the dais and the vast hall itself began to waver and then faded away. Before them a shimmering corridor opened up, made out of what looked like minuscule soap bubbles. "Come," Vígeldgeirr said, and they moved forward, Vígeldgeirr leading the way with the Archons bringing up the rear. The bubbles moved gently aside, though Astra herself seemed to be motionless.

"Ah, here we are," Vígeldgeirr announced, as if they'd arrived at a thought-tube stop. Where were they? She could just make out shadows around her that rippled and pulsed. Shimmering rooftops suddenly popped into solidity, and then, incongruously, a desk and chair, and now in the distance she

339

could hear the sound of many feet marching and a male voice shouting orders. She felt her feet touch carpet as the last of the bubbles dissolved. She was in a large, high-ceilinged room, an office of some sort, in front of a large open window. Far below was a vast plaza with soldiers—Fire Reaper troops—marching along in their thousands. The broad avenue leading to it ran past transparent buildings, and it was lined with people as far as the eye could see.

The City! She was back in the City! She stared round the room in amazement. She must be inside the Palace of the Archons, the immense black-sided ziggurat that dominated the whole place. Her parents had called it the *Svarthull*—the Black Hole—because it sucked all light and energy into it (though they called it that only when they could be certain of not being heard). She'd only ever seen it from the outside—its walls made of shining black lupiathon, its stepped towers silhouetted against the domed Sky. Her parents had told her that the blue dome with its images of clouds wasn't the real sky. But she hadn't believed them until the day she and her father fled the City.

"You are in my private quarters," Vígeldgeirr said behind her. "The Abode of the First Flame. You are to be my guest here. Anything you wish for, you have only to ask."

Astra turned around, still dazed. "But how did we get here? What was that corridor?"

"We Archons travel between our temples by means of energy pathways," Vígeldgeirr said smugly. "They exist all over Nordlandia. Eventually they will link temples all over Terrania."

Astra shuddered. *Let's hope that day never comes.*

"And now let me order your meal."

As Vígeldgeirr swung round to the imagescreen on the wall, Astra turned back to the window. How high up they were! There, in the distance—tiny, almost invisible—was the play-park where she'd gone with friends on sunny days. And not far from it was the housepod where she'd lived with her father and grandmother. Four years ago now. It felt like another life altogether. Was Amma still there? Her heart beat a little faster. Would she be able to see her? Or would asking about her bring Amma into danger?

The door opened and a slave in fire-coloured clothing came in, guiding a floating tray with various covered dishes. Vígeldgeirr motioned her to a comfortable thoughtchair, which moulded itself to her body before she even sat down. As the tray hovered in front of it, the slave lifted one of the covers. Stroorberrie Joywafers! How had they known it was her favourite food?

But now she looked at it in dismay. It wasn't really food at all. It was—well, she didn't know what it was, except that it was dead.

"Surely you must be hungry," Vígeldgeirr said sharply.

"Yes," said Astra quietly. "Only for real food. Made from things that grow."

Vígeldgeirr's face darkened. "This *is* real food. The best we can manufacture. And free of all the insanitary bacteria that contaminate the outside world." He motioned to the slave, and the tray was removed. "Perhaps you are too tired to eat. Let me show you to your room."

She followed him down a vast corridor, brilliantly lit, to a large, beautifully decorated bedroom, with a thoughtbed and the inevitable imagescreen on the wall. There was even a window opening onto the plaza, which somehow she hadn't expected.

"I hope you'll be comfortable here," Vígeldgeirr said. "Or," he added brusquely, "is the room likewise not to your liking?"

"What are you going to do with me?"

"*Do* with you?" There was that amused glitter in his eyes again. "Oh, my dear, how cynical you are! As I said before, you are our guest. We hope, in time, you might even come to appreciate our point of view." And with that he bowed and withdrew, closing the door behind him.

Astra sat down on the bed and stared around her, feeling disgusted and frightened. What *were* they planning? Not to punish her, it seemed, despite her behaviour at the so-called trial. No, they clearly wanted her here in the City, alive. Did they think they could persuade her to help them again?

General Sardonyx had claimed her father was here, too. "Taking instruction from the First Flame," the General had said—from Vígeldgeirr himself. She white-knuckled her fists. Did they think she'd go over to their side because her father, of all people, had?

But perhaps they'd threatened to harm him if he didn't cooperate. Perhaps they'd drugged him. "Never compromise with evil," he'd told Astra more than once. "Because in the end you lose your soul. And once lost, it can never be recovered."

The Sensor! Maybe she could find out where he was. She took it from her pocket and adjusted the finger holes. But as Áilu had warned her, even though the Sensor had worked in the Fortress, the Fire Reaper energy inside the Palace must be too strong. The Sensor simply sat inert in her hands. If her father really *was* here, she'd have to find him some other way.

Sitting on the cold sand under the stars, Neil drank the nauseating greenish liquid slowly, as Charlie had instructed. It was as thick as mud and he had to choke it down. He waited, but nothing happened. Certainly nothing like the horrible spinning and sliding he'd experienced during his time travel. He gave some to Freya, too, and then Charlie drank. Still nothing.

Except—just a minute. He could hear something. Something that sounded like—well, like thousands of people cheering. He opened his eyes, blinking. Where was he?

He was standing on a street somewhere, though unlike any street he'd ever seen. It was made out of some strange transparent material that gave slightly as he moved. He was in the middle of a dense crowd that jostled and shoved and edged forward. And there, marching past, were Fire Reaper soldiers, hundreds of them, a dozen abreast, lifting their knees high, their faces solemn, their eyes straight ahead. The sight of all those flame-coloured uniforms, all those fixed expressions, made him feel sick. Around him the cheering had intensified, almost deafening him. One or two people nearby looked at him oddly, so he joined in the cheering, though he hated doing it.

Suddenly that searing pain leapt up his leg and he felt sick to his stomach. He gritted his teeth, trying to pretend he was fine, sweat breaking out on his forehead. To his immense relief the last of the Fire Reaper soldiers marched past and the pain eased slightly. The crowd was beginning to break up, people moving away in twos and threes, their faces still flushed and excited.

And then he heard someone calling his name in an urgent whisper. There, on a corner beside a huge flickering screen— it was Charlie! Or most of him, anyway—all except his feet. A long golden tail and a pink-tongued mouth was emerging, too, and Neil stumbled as fast as he could toward them.

Charlie grabbed him by the shirt, pulled him into the shadows, and put his finger to his lips. Then, ducking down, he motioned to Neil to follow him. With Freya sticking close, the two of them hobbled in and out between the oddest-looking buildings Neil had ever seen—cubes of different sizes, all locked together like Lego and all transparent, and raised high on stilts. The air smelled strange, with a slight fragrance he couldn't identify, like bathroom freshener. And everywhere, mounted on street corners or the sides of buildings, were those vast screens with their flickering images.

He was almost out of breath when they came to what looked like a building site at the end of a cul-de-sac. It was strewn with plastic and metal waste, with the odd weed poking through— the first growing things he'd seen here. Charlie, limping more now, led them behind what must once have been one of those vast screens, now half sheared off, and flung himself down. Neil collapsed beside him, and Freya crept into his arms, her ears back, trembling.

"Where are we?" Neil whispered.

"Of all the places to end up," Charlie said, and rolled his eyes. "It's the City! Can you believe it?"

So *that* explained how Charlie knew where he was going. Neil shuddered. "But—what happened? I thought we—"

Charlie sighed heavily. "I figured we might have problems. But I sure didn't expect *this*." He shook his head. "Maybe that clove oil was bad."

Neil sat back, stunned. Not only had they not found Astra—they'd ended up smack-bang in the very heart of Fire Reaper territory! He rubbed his ankle, which still throbbed painfully.

"I forgot," Charlie said, glancing at him. "You got one of those damn codes, don't you."

"Yes. Don't *you*?"

"I disabled it. Got hold of a Coder and figured it out." He eased his injured leg into a different position. "We better keep out of sight for a while, with that code of yours. Besides, it's obvious we're not from here. And with a dog, too—no one's allowed to keep animals, unless they're higher-ups. Senior officers, priests, that kind of thing."

Neil's thoughts were racing. They couldn't sit here forever; they had to do *some*thing. "If the Fire Reapers were telling the truth," he said, sitting up, "then Hallvard's here somewhere. Maybe we can find him."

Charlie groaned and adjusted his leg again. "Something tells me we're not the best choice for a reconnaissance mission."

It wasn't like Charlie to give up so easily. His leg must be really hurting, Neil decided. "You've been here before," he said stubbornly. "You know the place. Where d'you think they might be keeping him?"

Charlie paused. "There's the underground prisons," he said slowly. "But I think he's too valuable for that. They'd want to make use of him. His scientific knowledge."

"Astra talked about a place where he used to work. Some kind of institute for research. Maybe they took him there?"

Charlie shook his head. "I doubt it. They wouldn't let him just go back to his own research."

Neil slumped. He wasn't getting much help. And just surviving here was going to be tough—never mind finding Hallvard. "Suppose we say we're from one of the villages?" he suggested. "We could earn some money." He'd seen buskers on the sidewalks in Vancouver, a hat on the ground in front of them, playing an instrument. "Freya can roll over and do tricks. She's pretty smart."

This time Charlie smiled. "You really got your thinkin' cap on, don't you, kid? But it's against the law here. You'd be in jail before—" He sat up suddenly. "But you know what? There is somethin' we can do. We'll say we came into town to sell Freya."

"Sell her?" Neil was horrified. Whatever else happened, he wasn't about to lose her again.

"There's a weekly market. Villagers come into the City to sell handicrafts and stuff. If we're stopped, that's what we say."

Neil looked dubious. "As long as we're not *really* going to."

"'Course not. We're just goin' to do a bit of snoopin'. See what we can find out. Think you can handle the code pain?"

Neil nodded, apprehensive. The pain was horrible, but it seemed to get a little easier each time it happened.

"And another thing." Charlie lowered his voice, looking around them. "This is the only place there's no imagescreens. Did ya notice?"

Neil glanced about, puzzled. It was true, but what did it mean?

"The screens work two ways. The Fire Reapers spy on people through them. The whole City's under surveillance."

"You're kidding." Neil stared around again, and slid closer to Charlie.

"I'm surprised this one hasn't been replaced." Charlie jerked his thumb at the screen above them. "Someone planted an explosive device here a while ago. The Aqua Libere, so the rumour went."

Neil remembered the young Libere woman who'd spoken at the Assembly meeting. Mesi. Had she been involved?

345

"So once we leave here, we don't talk. Okay? One finger up means yes"—he held his forefinger up—"and two fingers means no." Neil nodded solemnly. "And if they do stop us, we're from an Ash-Gatherer village far to the south."

A thought suddenly struck Neil. "You know, since we ended up here, maybe—" He hesitated, knowing it sounded crazy, and plunged on. "Maybe we *did* get attuned to Astra. Maybe we ended up here because she's here, too."

"Oh, sure." Charlie snorted. "I bet they gave her a deluxe room in the Archons' Palace, too. I bet they're waiting on her hand and foot."

It was Vígeldgeirr himself, the next morning, who proposed that Astra go out for a walk. "After all, this City *was* your home," he said smoothly. "I'm sure you'd like to visit your old haunts. And besides, a little fresh air would do you good."

"Thank you. I'd like that," Astra said, in the same falsely polite tone. She decided not to point out that no one in the City had any idea what fresh air was like. But what was Vígeldgeirr up to? They weren't doing this just for her health. Perhaps they planned to watch what she did. With the imagescreens, of course, they could keep an eye—and ear—on her anywhere.

Still, it would be wonderful to be outside, away from the Archons' headquarters. She grabbed the tildein cloak she'd been given to match her new tildein leggings and tunic, and took a CloudTube to the bottom floor. She crossed a vast reception area the size of the whole of Ashgård and walked through the massive doorway, where two guards on either side saluted her. And then—then she was outside, at last, crossing the Great Plaza and looking round her.

For the first time she noticed how afraid people were, how they hurried past, staying close to the buildings and never meeting each others' eyes. She'd once thought this City the most beautiful place in the world, with its controlled weather and amazing architecture and endless things to do or see. She'd felt sorry for people who had to live outside it. But compared to real grass, and real rain, and a real sky ...

Passing a tiny little hole-in-the-wall café, she realized she was starving. Her cloak had a FlammunirTab in it, so she slipped through the door and sat down at a table. There was no one in the place except for the waiter and an older man at the bar. Among the moodfood dishes on the menu were one or two traditional Nordlandish ones, including bean soup. Oh, how she missed Fru Berta's!

"I'll have the soup," she said to the waiter.

The man at the bar glanced at her without interest and turned back to his drink. "If you ask me," he said to the waiter in a low voice, "it's deliberate. Not an accident at all. Blowing up parts of the City like that."

Obviously she'd interrupted a conversation. "My wife works at one of the pleasurepavilions," the waiter said. "She says whenever there's bombings they play the music there extra loud."

Why were they talking so openly, and in front of a stranger? Then she noticed that the imagescreen was dark, the little flame icon extinguished. Someone must have disabled it.

"It's the Prophecies," the man at the bar said, switching to Old Nordlandish. He must have assumed she wouldn't know the older version of the language. "They *want* the City to fall. They're getting impatient." He dropped his voice to a whisper. "My son's a Flame-Defender with the Fire Reapers. He says the outlying areas are already gone."

The door banged open and a tall, fat Fire Reaper officer strode in. The waiter straightened immediately. "What can I do for you, sir?"

"Give me a moodcola. Large, with ice. What's the matter with your imagescreen?"

The waiter licked his lips and flicked his eyes nervously at the man at the bar. "Just went down a few minutes ago, sir. I don't know what happened."

"Well, you should have reported it immediately." The officer unclipped his devcom and barked some sort of order into it. Astra hurriedly finished the last of her soup, paid for it, and slipped out. Her mind was buzzing. Could it really be true what the men were saying—that the Fire Reapers were *deliberately* destroying the City, bit by bit? Her father had told Neil about the End Times that the Book of Prophecies had predicted. Why hadn't she listened more closely?

There was one place she might find an answer—at her grandmother's. Ordinary citizens weren't supposed to own copies of the Prophecies, but her grandmother had one. It was stored, along with the other forbidden books, in that locked box under the floorboards. Somehow Astra had to get her hands on it.

She walked steadily in the direction of her old house, trying not to betray her haste. Past the medstation, past the bodydesigner's, across the playpark where children were playing as she once had. And here was her street: Logalund. Their house was the pod at the end, an unusually large one because her parents, as scientists at the Institute, were granted such privileges. Now she couldn't help herself; she ran as hard as she could down the street and through the gate.

Was it her imagination, or did the garden look neglected? The door was locked, but it was easy to see from the transparent walls that no one was home. She walked around it disconsolately. The place definitely had a shabbier air, and it seemed as though the upstairs rooms were no longer used. Where could her grandmother be?

She didn't dare linger. She really shouldn't have come here— they would certainly know about it. Her grandmother was probably already under suspicion as a relative of someone who'd escaped the City. Perhaps she'd even been impris—but Astra couldn't bear to think about that, so she walked steadily back the way she'd come, trying to look confident and untroubled.

"What are you two doing here?"

It was a Fire Reaper officer, just coming out of some little café, who addressed them in UL. He was tall and redfaced and his belly hung over his belt. He wiped his mouth, belched, and planted himself in front of them.

Before Neil could say anything, Charlie stepped forward. He pointed to himself and Neil, then to the end of the street, then back to themselves. The officer frowned. "You're not from Nordlandia? Where are your permits?"

Freya growled, and Neil hastily grabbed her muzzle. Charlie shrugged and smiled and opened his hands and generally gave an impression of stupidity. The officer frowned again. "If you can't produce permits, I'm going to have to take you in."

Charlie began waving his arms agitatedly and jabbering what to Neil's ears was clearly nonsense. People nearby were glancing nervously at them and hurrying past, though an erect old lady paused, her shopping bag in her hand.

"You can tell your story to someone who speaks Drearish, or whatever it is you're talking," the officer said in annoyance, and pulled his devcom from his belt. But the old lady hurried forward, giving the man an ingratiating smile.

"They've obviously never been here before, officer. They don't know the regulations."

Neil shot her a grateful look as the officer glared at her. "Well, they'll soon learn. They ought to have a permit for the dog object, too."

"Then I'll take them to the right office," the old lady said brightly. "I think they might be a little—you know," and she tapped her forehead.

The officer nodded, obviously relieved at not having to deal with petty data entry. "If I find you on the street again, it'll be the worse for you," he said, glaring at Neil and Charlie again, and strode off.

"Follow me," the old lady said firmly, and set off down a

side street. About fifteen minutes later they came out near the remains of what might once have been a subway station—with no screen nearby, Neil noticed. "I *think* we've shaken off anyone who followed us," the old lady said, looking round carefully, "and I don't think you're *quite* as stupid as you made out."

Charlie grinned. "No, ma'am. You guessed right. We're mighty glad you came along and rescued us."

"I don't like those bullies. So I stand up to them whenever I can," the woman said. "Where are you from?"

Charlie and Neil looked at each other, and Charlie sighed. "That's a long story," he said.

"Very well. You can tell it to me at home, over a meal." And with that the woman set off again, on another convoluted route, until they came to one of those strange transparent cubes, larger than usual, set off on its own at the end of a street. Neil stared up at it, hoping this wasn't some sort of trap—though the woman didn't seem the type. She produced an old-fashioned key, unlocked the door, and hurried them inside.

"You've no idea how lucky you were," she said, heaving a sigh of relief. "And don't worry about the imagescreen." She waved her hand at its blank face on the far wall. "I've disabled it. It's against the law, but so far ..." She shrugged.

Neil and Charlie sank down gratefully on low, body-fitting chairs as the woman bustled around, preparing food. She set out a bowl of water and some scraps for Freya, too. "We had a dog when I was very small," she said softly. "A long time ago." She set out cheese and fresh bread and tomatoes—"I get this food on the black market," she said softly—and Neil and Charlie fell on it like wolves.

"Now you certainly aren't from the Drear Lands," the woman said. "I've heard Drearish before, and it sounds nothing like that. So suppose you tell me who you are and why you're here?"

Astra and the Prophecies

W e will waste no time," said Flame-Bearer Arnfasta briskly. "The sooner we begin instruction, the sooner you will be guaranteed redemption."

She and Astra were sitting in a small room off Vígeldgeirr's grand office, later the same afternoon. Vígeldgeirr had earlier professed to be very worried about Astra's long absence, though Astra was certain they'd known where she was. "I've been doing a lot of thinking," she told Vígeldgeirr contritely. "I went to my grandmother's house because I wanted to tell her how wrong she was, the way she raised me. I'm only just realizing how wicked she and my parents were. And I'd really like to learn more about the Fire Reapers."

"Well." Vígeldgeirr placed his hands together in that Fire Reaper gesture, raising them above his head and lowering them. "I didn't expect it to happen quite so quickly, my dear. May I say how gratified I am. I can assure you that you are making the right—the only—decision." He patted her patronizingly on the head and immediately arranged for lessons with one of his senior aides.

Astra had expected someone older, but Flame-Bearer Arnfasta turned out to be in her twenties and very pretty. She strode into the room in her uniform, followed by two slaves carrying a massive book on a silken cushion. The slaves set the cushion down on the table and departed. Arnfasta bent and reverently touched her forehead to the book, then looked at Astra. "Let's get started at once."

"Why do you touch the book like that?" Astra said, taken aback.

"We never call it 'the book,'" Arnfasta said severely. "Its name is the Book of Prophecies—or the VísinBók, to give it its true name. It was revealed to the first Guardian of the Flame many years ago in a dream, and dictated to his closest followers—we call them the Nine Scribes, the Ni Skrifarren. We bow to acknowledge its sacredness."

Astra's parents had taught her that all books were valuable, because each contained a little piece of the truth, so she merely nodded politely.

"We'll begin," said Arnfasta, opening the book solemnly, "with the Preface, in which the Guardian explains how the Prophecies were revealed to him." She began reading out loud, but Astra soon got lost in all the details, which went on for pages, and found herself falling asleep.

"You aren't paying attention!" Arnfasta said angrily, prodding her. "Vígeldgeirr himself is planning to test you on your knowledge."

"I'm sorry." Astra tried to rouse herself. "Perhaps we could start somewhere else." She tried to make her expression as innocent as she could. "The Prophecies talk about the End Times, don't they? I'd like to hear about that."

"That's like trying to run before you can walk," Arnfasta said scornfully. "You need to learn each chapter by heart. I myself memorized the whole thing by the time I was twelve." She pointed to the medal on her jacket. "That meant I could be one of the Flame-Youth. You, too, could strive for that."

Privately, Astra couldn't imagine anything worse. But at that moment the door opened and a slave entered with a message. After illumining and reading the metal wafer, Arnfasta rose abruptly. "I must attend an important meeting. Meanwhile, you are to stay here and study the Prophecies. And begin at the beginning," she warned before striding out of the room.

Astra stared at the book in dismay. It was thousands of pages long. How was she ever going to find out what she needed to know? Well, she had to seize the moment—she might not have another chance. She began riffling rapidly through the book, but soon realized that that was fruitless. She found the table of contents and ran her finger down it. The final chapter was called "The Afterburn." She turned to its first page.

In the hundredth year after the oceans rise, infidels will attack the Temple. They will be led by a creature who is half-man half-beast, and other misshapen things will obey him. The Temple will be razed to the ground, and the earth will tremble. When the Temple falls, the City will follow, collapsing in great noise and tongues of red flame. Thereupon a great battle will take place in the North, and a Bird of Fire will arise from the last trees, and its flaming wings will cover the earth, and white flakes will fall from the sky, and at the Last Stand the final flames shall devour them.

Astra lifted her eyes from the page and stared unseeing at the wall, her heart beating faster. *In great noise and tongues of red flame.* That could include explosions, couldn't it? The Prophecies said nothing about who would destroy the City. Perhaps the Fire Reapers believed they were fulfilling them by destroying the City themselves. *A Bird of Fire will arise from the last trees.* She didn't know what that meant, but she was sure the Fire Reapers were already making plans. Flaming wings and white flakes. Fire and ash, falling from the sky.

She shut the book, sickened and trembling. She had to find her father before the City was completely destroyed. And what about Amma? She had to get word to her somehow, too. How the three of them might escape the City she had no idea, but she had to find a way.

Apprehensively, she opened the book again, to the last chapter.

And in the falling City, those who are lost will be purified by the Flames, and will rise up in its smoke and be carried heavenward.

And on the Last Day the Daughter of Fire will be carried on her Throne to the centre of the City, and the God of Fire will take her to Himself, and her sacrifice will bless and sanctify the destruction. And the Daughter shall be an infidel, the child of an infidel, who has seen the Light and wishes to join herself to Fire. And she will be a mere child with hair the colour and shape of Flame, and all will bow down and worship her.

Astra slammed the book shut and stared at it in horror. *The child of an infidel who wishes to join herself to Fire ... with hair the colour and shape of Flame.* She touched her short red-gold hair and swallowed hard. Was this the real reason they'd wanted her in return for the other prisoners? Had they planned this all along? And by asking for lessons, she'd played right into their hands!

She had to get out of here as soon as possible.

But first she had to find her father.

"Well, I'll be damned. And then some," Charlie said.

They were sitting in the shabby armchairs after a delicious meal of Nordlandish rabbit and onions. It was the first time Neil's belly had been full since—well, he couldn't remember when. He felt sleepy and comfortable and safe. Freya did too, apparently; she lay asleep with her head on his feet.

"It's the damndest thing, how we ended up here," Charlie said again, shaking his head. "Beats me how it happened. And that was some dinner you fixed, ma'am. I ain't eaten like that since my Yukon days."

"Oh, you mustn't call me ma'am," the woman said, shaking her head and smiling. "My name's Saehild, but you must call me Amma. Just like Astra used to." And a shadow of sadness fell across her face.

"Wish I had better news of your granddaughter," Charlie

said quietly. "I hate to be the one to tell you. Not to mention your son."

"Hallvard's very brave," Amma said, sitting up straighter, "and he has great strength of mind. Wherever he is, I'm sure he'll survive."

"And Astra's brave, too," Neil said, rousing himself. "In fact," he added simply, "she's the bravest person I know." He hadn't known he knew that until he said it.

Amma's eyes filled with tears. "She's like her parents. Her mother, too, was very determined."

Outside the underground streetlights had flicked on, casting an eerie glow. "Well, we can't stay here forever," Charlie said, getting up. "For one thing, it's too dangerous for you, ma'am—I mean Amma."

"Oh, you needn't worry about me," Amma said. "There's nothing more they can do to frighten me. They imprisoned me for a while after Hallvard left, they took away all my techno privileges. But as you see"—she gave a weary smile—"I'm still here."

From somewhere in the distance—or were they hearing things?—came a faint boom. Then another, further off, so faint they had to strain to hear it. Amma shook her head. "They tell us it's construction in the outer suburbs, but no one believes that." She took a deep breath. "I'm sure the Aqua Libere have infiltrated again."

Charlie sat down. "They're *still* plantin' bombs? They were doing that before I was shipped to the Fortress."

"No one knows." Amma's voice had sunk to a whisper. "People say it's not just the Libere. But of course no one dares to really talk about it."

"Who do they think it is, then?" Charlie asked.

"Some people say"—Amma's voice sank even lower—"that it's the Fire Reapers themselves."

"At the Assembly meeting," Neil said slowly, remembering, "an Aqua Libere scout told us she'd seen troops, thousands of them, heading north. And a Fire Reaper prisoner told us they were planning a final battle there. Somewhere called—" He struggled to remember the name of the place, but couldn't. "He called it the Last Stand."

Amma gasped. "'When the Temple falls, the City will follow, and at the Last Stand the final flames shall devour them,'" she said, so softly they could barely hear her.

The three of them exchanged alarmed glances. "Then if there's a chance Hallvard's in the City, we've got to find him," Charlie said grimly, and stood up again.

"But it's after 2300 hours—long past curfew." Amma glanced apprehensively at the clock face, evidently still functioning, in the corner of the disabled imagescreen. "You mustn't go out, you'll be arrested. In the morning—"

"Charlie's right," Neil said stoutly, though he was far from feeling it. "If there's any chance at all—" He gulped and stood up. Freya got up, too, stretching and wagging her tail. Glancing down at her, Neil suddenly had an idea. "You know, Freya's a great tracker. If we had something of Hallvard's for her to smell ..."

"That's a fine idea, kid," Charlie said enthusiastically.

"If you're sure," Amma said hesitantly. She left the room and brought back a scarf, patterned with leaves. "Astra's mother gave him this," she said, handing it to Neil. "But the street's a dangerous place at night. There's the Sjørøver gangs as well as the patrols. You really must wait—"

"Begging your pardon, ma'am, but we can't just sit here," Charlie said. He was already pulling on the outer tunic of Hallvard's that she'd given him earlier. "The sooner we get started, the better."

Amma stared at him sombrely. "Then you must take something else with you." She hurried out again and came back with a Tabri—a much older model, covered with dust. "Hallvard left this here for me, but I've never used it. Please, take it." She thrust it into Charlie's hands.

For a moment Charlie hesitated. Then he shouldered the weapon, gave Amma's arm a squeeze, and opened the door. Moments later he and Neil, with Freya at their heels, were picking their way through the shadows in the direction of the Great Plaza.

Astra crept to the door of the little room and opened it. The long gleaming corridor stretched emptily away before her. When she peered across the hall into Vígeldgeirr's office, it, too, was empty—he must be at the same meeting. She tiptoed in, hesitantly, on hyper-alert for any sounds. There was no time to lose. She began rifling through desk drawers, not really knowing what she was looking for.

Her elbow accidentally banged the wall, and a screen flickered into life. An image of the room where she'd met with Arnfasta came up, then another image—her bedroom. So they _were_ spying on her. Not that she was surprised. Other rooms came up on the screen, one after the other, so many she couldn't believe they were all in the Palace. She saw the prisons, too—vast underground lightless dungeons where humans and other beings were chained to the walls. She shuddered and forced herself to look closer. Was her father among them? She scanned wall after wall, but she couldn't see him.

The sound of approaching footsteps made her flatten herself against the wall. A pair of Fire Reaper officers, talking in low tones as they passed, their bootsteps fading away down the corridor. She slipped back into the smaller office, heart thudding. What if she was caught in Vígeldgeirr's office? On the other hand, what else could she do? On her own, with no help, how could she _do_ anything?

No one asks for such tasks. Wasn't that what Áilu had said? _I can tell you, however, that the only way to reach your father is to undertake it._ Well, she _had_ undertaken the task. And she'd got this far, after all. All she could do was keep going.

Holding her breath, she made her way back into Vígeldgeirr's office. She touched the screen on the wall, which flashed up again, revealing still more rooms and laboratories and corridors. Most were empty—the Palace had been built for effect, not practicality—but now and then a few Fire Reapers appeared, monitoring screens, just like her. Could they see her? Probably not—spying from Vígeldgeirr's office must be only one-way, but just in case, she crawled under the desk and watched the screen from beneath.

Still more rooms, even storage rooms and closets, appeared. And now, it seemed, she was back at the beginning—the room where she'd sat with Arnfasta, her bedroom ... Her leg was cramping so she changed position, hitting her head on the underside of the desk. "Heilagr aska!" she muttered out loud.

Perhaps it was a password, because the screen suddenly went blank and then came to jerky life again. Room after warehouse-sized room came up filled with weapons and Fire Reaper uniforms, moodfood and containers of water, medical supplies and techno parts. They were ready for a siege, if need be. And now rooms came up where broken or outdated equipment and other junk had been tossed.

Just a minute. The camera had panned over what seemed to be just another storage room, except that it held a rumpled cot, a toilet, a shelf with a few books on it. The inevitable imagescreen, now dark. Astra leaned forward, holding her breath. A haggard figure was sitting at a table. Could it be—? With the straggly hair and beard she couldn't be sure. She waited on tenterhooks until the camera came round again. This time the figure looked up, briefly, as the camera passed. The face was thinner and more lined, the eyes sunken, but even with that beard she would have known him anywhere. Her eyes brimmed and spilled over, blurring her vision. She wanted to reach out and kiss the screen.

So he was here after all. And alive, even if he didn't look well. But where in the Palace was he?

The camera panned round the room once more and she stared avidly at the images, searching for clues. No windows, so it wasn't along an outer wall. A door with a tiny barred window—a peephole, really. Nothing else that gave any indication where it might be.

Where would *she* keep her most valuable prisoner if she were—she felt sick at the thought—Vígeldgeirr?

At the very top of the Palace. That was where the First Temple was, or so she'd been told when they'd lived in the City. No one was ever allowed there but the Archons. A prisoner kept there would have no access to anyone, except a guard.

She crawled to the door, still keeping out of sight of the screen, and peered into the corridor. Several slaves appeared, carrying some sort of equipment, followed by two guards. She shrank back as they passed by, then stood up and slipped silently down the hall. Surely there was a stairway somewhere. She didn't dare use the CloudTubes in case she ran into someone.

She opened door after door, heart beating—*if anyone's inside, I'll tell them I'm looking for Arnfasta*—but found only room after empty room. She was beginning to despair when, opening another door at random, she almost plunged headlong down a dirty staircase. It spiralled away upward as well, the steps cracked and broken. Clearly, no one ever used it.

She let the door shut behind her and was plunged into darkness. Fighting down waves of panic, she made her way upward by feel. From time to time a stair almost gave way beneath her and the dust brought on fits of sneezing and coughing. And still the staircase spiralled up and up and up ...

She was dizzy and disoriented when, after yet another spiral, she almost walked smack into a blank wall. She stared at it, bewildered. What was the point of building a staircase that went nowhere? She ran her hands over the wall but found nothing.

There must be *some* way through. Perhaps this staircase,

like the tunnels in the Fortress, had been intended only for escape from the lower levels. In which case ... She began searching along the floor at the base of the wall, centimetre by centimetre.

A sudden spark of light zinged into her vision, almost hidden under a layer of dust. A tiny glowing flame, no bigger than a pinpoint—just like the one in the Fortress! Trembling with excitement, she pressed it. A section of wall beside her suddenly seemed to thin out and vanish. She stared at it, baffled. More new techno stuff. Cautiously she put her hand out. It disappeared up to her wrist! She hastily withdrew it, then tried again, this time with her whole arm. The opening grew a little larger. She pushed at the sides and discovered that they moved back as if she was opening a sliding window.

She put her head through, then her whole body, and half-stepped, half-fell onto a vast golden floor. Behind her the opening sealed shut, but she barely noticed. She sat up and stared round in wonder. She was in the First Temple!

It was exactly the same as the one in the Fortress, except even larger and more dazzling. As a little girl she'd often stared up at the top level of the ziggurat, wondering what the Temple was like, but she'd never ever expected to one day be inside it. Everything—the floors, the walls, the ceiling—was coated with gold leaf. Just as in the Second Temple, the room was filled with thousands of shelves and what must be millions of vials of ash. Dazed, she began walking slowly round the room. Each vial, just as before, was labelled and dated. *White Birch, Beaufortia, 18 Efst-Flamme, Year 23 of the Fire Reaper Ascendancy. Scrub Olive, Northwest Drear Lands, 6 Þoka-Flamme, Year 11 of the Fire Reaper Ascendancy.* She thought of the orchard in Ashgård with its old apple and mango trees that had been destroyed the night of their escape, and shuddered.

It looked as though the Temple hadn't been used in some time. There was a thick layer of dust on the altar and a dead mouse nearby. That was reassuring, at least. It was less likely she'd be discovered. A CloudTube shaft was nearby, but when she pressed the button nothing happened. No doubt only the Archons could control it.

But she'd come to find her father.

She continued round the walls, looking for more glowing pinpoints or some other sign of a hidden entrance. At last she was almost back where she'd started, and still there was no sign of a hidden room.

Then a section of shelving caught her eye. There was something askew about it. She stared at it, puzzled. Yes, that was it—it stood ever so slightly farther out from the wall than the sections on either side of it. She began pulling out vials as fast as she could. There, behind a vial of Alpine Fir: another glowing pinpoint. She pressed it, trembling. The wall of shelves slid aside, and there—there was the door she'd seen on the computer screen, only from the outside, looking in. There was the tiny barred peephole. And inside, lying asleep on the cot, was her father.

To her astonishment the door wasn't even locked. Maybe the guards were getting careless. She opened it and stepped inside. Her father stirred and mumbled and opened his eyes. And saw her. He sat up, staring.

"Astra! Is it really—can it be—?"

"Yes, Pappa! Oh yes!" She flung herself across the room and threw her arms round him. He was so thin! And he looked so old ... Trembling, he touched her face wonderingly, anxiously.

"It's really you? Not some Fire Reaper devilry?"

"No, Pappa, no, it's me, it's really me." She tightened her arms and pressed her face into his chest. She was never, ever, ever going to let him go. "It's a long story, Pappa. But I'm a prisoner now, like you."

He gave a long sigh, and stroked her hair, and murmured "Elskede, elskede, elskede" over and over. "You're hurt, dear one," he said in alarm when he noticed her withered finger.

"Oh, that. It's nothing, Pappa." Astra pulled away and looked up at him. "They said you were *helping* them. They said you'd converted to their beliefs." She felt tears coming and choked them back. "It isn't true, is it, Pappa?"

"They threatened to harm you. They said they'd captured you. I thought I could protect you if I—if I pretended to go along with them." An expression of weariness and disgust crossed his face. "But I'm not a very good actor, I'm afraid. And really, without you it was impossible to work on the Memory Stone. I've been here ever since."

Astra clenched her fists. Her father's first thought had been to protect her. Now it was up to her to protect him.

"Somehow we have to get out of here, Pappa," she said urgently. "They're destroying the City. They're making the Prophecies come true."

Her father shook his head sadly. "I'm not well. I'm afraid I'm in no condition to try escaping, even if escape is possible. But *you* must try. You must save yourself, if you can."

"I'm not leaving without you." Her voice shook and she fought to control it. "Not after I finally found you. We can go back the way I came in."

A sudden ping made her look up sharply. The imagescreen on the wall was flickering into life. The image wavered and steadied. It was Vígeldgeirr, as large as—larger than—life, his head filling the whole screen. He was smiling broadly, as if at some joke.

"You're a clever young girl. *Very* clever. We really didn't expect you to get so far." He gave a high, mirthless laugh. "Such a shame you weren't truthful about joining us. We Fire Reapers have a great appreciation for truth." He turned his head, as if looking at someone off-screen. "Someone else would like to speak to you—someone you may remember."

Slowly his face dissolved into another, a younger man's face with a glittering tiger's-eye in his forehead. He wore the strange three-cornered hat of the Fire Reaper military, with the seven flames consuming a globe that indicated a general.

362

Chalcedon!

He stared at her as if he'd never known her, much less been an ally. "Alas," he said icily, and the tiger's-eye seemed to darken as he spoke, "it turns out that you've been *too* clever. You're trapped now like a fly in amber. Until, of course, the Prophecies are fulfilled."

Behind her she heard the door shut and the sound of a Coder locking it. Chalcedon's eyes blazed with triumph, and the tiger's eye flashed fire. Then the screen went dark.

Freya Leads the Way

Under the artificial moon the streets were deserted.

Even the Fire Reaper soldiers seemed to have disappeared. Gangs carrying knives and Tabris strode past, arms piled with looted goods, but they paid no attention to Neil and Charlie. From time to time shouts and the sound of shattering echoed through the night.

"They've already abandoned the City," Charlie muttered. "They're lettin' the outlaws run the place."

"Where are we going?" Neil whispered, the hairs on the back of his neck prickling.

"I figure we'll start with the Palace. Maybe the dungeons. I spent a delightful couple of months there myself."

From the distance came the sound of an explosion. Then another one, much closer, and a massive cloud of dust rose into the air a few blocks away. A woman hurried past clutching two small children by the arm. She glanced in terror at Neil and Charlie. "They bombed yours out, too?" she whispered.

"Uh—yeah," Charlie whispered back. "Where's yours?"

She nodded, as if she'd expected his answer. "They're bombing all over now." She pointed in the direction of the cloud. "That's where I lived. One of my neighbours warned me. A few of us got out."

Another explosion, this time on the corner ahead of them. As Neil and Charlie and the woman watched in horror, a collection of housepods slowly collapsed into rubble. They could hear screaming. The woman clutched her children and hurried off. Charlie and Neil stared at each other, stricken.

"We better move fast," Charlie said grimly. "Don't look like we got much time." And he broke into a limping run.

By the time they reached the Palace, the imagescreens showed it was well after 2400 hours. The building was a blaze of lights, with dozens of soldiers patrolling up and down in front of it. The plaza was deserted, but above it a huge black cloud rose and circled. Neil glanced up and stiffened.

"Vampyriae!" he whispered, aghast. He grabbed Freya's muzzle, but it was too late. She sniffed the air and barked twice, loudly.

"Who's there?" a soldier shouted from the distance. Neil and Charlie shrank back into the shadows. The searing pain shot up Neil's ankle again and he had to bite down hard to stop himself from crying out.

"Reveal yourself," the soldier shouted, "or we shoot!" The next minute there came the sound of boots running in several directions and more shouting. Charlie yanked a half-conscious Neil after him behind a pile of twisted and blackened rubble. They sat holding their breath, Neil clutching his ankle and breathing hard.

The shouts grew more distant, and Charlie hurried them through a tangle of narrow maze-like alleys. At last, panting, they found themselves in an older neighbourhood of crumbling housepods at the back of the Palace. A few Vampyriae were still screeching high overhead, but the only soldiers in sight were a little group clustered at a far corner of the building, inhaling threk. The pain in Neil's ankle was fading, to his great relief.

"This way," whispered Charlie. Moving quickly from shadow to shadow, they crossed the empty square behind the Palace and hid behind a large stone statue of Vígeldgeirr. It was a short distance from the statue to the nearest wall of the building. They crept round the side, looking for some way in. Charlie found a place at shoulder height where the lupiathon walls had developed spiderweb cracks. "They're gettin' careless," he whispered. "Or runnin' out of money. We heard they were billions of Flammunir in debt to the UCE. Now keep an eye out."

He pulled the old Tabri from his shoulder and brought the butt down hard on the lupiathon, eight, ten, a dozen times. Finally it shattered into large jagged sections that the two of them pried apart gingerly with their fingers. Charlie hefted Neil up to peer inside.

A storage room of some kind, crammed with odds-and-ends—discarded furniture, unopened crates of moodfood, old techno parts. Neil hauled himself through the opening, being careful with the jagged edges, and jumped down. Immediately the searing pain returned to his ankle, though this time it seemed to fade more quickly. He heard scrabbling behind him as Charlie lifted Freya up, and then it was Charlie's turn.

"I ain't as young as I once was," Charlie said, panting, as he struggled through the opening, dragging his injured leg behind him. "Hot doggety! Are those Fire Reaper uniforms?"

One whole corner was filled with racks of cloaks, boots, tunics. Neil tried on cloaks while Charlie, grimacing, adjusted a tri-cornered hat with a Flame-Protector's badge. Minutes later two newly outfitted Fire Reapers stood facing each other amid the jumble. Neil took out Hallvard's scarf and knelt in front of Freya.

"Freya, this is important. *Really* important." He held the scarf to her nose. "You have to find Hallvard, okay? Can you find Hallvard?"

Freya cocked her head, her ears pricked, her intense brown eyes searching Neil's as though she was deciphering what he'd said. Charlie cautiously opened the door and peered out. Moments later two Fire Reapers, the taller one limping, an odd moving bulge under the shorter one's cloak, could be seen walking down the deserted corridor. The corridor soon branched off in a dozen different directions, and after a hasty glance around Neil swung his cloak aside.

"Okay, Freya. Find!" She hesitated for only a moment, sniffing the air, then took off down one of the branches. Neil and Charlie hurried after her, both of them praying they wouldn't run into anyone.

"Good sled-dog genes, your girl," Charlie said admiringly as they panted down the corridor. "Hate to think what she could do when she's feelin' a hundred percent."

Round the next corner they almost collided with three officers stepping out of a CloudTube. One of them—older than the other two, with a Flame-Shielder's five-flamed badge—stared at them, eyebrows raised. "Didn't I just see a *dog* object go past?"

"Yes, sir." Charlie promptly saluted in Fire Reaper fashion and Neil hastily followed suit. *Crapola. What was he saying yes for?* "It escaped from the Research Labs upstairs, sir. We were ordered to track it down."

"Escaped?" The Flame-Shielder frowned. "Exceptional carelessness, I'd say." The two others with him nodded, looking grim. "I'm surprised they sent only two of you."

"Oh, there's others looking in different—er, areas," Charlie said quickly.

The officer hesitated, glancing at his companions. "You'd better send for reinforcements at this level of the Palace," he said to them curtly, and walked off.

Whew. That was close.

"How did you know there were labs here?" Neil glanced nervously behind them as they hurried after Freya.

"I didn't." Charlie grinned. "I took a chance. Hells' bells, hope we can find her."

She was at the far end of another corridor that angled off to the right, whining and pacing in front of a door. It opened onto a dirty staircase, obviously long unused, that spiralled away into the darkness above them. Freya shot through, racing up the winding steps. They could hear her claws on the stone far above them.

"Hope she knows what she's doin'," Charlie muttered.

They hurried through, shutting the door behind them. There

wasn't a scintilla of light anywhere. As they began climbing the narrow, crumbling stairs. Charlie kept losing his footing and exclaiming "Dagnam it!" each time. Neil found himself sneezing over and over, and blew his nose on the Fire Reaper cloak, which was probably a terrible offence punishable by death (or worse). And still the stairs spiralled away above them ...

At last, out of breath, they heard Freya just above, rooing excitedly. They turned the corner and there she was, thumping her tail happily—against a blank wall! Was it some kind of trick? The stairs had come to a dead end!

"Dagnam and blast it!" Charlie said, for the umpteenth time, and collapsed on the top step. "To think we climbed all that way ..."

"I don't get it," Neil said, puzzled. "She seemed so sure. It's not like her." Freya had never been wrong before. How could she be wrong now, when it was so important? He hunted along the wall but could find no opening.

Freya was nosing about and whining softly. She gave a short, sharp bark and stood up on her hind legs. The next moment a section of wall suddenly seemed to thin out and vanish. She began scrabbling through, her head disappearing, then her forepaws. "Freya!" Neil shouted in horror. He grabbed her tail only to watch in disbelief as his hand and arm vanished up to the shoulder.

"Charlie! Help!"

Charlie, who'd been examining the stairs lower down, spun round. "Hot jiggety!" He grabbed Neil, who by now had disappeared up to his armpit. Still holding Freya's tail, Neil felt himself yanked forward. Then he was tumbling through space, landing with a thud that knocked the breath out of him. Moments later Charlie came tumbling through the air on top of him. They both lay sprawled, trying to catch their breath.

They were in a vast golden hall, so bright their eyes hurt after the long darkness. There were thousands of shelves filled with millions of glass vials, a massive altar studded with onyx and rubies, and an enormous central fire pit. Neil sat up and stared round in amazement. It looked just like the Temple in the Fortress, only even bigger.

Charlie sat up too, clutching his head. The tri-corner hat had fallen off and his tunic had shed a button. He looked round slowly, blinking. "Holy moly. Whaddaya know."

The next moment the air was filled with Freya's high-pitched sobbing. Neil scrambled to his feet. Not far away her tail was sticking out between two sections of shelving, wagging madly. Had she found Hallvard? No. She'd found a door. Heavy and black, he saw as he hurried closer. It must be some secret room for the Archons or something ... with something inside that Freya wanted. He stood on tiptoe to peer through the tiny barred window.

Oh—my—god. Ohmygodohmygodohmygod....

The next thing he knew Astra was jumping up and down at the window, Freya was rooing hysterically, and Charlie was ordering them all to stand back while he levelled his Tabri at the door. Astra rushed through the melting fragments, laughing and crying and flinging her arms round them. Hallvard, looking dazed, rose slowly from his cot, blinking in disbelief.

It was Charlie who found his voice first. "Howdy," he said, stepping through the smoke and sticking his hand out. "The name's Charlie—Tombstone Charlie. You must be Astra's father. I'm honoured to meet you, sir."

"I, too, am honoured," Hallvard said softly, as if having two people and a dog come crashing into his cell was an everyday event. "Honoured to meet another scientist of time. Especially having heard from my daughter how you saved her life."

"She's, uh, makin' it sound more than it is, sir." Charlie looked down, abashed. "Anyway, I'm real glad we found you. Hope you don't mind us droppin' in so rudely."

"Mind? Oh, Charlie!" Astra flung her arms round him again. "I've never been gladder to see anyone in my whole life!"

"It was Freya who found you," Neil said stoutly, rubbing the dog's ears as she thumped her tail proudly. "Why did I ever doubt you, Freya?"

Astra looked searchingly from Charlie to Neil and back. "I've found out some terrible things. About the Prophecies. About someone they call the Daughter of Fire." She gulped and plunged on. "They say she's the daughter of an infidel, she has hair like flame. And on the Last Day the God of Fire is going to take her away." She stopped, stricken. "They're going to—to sacrifice her. And I'm certain they mean me."

Neil and Charlie stared at her in horror. "Monsters," Charlie said, his jaw clenched.

"But that's—that's crazy!" Neil burst out, feeling sick and helpless and angry all at once.

From behind them came the sudden ping of the imagescreen, making them all jump. A blurred image appeared, crackling with static, but it wasn't Vígeldgeirr. The picture sharpened—a barren, rocky coastline lapped by slimy green waves, the brassy sun beating down out of a burning sky, a clutch of abandoned houses just above the beach.

"Why, that's Varangerhalvøya!" Hallvard leaned forward in amazement. "On the edge of the Arctic DeadSea! I went hiking there as a boy. Though by then it was already an øy, an island, not a half-island like its name says."

The screen suddenly filled with a Fire Reaper announcer in ceremonial red uniform, standing beside one of the ruined houses. "And here we are in Hamningsberg, bringing you live coverage of the start of the Final Campaign!" She was flushed with excitement, her eyes gleaming. "How we've all longed for this glorious day! And thanks to our glorious Fire Reaper techno, all Terranians can join with us in our final triumph!"

"Lies," snorted Charlie, almost spitting at the screen. "Only the twelve Cities have imagescreens."

"Is it real?" whispered Astra. "Is it really happening now?"

From offscreen came the sound of robotic chanting. Fire

Reaper troops in endless phalanxes appeared, hundreds of thousands of them, marching in formation across the landscape. Special battalions dressed entirely in red carried wand-like torches, flickering palely in the daylight. The image changed to a vast forest of spruce and pine and birch, stretching as far as the eye could see. Then the announcer's face, quivering with excitement and outrage, filled the screen.

"This tree-smothered place represents the Old Age, that decadent and ignorant time when people believed the existing planet was worth saving. But now"—her voice rose to a shriek—"we are ushering in the New Age, when the planet will be cleansed and a new and better world will arise from the ashes! Stand with us as we—"

"We don't," Charlie said, striding over to the imagescreen, "have to watch this crap." He felt around the rim, struggled with something, let out an exclamation, and stuck his finger in his mouth. "The damn thing bites!" he said.

A tiny wriggling worm-like shape fell to the floor. Freya nosed it as it lay twitching and leapt back, growling. Charlie picked it up cautiously. Thin as a needle, with intricate little mechanisms for eyes. "They're using *living* parts now," he said in disgust. He tossed it to Freya, who caught it and broke its back with one snap.

"When we lived here I knew how to disable the imagescreens." Hallvard shook his head, distressed. "But now ..."

An explosion somewhere outside shook the Palace. It rattled the chairs and table, and a shower of dust fell to the floor. They all stared at each other in alarm.

"Well, we ain't just sitting here till *we* go up in a burst of electrons, too," Charlie said decisively.

Hallvard pointed to the destroyed door. "The guards often left that open. They knew I couldn't escape—they control all the exits. There isn't any other way out."

"What about the way we came up?" Charlie said, and strode off to investigate. He came back shaking his head. "It's a way to get in, if you know how, but not out. They musta planned to hole up here if they had to."

"The Archons have a way out." It was Astra, whitefaced. "They have a—I don't know how it works, but Vígeldgeirr called it an energy pathway. That's how he brought me here from the Fortress. They use the pathways to travel between Temples."

"*Energy* pathways?" Charlie muttered, and looked grim. "Hoo boy. They're closer than I thought to—well, to the kinds of things I was workin' on. Only they're usin' 'em for their own ends."

"Can't *you* do something?" Neil looked at him in desperation. "You *did* make that stuff we drank that got us—"

"Gimcrackery," Charlie said disparagingly. "I was damnfool lucky. Even gettin' to Nordlandia in the first place was a mistake." He looked at Hallvard sheepishly. "I wanted to find an *enlightened* future. That's what you get for doin' quantchemy by the seat of your pants." He glanced round the cell as if a plant or a potion might materialize. "Anyway, there's nothin' to use. Not even stone energy," he added sadly, and Neil felt a sharp pang at the memory of Piedra.

Astra pointed beyond the cell to the Temple walls. "There's the ash," she said.

The other three stared at her. "But it's *dead*," Neil said.

"It's been produced for evil ends, elskede," Hallvard said gently.

"By cracky!" Charlie's eyes widened. "The kid may be onto somethin'. Besides, what's the worst that can happen?"

Neil gave him a derisive look. "We end up dead too?"

"If we do nothing we're dead anyway," Charlie retorted grimly. "The worst is it won't work. Or not the way I expect. Astra, get me a bunch of those vials. You too, Neil."

Astra hurried off to the nearest wall, with Neil following her reluctantly. Hallvard shook his head. "The Plant Nation has undergone such horrifying torture," he said softly, "that its energies are nullified. These corpses cannot help us."

"There's bound to be energy traces left," Charlie said stubbornly. "Bits of wood that didn't get burned all through."

"There's a very old poem my mother used to quote. In UL it goes, '*Evil means always have evil ends. The evil that you use your use portends,*'" Hallvard said. His eyes were full of sadness.

Charlie jerked his head toward Neil and Astra, who were filling their arms with vials. "Those kids were sent on a mission. And it's my job to help 'em."

As Neil and Astra hurried back and forth, Charlie began emptying the contents on the gold-leafed floor. When the pile of ash grew as high as Freya's nose, he rubbed his hands together. "Okay. Now, with any luck ... Freya, I need you, too. Stand right there." He positioned her beside the pile, nose pointing east— the position of vision and illumination, he said, according to First Nations elders. "Now we gotta sit in a circle round the pile and hold hands. Neil, put one of your hands on Freya. I'll do the same thing."

Everyone sat, even Hallvard. "Close your eyes," Charlie ordered. He leaned forward and dropped his voice to a whisper. "You who lost your lives for the evil ends of deluded humans. You who have already given more than Living Beings should be asked to give. We ask you to join your spirits with ours in opening a pathway that will release us from this evil place. Help us to join our friends the Bi-Souls in their struggle to restore balance and harmony to—"

But Charlie never finished his invocation. At that moment a blast hit the Palace itself, sending shattered slabs of lupiathon and stone and glass flying in all directions. The massive onyx altar cracked in two. The vast golden floor tilted sideways as incandescent white light burst round the little group sitting there, lighting up their terrified faces.

Then everything was blackness.

The Prophecies Are Fulfilled

When Neil came to, he was lying on a wet, cold floor in the semi-dark somewhere, his whole body numb. He tried to sit up, but something was pinning him down. With an effort he opened his eyes. *What hap—where am— Frey—must find—*

He managed to turn his head and look to either side. Broken glass, shattered walls, piles of rubble lay everywhere. An imagescreen had melted into a puddle; broken wires dangled from what remained of the ceiling; a metal bar had been driven into a huge chunk of black stone just centimetres from his head. He stared at it for a full minute before realizing it was part of the altar.

The Temple! That's where they'd been ... Charlie had been talking ... then—then he couldn't remember. Shakily, he lifted his arms and examined them. They seemed fine, except for being covered in dust. But his legs were trapped by some heavy object he couldn't quite make out. He lifted himself awkwardly on his elbows. A desk, that was what it was. Flipped upside down. He managed to struggle and squirm his way out from under it, and pushed himself to his feet. Pain stabbed through his ankle—his *right* ankle. He bent down to look. It was badly bruised, maybe broken. But apart from that and his foggy head he seemed—amazingly—okay.

He stared about him. Unbelievably, he was at ground level— there, in the distance, was the entrance, with its distinctive gate. But where were the others? Were they hurt? Were they—

He pushed his horrible thoughts away and began moving cautiously through the rubble. A broken pipe was spewing water over everything. The first body he found was that of a slave, still clutching the tray he'd been carrying, his eyes wide with terror. Then the body of a Fire Reaper soldier, face down. Shaking harder now, he clambered over shattered equipment, across the pieces of a huge ruby flame that had once stood on the roof. Then he heard moaning.

It seemed to be coming from a pile of shelving. He scrambled toward it. A dust-covered arm stuck out at a grotesque angle. He hauled a shelf out of the way, then another. A man in a Fire Reaper uniform lay there, semi-conscious, a deep gash across his scalp, a shard of glass embedded in his cheek.

"Where—where am I?" The arm moved, weakly.

"Charlie!" Relief flooded him. "It's me, Neil! Are you okay? Are you hurt?" What a dumb question!

Charlie grimaced. "My legs. Somethin's happened to my legs."

He was trapped underneath the remains of what might have been a CloudTube station. Neil tried pushing at the wreckage and then pulling, but it was useless. He was hauling a shelf off Charlie's legs when he heard frantic rooing. A golden dog came hurtling round a broken wall and flung herself at him, her whole body quivering. She was covered in dust but she seemed unhurt, to his immense relief.

"Freya! Oh Freya Beya ..." He clung to her while she licked his face urgently. Then she turned and began licking Charlie's.

"Look"—Neil swallowed hard. "I'll go find some water, okay? And some bandages."

With an effort Charlie turned his head. "Listen, kid." He paused, breathing heavily. "You gotta get out of here. It's not safe."

"No! No way! Just hang on till I get back. Freya, stay with Charlie."

That storage room they'd found when they'd broken into the Palace—there'd been some first-aid supplies there, hadn't there? He staggered off through the ruins, hoping against hope it wasn't destroyed. The door was torn off and two of the walls were gone, but the rack of Fire Reaper uniforms was untouched. He hunted through the wreckage until he found a box, badly dented, with gauze and disinfectant. He found a basin, too, cracked but in one piece, carried it back to the broken pipe and filled it with water. Then he hurried over to where he'd left Charlie.

Freya was lying beside him, licking gently at the blood trickling from Charlie's scalp. "Good dog," he said. Charlie's eyes were closed.

"Charlie? It's me again." He knelt down awkwardly. "I've got some water."

After a few moments Charlie's eyes opened, though it took him a while to focus. "Neil? What are you doin' here?"

Oh god. "I've got some water, Charlie. Here, open your mouth." He lifted the basin, but all he succeeded in doing was sloshing the contents down Charlie's chest.

Charlie gave him a ghost of a smile, teeth white against the dust. "There's nothin' you can do, kid. Now scoot."

"Look, I'm going to bandage that wound, okay?" He fought back tears. "And then we can try getting out of here."

There were pills in the first-aid box. He didn't know what they were—the label was in Nordlandish—but he pushed one into Charlie's mouth anyway.

"Just hang on, okay, Charlie? We'll get you out of here soon, don't worry. That's a good girl, Freya, you keep licking ..."

He was fumbling with the bandage when Charlie spoke again. "If we—if we failed—" He stopped, heaved in a breath. "It was my fault, okay? My fault. Just remember that."

He was hallucinating, obviously. "It's okay, Charlie. It's okay."

"You're a—a skookum kid. The best."

This time Neil couldn't stop the tears. Furious, he brushed away the wet and got his arm under Charlie's head. "Can you sit up? Let's help Charlie, Freya. Atta girl."

Charlie smiled at him—a strange, tender smile, like nothing Neil had seen before. "Hang in there, kid. Don't give up."

His eyes drifted shut and something like a sigh went through his body.

"Charlie? Charlie?"

Freya flung back her head and let out a heartbroken howl.

How long he lay there he had no idea, only that when he finally pushed himself up his eyes were hot and swollen from crying and his head ached horribly. The rest of him was ice-cold, except for the side where Freya had been pressed tight against him. He got to his feet and stared down dully at the closed eyes, the battered face. What was he supposed to do now? Charlie had told him to get out of here, to save himself.

"I'm sorry, Charlie. I feel terrible. Terrible that you—" He choked up, and it was several minutes before he could summon a prayer from his father's funeral. He whispered what bits he could remember. Then, with Freya close beside him, he dragged himself and his injured ankle to the front entrance.

What he saw outside stopped him cold. As far in every direction as he could see, the City lay in ruins. Even the huge dome had been partly shattered, and night had fallen—real night. Fires burned here and there, and the odd underground streetlight blinked on and off at random. A few buildings stood intact, but mostly it was a sea of torn and broken lupiathon and glass and stone and other stuff he had no name for. Dead imagescreens hung at odd angles from broken walls. Among the wreckage, people wandered, dazed, or stood staring. One woman sat on the ground nearby cradling a child's shoe. Flocks of Vampyriae circled, dropping lower in the sky.

In front of him, the Plaza had been cleared of rubble and was surrounded by soldiers. A huge pile of logs was heaped in the middle. A bonfire would be nice, Neil thought dully. He was so cold; he'd never been so cold. People were straggling toward the Plaza from all directions, some of them injured, some leaning on others who were injured. They were chanting something, over and over, though it took him a while to make out the words. *"Daughter of Fire, save us! Daughter of Fire, save us!"* It made his blood freeze.

And now from around the corner of the building came soldiers, dozens of them, twelve abreast, each carrying one of those wand-like torches. Behind them came yet more troops, Tabris at the ready. Then a squad of children and teenagers dressed in white, the Fire Reaper flame on their collars, each carrying some sort of ceremonial jar. The chanting intensified. People elbowed their way forward to get a better look. Two men in white, with red sashes across their chests, carried a scarlet cushion on which a gigantic gold book lay open. The Archons came next, walking two by two in their red robes, slow and erect and proud, and finally Vígeldgeirr, surrounded by yet more soldiers and acolytes. He wore a glittering headdress of gold and rubies, and he carried a bejewelled bowl of flame.

The procession halted. Vígeldgeirr faced the vast crowd and held the bowl high above him. In the sudden silence hundreds, maybe thousands, of people dropped to their knees. Some were holding out their arms or weeping; many gave the Fire Reaper salute. Vígeldgeirr turned and placed the bowl reverently at the foot of the pile of logs. Then he motioned to the two men holding the book. They held it upright so that Vígeldgeirr could read aloud. He lifted his hands in the Fire Reaper gesture and began.

"In the hundredth year after the oceans rise, infidels will attack the Temple. They will be led by a creature who is half-man half-beast, and other misshapen things will obey him. The Temple ..."

But the crowd wasn't listening. They were staring in the direction the procession had come from. All of a sudden a huge roar went up. A massive golden throne was coming round the corner, carried on the shoulders of a dozen slaves. Its embedded rubies seemed to flicker as it moved. The chanting began again, deafening this time. A tiny figure sat on the throne—a girl in an elaborate red dress that spilled to the ground, with a crown of flame-shaped rubies on her head.

Astra!

Neil stared at her, paralyzed with horror. How had they—? He glanced wildly at the ruins behind him, then back at the throne. They couldn't have—it wasn't possible— But it was unmistakably Astra. She stared straight ahead, unseeing, her eyes glazed. People shrieked and howled and had to be prevented from throwing themselves in front of the throne by the soldiers. *"Daughter of Fire, save us! Daughter of Fire, save us!"*

Behind the throne a man stumbled along between two soldiers, his wrists bound. Hallvard! The slaves set the throne down beside the pile of logs. More ear-splitting shrieking and chanting. Vígeldgeirr and the Archons bowed low before it, their lips moving, though Neil couldn't tell what they were saying. Astra raised her head and stared about, obviously bewildered.

Vígeldgeirr must have given some signal, because suddenly the slaves bent, hefted up the throne again, and began hoisting it to the top of the pile. The entire Plaza seemed to convulse in sobs and howls and moans. The soldiers with the torches moved forward, the flames flaring in the darkness.

They were going to set fire to the pile ...

Neil clung to the broken entranceway, numb with despair. The soldiers were lowering their torches. The kindling at the bottom caught—even at this distance Neil could hear the crackling. A log burst into flame, then another, and thick grey smoke began swirling skyward.

Stop! his mind shrieked. *Stop it, someone! Save her! Save Astra! Save—*

Suddenly Freya darted forward out of the broken doorway. "Freya, come back!" he screamed, but it was too late. She raced headlong into the Plaza, barking furiously. Freya, who was so afraid of smoke! Some of the nearest soldiers scrambled backward, clearly terrified. As confusion broke out, the crowd surged forward.

Dragging his injured ankle, Neil charged after Freya, heart hammering. That familiar pain was flickering in his other ankle now, but he pressed on. Fights were breaking out between people pushing forward and soldiers trying to push them back. Vígeldgeirr was shrieking at the nearest soldiers and pointing at Freya. They aimed their weapons at her, but she was dodging in and out of the procession. The next minute she'd reached Hallvard and seized his tunic in her teeth, growling like mad.

"You mustn't touch her!" Neil, arriving just in time, gasped the words out as one of Hallvard's guards swung at her with the butt of his Tabri. Sudden inspiration seized him. "She's a Flame Dog. The God of Fire sent her."

"Never heard of a Flame Dog," the second guard snarled as other soldiers drew menacingly closer. "Dogs are forbidden. And who are *you* anyway?"

At the edge of his vision Freya was tugging a bewildered Hallvard away from the procession. He had to keep talking to give her time. "She runs at the speed of flame to protect the people the god protects," he said. The words seemed to be coming out of his mouth without his bidding. "That's why you mustn't touch her. She's been purified by going through fire. She's—"

The Coder at the guard's belt suddenly began beeping. He stared at it, then at Neil, light dawning. "You're a *prisoner!*" He leapt forward to grab Neil, the other guard right behind him, but a scuffle had broken out near the men holding the Book of Prophecies. It flew up in the air, its pages fluttering, collided with one of the torches on its way down and burst into flame.

The crowd began shrieking and screaming—something had gone horribly wrong. It was a dreadful omen, a sign the God of Fire was angry. The guard, stunned, let go his hold on Neil as the crowd stampeded in every direction, trampling each other in their rush to escape. Even many of the soldiers were throwing down their weapons and fleeing along with the crowd. Above them all, the Vampyriae circled, screeching and flapping.

Neil rushed through the panic and confusion toward the

burning pile. It was smoking heavily, but only a few logs at the bottom had caught. Freya and Hallvard, thank god, had reached the safety of the ruined Palace. He began scrabbling up, almost passing out from the pain in his ankle. When he reached the top, Astra merely stared at him, bewildered—they must have drugged her, Neil thought. He grabbed her arm and almost yanked her off the throne. Somehow, slipping, half-falling, they made their way back down the pile, though Astra's dress kept catching and he had to stop each time to disentangle it.

At the bottom Vígeldgeirr was waiting, surrounded by his elite guard, the Archons huddled behind them. "You're a meddling little prick! You're the anti-Fire!" he roared, his face contorted with fury. "Seize them!"

"What for?" Neil said, pushing Astra behind him. An immense calm had descended on him. "Don't you see nobody believes in you now?" He waved his hand toward the sea of fleeing people. "If you and your god can't protect them, you're not much use to them, are you?"

Vígeldgeirr went white and then red. His eyes seemed to bulge out of his head. Some of the guards moved forward, weapons raised. "You're too late," Neil said to them, marvelling at his own calm. "There's no point anymore. Why do you serve such a weak leader?"

A violent argument broke out. Two or three of the guards flung down their weapons in disgust and began walking away. "Come back at once!" Vígeldgeirr roared, but they didn't respond. Neil grabbed Astra's hand and pulled her after him in the direction of the Palace. When he looked back, Vígeldgeirr stood alone beside the smoking pile, the Archons huddled near him on their knees. There wasn't a soldier in sight.

Neil led Astra and Hallvard through the tangle of maze-like alleys behind the Palace that Charlie had guided him through the night before. With the air full of smoke, breathing was difficult, and Astra especially was still groggy. Only Freya, a piece of some Fire Reaper uniform snagged on her collar, seemed recovered from her ordeals, trotting alertly ahead.

The streets were littered with discarded things—shoes, looted goods, even weapons. Neil found a perfectly good Tabri hanging on a broken wall, the familiar flame on its stock. Hallvard, stumbling to a halt, leaned unsteadily against a ruined house-pod. "I can't go any further," he muttered, rubbing his wrists where the handcuffs bit into them.

Astra, still looking dazed, sank to the ground. "Where are we?" she whispered.

"Just a bit farther," Neil said, though he had no idea where they were going. "We just need to get farther away from the Plaza."

"You saved our lives." Hallvard shook his head, his face grim. "My daughter and I—" He closed his eyes and shuddered. "It was a very close thing."

"But how did you—? I mean, the Palace exploded but you got out!"

Hallvard shook his head again. "I don't know. *They* must have got us out. The next thing I knew I was walking in that dreadful procession." He shuddered again.

Perhaps they'd used that energy pathway Astra had talked about. It had obviously all been planned, down to blowing up the Palace. And Charlie, dear brave Charlie who'd been so kind to him ...

"Charlie didn't make it," Neil whispered. His eyes were brimming. "He was trapped in the wreckage. Me and Freya—we tried to—" He couldn't go on.

Hallvard sucked in his breath. "He was a courageous man," he said softly after a few moments. He paused, staring sorrowfully into the distance. "May he be at peace."

It was Freya who broke the dark mood, playing pounce games with a scrap of cloth blown by a sudden breeze. "Freya was the one who *really* saved you," Neil said, still tearful. "She was braver than all of us."

Hallvard's face was sombre. "They must be horrified by this lapse in the Prophecies."

"Amma!" Astra cried out suddenly. She seemed to have woken up all at once. "Where's Amma? We have to find Amma!"

"I fear the worst, given all this destruction," Hallvard said gravely. "But yes, elskede, we must find out what happened to her. Then we need to get out of the City as soon as we can."

They reached the housepod, or what had been the housepod, half an hour later. People were emerging from the ruins around them in twos and threes, clutching bags and babies and anything else they could carry. Nothing of the housepod was left standing. Astra found her old cuddleswing smashed into tiny pieces. The three of them stood staring in horror.

"Charlie and me ate dinner here just last night," Neil said miserably.

"Here?" Hallvard looked incredulous.

"With Amma?" Astra whirled. "So she's alive?"

"She *was*. She rescued me and Charlie and Freya from a soldier who was trying to arrest us."

"That sounds like my mother, all right." Hallvard permitted himself a small, grim smile. "All the women in my life, in fact." He ruffled Astra's hair with tender sadness. An elderly man hobbled past, leaning on a cane. "Do you know what happened to the woman who lived here?" Hallvard asked urgently, but the man hurried on without looking at them.

Tears in her eyes, Astra pressed herself against her father. "We have to find her, Pappa."

"We can't risk staying here, elskede. Perhaps we'll meet her on our way out of the City."

Amma's probably lying among the wreckage of the housepod, Neil thought, but he said nothing. Astra, sobbing, hung on to Hallvard's arm and they set off, disheartened and exhausted. Crowds of people were streaming toward the gates, which made for slow going. Many were injured, others traumatized or angry, and everyone was frantic to get out. Roving Sjørøver gangs and groups of soldiers were threatening and looting passing families.

By the time they reached the edge of the City, the sun was rising, promising a hot northern day. The gates stood wide open; those guards, too, must have fled. Thousands of people were pouring through the gates, mostly on foot, though some had commandeered one of the Fire Reapers' floating vehicles or the High Militia's mules. High above them fluttered a vast flock of Vampyriae—"waiting for bones to pick," Hallvard said darkly.

As they stood hesitating, a cart laden with furniture drove past, its elderly driver leaning over the reins. "Can we get a lift with you, good sir?" Hallvard called out.

The driver stopped and stared at them out of the folds of his hood. "How do I know you're not looters? Or murderers?"

For answer Hallvard held up his handcuffed wrists. "We're escaping with nothing," he said. "This is all I have left. My son, my daughter, and our dog."

"What'll you pay me?"

Reluctantly, Neil held out the Tabri, which he'd hidden behind his back. The driver grabbed it and looked at them suspiciously. "I'll take you as far as the first Ash-Gatherer village and no farther. Get in."

They joined the vast crowd of people moving away across the barren wasteland that ringed the City. It was getting rapidly hotter, without a breath of wind. Neil looked longingly at the container of water sitting in the cart beside him.

"You're lucky I know my way," the driver remarked, ignoring their silence. "Most of these people've never set foot outside the City before." In fact some of them were already turning back, shouting warnings to the driver. There were wild beasts ahead, devils, monsters as tall as the City gates, waiting to devour them. The City might be in ruins, but it was safer than the wilderness.

Some hours later they stopped to give the mule a rest. They'd been descending for some time—the City had obviously been built high up—and the land was baking. The driver permitted each of them a few sips of water but refused to share his mood-food. "All's fair in love and war, and this is war," he said.

A handful of other people wandered up, covered in dust and sweat. "It's all the fault of that Daughter of Fire," a young woman said, pulling a dirty blanket over herself and two small children as shade. "None of this would have happened if she'd sacrificed herself like she was supposed to. I saw her climbing down when I looked back."

Astra pressed herself closer to her father, hoping no one noticed her.

"Nonsense!" an older man said disgustedly. "The God of Fire's angry with us, that's obvious. He's punishing us for our evil ways." He made the sign of the Flame and closed his eyes.

"Abjörn here's right," muttered another man, thin and wary-looking. "I was right at the front, I saw a fanged beast leap out of nowhere to devour Vígeldgeirr. All golden, like fire itself."

Neil quietly pushed Freya between his legs.

"It's balderdash," a large middle-aged woman said tartly. "All that Fire God stuff—who d'you suppose that nonsense benefited? Not you and me, that's for sure!"

"That's blasphemy!" the young woman with the blanket shouted. "I don't want my youngsters hearing such filth!" She got to her feet, hauling her children up, and marched off.

"Funny," the middle-aged woman said, catching sight of Astra, "but you look a bit like the Daughter of Fire yourself. Maybe we ought to build a fire right here and make everyone happy!"

The woman was being sarcastic, but Astra shrank back, wishing she'd been more careful about covering her hair. "It was all a ruse," Hallvard said quickly. "The Fire Reapers wanted to deceive you all. They wanted to make the Prophecies come true."

"You sound like infidels, both of you," the older man said angrily. "That's why we got into this mess in the first place—because of the unbelievers."

An argument broke out between those who still believed in the Prophecies and those who didn't. Despite the catastrophe of the City, most of those gathered round seemed to be in the former group. "Go on, be off with you," the man continued sullenly, staring at Hallvard. "We don't need your kind round here."

"I wouldn't have let them in the cart, if I'd known," the driver said indignantly. He climbed back in and drove off.

"We'll be leaving now," Hallvard said quietly. "We don't want to cause trouble."

They walked all day, and in the evening collapsed in a hollow under some thorny bushes. "There's a village to the south, about a day's walk away," Hallvard said. He gave his daughter a tender, weary glance. "We passed through there when we fled the City the first time."

They spent the night huddled together, sleeping fitfully, startling at any noise. In the morning, their stomachs growling, they started out. For water, Astra dug at the roots of desert plants and found tiny brackish trickles. Late in the evening they arrived at what was left of the village—the place lay in ruins. It had been empty for some time, judging by the weathered state of the houses. They wandered disconsolately through the place, finding only a handful of dried turnips to eat. Freya caught a couple of desert rats, which they roasted over a fire made by rubbing two stones together.

Neil's injured ankle was badly swollen, and he was having difficulty walking. Astra, too, was wobbly from the drugs, and Hallvard had been weakened by his long weeks of imprisonment. It was clear they wouldn't be able to travel much farther. "How far's the next village?" Neil asked anxiously.

Hallvard shook his head wearily. "I'm not sure. We avoided most of them the last time, so as not to draw attention to ourselves."

Astra, lying on her side, felt the edge of something hard pressing into her. The Etheric Sensor! In all the fear and confusion she'd completely forgotten it. She sat up at once and pulled it out. "Look, Neil! I got it back! Maybe I can find a village near us."

She began fiddling with the finger holes while Neil explained to Hallvard about the Sensor and where it had come from. But it still wasn't working, and Astra crumpled into tears of frustration.

How long can we survive out here? Neil wondered grimly. Danger behind, danger ahead—not much of a choice. They slept restlessly and breakfasted on the last of the turnips. Astra returned from a pee behind some bushes to report she'd seen footsteps—fresh ones. "*Human* ones," she added, glancing round nervously. "You don't suppose they're Sjørøver, do you?"

"Out this far? I doubt it," Hallvard said. "But I'm going to see for myself."

"Then I'll come, too," Neil said, but when he tried to stand his ankle collapsed. In the end Hallvard went off with Freya. As the minutes passed and he didn't return, Astra said anxiously, "Maybe I should go and look for him."

"No," said Neil, with more confidence than he felt. "I'm sure he'll be back any minute." He forced himself to focus on the walking stick he was whittling with a sharp flake of stone. After a few moments Astra took out the Sensor again and began studying it, looking up worriedly from time to time.

It was ages later when they saw two tiny figures through the distant heat haze. There was Hallvard, there was Freya—only now, coming up behind them, were three, four, half a dozen others. Neil's heart lurched, and he and Astra exchanged frightened glances. Had Hallvard been captured?

They crept backward into the shadow of the nearest ruined

house. Perhaps there was still time to escape ... But now they could hear distant laughter and chatter in Old Nordlandish. Friends of some kind, then, but who? They didn't look like Ash-Gatherers.

"Hey," Neil said as they got closer, "they're Aqua Libere!" They wore those high blue-grey boots and their heads were wrapped in lengths of blue cloth. Freya danced back and forth, rooing enthusiastically.

"They were out on a scouting patrol," Hallvard explained, smiling, as he came up. "And look!" He held up his hands, freed by a sharp Aqua Libere knife.

"Just keeping an eye on things," one of the women explained. "And looking for a fresh water source we'd heard about." She waved her hand at the others, two women and three men, all young and wiry and fit. They carried a variety of weapons— battered Tabris, bows and arrows, an old pistol—and one of them held a freshly killed rabbit.

"Hallvard says you're injured," the young woman who had spoken said, kneeling down beside Neil. He suddenly saw her as he'd seen her days ago, at the Assembly meeting outside the Fortress.

"You're Mesi!" he burst out. "You told Hreinn-Sál about the troop movements through that mountain pass!"

Mesi nodded and grinned. "I'm always happy to spy on Fire Reaper allies. Vaclav here's a medic—let's see what he can do for you."

While Vaclav tended to Neil's ankle, Mesi and two of the others went off to catch more game, and the remaining two built a fire. Mesi and her companions were soon back with three more rabbits and half a dozen small birds, and the air quickly filled with the delicious smell of roasting meat. As they ate, Hallvard told their visitors what had happened in the City and what they'd seen on the imagescreen in his cell in the Temple.

"So that's why we saw the Bi-Souls heading north a couple of days ago." Mesi frowned and wiped grease from her mouth.

"We assumed they were following the United Chinese Empire troops."

"We saw thousands of Fire Reaper reinforcements, too," one of the other women said quietly. "Fifty thousand at least. And hundreds of Varg-Minne and Vampyriae."

Neil felt sick. What chance did the Bi-Souls have against such numbers? But the Aqua Libere didn't seem concerned. Mesi and one of the men were talking in low tones, and after a few moments Mesi looked up. "None of you are in any shape for walking. So we've come up with a plan, Savio and me." She leaned forward and sketched a picture in the sandy earth with a stick. "We're going to build litters, like this one, and carry you."

Hallvard stared at her. "But you'll be exhausted within a day or two."

"We'll manage." Mesi gave a sly smile. "We have our own source of help. Water." Neil and Astra and Hallvard exchanged baffled glances. "You see," Mesi explained, "when it's spoken to and respected, water is only too willing to help us. I believe it was a scientist of your era"—she looked at Neil—"who discovered that water molecules can be imprinted with information. Dr. Masaru Emoto. He discovered *hado*—the energy and vibration in all things." She paused and drew a bottle of clear liquid from her tunic. "This is imprinted water. We have asked it to give us energy and courage. We carry it with us always. It allows us to travel tirelessly for days, and to go without food if necessary. So you see, carrying you will not be difficult."

"Where are you headed?" Hallvard asked.

"We think we should take you north," said Savio. "If the Last Stand is upon us—well, we ought to be there. They'll need all the help they can get."

"With our knowledge of how water behaves," Mesi said softly, "we hope to be of assistance. And besides" —she glanced gravely at Neil and Astra— "the two of you have a mission to complete, or so we understand." She stood up briskly. "But we mustn't waste more time. Savio, take Vaclav and Siobhán and see what you can find for our purposes among the ruins. Quan and I will remove all traces of the campsite, and Ritsuko will take the first guard duty."

A mission? Neil thought. Their mission so far had been a complete failure. Charlie was dead, Piedra had been lost in the Fortress, and the Fire Reapers were as numerous and powerful as ever. What use would he and Astra be in the final battle?

Through the Sigr-Bruni Pass

he litters were ready by evening. Savio and the others had fastened three groundsheets from their packs to the rusted steel rods they'd pried from the ruined walls. After a quick meal of dried biscuits, they set out. The night was dark and starless, yet the Libere seemed to have eyes like cats, and travelled swiftly and surefootedly over the hillocky ground.

Neil rode in the last litter, carried by Vaclav and Ritsuko. He'd expected to be jolted over the rough terrain, but it was like being on a boat on the ocean, rocked back and forth as the land rose and sank. He marvelled at their strength and tirelessness. They walked all through the night, and it wasn't until the sun was high in the sky the next morning that they called a halt.

"We'll rest for a few hours, during the hottest part of the day," Mesi told them, "and then we'll be on our way again." Hallvard offered to take a turn standing guard, but Mesi shook her head. "We're trained for this kind of thing. No offence, but you'd miss more than we would." And with that she herself took the first lookout duty, while the others curled up in the thin blankets they'd taken from their packs. Neil and Astra and Hallvard were each given one, too. The blankets were so fine and supple they could be folded to the size of an eyelash, yet they were wonderfully warm against the chill.

It seemed to Neil he'd been asleep for only a moment when Ritsuko shook him awake. They had a quick meal of the biscuits and another mouthful each of the imprinted water. "No more than a swallow," Ritsuko told Neil firmly. "It takes time for the body to adjust to its power." Yet Neil already felt more alert, and his ankle had improved, too, though perhaps that was due to rest and Vaclav's treatment.

They travelled all evening and through the night, stopping only briefly. The land beneath them changed from bare hillocks to swampland studded with grassy tussocks, with purple foothills visible in the distance. "Beyond those foothills," Mesi said, "lie the Skapraun Mountains, and in the middle of those is the Sigr-Bruni Pass." The mention of the pass was unnerving. With every minute they were getting closer to the fighting, and though Neil wanted with all his heart to be there, he also dreaded it.

They stopped for a few hours in the middle of the day and then set out. Neil, dozing and waking, lost track of time. Another night followed, or was it two? Late on an afternoon, they finally reached the lowest range of the Skapraun Mountains, its high peaks piercing the sky. Far in the distance, following Mesi's finger, he could just make out a yawning abyss between high granite walls—the Pass itself. It seemed impossible that they could climb so high, but Mesi laughed. "We're old hands. When you live as freedom fighters, you learn all kinds of skills."

They began climbing as the late afternoon sun streamed down, shedding its gold autumn light over everything. There were trees here, to Neil's amazement, though these weren't the pines and spruce and birches he knew from the Yukon. Ritsuko named them: stone pine, eucalyptus, others that Neil then forgot. Every so often small streams waterfalled down the mountainsides. At each stream the Aqua Libere paused to kneel and whisper a few words—"of gratitude," Ritsuko told Neil. "We let them know that we are grateful for their presence in the FeverWorld."

"The FeverWorld?" Neil asked.

"The time period we are now living through." Ritsuko's bright expression dimmed. "That is what we and the Fossefallen call it. Our beloved Terrania has been sickening for a long time, and now she is in the throes of deep fever. We pray the fever will break some day, and that Terrania will recover her health."

She looked so sad that Neil took her hand. "It's our fault, isn't it? The people who lived before this time, I mean. Things were changing even then."

Ritsuko sighed. "Blame is of no importance now. Humans, always and everywhere, are guilty of hubris—of dangerous pride. We think we can live outside the natural world ... until we are forced to learn otherwise."

Neil fell silent. If he ever got home, which seemed impossible, he'd do everything in his power to let people know what was going to happen in the future unless things changed.

They followed ancient trails around the mountains, trails that only the Aqua Libere knew. "That's why the Fire Reapers renamed these the Vexation Mountains," Vaclav said with his lopsided grin; a scar tugged at one corner of his mouth. "They found it very difficult to get their troops through." Neil and the others were all more than able to walk now—the bruising on Neil's ankle had almost completely gone—but the Aqua Liberes' nimblefootedness meant that it was faster to ride in the litters.

They reached the Pass two days later. It was barren and cold, this high up, and the late-autumn winds howled around them. Vaclav had told him they were above the Arctic Circle—farther north than Neil had ever been in the Yukon. It was weird there was no snow or ice here. There had been once, Savio said softly, when Neil told him that. His father and grandmother and two of his great-grandparents had all been Aqua Libere, Savio said, and the memory of snow had come down to him through them. So much snow you could travel the Skapraun Mountains from their peaks to the sea on wooden sticks. There'd been reindeer, too, and elk and lynx and wolverines. And fish, of course—cod and coalfish and haddock—in the fjords. "But now there is nothing." Savio shook his head sadly. "They say the last lynx was shot here over two hundred years ago. Its pelt used to be in a museum, but now it's a rug for some high-ranking Fire Reaper officer."

There were still voles and mice, though, lots of them—Freya was very good at catching them. She pounced on them like a fox, brought them proudly back to the group, and managed to keep herself in food. The Aqua Libere hunted birds and mountain hares, which they roasted at night under rock shelters, where the smoke couldn't be seen.

It was evening when they began descending the Pass. Spread out below them was the vast coastal plain, stretching away as far as the eye could see and dotted here and there with villages. Ritsuko explained that, because the villages flooded in spring and fall from ocean surges, people lived in houses built on high stilts. In the summers, because of the heat, they retreated to the mountains. Around the villages were rice paddies studded with tiny black dots—people, harvesting the rice. Beyond the villages were kilometres of rockstrewn sand, and far in the distance the horizon was blotted out by ocean fog or mist.

An odd mist, though, with occasional flashes of red or gold or white, like fireworks. Mesi, who seemed to find everything funny, grinned at Neil's words. "That's not mist. It's smoke, from the burning trees. And those flashes are weapon fire."

Neil swallowed, hard. The smoke stretched across the entire horizon. What had happened to Hreinn-Sál and Guldsterre and the others? And to the island of the Last Stand?

"The villagers can tell us," Mesi said. "Some of their people have probably joined the fighting."

The first village they came to was bursting with refugees— village people who lived closer to the battle. Each house was crammed with occupants, and no one was very pleased to see another group of arrivals. Still, room was made for them in the largest house. A couple of women brought bowls of rice and rabbit stew and glasses of rice wine. The air smelled strongly of smoke, and the villagers complained that it was ruining their crops.

"We knew there was trouble brewing when the UCE troops arrived," remarked one of the women, handing round the bowls. "None of us had seen them this far north before. Torsten here says the Fire Reapers believe it's the End of Days."

"Those lunatics always left us alone before," the man called Torsten said sourly, as Neil and Astra fell on the food. "We were protected by the mountains. Mostly they forgot about us."

"And then," said an older man who was smoking a pipe, "they marched in here demanding food. They tramped through the paddies—destroyed all my crops."

There were nods and angry mutterings of agreement. A number of other farmers had suffered the same fate. "My Markus— that's my oldest boy—said enough was enough, he was joining the Bi-Souls," said another woman, her face troubled, "and we haven't seen him since. We've never seen the Bi-Souls, either, though we've heard of them often enough."

"From the Aqua Libere," interjected Mesi, who had finished her stew and was helping herself to more wine. "We're the messengers," she added, glancing at Neil and Astra and Hallvard. "Here they call us the Hermodda."

"Like the god Hermod, who rode for nine days and nights to get to Hell," explained Torsten. "Which is more or less where you've arrived," he added bitterly.

"And the battle?" asked Hallvard gravely. "What's happening at the front?"

"Ah, that we can't tell you," Torsten said, shaking his head. "All we hear are rumours. One minute the Bi-Souls are winning and the next minute it's the Fire Reapers. You know the old saying—the first casualty of war is truth."

It was getting very late, and people were settling themselves to sleep wherever they could, on floors and rustic furniture. A shed outside the house, the only space left, was offered to the new arrivals. It smelled strongly of goat, but Neil didn't care. He fell asleep right away, his belly satisfyingly full for once. Again it seemed only a moment later before Ritsuko was shaking him, though this time he found himself quickly wide awake—whether because of his daily dose of imprinted water or because the battle lay just ahead, he didn't know.

He looked at Astra, busy pulling on her tunic in the pre-dawn light. Neither of them said anything, but each knew what the other was thinking. If the battle was going badly for the Bi-Souls ... it didn't bear thinking about. All hope would be lost. Perhaps the Prophecies had been telling the truth after all.

At first they kept to the edge of the foothills, where the air was clearer and they could take shelter if need be. Neil's ankle felt sound, and he had never been more alert and alive. Hallvard and Astra, too, looked healthy and rested. The litters had been taken apart and the groundsheets stuffed back in packs, and the group set off, Freya in the lead beside Mesi.

They walked all morning. Neil was astonished that he felt so little tiredness. The smoke, blowing in from farther north, grew thicker, and for the first time they could hear the distant whine of Tabris. At a rocky outcrop on the plain, Mesi called a halt.

"Quan and I are going to scout ahead," she said. "I want to get a better idea of what's happening. Wait here." And with that they were gone, so swiftly and silently they seemed to have merged with the ghostly grey light.

Neil sat with his back to the rock, his fingers through Freya's collar, trying not to imagine the worst. How far were they from the Island of Birches? Did all that smoke mean it was already over? A few moments later, or so it seemed, Mesi and Quan were back and answering his questions.

"That smoke's deceptive," Quan said, trying to catch his breath. "They've begun a token burn to the northeast of the battlefield. There's a narrow isthmus there. The Bi-Souls and some of the local villagers are holding it to prevent the Fire Reapers from reaching the island."

"How far are we from the battle?" Astra wanted to know.

"Quite close," Mesi said. She actually seemed worried for once. "Perhaps twenty handsprings or so." And when Astra and the others gave puzzled glances, she added, "A thousand metres, maybe, by how your people measure distance. I'm afraid it looks—" A sudden volley of Tabri fire drowned her out.

"And the slain?" asked Hallvard softly when he could be heard again.

"There are many," Mesi said. She glanced down, and when she looked up again her eyes were wet. "Mostly villagers and other humans. They lack the armour and weapons of the Fire Reapers." She turned to the other Libere. "I saw one of our own. Niállim, the son of Naiad of the Fossefallen."

"But he's no more than a boy!" Siobhán cried. "Fourteen at most!"

"We must fetch him," declared Savio, springing to his feet, and moments later they had all disappeared into the smoke. Freya tugged urgently against her collar, whining frantically. After what seemed like an age they returned, carrying the boy Niállim. He was still alive, but badly wounded. The character-istic white Lumini burns puckered his chest, and he had Tabri slivers in his legs and groin.

Vaclav hauled out his medical kit, while Mesi pulled a tiny glittering needle-like object from a fold of her headcloth. "Stay here with Vaclav, where you're safe," she ordered Hallvard and the children. And then they were gone again, swift shapes glid-ing into the boiling clouds of battle.

"I'm going, too," Neil said, and stood up, though he felt light-headed in the heat.

"You're doing no such thing," Hallvard said sharply, grip-ping his arm. "Look what happened to the boy here. Besides, you have no weapon."

If only he had his beautiful Yukon knife, the one his uncle had carved! Maybe what Mesi had pulled out was a sort of knife. "Vaclav must have a weapon he isn't using," he said, lift-ing his chin defiantly.

But Vaclav, busy extracting the Tabri slivers from the boy's legs, shook his head. "Our weapons respond only to us. Each is powered by a water source sacred to its owner."

"But our friends are out there!" Neil shouted, almost beside himself. "We can't just sit here! We have to help them!"

"Neil, you can't," Astra said pleadingly, her voice rising in panic. "You can't, you'll be killed—"

"I don't care." Neil's eyes blazed. Why hadn't he gone with Guldsterre when she'd invited him? "We were sent here on a mission. We have to."

And before anyone could stop him, he had darted forward into the thickening layers of smoke.

Neil pounded across the rocky sand in what he thought was the direction of the battlefield. Where were Hreinn-Sál and Guldsterre and Picea and their troops? He dodged and weaved through the smoke, keeping low to avoid the hot-white blasts of Luminis that shrieked above his head. Outlines were emerging from the gloom—a Fire Reaper trooper in hand-to-hand combat with a blue-jewelled Mínera, an Ash-Gatherer not much older than himself brandishing a hoe as a weapon. A Fire Reaper trooper raised his Tabri and a cougar-Bestia vanished in a burst of electrons. An Arbolé staggered past pursued by a Varg-Minne, sap oozing from his wounds.

The shouting and confusion was deafening. Busy watching for Fire Reaper soldiers, zigging and zagging, Neil nearly fell over a platoon of mole-Bestia planting paralysis mines.

"Time Boy!" one of them squeaked, standing up on his hind legs. "We met outside the Fortress, remember? What are *you* doing here?"

Panting, Neil threw himself flat on his stomach as spores from some kind of weapon zoomed overhead. "Hreinn-Sál ... the others ... where are they?" he gasped, coughing from the smoke.

"Last I saw, they were defending the isthmus," the mole-Bestia shouted. He pointed off into the distance.

"I'm with the Aqua Libere ... back there ..." Neil jerked his head. "With a medic."

The mole being shook his head. "Too many wounded to fix. It's terrible. Never seen anything like it."

At that moment a Fire Reaper soldier, his chest aflame, staggered toward them and fell headlong. As the mole-Bestia scurried for safety, the soldier lay still, sprawled on the ground beside Neil. Something rolled from his hand—a something the size of a ballpoint pen, black and shimmery. A SerraTube! Neil threw himself on it and hoped he could remember how to use it.

Shuddering, he gripped the SerraTube tighter and crawled forward on his belly. A platoon of soldiers, heads encased in plumed helmets like feathered insects, ran past. One lifted his hand and flung a tiny metal ball at a diamond-studded Mínera. As the casing disintegrated, a cloud of writhing black snake-like things fastened themselves to the Mínera's neck. He clutched at his throat in agony and fell to his knees before collapsing. In moments all that remained was his skin, like an empty chrysalis, and a handful of diamonds.

Neil stared down in horror at the lifeless face. It was familiar, this face. Then he remembered. It was one of the Mínera officers who'd accompanied them from the Timeless Caverns to the Valley of the Slaves. Yet another who'd been betrayed by Chalcedon.

A boiling hate stirred in Neil's guts. Still on his stomach, he gripped the SerraTube and focused all his energy on it. This is for that soldier, he thought to himself. And for Charlie. And for Hreinn-Sál and Arduinna and Guldsterre and all the others who've helped us. The next moment a beam of light shot out of the glowing tube, striking the nearest feathered soldier. He screamed and dropped his weapon, his plumed helmet cracking open as he fell. Neil aimed the tube at another soldier, and another. A fourth soldier caught sight of him and launched one of the metal balls, but the tube blew it to smithereens in midair.

The rest of the platoon turned and fled as Neil, shaking uncontrollably, got to his feet. He'd cleared a small space around him, but a sharp pain stabbed the arm that held the SerraTube. He looked down. The muscles of his forearm were withering and turning white—just like Astra's finger had.

Astra stared helplessly through the smoke, straining to see. Neil had disappeared so quickly she was still in shock, and what with the scream of weapon fire and Freya yelping and struggling, she could barely think. I need a weapon—something—anything, she thought, fighting down panic. And then she remembered the Sensor. Except it hadn't worked when she'd tried the last time.

She yanked it out, trying hard to concentrate, to let her vibration attune itself to the Sensor. Her fingers were slippery with sweat and the Sensor shook in her hands. *Be calm ... be calm ...* She could see nothing, only a whirling cloud of sand and dust and smoke. Perhaps Silfra the Learned's charge was wearing off? She took a deep breath and tried again, shutting out the sounds of battle as best she could. She suddenly remembered the Memory Stone and how she'd had to almost feel her way inside it. You couldn't rush it. You had to—

There. There *was* something. A shape was coalescing out of the whirling cloud. Zircon! His jewelled face was beet-red, and he was battling hand to hand with a Fire Reaper officer. And there was Picea, taking aim at a UCE soldier with his Chlorophyllider. There, dear god, was Hreinn-Sál at the head of a phalanx of Bestia, his heavy coat matted with dust and blood. And there beyond him, not a hundred metres away, lifting his Tabri, was none other than Chalcedon!

Astra let out a sob and leapt from behind the rock, dimly

aware of her father's shouts behind her. She choked down another sob and ran on, dimly aware, too, of a golden shape that caught up with her and hurtled past. At the edge of the battle, panting heavily, she glanced round wildly. Where were they? *Oh no—please no—*

Out of the sky above her, squawking and screeching, hurtled a squadron of Bird-Bestia. Tårnfalk—dear Tårnfalk!—was in the lead. They dive-bombed Chalcedon, while those in the rear fended off an attack by a flock of Vampyriae. Caught off guard, Chalcedon threw up a gloved arm against Tårnfalk's battering wings. Moments later Freya leapt at him, teeth bared, growling ferociously. She seized him by the throat and pinned him to the ground, jaw open in a snarl just millimetres from his face. He was hauled to his knees by half-a-dozen Bestia troops and dragged off the field, bleeding heavily.

Numb with relief, Astra turned to see Neil staggering toward her, sweat streaming down his dust-caked face. A shining needle whistled through the air between them and they threw themselves to the ground. It lodged in the neck of a Corporatist Special Elements soldier, who staggered forward and fell heavily across Astra. She could feel his blood soaking through her tunic. Shuddering, she wriggled out from under him, feeling sick to her stomach.

"That stopped *him*," said a voice with satisfaction. It was Mesi, yanking the needle from the soldier's body. She grabbed Astra, then Neil, and, covering with her weapon, retreated from the battle with Freya at her heels. "He was about to fire at you," she said, glaring at Astra when they'd reached safety. "What in the name of the divine Atla are you two doing here?"

As they emerged out of the smoke, Hallvard came hurrying up, his eyes huge in his white face. "Elskede! Dearest one! You're hurt!"

He moved to swing her up in his arms, but Astra put a hand out. "No, Pappa, no. I'm okay. A soldier fell on top of me."

"Thank god," Hallvard muttered fervently. He pulled her

to him and glanced over her head at Mesi as Neil stood there swaying, clutching his withered arm. "Thank god—thank all the gods—you saw them."

"She saved me, Pappa. She threw that needle thing. She killed a Corp—" But overwhelmed with relief and grief and terror, Astra pressed her face against her father.

"That's it," Hallvard said in a brook-no-argument tone. "We must get you both out of here. We're leaving—mission or no mission."

The Last Stand

efore they could stir a step, Ritsuko came racing toward them, Savio hot on her heels. She was waving an arm frantically toward the northeast and shouting. "They've broken through! They've broken through!"

A wind had sprung up, thinning the smoke, and for the first time they could see the narrow bridge of land the Bi-Souls had been holding. Now thousands of Fire Reaper troops were pouring across it, chanting, their torch battalions setting fire to trees as they went. Behind Neil and Astra and the others, marching toward the battlefield from the Sigr-Bruni Pass, were yet more troops—UCE soldiers, Corporatist Special Element Forces, and many others—so many they couldn't see the end of them.

"Reinforcements," Hallvard breathed, his face ashen. "They'll hold the isthmus after the others have crossed. And they'll box us in so no one can escape."

It was over. It was really over. Even Mesi had sunk to the ground, her hands over her face. Astra and Neil stared at each other in disbelief. Was this it? Standing here helplessly while the Fire Reapers marched in their thousands toward the Island of Birches?

"We're totally outnumbered, I'm afraid." Quan arrived, panting and out of breath, and shook his head wearily. "Even the Antarctica Wealth Region sent troops. They used to be the Fire Reapers' bitterest enemies." He pointed to passing battalions in shorts and wide-brimmed hats, looking to Neil for all the world like old-fashioned park rangers, except for the lethal-looking weapons they carried.

A handful of Mínera came limping toward them, the gems in their foreheads and wrists and throats dull and lifeless.

403

Vaclav, arriving with his medical kit and imprinted water, at once set to work. "The boy Niállim's been taken away by some of his Fossefallen people," he told the others. "Mesi, what's that wound in your leg?"

It was from a Corp.SE weapon. "Nasty things, those," Vaclav muttered. "Living microbes that eat away at your flesh from the inside. You don't feel a thing until it's too late." He slapped some sort of patch on Mesi's leg—to numb it and halt the feeding, he said—and then had Mesi swallow something to kill them. "The Nano-Irradiator works perfectly, if you take it quickly enough." Mesi scrunched up her eyes and whimpered like a puppy— Mesi, who was so brave about everything else!

Other Bi-Souls trickled from the battlefield, too exhausted to speak, many of them badly injured. Vaclav and a handful of medics from the three Bi-Soul Nations went to work, assisted by some of the Fossefallen who had stayed behind. Astra and Neil and Hallvard helped where they could, tying tourniquets under Vaclav's direction or fetching more water. Freya went from being to being, cocking her head worriedly at the gasps and moans and licking faces.

Hreinn-Sál himself, accompanied by his lieutenant, the eagle being Ørn-Sál, was the last to leave the field, having scoured it for wounded Bi-Souls. One of his haunches was bleeding badly and he had a broken antler, yet he still held himself with the dignified pride Astra and Neil had come to know so well. He placed a hoof on each of their heads and gave a smile of intense weariness. "We give thanks to the beings of the Many Realms that you and the dog being are safe. And unhurt."

In the shelter of a tumble of rocks he called an Assembly meeting. It was a much-diminished group. Picea and Hjästäl had both been seriously wounded; no one had seen Guldsterre or Bjarkansál, and it was feared they'd been taken prisoner. That left Álmveig, Rhodium, Ørn-Sál, and Hreinn-Sál himself. Rhodium's left arm was in a sling from a Vampyrion bite, and one of Ørn-Sál's wings was badly Lumini-burned. As for

Álmveig, she looked so withered no one knew how she was still standing upright.

Neil, Astra, Hallvard, and representatives of the Aqua Libere were asked to join the Assembly meeting as well. "Meetings!" muttered Mesi. "I hate meetings, they're always useless." But she and Quan went along anyway, while the others stayed behind to keep an eye on the patients.

"I'll keep this brief," Hreinn-Sál said when everyone was assembled. "I'm sure it's obvious to us all that we have no chance of defeating the assembled Fire Reaper forces."

A collective outbreath of sorrow and despair and devastation rippled round the group. Even Freya lifted her muzzle and gave a long, mournful howl. Hreinn-Sál raised a hoof for silence.

"That does not mean," he said sternly, "we are giving up. We all know—or should know"—he looked severely round the little group—"that our thought forms influence our actions, and that our actions in turn influence events. Accordingly, I have asked Ørn-Sál to make a report." He inclined his head in the direction of his fellow Bestia. "Ørn-Sál supervised an interrogation of Chalcedon in the prisoners' quarters."

There were murmurs of surprise and outrage. "That traitor!" muttered Rhodium between clenched teeth. "I hope we are not being asked to give credence to anything he said."

"I concur." Ørn-Sál nodded his feathered head. "However, the results were, to say the least, unexpected." He paused and glanced round the group, as if relishing what he was about to say. "According to Chalcedon, there's been a falling-out between him and Sardonyx. The General proclaimed *himself* the First Flame just before the Fortress was destroyed. In effect, he has overthrown Vígeldgeirr, and he has many troops supporting his rebellion. Chalcedon, however, was shut out of any leadership role in the new government. And he wants revenge."

"How do we know he's telling the truth?" Álmveig asked, her withered elm leaves rustling. "Everyone knows that interrogation results must be validated by other means."

"Perhaps if we knew what had happened to Vígeldgeirr ..." Hallvard put in hesitantly.

"I fail to see how any of this information is helpful." Rhodium sat stiffly, his shoulder encased in bandages. "In fact it may well be designed to sow confusion."

Hreinn-Sál nodded his head slowly. "We are all aware that the Fire Reapers employ deceit—blackformation, as they call it. But Ørn-Sál is convinced that Chalcedon is telling the truth."

"Let me explain." Ørn-Sál preened his wings and settled them again. "According to Chalcedon, the Fire Reapers were carrying out research on manifesting the past. Apparently, the General has something called a Memory Stone in his—"

"But that's mine!" Hallvard jumped to his feet. "They stole the Stone from my secret lab in Ashgård after they arrested me!"

"The Fire Reapers made it more powerful." Astra spoke up nervously. "Then they tried to make me use it to help them. They wanted me to—"

"Chalcedon knows where the General keeps it!" Ørn-Sál interrupted. "He's prepared to lead a raid—"

But he got no further, because a hubbub of voices broke out. Hreinn-Sál bellowed for order several times before everyone quieted down.

"Chalcedon was told that Astra had succeeded in manifesting the boy," Ørn-Sál went on, after Hreinn-Sál nodded at him to continue. "He suggested that she might be able to manifest something that would defeat the Fire Reapers. An entire army from the past, for example."

Another agitated hubbub broke out. "Anyone would think this was a social occasion," Hreinn-Sál snorted once order was restored, in his nasal reindeer grunt. "Now what's all this about Astra manifesting the boy child?"

It took quite some time for Hallvard and Astra and Neil to explain everything, especially the part about manifesting—or rather *not* manifesting—Neil.

406

"So despite your naive optimism, Chalcedon wasn't telling the truth, as we might have expected," Rhodium said, giving Ørn-Sál an I-told-you-so look.

Ørn-Sál looked deflated. "It all sounded like the answer to our prayers. A device that could manifest an army!"

"I did manifest *some*thing," Astra said reluctantly. It seemed such a tiny achievement, now. And totally useless in their present situation. "It was when the General came to see a demonstration. I didn't want to help them at all. But instead I—I manifested a yam." She gulped and rushed on. "It's really stupid, I know, I don't even know why I'm telling—"

"A yam?" Hallvard turned to his daughter, his mouth open. "An actual real yam?" Astra nodded sheepishly. "But elskede, don't you see? Don't you see what a breakthrough this is?" His eyes were shining; he seemed to have come alive again. "If you can do that, there's no telling what else you might be able to do!"

"A yam," said Rhodium sourly. "Perhaps we can manifest a field full of yams and throw them at the Fire Reapers."

"It's all nonsense anyway," Álmveig said impatiently. "It's a pack of lies. The Fortress was destroyed and all the Fire Reapers' research along with it."

"That's what Chalcedon thought, too," said Ørn-Sál. "But then he discovered the General had taken possession of the Stone just before the order to destroy the Fortress was given."

"Why is he telling us all this *now*?" Mesi wanted to know. "Why didn't he defect to our side *before* the northern assault?"

"This is a complete waste of time." Rhodium stood up angrily and turned to Hreinn-Sál. "With respect, Hreinn-Sál, I'm beginning to question your ability to lead us. We need a strategy, not moonbeams and blackformation."

An alarmed silence fell. Hreinn-Sál stood up, too. Rhodium's hand went to his weapon, and for a terrible moment it seemed they might fall on each other.

"The last thing we need," Álmveig said with annoyance,

"is to fight among ourselves. Honestly, sometimes you male Bi-Souls are almost as bad as humans."

She sighed heavily, her leaves rustling, and if the moment hadn't been so fraught Neil would have laughed out loud, because it sounded just like what Piedra might have said. It was Mesi, surprisingly, who eased the tension. *"We'll* lead a raid," she said, jumping up. "Quan and I."

"Your bravery and skill are unquestioned, Mesi." Hreinn-Sál looked at her with respect. "Which is precisely why we can't risk your doing such a thing when we still don't know if the information is reliable."

"Do you have a better idea," Rhodium asked ominously, "for determining whether or not the information is true?"

"If we *could* get the Stone back," said Hallvard quietly, "it might prove to be a turning point."

Hreinn-Sál said nothing. He lowered his antlers and nodded, almost imperceptibly, at the Aqua Libere.

Mesi, Quan, and Ritsuko set out for the front as soon as they got their map coordinates, shrugging off all suggestions of caution. Hreinn-Sál gave orders that all remaining able-bodied troops were to assemble for an assault on the isthmus they'd failed to hold.

"We've nothing to lose," Hreinn-Sál said grimly. "We're sitting ducks if we stay here. I'd rather we fight on our feet than die on our knees." Messengers had been dispatched to summon all possible reinforcements from the Bi-Soul Nations as well as the Ash-Gatherer villages.

Neil thought it was a disastrous decision. Hreinn-Sál had said they were outnumbered, so why were they doing something so suicidal? They ought to wait for reinforcements. They ought to wait till Mesi and the others got back. He said as much to Hallvard and Astra. Hallvard nodded, his face drawn with weariness. "I suspect the Bestia view prevailed, since they're the majority on the Assembly," he said softly. "Wiser heads might have decided otherwise."

He put his arms round Neil and Astra and pulled them close. Freya jumped up and Hallvard took her into his embrace too. "Whatever happens, I want you to know how proud I am of you." His eyes were bright with moisture. "Against all odds, Neil, you and Freya found us—Astra and me—in the Palace. You, daughter"—he squeezed her hard—"have had to endure the terrifying demands of the Fire Reapers. For all the horrors that humans have perpetrated, the two of you are a credit to our species, and the dog Freya to her own Nation." He smiled down at Freya and said something else, but neither Neil nor Astra heard any more because they were both sobbing.

The troops that were finally mustered were a ragtag group, all of them exhausted by long days and nights of battle. How this handful of scruffy Bestia, limp-leaved Arbolé, and dulled Mínera was ever going to stand up to the might of the Fire Reapers and their allies—it was crazy, it was dumb beyond belief. There were Ash-Gatherer villagers, too—Neil thought he recognized a man from Ashheim—and the remaining three Aqua Libere, and even several Fossefallen priests and priestesses who'd never fought before. It's a joke, Neil thought. A complete joke. What was Hreinn-Sál thinking?

But leaving was out of the question, despite Hallvard's earlier insistence, since they were now surrounded. They set off under the beating sun, almost blinded by the brassiness of the sky. With so little imprinted water left, everyone was allowed only a drop or two. Neil was drooping with thirst, and Freya's tongue hung almost to the ground. Siobhán and Savio went off to scout among the rocks of the coastline, looking for a particular beetle that collected water in the bumps on its back from condensed fog. "We'll leave them enough water for their own use, of course," Siobhán explained.

A wind had picked up, sweeping the thickening smoke

toward them and making their eyes water. "How far are we from the Island?" Astra asked Álmveig, who happened to be nearest. Álmveig made some rapid calculations in her head. "Perhaps eight kilometres in your system of measurement."

Eight kilometres! The first troops of the Fire Reaper army must already be very close ... except that they'd have to find a way to reach the Island. Álmveig shook her head again at Astra's fear. "It's not more than a kilometre from the land, and the sea's very shallow at that point. They can wade across."

Astra gave Neil a terrified glance, wondering if he'd over-heard. Neil, who had, merely tightened his lips and gave a brusque nod. *Crazy, crazy, crazy* ... His thoughts were inter-rupted by a sudden distant roaring and chanting and singing that went on and on. The Fire Reapers must have reached the Island, or at least the coast across from it. He felt sick to his stomach. Hallvard placed a hand on his shoulder, but even that didn't help to steady him.

They crossed the isthmus and entered more wooded terrain, the smoke thickening by the minute. Flames crackled through the trees on either side of them. How must the Arbolé feel, watching their fellow beings—their relatives—burning like liv-ing torches? But they had neither the time nor the water to put them out. Álmveig was visibly quivering, her leaves curling at the edges. Neil glanced back and saw a vast sea of enemy troops—Antarctic Wealth Region soldiers, Corporatist Special Elements forces, packs of Varg-Minne. The isthmus was sealed off. There was no turning back now. And no way for reinforce-ments to reach them, either. He turned his face back to the northeast, his insides roiling as if someone was violently shak-ing him.

The roaring and the chanting in the distance, which had qui-etened down, picked up again, closer this time. Through a gap in the burning trees they could suddenly see the dim rounded shape of the Island in the distance. Thousands of soldiers were wading across the channel, still chanting. Neil couldn't make

410

out the strange New Nordlandish words, but Astra whispered them to him in UL, her face filled with horror.

We are fire-born, Purifiers,
We raise torches, raise them higher,
We bear flame to save the world,
We release the Bird of Fire!

The first of the troops—a regiment of torch-carriers—had reached the Island. The trees nearest to shore suddenly burst into flame, and the chanting grew deafening. Against the darkening sky the blazing limbs and crowns seemed to writhe in the smoky air. Hreinn-Sál hesitated, and the little army halted and stood there in confusion. The Arbolé crouched together, arms round each other, a quivering knot of limbs and leaves. Neil and Astra stared wildly at each other. If Hreinn-Sál himself had lost courage ...

A figure, dripping wet, suddenly emerged from the greyness behind them. Neil and Astra almost jumped out of their skins. Mesi! She was panting heavily, her headcloth plastered to her skull, her familiar grin gone. Behind her Ritsuko and Quan appeared out of the smoke, equally soaked.

"Here. We got it." She held out the familiar silken pouch to Astra, her chest heaving. "What can you do with it?"

For a few moments Astra was struck dumb. "I—I—I don't know," she stammered. She drew out the Stone, not quite believing it, her heart thuddering. It was its glittering, brilliant self. "Pappa, look, it's back!" she blurted, eyes shining, but her lower lip trembled. Overcome, she held it to her cheek, and at once it begin to heat up. It was still charged with pixillite!

"Can you do it? Can you manifest something to help us?" Mesi demanded. Excited murmurings rippled round Astra as Arbolé and Bestia and human and Mínera marvelled at the Stone's arrival and offered suggestions.

"We need a weapon—the most powerful weapon ever

invented!" an Ash-Gatherer villager shouted. The Arbolé and the Fossefallen urged some non-violent method for stopping the Fire Reapers. The Bestia and the Mínera and most of the humans argued for any method that would destroy them immediately and completely. Astra and Hallvard kept trying to be heard over the din, explaining that they couldn't manifest something new, only something from the past—if anything at all.

"A herd of dinosaurs," Neil suggested, and promptly regretted his stupidity. Of course Astra couldn't do that, when all she'd produced so far was a single yam!

"A wisdom being. Jesus or Muhammad, perhaps. Or Buddha or Sophocles"—this from Hallvard. But the Bestia and the Mínera looked scornful.

"A lethal disease? Something that will affect only the Fire Reapers and their allies?" Álmveig asked cautiously. But anything that affected the Fire Reapers would also affect the humans—Hallvard and the children, the Ash-Gatherers, the Aqua Libere, the Fossefallen—on their own side.

Savio came rushing up with a container of the water he'd just collected. "Here, Astra. Freshly imprinted. And with beetle energies in it, too. Take a good mouthful. And another." Astra drank obediently, but her mind was scuttering like a beetle itself. What in the Holy Ashes could she do?

"Pappa, I can't! I can't, I don't know what, I can't!"

"What did you do when you manifested the yam?" Hallvard said, his voice low and urgent.

"I thought about the garden," Astra faltered. "The vegetable garden in Ashgård. I wasn't even trying."

"Forget gardens and vegetables!" Ørn-Sál exclaimed. "The biggest army in the world—that's what we need! What are you waiting for?"

But that was impossible. She stared at the Stone's pink and dazzling heart. She'd never felt so hopeless, so useless. They were all depending on *her*—a twelve-year-old girl who had once thought she knew almost everything and now knew she knew almost nothing. "First, the thought form," Hreinn-Sál said softly behind her, and put his huge hoof on her shoulder. But she could think of nothing.

She held the Stone out, trembling. "Maybe—maybe if we all stand in a circle," she said to her father and Neil. "Like that first time with Neil in the lab. Maybe if we all hold it. Maybe something will come to us."

Neil and Hallvard obediently cupped a left hand each under the Stone, though Neil's shook and even Hallvard's didn't seem very steady, and grasped each other's right arm. Neil shut his eyes and tried desperately to visualize something. Concentrate, concentrate, he told himself. But what came was a vision of carrots and potatoes and zucchini and broccoli, holding hands and dancing mockingly in front of him, like some stupid commercial. He shook his head angrily, his eyes blurring. He couldn't do this, he couldn't, it was useless. The sweltering heat, the choking smoke, the gutwrenching fear—it was like those nightmares he'd had before moving to the Yukon, come to ghastly life.

All he *really* wanted to do was disappear into the past, see his father again. There, just for an instant—a burst of that low murmuring singsong, as if it had been turned rapidly on and off. And now came that weird feeling of slipping down into his own body, of his own cells and molecules jostling into place alongside the Stone's, forming an intricate, shimmering structure. It began shifting like a kaleidoscope into other patterns, resolving into—*ohmygod*.

He was standing with Freya on their favourite trail in the Yukon, in the hills above the Hidden Lakes, the snow falling softly all around them. And there was his father, for some reason. No longer ill but striding vigorously toward him in a red parka, his cheeks pink, his eyes shining. He gave Neil one of his old affectionate thumps on the shoulder. "Think we can make it up that hill?" And he pointed to a distant peak through the thickly falling flakes.

Neil hesitated—it seemed awfully high and far away—but his father had already swung off along the trail. Neil hurried after him, Freya rushing back and forth between them, barking excitedly. The snow was growing thicker by the minute. His father kept up his long, steady strides, leaving Neil gasping to keep up. Every now and again, just when Neil was about to give up, his father turned round and smiled at him. Don't be a wimp, he told himself sternly. Besides, the last thing he wanted to do was lose his father again. So he struggled onward, stepping in the deep footprints his father made, his eyes not on the distant peak but on the back of his father's cheery red parka (though he didn't remember his father ever having a parka, let alone a red one). Even Freya was flagging now, but still they strode, on and on through the falling snow, as night came down and the distant peak disappeared and all that was left were the thick white flakes spiralling down out of the black starless sky ...

He turned to check how far they'd come—kilometres and kilometres—and when he turned back, his father wasn't there. Neil stared about him. How had he disappeared so quickly? The flakes were already filling in the footprints ahead of him. Soon they'd be obliterated, and there'd be no evidence his father had ever been here. He shivered violently—he was suddenly bitterly cold. He felt a terrible, aching, lonely, desperate sadness. Wherever his father had gone, he couldn't follow. He knew that now. With an effort he opened his eyes.

Someone was calling his name, over and over. It was Astra, jumping up and down for some reason and shouting, "Look! Look! It really exists! It really exists!" There was Mesi, too, grinning like a madwoman, and Hreinn-Sál and the other Bestia roaring and bellowing, and the Arbolé dancing in a circle, and Hallvard slapping him on the back so hard he almost fell over. Had they all taken leave of their senses?

And then he felt it, felt it on his face and shoulders and eyelashes. Snow. All around them and as far as he could see, falling and falling. He'd never seen such thick wet flakes. It was falling

414

on the rocks and sand and trees and along the coast. It was falling on the thousands of soldiers still wading across to the Island. And it was falling most thickly on the Island itself. A heavy white blanket was being laid over the burning trees, changing the smoke they were giving off to steam, snuffing out the flames.

"You did it! You did it!" Mesi threw her arms round him in a bone-crushing hug. "I told you it would work! I told you the water would help us! Look!"

The snow was having an opposite effect on the Fire Reapers and their allies. The soldiers who'd reached the Island were turning tail and fleeing, just as they had in the City. They had to fight their way back through the oncoming troops, including several packs of Varg-Minne. Huge battles broke out. Astra, watching through the Etheric Sensor, reported that officers and troops were battling hand to hand as blasts of Tabri fire soared over the channel. The sea began filling with bodies, and soon its slime-green surface was streaked with red.

By the time the first of the fleeing troops reached Hreinn-Sál's army, the snow was already knee-deep. Soldiers slid and fell in the unfamiliar substance and picked themselves up again, their faces white with terror. Others threw down their weapons and tried to claw their way over their comrades. "Run, you fools!" one soldier shouted to Astra and the others. "Can't you see? The Holy Ash—it's turned to ice!"

"He's turned against us!" screamed an officer with a haunted look on his face. "The God of Fire—he's turned against us!"

Several others fell to their knees in the snow and began praying. "The world—it's ending, it's ending," whispered one of them. "But it's ending in ice, not fire."

"Poor souls," whispered Hallvard, watching them in wonder. "It's only snow. Frozen water. The stuff of life. But they've turned it into death."

Savio and Ritsuko had discovered how to make snowballs and were throwing them giddily at each other when a pack of Varg-Minne broke off and came loping toward them all. They were howling like wolves, their three Gribbhålla mouths slavering. Astra and Neil turned to run, but in a single bound, one Varg-Minne caught Astra, another Neil, and held them down with their great wolf paws. The rest of the Varg-Minne surrounded Hreinn-Sál's little army, who were ordered to drop their weapons. Freya was lifted in a Varg-Minne muzzle and dropped whimpering on the snow.

Moments later a transporter came gliding through the falling snow and landed beside them. The skin of the transporter unsealed and out stepped Flame-Protector Vígdís, her body rigid with fury. Even the Varg-Minne seemed to quail before her. Behind her was none other than General Sardonyx himself, his neck swathed in bandages. The red and black and white banded stone in his forehead glittered angrily.

"You left me for dead," he snarled at Mesi, who was staring at him with her mouth open. "Alas for you, I'm not so easy to kill. Our research chemists long ago came up with the antidote to your *Háls-Stinga*, your Neck-Stabber."

Hreinn-Sál threw back his head and roared, while on either side of him Ørn-Sál and Rhodium lifted their weapons. They were knocked out of their grasp by a Varg-Minne paw.

Sardonyx looked at them all with contempt, and turned to Astra. "So you were capable of manifesting something," he said, his upper lip flickering with rage. "A very clever trick, frozen water—but a temporary one, of course. Your precious trees can't be protected forever."

"Leave my daughter alone, coward." Hallvard stepped forward, his eyes flashing. "Choose someone else to intimidate."

At a sign from Sardonyx, one of the Varg-Minne lunged forward and cuffed Hallvard across the face. His hand leapt to his cheek as blood poured from it. Astra cried out, struggling against her captors, as Sardonyx stared levelly at Hallvard. "Such a pity that an intelligent man like you aligned yourself with this pathetic band of rebels." He shook his head sadly, as if genuinely pained. "And to think that you all fought for nothing!"

416

"We are fighters for freedom," Hreinn-Sál growled savagely, lifting his antlers high. "For the freedom of all life. Even if you kill all of us, the desire for freedom will not fade."

"Freedom?" The General laughed deep in his throat. "Freedom for what—to be outcasts and misfits? Half-formed *things*, like the Varg-Minne?" The creatures snarled at this, their huge jaws dripping and their red eyes flashing at their masters. Poor things, Astra thought suddenly, created only to be weapons.

"Release them!" commanded a steely voice behind the General. Sardonyx and Vígdís whirled, while Hreinn-Sál and the others gaped in astonishment. For there, right behind Sardonyx, still highlighted by the glow of the energy pathway, was Vígeldgeirr, with the Archons ranged round him.

"You, even more than these half-formed things, are a traitor!" Vígeldgeirr pointed to the General, quivering with fury. "You are guilty not only of insurrection but of subverting the will of the God of Fire himself. As are you, Vígdís, and all those who supported this—this heretic!" His hand shook with emotion. "Seize them!"

The Varg-Minne let go of Neil and Astra and lunged toward the General and the Flame-Protector. With a strangled cry, Sardonyx lifted his Tabri and fired at Vígeldgeirr, but the beam merely bounced off the energy pathway. The next moment the Varg-Minne had pinned him and Vígdís and forced them to their knees. Vígeldgeirr moved toward them from the fading energy pathway, his face a mask of hatred.

Neil yanked the SerraTube from his belt and aimed it at Vígeldgeirr. The beam of light struck him in the chest and he fell headlong, writhing and clutching, withering before their eyes. The Archons dropped to their knees, whimpering like children. Neil whirled to face the General, who had broken free from the confused Varg-Minne, but Álmveig had already fired her Chlorophyllider. Sardonyx exploded, floating away on the breeze like so many dandelion spores.

417

Ørn-Sál and Rhodium handcuffed Vígdís, who stood watching the Archons with contempt. "I despise cravenness," she said, and glared haughtily at her enemies. "Do what you wish with me. I have nothing to fear, because I am in the right. Imprisonment or death means nothing to me." And she lifted her chin and held her head high as she was led away.

Neil lowered the SerraTube and looked anxiously round him. What damage had he done? Astra suddenly let out a cry and rushed over to her father, who had turned white and was swaying on his feet. He clutched her shoulder for support and smiled weakly. "My darling girl," he whispered. "My elskede ..."

"Pappa! Pappa!" Astra tried to hold him up but he fell to his knees, still gripping her arm. "What happened? What's the matter?"

Even as they watched he seemed to be shrinking, his face turning white and ghostly. Neil flung the SerraTube away from him in horror. "It's my fault, Hallvard," he whispered, fighting back tears. "It's all my—" He couldn't go on.

Hallvard, fighting for breath, shook his head. "There was no other way, child." He tried to lift a hand to Neil's. "You mustn't ... blame yourself. You did right."

Vaclav appeared, carrying his medic's kit, and knelt down beside Hallvard. "SerraTube dehydration," he muttered, and shook his head. Astra, feeling her father's grip loosen, cradled his head in her lap, tears seeping down her cheeks.

"Help's come, Pappa. It'll be okay, you'll see. It'll all be okay."

Hallvard was whispering something, and Astra had to bend down to his mouth to hear him. "Promise me one thing, elskede." He was smiling a gentle, almost dreamlike smile. "Promise me you'll bury me on the Island of Birches."

"Don't go, Pappa! You can't go!" Astra shrieked, and flung herself across him. But already he lay unmoving, a gaunt, shrivelled figure in too-large clothing. Neil, quivering with sobs, wrapped his arms tightly round her. Astra gathered her father in her arms, bent her head over him, and wept.

The Parliament of Beings

he long regime of the Fire Reapers fell that night.

There were rumours of further reinforcements from elsewhere in the Arctic Wealth Region, but if they set out they failed to arrive. With the deaths of Vígeldgeirr and the General, the troops holding the isthmus fled, looting as they went. A few fought hard, but Hreinn-Sál's exhausted forces overcame them. The Varg-Minne and the last of the Vampyriae were finally brought down by the combined efforts of the Bird-Bestia and the deadly Dhilalia of the Mínera. Neil, shuddering, refused to touch the SerraTube, but it was no longer needed.

As for the Island of Birches, the snow continued to fall there long after it had stopped everywhere else. The flames along the shoreline, now doused, left a narrow band of burnt trees. Neil and Astra remained well away from the battles, kneeling beside Hallvard's body with Freya between them, watching the moon rise above the Island.

"When all this is over, we'll go there. Just you and me," Neil said. "We'll do what your father asked."

"If he's buried on the Island," said Astra slowly, "then I want to be nearby. Maybe I can live with the rice farmers."

Álmveig came toward them slowly, the strange harp-like Chlorophyllider slung across her. She was leaning on Mesi and limping. "You're hurt," said Astra with concern, staring at one of the tree-root-like feet, now oozing moisture.

"I believe Mesi saved me by dousing it with water," Álmveig said softly as Mesi eased her to the ground.

By the time the last of the Fire Reaper troops had fled or been finished off or captured, the moon was a pale disk in the western sky. Astra, curled up on the ground, had finally fallen asleep, Freya pressed tight against her. Hreinn-Sál, returning wearily with a handful of the Bestia, bent over and touched her tear-stained cheek. "Poor child," he said gently. "This has all been too much for you." He shook his head, angry. "I wonder if they understood, Áilu and the beings of the Many Realms, what they were asking of you."

It was the Arbolé who arranged the trip to the Island of Birches the next day. They had their own ceremony to conduct, Álmveig explained, and they would consult the Trees there about Hallvard's request. Astra and Neil were invited to join them, though Freya, for once, was left behind. "I'm afraid she may be a disruption," Álmveig explained gently. "Our ceremony requires deep focus and attention." Freya announced her indignation by howling miserably as the coracles, lightweight woven boats borrowed from the rice farmers, pulled away from shore under grey skies.

Astra sat in Álmveig's coracle, staring out at the ocean with its great green patches of dead algae. Her father's body travelled in a coracle manned by Picea. Neil travelled with Bjarkansál, who had—to everyone's immense relief—staggered into camp the evening before.

Though she couldn't see Neil, Astra was certain they were thinking the same thing. Surely this was the end of their mission. If so, what happened now? But she didn't want to think about any more sadness. She glanced behind her at the coracle carrying her father and tightened her fingers round the wedding ring she'd taken from his left hand.

They arrived in the evening, beaching the coracles along the burnt shoreline where dozens of blackened trees stood, twisted and shrivelled. Most of the snow had melted, though there was the odd patch here and there. Astra and Neil stared in wonder at the virgin stands of birch and spruce and pine, the under-growth of scrub willow and wild rose bushes. So this was the Island that held the last stand of the once-great boreal forests—forests that had stretched, Neil knew, around the circumpolar world, from North America to Scandinavia to northern Asia. If the Fire Reapers had succeeded in their terrible task, this threatened place would now be a scorched desert. And the Fire Reapers would be rejoicing at the new world emerging from the ashes of the old.

They set up camp in a small natural grove, out of sight of the burned shoreline. Half-a-dozen of the Fossefallen had come with them, too, and after the evening meal, as everyone sat or half-lay in a circle, one of them told a story. "Long ago, when Terrania was young," she began, "a giant ash tree linked and sheltered the three worlds—the world of the gods, the world of humans, and the underworld. Its name was the World Tree, and its branches extended far into the heavens. At its roots lay three wells: the Well of Wisdom, the Well of Fate, and the Roaring Kettle, the source of many rivers. The Deer of the Four Winds lived in its branches, and the Eagle of Wisdom, and they say that the dew that fell from its leaves was the nectar of the gods.

"But the gods then were young and foolish, and the day came when, as it had been foretold, they would do battle with the giants. On the Day of Doom the fire giants, led by Surt, set forth from the south, and Surt carried a sword that blazed like the sun itself. From the three worlds, gods and giants, dwarves and demons, rode toward the huge plain of Vigrid where the last battle was fought. Then Surt set the World Tree on fire, and all the worlds burned, and friends and foes alike perished, and Terrania was destroyed.

"So you see," the Fossefallen priestess concluded, "the Fire Reapers believed that history would repeat itself, and that if Terrania burned again, a new world would come forth, as it had once before. They failed to recognize that history never repeats itself in exactly the same way. They did not know that two humans and an animal being from the Time Before FeverWorld would be summoned to our aid—the quantchemist Charlie, the boy Neil, and the dog Freya. They did not know that these three would be joined by the girl Astra from our own time, and that to these four would be given the mission of saving Terrania."

The tale-teller bowed her head toward Neil and Astra, seated together. Neil shifted uncomfortably as all eyes turned to them, and Astra felt her cheeks blaze.

"Like all tyrannical regimes, the Fire Reapers underestimated the strength of those who opposed them," the tale-teller went on. "I speak not only of the Four, but also of the Arbolé and the Bestia and the Mínera, who dedicated their lives to bringing forth a new world through creation, not destruction. I speak also of the Aqua Libere, our far-flung allies, who work together with us to protect all sources of water. And I speak also of brave humans such as Hallvard Bjarnason, who tried to prevent his work from falling into Fire Reaper hands."

Here Astra couldn't help herself—she broke into quiet sobbing, and Neil put his arm round her. "Of those given such mighty tasks, much is demanded," the tale-teller said gravely, and bowed her head again. "But know that the tale of your deeds will be told round hearthfires for many generations. You are both human children, but by your deeds you have joined the Immortals."

Then a goblet was passed from hand to hand containing a drink called *nektar* whose recipe had been handed down from the time of the World Tree. Astra thought it tasted like her favourite mango shake, and Neil was sure the flavour was just like chocolate milk, and everyone agreed it was the most delicious drink they'd ever had the pleasure of swallowing.

Just before sunrise everyone rose—Neil and Astra still blinking the sleep out of their eyes—and gathered on the shore among the burnt trees. One of the Fossefallen, carrying a small golden bowl and accompanied by two other Fossefallen as well as Álmveig and Picea, moved from tree to blackened tree, anointing each one with liquid. To each tree she murmured something in Old Nordlandish that Astra couldn't quite follow, though she was sure she heard the word *tilgi*—forgive—several times.

"We have promised the Trees," Álmveig explained to Neil and Astra afterwards, "that this Island will be forever sacred, and that no one else will ever set foot on it, unless it is for the Trees' protection."

"But my father ..." Astra trailed off, tightening her hold on the ring.

"We have already spoken to the Trees," Álmveig said gravely. "They tell us they would consider it an honour to keep watch over your father. Come." And with that she set off into the forest, Astra and Neil hurrying along behind her. Neil felt a strange happiness creep over him. Walking between the tall, white birches was like being on that trail above the Hidden Lakes. The golden leaves of the birches showered down around them, as if the trees were greeting them.

Climbing up a hill in the hot sunshine was hard work. At last they reached the top, where a soft breeze blew and they could see around them in all directions. The stands of birch and pine fell away beneath them, a squirrel chittered somewhere, a warbler landed on a branch and regarded them with bright eyes. For a brief, wild moment, Neil wondered if he'd been whisked back to the Yukon after all.

"What do you think, Astra?" Álmveig turned round, her arms held wide. "Would your father like it here?"

Astra's heart was too full to speak, but really, it was the perfect site. The breeze would bring the scent of pine and the songs of birds to him, the trees would watch over him, and no one would ever disturb this sacred place. Besides, if she lived nearby she could look out and see it every day of her life. She nodded, tears trembling on her eyelashes. Together, the three of them chose a south-facing spot, and Álmveig marked it with an arrow made of twigs.

That afternoon they returned with all the others, Hallvard's body borne aloft by several Arbolé. Other Arbolé dug down into the earth, thick with lichen and pine needles. They lined the grave with moss before gently placing Hallvard in it. Then they knelt, and the Fossefallen said a long prayer in Old Nordlandish, and Álmveig spoke one in her own language of Álm and another in the Leaf-Language that all the trees shared.

And then the strangest thing happened. The breeze had dropped, yet there was a sudden scattering of birch leaves from the trees around them. They lay in the grave like tiny gold flames.

After the grave was refilled, Astra was left to say a few words of her own and to gaze out one last time over the hills and the Island and the surrounding ocean. "That's where I'll be, Pappa," she murmured, pointing toward the blue shadow of the mainland. "I'll find a little house there, and every day I'll look out of my window at the Island."

At the shore, while the Fossefallen waited for them beside the coracles, Álmveig put an arm round each of the children. "We will stay behind, we Arbolé, for a while. We must enlist the help of these Trees if we are to restore order and harmony to the world."

"Won't we ever see you again?" Astra asked anxiously.

"I do not know the future, child," Álmveig said gently. "My first duty is to the Trees. But Picea will travel back with you as our representative at the next Assembly meeting. For the Bi-Souls must now decide how Nordlandia is to be ruled."

Astra's lower lip quivered, and Neil set his jaw firmly, feeling any display of emotion from someone who had helped defeat the Fire Reapers was—well, not heroic. With a last glance at the

Island, they climbed into the coracles. As the little group of vessels drew away from shore, Álmveig and the Arbolé stood waving until they blended with the trees and disappeared.

It was a grim scene that greeted them on their return. The Bestia and the Mínera were still removing bodies from the battlefield, carrying them to a distant corner where a huge pyre burned, a vast column of smoke and ash drifting skyward. At a makeshift field hospital set up for both their own troops and enemy wounded, Vaclav sat outside one of the tents, looking exhausted. "We've had many deaths," he said wearily. "We have no antidotes for some of the newer Fire Reaper weapons."

"Has Guldsterre turned up?" Neil asked anxiously. Yes, she had. She, too, had escaped from the prisoners' quarters after the Fire Reapers' defeat. "One of her captors tried to gouge out the gold vein in her forehead," said Vaclav in disgust. "But they're tough beings, those Mínera. As you'll soon see," he added, grinning.

What did that mean? But Vaclav clammed up and wouldn't say anything more. A horn sounded, marking the summoning of the Assembly. "Off you go," Vaclav said, waving them away. No, the Aqua Libere wouldn't be sending anyone. "We're needed here, at the hospital," Vaclav said. "And besides, we're allergic to governments and rules. After all this is over, our kind will still be needed."

Freya, overjoyed that the children were back, dashed off, rooing loudly. A large circle of sitting-stones had been set up on a rocky promontory. The wind was carrying the smoke in the opposite direction, but Neil and Astra made sure they were seated with their backs to the grim business below them.

The arrival of the Assembly members was a sobering sight. Several Bi-Souls were missing and presumed dead, including Zircon and the gentle young Melke, which brought Astra to tears all over again. Others, such as Hästsjäl, were still recovering. But Guldsterre was there, pale but determined—she gave each of the children a long embrace—and Rhodium, and Ørn-Sál, and Picea. And Hreinn-Sál himself, wearing a patch across one eye, which made him look like a bandit.

"We have many things to discuss," Hreinn-Sál said as he called the meeting to order. His coat was rubbed bare in places, and even the remaining intact antler had lost a tine or two. "I wish to hear from those present about our most pressing needs."

"A count of our losses," said Picea gravely. "Prayers for the dead, and—"

"The choosing of an Interim Council is far more important," interrupted Chalcedon, "now that the old regime has been destroyed."

"Bringing the remaining Fire Reaper leaders to justice," said Ørn-Sál, and his eyes blazed.

"All of these are important," said Guldsterre softly after a moment or two. "But there is one matter—or rather two—of pressing urgency." She looked at Neil and Astra. "Two children sit with us who have made great sacrifices to aid us. We must return the favour."

There was a silence as everyone regarded the children. "You do well, Guldsterre," said Hreinn-Sál, "to remind us of this." He turned toward Neil and Astra. "We will deal with the child of our own time first. Astra, what is your wish about your future?"

"I want to live near the Island," said Astra. Her voice, quivering, gained in firmness. "I can't go back to the City. And in Ashgård ..." She faltered. "There's nothing left there, either."

Guldsterre, who was sitting to one side of Hreinn-Sál, leaned toward him and whispered something. Hreinn-Sál listened, nodded, and grinned broadly. "This would seem to be the right time to introduce our visitors," he said. He turned round, and everyone else did the same. Astra, following his gaze, leapt to her feet. For there, coming toward them, was Fru Berta, and she was arm in arm with Amma!

426

Astra flew toward them as if on wings, and seconds later was wrapped in their joint embrace. "What—how—where—" she stammered.

"Oh, it's a long story, and not one I'll tire you with now," chuckled her grandmother, as Astra pulled away to stare at them in joy and amazement. "Though Fru Berta tells me that someone named Áilu may have had something to do with it."

Neil had come running up, too, and flung his arms round Fru Berta. "Such a brave lad," she murmured, holding him close and ruffling his hair. Freya began rooing loudly, demanding to be included, and the rest of the conversation was lost in the clamour and laughter.

Fru Berta and Astra's grandmother were invited to take seats at the meeting. When everyone had sat down again, Astra said softly, "I want Fru Berta and Amma to live with me in the village nearest the Island. If *they* want to, that is."

"Yes! Oh, yes!" the two women said at once, nodding vigorously.

"Then it shall be so," Hreinn-Sál said, as everyone in the circle smiled at each other. "I can think of no better solution. We will discuss a house of your own with the rice farmers."

Amma, sitting on one side of Astra, gripped her granddaughter's hand tightly, and Fru Berta, sitting on the other side, did the same. "I can think of nothing better than living with my grandchild," she said softly, "and with the woman who cared for her during those long years away."

"But what," said Astra in a small voice, "about Neil?"

"That," Hallvard said heavily, "will be more difficult. No doubt, child of a former time, you wish to return to your own world?"

Neil squirmed uncomfortably. Living with Astra and Fru Berta and Amma would be wonderful. But it wasn't where he belonged. Somewhere, in some unimaginably distant past, or so it seemed, his own family waited for him, and suddenly he longed more than anything to be there.

"I want to go home," he said. Fru Berta, sitting next to him, squeezed his arm.

"The boy travelled to our time by means known only to another traveller from the past," Hreinn-Sál said slowly, "and that one is no longer with us." He gazed round at his fellow Bi-Souls. "The Memory Stone, which proved so critical in our struggle with the Fire Reapers, cannot—at least not yet—manifest beings in either time direction."

Neil's heart sank. Hreinn-Sál had said nothing new, yet somehow he'd hoped against hope. But with Charlie gone and his knowledge lost, what hope was there?

"There *must* be a way," he said, his voice trembling. "I mean, it must be possible to reverse whatever Charlie did."

"But no one knows what that is." Hreinn-Sál frowned and shook his head.

There was a flurry of whispering round the circle. Guldsterre leaned forward and murmured in Hreinn-Sál's ear again. Neil caught only a few words: "quite ill" and "untested" and "get his hopes up."

At last Hreinn-Sál, glancing at Neil with concern, nodded and banged his hoof against his seat to gain everyone's attention. "Guldsterre has offered us a possible solution," he said. "But"—and he raised his hoof in caution—"we do not know if it will work. It is quite untried. And it involves the powers of another, who is still recovering from her ordeal as a Fire Reaper prisoner."

Another flurry of excited whispering. A young Bestia soldier was sent scurrying off in the direction of the field hospital. After what seemed—especially to Neil—an endless wait, he returned, accompanied by a tall, thin figure in a long dun-coloured robe, the hood pulled across its face. The figure went and stood beside Guldsterre, visibly trembling.

"It was good of you to come," Guldsterre said softly, taking the figure's hand—a feminine, shapely one. To the gathering she said, "This human was held prisoner by the Fire Reapers in the

Research Laboratories of the Fortress. She managed to escape when it was destroyed, though she was badly wounded, and eventually found her way to a troop of Mínera, who brought her to me."

The figure pulled back her hood. She had a pale, angular face, large dark eyes, and a mass of thick dark-chestnut hair that fell below her shoulders. "Forgive me," she said, "but I am still recovering and will not be able to speak long. My name is Montserrat Lavallet."

Hallvard's former colleague! Neil couldn't take his eyes off her, while Astra leapt up. "I'm Astra, I'm Hallvard's daughter," she said breathlessly. "Look!" She pulled the Sensor from her pocket with a flourish. "Áilu gave your Sensor to me, she said I ought to have it. The Fire Reapers stole it, but I got it back," she finished triumphantly.

Montserrat's pale face registered astonishment. "How amazing ... Hallvard's child," she murmured. "And that you should have acquired the Sensor ..." She shook her head, as if not quite able to comprehend this turn of events.

Neil sat on the edge of his rock, trembling with anticipation. Montserrat took something from the pocket of her robe and held it in the palm of her hand as she spoke. "I first worked on a device that would allow us to enter the energetic realm. That device, the Etheric Sensor prototype, is what Astra has. But I wasn't satisfied. I wanted it to work in the dimension of time as well as space. I was intrigued by Hallvard's work with his Memory Stone."

All this sounded very weird to Neil. Besides, what did it have to do with his dilemma? He glanced round impatiently, wondering if anyone else was feeling the same way, but all eyes were glued to Montserrat. "This is the next prototype of the Stone," she said, and held it up. The device was as tiny as a pebble and glittered as the sun struck it. "I worked on it secretly during my captivity. By day"—she made a face—"I worked in the Chronological Weapons Unit, which was trying to use time

429

reversal as a weapon." She gave a small smile. "I'm happy to say that, during my time there, we made little progress."

She paused again and looked round the gathering, as if trying to reassure herself she was among friends. "This version of the Stone allows us to tap, not into the past, but into the future. It does so by displaying, as in a hologram, alternative memories that have been stored at the energetic level." She stopped, looking exhausted. "Such energetic memories, which are images, can be summoned and superimposed over the present in order to know our future—or to change it."

Several of the Bi-Souls looked distinctly uneasy. "It isn't— it isn't contaminated by Fire Reaper energy, by any chance?" Picea asked.

Montserrat shook her head. "It was never used by the Fire Reapers. It has never been deployed at all. It's entirely at the experimental stage."

"So what you intend to do, if I understand correctly," said Hreinn-Sál slowly, "is to summon such a future memory of Neil."

"Yes. A memory of Neil returning to his own time—if there is such a memory. This device will tell us if there is. And then, according to my experimental data, Neil will be able to step into the image of himself and be reabsorbed by it, and in that way be returned to his own time."

Neil stared at her, his heart thundering. "And if there isn't? Does that mean—?"

"It means that return was not your choice. Or did not succeed," Montserrat said quietly. "At least as far as this device can tell us."

It was all very confusing. "Do you wish to proceed, child of the past?" Hreinn-Sál asked, and it seemed to Neil as if the weight of the world rested on his answer.

"Of course he does!" said an indignant voice—a voice Neil would have recognized anywhere. It came from the pocket of Fjellgeit, who was standing quietly outside the circle, coated in travel dust. "My troops found a friend of yours," he said, "during our mopping-up operations." He reached into his pocket and held out a piece of granite. "He insisted I bring him here."

"Piedra!" cried Astra.

"They're such stuffy places, pockets," Piedra said, as if he'd seen them all just yesterday. "Quite awful."

It was the same touchy, huffy Piedra of old, Neil thought happily. Fjellgeit placed Piedra in his hand, the stone's copper vein winking up at him. "Put me in your pocket," Piedra whispered. "I rather like the idea of being younger. Shave a few years off my thousands."

"The whole thing sounds rather dangerous to me," Picea said dubiously. "We can't test an experimental device on a mere child."

"Suppose it goes wrong?" said Rhodium. "Suppose the child ends up in another time altogether?"

"Do any of you have a better idea?" said Piedra sharply. "The child wants to go home. We ought to give it a try, at least."

It was risky—Neil understood that. But Piedra was right. "As long as Freya goes with me, too," he added quickly.

"Then we must proceed at once, before my own energy weakens further," Montserrat said. "Would everyone please clear a space for us."

With a clatter of hooves and a rustle of leaves, everyone rose. "You'd better say goodbye, all of you," said Montserrat gently. "If the process works, it may be very fast."

Astra burst into tears at once. "I'll never, ever forget you," she whispered to Neil through choked sobs, and flung her arms round Freya, too, who licked her wet face.

"My Toivo would have been proud of you, lad," Fru Berta said gruffly, and turned away before crumpling into tears herself. Rhodium saluted him; Picea touched a leafy hand to his cheek. Guldsterre held him at arm's length, regarding him with a tender, sorrowing smile. Last of all was Hreinn-Sál, who placed his hoof on Neil's forehead and pronounced him an honorary

431

member of the combined Bi-Soul forces. "You will long be remembered among our Nations, child," Hreinn-Sál told him. "Go well, and may you return to your own time safely."

Neil, his throat swelling, couldn't think of a thing to say. How could he possibly say goodbye? It seemed inconceivable he would never see them again—not after everything they'd been through together. "Say goodbye to Mesi and the others for me," he said lamely. "And—well, thanks for everything."

At the last minute he remembered the envelope for Montserrat that Markko had pressed into his hand when he and Astra left Ashheim. "Markko—he gave me a letter for you—only the Fire Reapers took it," he managed to stammer, as Montserrat's eyes widened and her hand flew to her mouth. Then he stood where Montserrat gestured he should, looked round the gathering through a blur of tears, and tried to memorize all the faces.

Montserrat came up beside him, carefully adjusting the Sensor. Neil, his hand on Freya's collar, stood nervously, trying not to expect anything. Montserrat adjusted the Sensor again and waited. In the distance the Bi-Souls and the others watched, stirring uneasily. Neil shifted his position—one of his feet was going to sleep.

Suddenly he was aware of a strange tingling all over his body. And there, standing across from him, was an exact replica of himself—right down to the very clothing he wore—with an exact replica of Freya sitting beside him. He stared in shock at the image, and Freya let out a short, sharp bark. It shimmered in front of him, a three-dimensional hologram, yet the grass and bushes of *this* world were clearly visible through it.

"You may have only a few moments," Montserrat said in a low, breathy voice. "Walk toward the image. Then wait until I tell you what to do."

Neil did so, Freya at his heels, never taking his eyes off the wavering image. His replica on the other side paid no attention; it seemed to be staring into space. "Now," said Montserrat, louder, "hold onto the canine being, and with your other hand, grasp the shoulder of the boy in the image."

Neil tightened his grip on Freya and reached out. As his arm entered the hologram, he had the strangest sensation—as if his arm had suddenly removed itself from his body. It began to shimmer and waver like the image itself. He touched the shoulder of the hologram boy and an electric shock roared up his arm, almost making him let go.

"Are you all right?"

Montserrat's voice seemed to come from a long distance away, but he nodded.

"Now I want you to step into the image *all at once*. Leave no part of yourself behind. Do you understand?"

He nodded again. Beside him Freya was tugging and rooing, obviously frightened. He gripped her collar as hard as he could and pretended it was the game they'd sometimes played out in the backyard, where he'd taught her to jump over upturned barrels hauled from Charlie's shed.

"Jump, Freya!" he shouted, and jumped himself. He felt a pain like a bolt of lightning, and a peculiar sensation of jerking through the air, as though he was in some old, flickering movie. He landed with a sudden thwump, and looked around.

He was sitting at his own table, in his own kitchen, in his own home in Whitehorse. Sunlight shone through the icicles at the window, blinding him momentarily. He glanced down quickly. Thank god, there was Freya, looking a little stunned herself. He stood up, experimentally, and felt himself all over. He seemed to be all in one piece. His withered arm had returned to normal, and the scars and bruising from his adventures had disappeared.

He went slowly up to his bedroom, still dazed, and took off the tunic and pants. They crumbled into dust on the floor as he did so. He pulled on a pair of jeans and a T-shirt, his mind in turmoil. Wait a minute—he'd forgotten about Piedra! He hunted about anxiously on the floor and found him, to his great relief. There was the copper vein, the familiar granite shape. "You okay, buddy?" he said, picking him up, but there was only silence.

Freya was already rooing, demanding to be fed. Time travel hadn't affected her appetite, obviously. Something about her was different, he thought as he scooped kibble into her bowl. He stared at her while she ate. Her tail was shorter! Not a whole lot shorter, but three or four centimetres were definitely missing. The tip of her tail must have been sticking out when they jumped.

He walked slowly through the empty house, marvelling at the ordinariness of it all. It was just as he'd left it—even his schoolbag still hung on its peg by the door. But it had been nighttime when he'd left, and now the clock said four-fifteen. What day was it? And where was everyone? The table in the dining room was set for six people—they must be having guests for dinner ...

The thought struck him like a bomb. *Montserrat had sent him back to the day before—the day of his birthday.* Uncle Dan and Aunt Trish and Luka were coming for dinner. That morning Uncle Dan had given him the knife with the handle he'd carved from sheep horn ....

Neil rushed upstairs. There was the knife, safely tucked into the top drawer of his dresser, along with the titanium watch with Ryder Hesjedal's signature that his mother had given him. He heaved a sigh of relief. Nothing had changed after all. The world was just as he'd left it. How he'd love to meet Ryder and tell him about his adventures!

The phone rang suddenly, startling him. He knew it would be Luka. He even knew what Luka was going to say.

"We're going skiing up at Mount Sima on Saturday," Luka said. "Me and my dad. Want to come?"

The End

ACKNOWLEDGEMENTS

f I hadn't arrived in the Yukon on a bright May morning twenty-some years ago... and if I hadn't lived in an old house with a false window... and if a certain Yukon trail-mix dog hadn't come into my life... well, I wouldn't have written this book!

My special love and thanks to Erling—my first reader—and our husky/lab Freya, for allowing me to send her on such an adventurous journey! (In real life she prefers peace and quiet, unless she's hunting squirrels).

I'd also like to thank:

- Stephanie Fysh, children's editor extraordinaire, who helped me see the story anew and who believed in it as much as I did.
- Mark Vessey, principal of Green College, University of B.C., and the Haig-Brown House of the Museum at Campbell River, for productive and stimulating writer residencies when I wrote earlier drafts of the novel.
- the Yukon Advanced Artist Award program (through Lotteries Yukon) and the Canada Council for the Arts, for grants that enabled me to work on this book.

A fond shout-out to a group of boys from the B.C. Boys' Choir, whose enthusiasm for the novel at an early reading kept me going when my own faith wavered.

And finally, my deep gratitude to Alison Uttley, Andrew Lang, George McDonald, Elizabeth Goudge, Enid Blyton, Anna Sewell, and all those other writers who made me want to cast my own spells when I grew up.

A NOTE ON THE BOOK

I found a lot of books helpful while I was writing *The Fire Reapers*. They included Gwynne Dyers' *Climate Wars*, John Michael Greer's *The Long Descent*, Stephen Harrod Buhner's *The Lost Language of Plants*, Diana Beresford-Kroeger's *The Global Forest*, Mark Stavish's *The Path of Alchemy: Energetic Healing and the World of Natural Magic*, and Stanislav Grof's *The Holotropic Mind*, among many others. I also found many useful websites and articles, including coverage by The Guardian and the BBC, and reports such as "The End of the Hinterland: Forests, Conflict and Climate Change" by The Rights and Resources Initiative (*www.rightsandresources.org*).

The language that the Fire Reapers speak (New Nordlandish) as well as that of the Ash-Gatherers (Old Nordlandish) combines Old Norse, modern-day Norwegian/Swedish, and invented words.

Stories, in the end, arrive in mysterious and roundabout ways. The trees, rocks, and plants of the Yukon, and the Yukon River, probably have as much to do with this story as anyone. But they aren't telling.

About the Author

orn in the UK, Patricia Robertson grew up in British Columbia and received her MA in Creative Writing from Boston University. She is the author of two collections of adult fiction. Her first collection, *City of Orphans*, was short-listed for the Ethel Wilson Fiction Prize. Her work has also been nominated for the Journey Prize, the CBC Literary Awards, the Pushcart Prize, and the National Magazine Awards (three times).

The Fire Reapers is her first work for younger readers; she is working on a second, *How To Talk To a Glacier*. She lives in Whitehorse, Yukon, with poet Erling Friis-Baastad and the real-life Freya.